Money,
Love

Also by Brad Barkley
Circle View: Stories

Money,
Love

A NOVEL

Brad Barkley

W • W • NORTON & COMPANY NEW YORK • LONDON

"James Dean," by Jackson Browne, John David Souther, Don Henley, and
Glenn Frey © 1974 Swallow Turn Music. All rights reserved. Used by
permission of Warner Bros. Publications U.S. Inc., Miami, FL 33014.

For information about permission to reproduce selections from
this book, write to Permissions, W. W. Norton & Company, Inc.,
500 Fifth Avenue, New York, NY 10110.

The text of this book is composed in Joanna
with the display set in Gothic Blond
Desktop composition by Gina Webster
Manufacturing by Courier Companies, Inc.
Book design by Rubina Yeh

Library of Congress Cataloging-in-Publication Data
Barkley, Brad.
Money, love : a novel / Brad Barkley.
p. cm.
ISBN 0-393-04929-9
1. Door-to-door selling—Fiction. 2. Fathers and sons—Fiction.
3. Sales personnel—Fiction. 4. North Carolina—Fiction.
5. Teenage boys—Fiction. I. Title.
PS3562.A67137 M66 2000
813'.54—dc21   00-025619

W. W. Norton & Company, Inc.
500 Fifth Avenue, New York, NY 10110
www.wwnorton.com

W. W. Norton & Company Ltd.
10 Coptic Street, London WCIA 1PU

1   2   3   4   5   6   7   8   9   0

Again, and always, for Mary

Acknowledgments

Writing, day by day, is such a solitary undertaking that it's always surprising to look back once the book is finished and see just how many people had a hand in it. Much gratitude to my parents for taking me to all those county fairs; to Lucas and Alex for helping me keep a part of myself eight years old; to Susan Perabo for her help with the early chapters a hundred years ago in Arkansas; and to the Thursday Night Group: Barb, Maggie, Keith, Karen, Mary, Jack, Micheal, and Frank. Not bad for a bunch of poets. Thanks to Kat and Wendy for curing my slump. I am grateful to Peter Steinberg for his hard work, faith, and calm perseverance in the face of my daily bouts of worry and paranoia, to Michael Parker for his clear-eyed encouragement, and to Patricia Chui for her smart insight and guidance; she promised this would be fun and turned out to be right. Thanks also to the English faculty at Frostburg State for their encouragement and to the Maryland State Arts Council and the National Endowment for the Arts for their financial assistance.

Money, love....No money, no love.
—Howling Wolf

The large print giveth, and
the small print taketh away.
—Tom Waits

Money,
Love

Chapter 1

The summer after Nixon resigned, my father began selling the Mr. America Body Sculpting kits, carrying them in the trunk of his Chevy Impala and wholesaling them door to door. August was the wrong time for such work, walking our low North Carolina hills in his brown suit, lugging the boxes of weights, stepping along broken sidewalks and driveways into basements and attics where he would assemble the kits for his customers and drink the glasses of iced tea they offered him. For all of his forty-one years, he'd had an unerring knack for predicting trends after they'd already occurred, conceiving hotshot ideas and then failing to capitalize on them, a natural inclination to wrong turns. At a time when it seemed everyone in the country had discovered jogging and yoga, the whole idea of lifting weights—grunting, sweating, pumping iron—seemed almost right-wing, as out of fashion as the Mr. America ads I saw in the back of my *Popular Mechanics*. They were always the same, those crudely drawn comic strips showing exiled fifties kids leaving the malt shop and heading toward the beach, where the crew-cut guys would fight over girls in Annette Funicello hairdos and two-piece swimsuits too modest to be called bikinis.

Even I understood the irony of those ads in that time, and I didn't know anything. I was sixteen years old, growing up in a city of subdivisions with names like Green Valley and Forest Glen, near a shopping center where each Christmas Santa Claus would drop in on a parachute. I let myself be carried through days by what amounted to a dumb acceptance of life, like a cow in a field. I wore a ponytail then, not as any kind of statement, but because my mother, Gladys (who insisted I call her by her first name), fancied herself an artist and poet and thought that raising a nonconformist child made her seem more the part. Her poems were published in mail-order anthologies she had to agree to buy for $29.95, an extra $10 for her name embossed in gold on the cover, her poems scattered in among a thousand others, nearly all of them on the subjects of Grandpa's farm, old dying dogs, and the American flag. One year she won the "Platinum Poetess Medal" and flew her first jet flight to Chicago, paid $275 (plus air fare and accommodations), and walked onto a plywood riser in the Airport Ramada to receive a framed certificate and a fountain pen. She went along with all this, I think, pretending, knowing that her poems were not very good, but wanting the pleasure of them anyway. Gladys believed that her final reward abided in me, that after nine and a half months of pregnancy and thirty-one hours of labor and a couple decades of free-spirited well-meaning parenting, I would finally become a "serious artist of some importance." This was her phrase, and she repeated it as though I'd come with a warranty. But the closest I came to an artistic impulse was dancing on my mattress in my underwear, whanging away at an imaginary guitar while Grand Funk or Led Zeppelin howled on the eight-track.

In the Mr. America ads no one did bong hits or tabs of acid, no one drank beer and drove around at night throwing the empties at stop signs. Instead they drove to the beach in paneled woodies filled with surfboards, enduring an endless summer. They had never seen leftover spray-painted microbuses and tiny Japanese cars, had never been stuck in a gas line on some cold Monday morning. Everybody in Mr. America world was white; no one had long hair, no one was poor. It was a world, stuck there in glossy black and white, into which my father would have fit nicely; people had not yet learned to give up their trust of politicians, policemen, salesmen. He could have made a killing selling embossed Bibles or hair tonic or fallout shelters. The world would not change so much, so quickly. He finally caught on, that summer of 1975, too late, when the sixties were finally over and he began wholesaling surplus army clothes and neon tie-dyed T-shirts, the same year everybody began blow-drying their hair and wearing leisure suits. Mr. America world had vanished forever. I didn't know how to tell him.

But my father could sell. I needed no more evidence of this than the fact that he'd sold Gladys on the idea of marrying him, even though her family cut her off from the money they'd made selling Standish's Lawn Builder and other fertilizer supplies, kicked her off the property at Pawleys Island one October. But for my father, nothing—not even winning Gladys—was ever enough. He grew impatient in his selling, made mistakes, got fired. He went through so many jobs that finally he had printed up a generic business card:

Roman Morrill Strickland
Salesman

In the corner was a fancy four-color graphic of a cherub adorned with hearts, garlands, and bows. My father said he intended the cherub to symbolize him, to be something that would stick in the minds of his customers, an idea he dredged from one of the motivational and super-salesmanship books he constantly read. I didn't tell him that at a stocky five foot ten, with slicked-down black hair beneath his fedora, a solid gut hanging over his belt, and dense fur covering his chest, he was hard to imagine as anything remotely cherubic. Roman was handsome, in a way that had gone out of style——his wide-shouldered burliness, gold tooth in the corner of his mouth, suspenders beneath his suitcoats. He wore a pinkie ring and paid money he could not afford for manicures. During up years he drove a big Lincoln Continental with suicide doors and opera lights. He still believed suaveness and manners carried currency with women, and, for a certain portion of his life, it did.

The weight sets weren't moving. Roman had assembled one of them in the damp basement of our house, beneath the pink lightbulb my mother kept screwed in the overhead socket because she liked the light it threw on her sheets when she folded laundry. She believed in small pleasures. At night after supper my father went downstairs and lifted weights, wearing a T-shirt, his pants tucked into a pair of old leather lace-up wrestling shoes he'd kept since high school. The set consisted of barbells and free weights which were no more than disks of cement wrapped in maroon plastic. There was also a bench that would tilt and recline for preacher curls and bench presses, a jump rope with weighted handles, a medicine ball, hand grips, a leather belt, and a full-size drawing of a man with his major muscle groups colored in pinks and browns and labeled with Latin names. This my father taped to the water heater, so I had to walk under the stairs to see the major muscle groups of the man's left shoulder and arm. Every evening I followed my father to the basement and read aloud the instructions for doing the exercises properly, to achieve, the booklet said, "the full Mr. America ISOTONIC™ Benefit!!!" Roman grunted with each lift, and beneath the pink bulb the redness of his face deepened. There seemed to be some kind of disappointment built into the set, as if making yourself anything like the pictures of Mr. America on the box (that hairless, tanned body, biceps like tennis balls) was simply impossible. I could not imagine Roman ever looking like that. Plus, the sound of the weights wasn't right; instead of the clang and ring of iron, the plastic-covered free weights gave forth a quiet *pock* when they hit into one another. Within a week the bar had begun to rust and the cement had broken inside several of the weights, so that they rattled like a box of stones. Roman wore a faint stripe of oil across his T-shirt where the bar rested on bench presses.

My job was to spot for him, and the first night he'd assigned it to me, he sat me down on the bench, looked me in the face, and wrinkled his eyes with deep concern (his "closing face," he called it). He told me he was putting his life in my hands. He took my wrists and held up my hands for me to see. I felt like some crack demolition expert, a gifted heart surgeon, and dismissed the thought that if he were to drop those 210 pounds squarely on his windpipe, there would be nothing I could do except run to the phone or scream. But when the reps slowed, I acted as if I were helping him, as if I really could save his life. He paid me two dollars an hour.

One night I stood behind him watching the bar rise and fall, bobbing my head to the sound of Deep Purple playing on the portable eight-track plugged in above the workbench. Roman puffed and grunted, smoking Pall Malls between sets, a thin film of sweat coating the vinyl bench of the weight set. Ours was not a normal basement with stacks of runny paint cans, tools, sawdust, and broken toys. Instead we were surrounded by leftover samples of all the things my father had sold, from jobs he'd held and lost. One shelf contained boxes of an all-in-one kitchen appliance called the Juice Moose, which actually worked, but came with a pink-and-blue cartoon moose permanently embossed on the front. Below that were the Havahart traps for rats and mice and the polystyrene golf balls guaranteed to shave five strokes off your game.

Gladys stood beside us snapping sheets under her pink bulb, folding my father's boxer shorts and starching his collars while she ironed on top of the washer, turning inside out my rock-band T-shirts so the iron-on decals wouldn't melt. She tried to hide under the basket of clothes her own underwear, the black front-hook bras and lace garter belts. It was only lately that I had connected the contents of the laundry with what my mother must have been wearing under her clothes, under the tan khaki skirts and tennis shorts and Peter Pan collars; it didn't seem to fit, as if there had been some mix-up and the washing machine had transported away what I imagined to be my mother's *real* underwear: white, wiry bras with wide straps and—God knows, I really thought this—bloomers. The black and silvery lace she tucked beneath the pile of clothes seemed like some other life she was hiding away. While I watched her, Roman grunted and the bar began to tip. I helped settle the bar while the tape deck clicked onto "Space Truckin'." I plucked the pocket of my jeans with an imaginary guitar pick.

"Turn that crap down," Roman said. "They sound like a bunch of maniacs."

"The very thing your father said about Buddy Rich," Gladys said. "Gabe's absorbing the music of his culture. It's part of his education."

"Study the way money works, son. That's all you need to know."

"Really, Roman," Gladys said. "Gabe, ignore him."

"I'm serious," Roman said. "One of your teachers starts poppin' off about . . ." He shrugged and stubbed out his Pall Mall on the leg of the weight bench. He swung his legs across and sat up. "What are they poppin' off about these days?"

"The Bastille . . ." I said. "Robert Frost . . . cosines."

"Okay, there you go. One of them starts on Robert Frost, you raise your hand—always polite, customers remember that—you raise it and say, 'How will this help me make money?' No answer? Walk out." He took a towel out of the fresh laundry and wiped his neck.

"Don't you listen to him, Gabe," Gladys said. "Think what money did to Richard Burton and Ernest Hemingway."

"God, yes," Roman said. "They had to get paid to be on TV, marry gorgeous women, drive sports cars. It was awful."

"I can't walk out of school, Dad," I said. "I'll get busted."

"Then *I'll* teach you," Roman said. "Home schooling, right here. Lesson one. You knock on a door, lady in curlers, face like a gravel driveway, and you're there to sell her what?"

I looked at my mother, and she rolled her eyes. This was an old drill. "Venetian blind cleaner attachments," I said.

"Fine, good," Roman said. "But you know by looking she's a tough sell. Ask for a few minutes of her time, offer a free gift, blah blah blah, she asks if you want to talk on the porch or come inside. What do you say?"

I shrugged. "Go inside?"

Roman smiled at me, his gold tooth showing. Then he raised up his arms and started gyrating, circling his hands, twisting side to side from the waist like some Egyptian snake dancer. "Oh that's up to you ma'am. I'm *completely flexible*." He stopped his dance. "You get it? The slightest giggle from that woman, the least baby smile, and bam—money in your pocket."

I laughed.

"Wonderful, Roman," my mother said, shaking out a pillowcase.

He ignored her. "There might be a quiz over this material," he said.

Gladys shook her head. "Roman, *stop* putting these ideas in his mind. Gabe, look at me. Promise me you won't go chasing after money. This is important to me."

"Okay," I said, and shrugged. I was sixteen and life held little weight. I could promise anything to anybody.

Roman picked up the spring-loaded hand grips and began squeezing them. His arms had expanded in the three weeks he'd been lifting, but without the definition of muscle, like Mr. America on the box. They grew instead like loaves of bread, thick and doughy, his chest barreling outward. He was quickly approaching being able to press his weight.

"All right, son, here comes math and philosophy at one crack. Just suppose I told you I only sold one Mr. America kit in the last two weeks. Sixty bucks commish take away gas and oil with the trunk loaded down leaves about twenty bucks, half a month's work, divided fifty hours a week. Then suppose I said this meant the light bill wouldn't get paid, our credit is going to shit, and no food. Then you think you could say that money is important?"

My mother dropped her skirt on the floor. "Roman, not again. Please not again." Unpaid bills were usually the topic of the muffled arguments I heard through their bedroom wall.

He waved his hand, the grips jingling. "Purely hypothetical. What do you say, son?"

As I started to answer, Gladys picked up the flowered skirt, crushed it into a ball, and threw it across the basement against the underside of the stairs. It dangled there, caught on a splinter. In two strides she made it across the room and punched Roman hard in the shoulder.

"God*damn* it, Roman. You stop this. I want you to *tell* me."

He looked at her and rubbed his shoulder. "Everything's taken care of, Gladys. Don't worry."

I understood enough of their marital code to know that this meant trouble, that my mother would have to take a temp job again, usually working in the ice cream warehouse at United Dairy. I knew that they would have a yard sale and I'd be forced to pitch in something, old roller skates or eight-tracks I didn't listen to anymore. On top of all that, I knew that Roman had an amazing aptitude for losing jobs and that Gladys hated it more every time it happened. Among the other leftovers on our basement shelves we had a dozen dust-covered green lawn chairs woven with a product called Supra-Webbing. Roman had done well one summer selling them on a commission-only deal for the inventor, who, to prove his product, had tied a length of the webbing to the bumper of his truck and pulled down a rotted fifty-foot silo on his farm near Asheboro. Going door to door, Roman carried with him color photos of the silo crashing in the gravel lot, and sold fourteen boxes of chairs his first week out.

The second week he took me with him, to drive him around (I was fourteen at the time). He decided to target the Bermuda Run Extended Care Facility. This had been Roman's brainstorm, to sell chairs and webbing replacement service contracts to every retirement village and nursing home in the state, places, he said, where everyone had nothing to do all day but sit. He liked his idea so much that he called Paulie Mathers, the Lincoln dealer, and put in an order for a new baby-blue Continental with electric windows, pecan trim, leatherette seats, and whitewalls.

The manager of Bermuda Run was a middle-aged, overweight woman in a green flowered housedress with Kool 100s sticking out of the pocket. As Roman worked his way through his pitch, she examined the lawn chairs, blowing smoke through her nostrils, and said in her tiny voice that they looked "flimsy."

My father handed her the pictures again. "Look at that silo, Margaret. Flimsy? Time and the weather can't knock the damn thing down. Pardon my French. No problem for Supra-Webbing. After we did this experiment we made chairs from this very webbing—didn't want to waste any—and those are the very chairs I use in my home today."

She picked up one of the chairs and shook it, her other hand holding the photos and her cigarette. "I don't know. You think they would hold me?"

Roman looked furtively around the room. "Margaret, I'm not supposed to divulge this, but NASA has contacted us about Supra-Webbing, for moon landings, space module parachutes, top secret programs, that sort of thing. This was the first lawn chair on the moon."

She studied the photos of the downed silo. "Do you think that's real, or they staged it?"

"The pictures don't lie. The silo was estimated to weigh three tons."

"No, I mean that whole man on the moon thing. Some people say it was a movie set."

Roman hesitated. "I can't say I've thought about it."

"'Cause if it was a movie I had no business getting up at two a.m. to watch. Wouldn't get up at that hour for Tyrone Power."

Roman bit his lip and glanced at me. He'd been thrown off his rhythm, as important to him in his pitch as to a major leaguer hurling a fastball.

"Margaret, these chairs are so comfortable that in my very own home we've given away the couch. Gave it away to charity. They're what we, my family and I, personally sit in." He lowered his voice. "Look at my son over there."

This was the solemn part of the sell, where Roman could somehow link lawn chairs (or electric can openers or aluminum siding) to the health and potential of America's youth.

Margaret looked at me and smiled, blowing smoke through her nose.

"You think I'd trust his safety and comfort to any lawn chair?" Roman asked.

She laughed at him.

Laughed out loud, her mouth exploding in smoke and noise, laughed without a joke. Everyone who got pitched laughed at some point, at the corny, front-porch stories Roman told, at the audacity of the pitch, at their own willingness to be carried along. According to Roman, after people bought something, they loved the person who had sold it to them. But Margaret, this woman in the flowered housedress, had stepped outside all that, forgotten her function as customer, blown her unwritten lines. My father called this "breaking the bubble."

Roman's face reddened. "Ben Franklin was a very wise man, I think you'll agree, Margaret."

I nearly laughed at him myself. The Ben Franklin close was a last resort, an amateur's way out, a spitball. Even I knew she was nowhere near closing.

Roman pressed on. "Ben Franklin, faced with a tough decision, would do a typically wise thing, Margaret. He'd sit and make a list of all the positives and all the negatives, then see which outweighed the other and go with that."

He drew pen and paper from his jacket. "Number one, you said you like the color of the chairs. That's a positive." He wrote it down. "Number two, you like the superior strength."

She frowned. "I never said that, Mr. Strickland."

He ignored her. "Number three . . ."

Margaret looked at me. "You know he fathered thirteen illegitimate children? Read it in the *World Examiner*."

I froze, convinced for a moment she was talking about Roman.

"I don't call that very wise," she said to Roman.

He began to put away his photos and samples, cramming them into his bag, winding the Supra-Webbing samples into tight rolls.

"You call if you change your mind," he said.

She shook her head. "I just don't think they'd hold me," she said, as if her decision had hinged on this point. It was the moment we should have walked out, but Roman, as ever, had to have the last word.

"They might hold you, lady," he said. "The question is, why in hell would they *want* to? I mean, *I* sure as hell wouldn't want to hold you. I'm sure your husband doesn't."

"Dad," I said.

He looked at me. "Can you think of anyone, Gabe? So maybe you're right, Margaret. Why should we pick on these poor chairs?"

In the parking lot he stopped and stood by his car, just staring off.

"You shouldn't have said that," I told him. "You blew it."

"I know it, Gabe. I know it." He scratched his head. "If they would just be quiet and *listen,* then I could tell them what they need, they could buy it, we'd all be happy."

"But they don't *have* to listen. You always forget that."

"No, you're right, son. We're living in a fallen world, and they don't have to listen." He smiled at me, then walked back inside, apologized, and gave Margaret one of the sample Supra-Webbing chairs. But it was too late for apologies. The next morning she had called and complained to his boss, and before lunchtime that day he'd been fired and had canceled his order for the Lincoln. For Roman, another routine week.

Gladys hit him with her fist again, softer this time. "I mean it, Roman. If you do this to us again, something's going to change." She shook her head. "I can't live this way."

"Mom, he said everything's under control."

"You're smarter than that, Gabe. You've lived here sixteen years." She looked at my father, who had the towel draped like a turban over his head. "Tell me, right now," she said.

"If you keep disturbing the class," Roman said, "I'll have to take you upstairs for a paddling."

He possessed a salesman's sense of timing, where a bad joke could break the ice, where pushing too hard could force the deal, where walking away was always possible. None of this worked at home, with her.

My mother stared at him, not wanting to let him off this time, wanting, I could tell, some real threat behind her words. She wanted to be able to dock his pay, to assign him a shit territory, to fire him—something he could understand. Instead she turned and stomped up the stairs above us, leaving her iron smoldering on the washer, burning through my father's bowling pin tie.

"So what's your answer, son?"

I stepped and lifted the iron, shut it off. "I guess the money's pretty important," I said.

He smiled and opened his hands to flex the muscles in his forearms, the odor of burned polyester all around us.

"Class dismissed."

Roman gave up the Mr. America kits after having to have the rear shocks replaced in the Chevy, and went back to household products. He hated household products because they were always steady sellers. You would never lose money, he said—housewives always needed oven cleaner and vegetable brushes—but by the same token you could never make money either. Not real money. In Georgia during the early sixties, he had a job selling Bibles door to door to the wives of cotton farmers and factory workers. He hit on a town called Byleah the morning after the Reverend Bobby Mortimer had blazed through with his tent revival, one long night of hellfire, healed goiters, and dyslexic schoolchildren cured of their demons. So after three and a half weeks of break-even, Roman pulled into town with his trunkload of gold-embossed red-letter Bibles and sold out in just over two days. He ordered more, loaded his car from the front seats back, got his hands on Bobby Mortimer's schedule, and followed that tent revival twelve hundred miles across the South, sweeping in behind like he was God-sent, selling Bibles without opening his mouth, pulling down fifteen hundred a month for almost half a year.

But nothing like that was possible with household products. "No matter how you look at foaming bathroom spray," he said to me once, "God's just not in it." And no challenge in pushing the products either; women were either out of cleaners or toothbrushes or they weren't, and he could please come back in a month.

"Take something like space-age lawn chairs, Gabe," he said to me, "or a framed copy of the Declaration of Independence." He shook his head. "There, you *create* a need, make it out of nothing, where it never existed before you opened your mouth."

He believed in the sale, lived his life in dedication to it. Once, to prove a point to Gladys, he bought up six cases of Thin Mint Girl Scout cookies, then went around the neighborhood in his shirt-sleeves, hat tipped back, and in three hours sold all six cases for double price. He gave the money to my mother. God only knows what he told the people who bought them.

So he came back to household products the way you come back to bad love. He sold them only because it appeased my mother, who seemed to like the idea of paying bills on time. Within a few weeks she'd managed to stock the freezer with hamburger and to get our couch and console stereo back from the repossessors. She was happy during that time, happy that she'd avoided part-time work at United Dairy, happy that my father was assigned local territory, that the paychecks were regular. This stirred Roman's belief that it was the money making her happy, instead of just the steadiness. He believed too that more money meant more happiness. This was his way of thinking: if he had a headache, he swallowed four aspirin, thinking this would cut his recovery time in half. Household products offered stability, so there had to be a way to squeeze even *more* stability out of them, if only, he said, you're willing to roll the dice a little and shake things up.

Roman began his next set of twenty reps, speaking in grunts and expelled breaths. "It's a matter of pushing harder," he said. I was spotting for him and reading aloud from *Winning As a Way of Life*, which had arrived two days before with my mother's book club selection, and which he'd already underlined and dog-eared. The book consisted of easy-to-remember rhyming homilies on the subjects of selling, winning, and making money ("If you want to earn your dough, get up in the morning and GO, GO, GO!"). Gladys was upstairs somewhere, working on a poem based on Billy Graham's new book, *Angels: God's Secret Agents*, which had been her monthly book club selection.

"But you told me demand was a constant," I said. "Either you have stuff to clean your oven or you don't."

He grunted, dropping the bar on its rests. "Read that last sentence again," he said.

"'Though we might use emotion, devotion, or some secret

potion, nothing does more than old-fashioned promotion.'" I looked down at him.

"See my point? It's *all* advertising, Gabe. Just look at your Uncle Dutch. Son of a bitch couldn't sell shit to a green fly, but look at the business he does."

Uncle Dutch was older than Roman by six years. He owned a Ford and Plymouth dealership on the outskirts of Kernersville where he had five acres of new cars and an OK Used Car lot. Ads for his dealership ran on late-night TV during *Twilight Theater*, for which he was the sponsor. Gladys was the only one who still got excited when his new ads ran. The commercials always featured Dutch doing things like jumping out of an airplane dressed as a turkey, or sitting atop one of his billboards on the highway, wearing a tuxedo and eating dinner by candlelight. In the latest ad, one of his Plymouth Furys had been immersed in a glass water tank, and Dutch sat behind the wheel wearing scuba equipment, waving at the camera. The joke of every ad was that Dutch never smiled, played everything with a serious deadpan, as if all these things had been done to him and he was the hapless victim of some prank. In truth, Dutch *was* as serious as he seemed; he had no discernible sense of humor. The stunts were designed by his advertising agency and he went along only because they sold cars and put money in his accounts. He was as rich as Roman wanted to be. Everywhere across three counties were the billboards of Dutch's solemn face, his black hair and silver sideburns, white suitcoats and brown ties. When I was a little kid he would come to our house for a visit once a year at Christmas, but at age forty-three he had married Miss North Carolina, and afterward the two of them spent Christmas in Las Vegas. Three years later Miss North Carolina divorced him, and for a year after that Roman worked for him selling cars. Roman quit finally, saying that it bothered his conscience to sell a Plymouth to anyone. The real reason, I knew, was that he didn't like having to work for his brother.

Roman sat up on the weight bench and wiped his face with his shirt. "Now with door-to-door, you can't go on TV. You've got no radio, magazine ads, billboards, subway posters, buses, taxicabs." He counted them off on his fingers. "So, where's the advertising?"

I shrugged, not wanting this to go much further. I think he really did believe that these basement sessions were the best part of my education, that they could take the place of school and put me, at sixteen, on the road to easy money.

"Me," he said. "*I'm* the damn advertisement, right? So I pump myself up to sell muscle kits, look nice and holy for Bible gigs, like a rocket scientist for encyclopedias and globes. Where does that leave us with household products?"

I handed him a towel. "I don't know. Look clean?"

He shook his head. "That's a given. I don't look clean, they don't open the door."

"Look friendly?" I said.

He laughed and lit up one of his Pall Malls, tossed the match into the floor drain. "You can do better than that, son."

I was getting tired of this. "You planning to test me on this stuff?" I said.

He pointed at me. "The rest of your life, that's the test."

"I can't think of anything," I said. This was a lie. I was thinking of my father in the heat of a North Carolina summer lugging across endless lawns, avoiding sprinklers and kids and stray dogs. I imagined him walking up sidewalks and driveways, his gait dictated by the sample case, his muscled body clothed in houndstooth jackets, Arrow shirts, skinny neckties, and two-tone shoes, looking like he'd just stepped out of two decades ago. I imagined the women behind the screen doors in the neighborhoods where their children played buying their vegetable peelers and pot holders from Roman, putting off buying them at the supermarket and waiting for his monthly visits because they felt that a man his age shouldn't have to support his family this way, wearing out his shoes, pounding on the doors of strangers.

"Son, I *can* think of something." He stood up and pointed at me. "I by God can. What did the book say, 'winning strategy'? You wait here." He ran upstairs, and ten minutes later had not returned. While he was gone I lay down on the padded bench, stretched my palms against the weight bar, took a breath, and pressed upward. The bar would not budge; I couldn't even lift a side of it, couldn't rock it on its rests. I shifted my weight, slid farther up, and tried again, spitting and grunting, straining so my eyes hurt and I thought the veins in my neck would burst.

I let go the bar and lay there looking at it, thinking of that first day with the set when he'd charged me with saving his life, and I knew that I could not help him in the least if he got in real trouble lifting weights. His windpipe could be crushed, his neck broken, and no amount of adrenaline would help me, the way it helped the people who told their miracle stories in the *Reader's Digest*s that Gladys kept on her nightstand. The stories always involved babies trapped under cars or grandfathers crushed under their tractors, and a series of unlikely weaklings—young housewives, boys who'd been cut from the football team, or old ladies a couple weeks out of surgery (*Reader's Digest* relished this kind of irony)—who found in themselves the muscle to drag Chryslers across sidewalks, to push John Deeres out of ditches. My mother loved these stories, believing, I think, that her entire adult life had been purchased from out of these mysterious reserves of secret strength, only she had withdrawn hers little by little, over the years, instead of all at once in a miraculous burst. But it was miracle enough for her that she'd stayed with Roman, that her only son was destined for artistic greatness.

A half hour later he came back down the stairs. He'd traded in his dark wool pants for a pair of white sweatpants tucked into his wrestling shoes, and a fresh white tank top. His thick, wiry black hair was all gone. He had completely shaved his head, bald, the whiteness of his scalp shining under the basement lights.

"Who wouldn't buy cleaners and brushes from Mr. Clean *himself,* Gabe?" he said. "Name me one person."

I could only stare at him. He had apparently shaved using his safety razor; all along the back of his head, nicks and cuts bled in tiny rivulets. On the top and sides, he'd stuck patches of toilet paper to the cuts, each patch with a perfect dot of blood in the center, like fish eyes. Behind his ears were tiny islands of hair he'd missed. He wore in his right ear one of Gladys's clip-on earrings, not a hoop, but gold dangles with pearls on the ends.

"Okay, it needs a little work," he said. "But the basic idea's a winner."

"Roman . . . damn," I said. "You look like a freak."

He tried to give me his look of fatherly disapproval while I tried not to fall on the floor laughing. In the absence of other hair, his thick, black eyebrows, heavy enough that he usually combed them down with a dab of hair oil, looked as if he'd pasted them on as part of a disguise.

"Is Speedy Alka-Seltzer a freak, Gabe? Is the Michelin Man? The Marlboro Man? Come back and talk to me after you've logged twenty-two years in this business."

"They don't sell Michelin tires door to door."

He crossed his arms, grown thick as fire hoses, and for a moment he really did look like Mr. Clean. He cocked his head at me, the pearls of the earring swaying.

"So what's your point, Gabe? You think Michelin just sprouted up overnight? Big factory, couple hundred thousand employees, just like that. Or maybe they started small, with a good idea and some gumption in their pocket?"

He was pulling words out of the motivational books he'd read, words from the Tab Taylor symposiums that were held every so often at the War Memorial Auditorium. Tab Taylor sold books and pamphlets and audio tapes that you were meant to listen to in your sleep. They indoctrinated listeners into the Tab Taylor system, which Tab himself had used to "corner the market in personal motivation," whatever that meant. Some nights I would go for a midnight snack, and find Roman on the couch, snoring, the big black headphones pushed up covering his nose. I never pointed out to him that if Tab Taylor had made millions in real estate and home businesses, he wouldn't need to travel around the country peddling his bullshit in hotel banquet rooms.

Gladys came downstairs to tell us that dessert was ready. Halfway down she stopped and stared at Roman, her face caught somewhere between speaking and smiling. She looked at me, as if Roman's appearance were some elaborate hoax I had rigged up and would reveal at any second.

"What's going on?" she said.

"Gladys, now you're going to listen to me on this one," Roman said.

"What the *hell* are you doing?" she said, her hands white on the railing. "Don't tell me. A hundred and fifty a week isn't good enough for you. Paying off bills isn't good enough. Nothing is *ever* good enough, is it, Roman?" Her cheeks reddened, as if she'd been slapped.

Roman turned to me, looking for help. The blood from the cuts had dried in dark brown lines, like he'd sprung leaks. He looked back at Gladys.

"Think for a minute, baby," Roman said. "You're in your bathroom, slaving away trying to clean the toilet, scrub the shower, then out of the blue *Mr. Clean himself* shows up on your porch step. Now what would—"

"I'd call the goddamn police. Roman, I swear to God I will *not* let you fuck this up this time. I won't *let* you."

I don't know what she expected him to do, short of going

upstairs, digging his hair out of the wastebasket, and gluing it back to his scalp. Hearing the profanity out of Gladys's mouth, I felt the same shock I'd felt when Roman had first come down the stairs. I suppose she had always spoken this way when they argued, but I was only just now noticing it, having recently picked up swearing at school the same way I picked up trying cigarettes and beer. I was working hard to acquire as many bad habits as possible, and here was my mother, already adept at several of them herself. I must have stared at her a full minute, trying to see into this secret self of hers, the evidence of which existed in the form of her outbursts of profanity as proficient as any I'd heard in the gym locker room, and the black, lacy under-wear folded and hidden away at the bottom of the laundry basket. I felt it so strongly, I wanted to ask her, "Who *are* you?"

Just as I noticed her gearing herself up for another barrage of anger at Roman, one of the pieces of toilet paper stuck to his head slipped loose and fluttered down, settling on the weight bench. Gladys pressed her lips together. Another piece of paper fell, then another, fluttering away from him. Gladys folded her hands over her mouth and bent at the waist, laughing.

"At least you're nicely *accessorized*," she said, nearly screaming the last word. My father looked at me and shook his head. I didn't know what it meant either, but I started laughing just because she was. Roman squared his shoulders and folded his arms, the gold earring flashing beneath the pink bulb.

"Fine," he said. "Keep laughing. You'll see."

"Just wear your hat tomorrow, honey," Gladys said. "Tell everyone you had surgery. You always say, sympathy sales are money in the bank."

The next morning Roman got dressed while Gladys was out shopping at the farmers' market. He walked into the kitchen in his Mr. Clean outfit and tossed me the car keys. He'd made a hoop ear-ring from a paper clip.

"You're wheel man today. I'll write a note for your summer school. I want you to see your old man in action. We'll clear five hundred today, easy."

Ever since I'd turned thirteen and could reach the pedals, Roman would sometimes have me tail him with the car, driving five miles an hour while he walked from house to house. This saved him the time of leaving the car and then walking back to it. I could hurry him along to the next block after he'd finished working one. Sometimes he would ride standing just inside the open door of the Chevy (or Lincoln, when he was having a hot year), clinging to the roof of the car, his sample bag resting on top. I loved how those days felt, as if the chase after money really were a chase, that it might get away if we let it. The trunk of the car was always filled with old samples from jobs he no longer held, the front dash covered with Styrofoam coffee cups and bean-bag ashtrays full of cigarette butts. I was expected to stay far enough back that it still looked like he was on foot. I was to avoid scraping the wire wheel covers against the curb, and was allowed in the summer to run the air-conditioning for ten minutes every hour. More, Roman said, and I'd be cutting into his overhead. He paid me, as he did for any job, no matter how small. When I was younger, he would make me come with him to the doors as he covered his territory, especially on rainy days. Sympathy sales *were* money in the bank. All of this quit when I reached nearly his height and let my ponytail grow out, because, he said, "nobody feels sorry for a wet hippie."

He had big plans for that day in his Mr. Clean outfit. He wouldn't allow me even to finish my eggs before he had me in the driver's seat, tooling slowly through subdivisions with names like Whispering Pines and Rolling Hills. Inching along in the Chevy, I decided that they must name the subdivisions for whatever it was they had to demolish in order to build them. Roman walked along carrying his clipboard crammed with order blanks, his case filled with triple samples so he could sell right on the spot.

I hung back the right amount of distance and watched him approach the first house. It looked likely: toys in the driveway, laundry flapping in the side yard, a little red windmill mailbox. Roman liked easy marks, and these were the signs. ("Nice people in nice neighborhoods," he said to me once, shaking his head, "sometimes it's like fish in a barrel.") He rang the bell, set his case and clipboard on the stoop, then struck a pose. He balled his fists and stood with his hands on his hips, chest puffed out. I imagined him trying to arch one of his slicked down black eyebrows. He rang the bell again, and I saw the bay window curtain part for a moment and then close. No one came to the door. As he made his way down the block there were four more no-shows, and two quick-slams, Roman's term for people who opened the door and immediately regretted it, who kept him from even launching into his pitch. He started running from house to house, breaking his own rules ("never panic," "never cut across lawns"). He crossed streets into the next block before he'd even finished the first. An hour later he still hadn't broken the ice, had not sold as much as one Screw-top Gripper, the cheapest item in his bag. I had to gun the Chevy to keep up with him, and got caught up in his panic, forgetting and letting the air-conditioning run until I had goose bumps along my arms. I wasn't sure what it was he was afraid of, what I was afraid of; he'd been skunked before on bad days, which he said averaged out and didn't matter. But I think this one time it wasn't money; instead, he wanted to prove to Gladys that his idea would work, that he didn't have to settle for just paying the bills. Good enough *wasn't* good enough. I dug a butt out of the ashtray and lit it. Near the end of Hickory Lane, he walked to the car and sat down heavily in the front seat. I heard his T-shirt stick to the vinyl. He opened the glove compartment and pulled out his bottle of Crown Royal, which he kept in its purple velvet bag, along with what he had always called his Binaca chaser. He offered me a drink and I took it.

"You ever see a hurt dog crawl up under a house?" he said.

I shook my head and handed back the bottle. We had never owned any pets, not even a gerbil or a goldfish.

"A dog gets hurt, gets scared, he crawls up under something and there's no getting him out. You got to wait for him to decide to come out. You see what I'm getting at?"

I shook my head again. "No."

He frowned. "Pay attention. This is important." He pointed the bottle at the row of houses. "They're scared to give in to this pitch. They *want* to, but they're scared. This is something new. The newness is what they're afraid of."

I wanted to say that maybe they were scared because he looked insane. Criminally insane, like some escapee still in prison whites, his head shaved for tomorrow morning's electrocution. Instead, I nodded, and took another drink.

"We've got to get them out, bring them to us," he said.

We found a subdivision we hadn't yet covered (Quail Run) and started at the top of Elderberry Drive, which curved gently downward, lined with cul-de-sacs. I drove as slowly as I could, making no jerky movements with the brake or gas pedals, while Roman stood—hands on his hips, smiling and arching his eyebrows—squarely on the hood of the white Chevy. He waved, lifting his arms like the Grand Marshal of some parade. I turned the radio up as loud as it would go, leaned against the horn ring, flashed the headlights. I turned on the emergency flashers and windshield wipers. Slowly, like squirrels out of trees, the people in the houses stepped out onto their porches and stood pointing and shaking their heads. A few people followed us down the block, swept into our wake, following the way they would follow searchlights in the night sky, not knowing what they might find. As we reached the bottom of the hill, I cut the engine and let us drift silently to a stop. Ten or twelve people, housewives and retirees, a few kids on bikes, had followed us down and now surrounded the car. Roman launched into his pitch, using this booming Mr. Clean voice. He asked them what they did about the dirt they could not see. He handed everyone a new dollar bill, telling them they could keep it, or triple its value in five minutes' time. The people stood looking at each other and at the free money that had found its way into their hands. A few walked away, but most didn't. Roman sold oven mitts and vegetable brushes, took orders for turkey basters, electric whisks, left-handed can openers, personalized asbestos pot holders. One of the kids even asked for his autograph. We covered two more adjoining neighborhoods in the same way, drawing bigger crowds each time.

"Do you believe this?" he said, back in the car. "Drive to Starmount Forest. That's where they're keeping all the money."

"I've never driven all the way through town before," I said, though my real problem was the bottle of Crown Royal we had half finished. My head buzzed and the Chevy seemed to want to steer itself.

"You get your license next year, right?"

I nodded. I should have had it already, but had never bothered with the Driver's Ed classes.

"So you're starting early. Drive," he said. He lit a cigar and completed the work on the stack of pink sheets in his clipboard. A five-o'clock shadow covered his head, the cuts now just thin scabs.

He had more trouble selling in Starmount Forest, where I imagined the people's lives bathed in refinement. For them, I figured, entertainment was the ballet or the symphony, and some cheap spectacle—a bald man on a noisy car—didn't count for much. When we rode through the golf course section an elderly security guard in a golf cart with flashing lights pulled me over and told me to stop honking the horn. He paid no attention to my father standing on the hood.

"He could've run me in for drunk driving," I said.

Roman shook his head. "Number one, he's just a pretend cop. Probably write you up if you hooked your tee shot. And number

two, drunk driving is what rich people do for fun." He thought
about this for a minute. "Don't tell your mother I let you drink."

We had a couple of hours of light left, but it was nearing the
dinner hour, when you should never ring a doorbell. "You interrupt
their food," Roman said once, "you can't sell them immortality."
We finished off the first bottle of Crown Royal and started on the
second. This was celebration for him. He'd sold two hundred dollars' worth of goods right out of his sample case, and taken orders
for another four hundred. This was a good month's salary in a little
under five and a half hours. As I headed out of Starmount Forest, he
pointed to a driveway on the right.

"Turn here, son."

The driveway ran half a mile to a big Victorian house overlooking
the eighteenth tee. It belonged to Dr. Ballister, who had retired as a
pediatrician ten years earlier. For a time, he'd been my doctor. He
always wore a silver eyeshade, like the doctors in children's books. He
washed off the tongue depressors in the sink to reuse them and
smoked Camels in his office, letting the ashes fall to the floor. The
office, in the parlor of the house, had been dark and foreboding, full
of oriental rugs, maroon couches, tasseled lampshades. As far as I
could tell, he hated children, which I always assumed to be his reason
for becoming a pediatrician. He was famous now for sitting all day
Saturday on a bench downtown, eating pork sandwiches. He had tons
of money and a filthy house. This was enough for Roman.

"He's a gold mine, Gabe," he said. "The cruddiest old man I've ever
seen. You think he couldn't use a few hundred household products?"

"But Roman, he's not going to buy anything."

He shook his head. "You are your mother's son. Just drive."

I wanted to talk him out of it, convince him to go home and
show Gladys that he'd been right about the Mr. Clean costume,
show her the roll of bills and checks in his pocket, get her to admit
all over again (which, through the years, she'd learned to do in her

sleep) that he could sell anything. I wanted him to use the money
to pay off bills and get the rest of our furniture back and take us to
dinner where they could drink champagne toasts. It ought to have
been enough, but nothing ever was.

He gave us each a final swig of the Crown Royal and put the bottle back in its purple bag and then into the glove compartment.

"You always make this final push, no matter how tired you are."

"Or drunk," I said.

He nodded. "Whatever. The important thing, it's the difference
between a good salesman and a great one."

I was thinking that by now Gladys would know that I had not
been to school that day, and she would know that Roman had kept
me out. She hated it when he did this, and sometimes wouldn't
speak to him for several days afterward. It wasn't school; I could
tell her that I didn't want to go to school on any given day, that I
wanted instead to go lie down somewhere beside a stream and look
at the sky and let myself think, and she would get on the phone and
call the vice-principal to make an excuse. She thought that these
days of contemplation were another form of education, and I did it
as many times as I thought I could get away with.

Roman slipped out the door and onto the hood, striking his Mr.
Clean pose. As we started down the driveway he held up his hand
for me to stop. He climbed down.

"Dr. Ballister is not a showy man, Gabe," he said.

"Not much," I said.

Roman nodded. "This approach is wrong for him." He asked me
to hand him his suit jacket from the backseat, which he slipped on
over his T-shirt. He sat down next to me. "It's always strategy,
Gabe," he said. "Try to think like your customer."

In the yard of the big house grew patches of bamboo, and scattered in among them leaned old signs from Esso and Mobil stations
and a huge statue of Bob's Big Boy with his plaster hair mostly

chipped off. I maneuvered in between them, right up to the house. Dr. Ballister sat on his porch steps watching our approach, the porch boards warped, weighted with rusted-out washers and a Coke machine. On the porch swing was a greasy sack I recognized as the one he carried his pork sandwiches in when he ate downtown on Saturdays. He wore a gray wool coat with blue jeans and a gray hat with a feather in the band. Across his lap he cradled a crossbow.

"Gentlemen, I don't care if you're selling soap or Jesus, just turn it around."

Roman stepped out of the car and drew his sample case through the window. "Tough sell," he whispered to me.

"Dr. Ballister, you recall we've met," Roman shouted. "Roman Strickland, and my boy there whose tonsils you removed. I came out to ask you to ask yourself one vital question: 'Am I getting the most for my cleaning dollar?'"

"One warning, now I call the authorities," he said. He took aim and fired his arrow at the Big Boy statue, chipping away another piece of plaster hair. He stood and went in the house.

"That supposed to scare us?" Roman said to me.

"No, Dad, I think it's just his hobby. And that *does* scare me. Let's go home."

Roman looked at me, his hair stubble like a dark halo around his head. "Haven't I taught you any better than this?"

He stepped onto the porch, opened his sample bag, and began spraying Rust-Away on the Coke machine. Roman believed in the power of demonstration over the pitch; in that regard he was the most selfless salesman I've ever known, all his ego taken out of the sale, every movement and word in service to the product. Whenever a TV commercial would become a fad and its slogan a national catchphrase repeated on bumper stickers and T-shirts, Roman would shake his head and call it a bad pitch. "It sells the advertisers," he'd say, "not the product." He had just begun sweeping the porch ceiling of its cobwebs, using the E-Z Reach Telescoping Dust Mop, when Dr. Ballister came back out through the screen door with his crossbow reloaded.

"You're still here," he said. "And now you're defacing my home." He shook his head and fired at Big Boy's left knee. "Well, these are your choices. Not good ones, but choices nonetheless. This carries us into the arena of existentialism."

"Dr. Ballister, what if I told you that *one* product would let you clean this entire house, top to bottom? It's almost spring-cleaning time."

He would say this no matter what month of the year. I could see that Dr. Ballister wasn't even hearing the pitch, had probably not heard anything outside his own jumbled thoughts in a good long while. Roman handed him a free Miracle Peeler, which he stuck away inside his coat.

"Evidence," he said. "That's fine." I thought back to when I had my tonsils removed by Dr. Ballister, the gray room I shared at Moses Cone Hospital with a red-haired kid who had blown out his eardrum with an M-80. Dr. Ballister wouldn't allow me any ice cream because he said it hindered the healing process. Thinking of that, I was certain that Dr. Ballister had, in fact, called the police on us. It hadn't been a bluff.

I honked the horn. "Dad, let's go home. Mom's waiting, dinner's waiting. Come on." As I honked again I saw in my rearview the black-and-white cruiser turn down the long driveway.

I later learned that Dr. Ballister called the police out to his property at least once a week, usually because he believed someone was trying to steal his Esso signs, or because, sorting through old papers, he'd come across an unpaid bill and demanded the arrest of some long-dead debtor. So it must have been a relief to the policeman to find us there, to find real trouble. When the officer pulled up and got out of his car, my father was spraying Antz-No-More along Dr. Ballister's windowsills. Everything would have been fine,

I think, except for our appearance—Roman's shaved head, my ponytail held back with a rubber band.

"Are y'all Hare Krishnas or something?" the policeman asked. The name on his tag said Ofc. Mitchell.

"I want you to put these two in prison," Dr. Ballister said.

"Let me handle this, Leo," he said. He wore a blond crew cut and a red mustache and looked to be only a few years older than me.

"Nothing more sinister than free enterprise," Roman said. I could see out of my own drunkenness how far gone he was, and how happy, caught up in this impossible sell.

I started the car. "Let's go, Dad," I said.

Officer Mitchell reached in and turned off the key.

"You're driving? Mind showing me a license?"

"I don't have one," I admitted.

"I was too drunk to drive," Roman said. "I let him take the wheel in the interest of public safety."

"But he can't drive."

"Oh, he does okay. Gets paid, too."

Dr. Ballister waved his Miracle Peeler at Officer Mitchell. "Is a man's home his sanctuary or not? Let's let the law answer that one."

"Well, here's my idea," Officer Mitchell said. "I take you two in my car, to HQ for a few tests, and we have this big dinosaur towed."

Before I could stop him, Roman reached into the pocket of his white sweatpants and pulled out the roll of cash he'd accumulated that day in the suburbs. "How much you want, young man? What's the cost on the trouble we've caused?"

I believe to this day that he didn't intend it as a bribe. For him, everything had a price, everything could be made a transaction. Money equaled everything. Officer Mitchell didn't see it this way, though, and after a fifteen-minute ride in his squad car, I found myself sitting in an office chair, sandwiched between the station coffeemaker and the water cooler. I read the day-old sports section they'd handed me, pretending to be interested, drinking coffee out of a wax cup. Roman was behind the locked door of the holding cell, his head bobbing as he paced back and forth. Officer Mitchell had taken the roll of bills as evidence, and now we had no money for bail.

When Gladys arrived she walked up and looked at Roman through the little door. She stared for several minutes, trying, I knew, to imagine what had gotten us to this point, how a day that began with a breakfast of granola and iced coffee had worked its way out to this. She walked over and took my hand, her face set in hard lines, her pulled-back hair the same length as my own. She dragged me up in front of Officer Mitchell's desk, where he was finishing his typing.

"I'll take this one with me," she said. "The other one you can keep awhile."

We walked over to the cell. Roman stopped pacing and pressed his face to the Plexiglas, scratched white and bored through with Swiss-cheese holes. "My idea worked. I was up five hundred and eighty, Gladys," he said. "Tell her, Gabe."

"He was," I said, trying to speak drawing my breath inward so she wouldn't smell the liquor on me. "He was way up."

"That's fine," she said. "Only I'm sure now that it's gone somehow. I have no money to bail you out, so I'm going to call Dutch to help us."

"Don't do that," Roman said. "Do not call him, Gladys, you hear me? I mean it, by God." He stuck his index finger out through one of the holes in the Plexiglas and wagged it at her. I tried to picture his anger, the bulge of his fat muscles, but could see only this little wagging finger, like some cartoon worm in an apple.

"Let's go home, Gabe," she said.

"He really was having a great day," I said. Gladys rolled her eyes.

"No Dutch, Gladys," Roman shouted as we walked away. "Don't call him. Give me your word you won't call him."

I knew then how bad it might be if she did call; this was the first time I could remember Roman asking to be given anything. For him, I thought, her word was priceless.

Chapter 2

Gladys went back to work during the evenings at United Dairy, working first in the milk capping room and then the warehouse freezer, where half gallons of ice cream were kept before shipping. The freezer hummed at a steady temperature of forty-five below zero, and every evening Gladys waved goodbye to me after dressing herself in olive drab polar pants and fur-lined boots she'd bought at Sgt. Ready's, the local army surplus store. She carried the matching polar jacket, beneath which she wore a wool sweater and one of my thermal undershirts, and beneath that, I guessed, the lacy black things she hid in the bottom of the laundry basket. She also had to wear a wool ski mask and fur hat and gloves. Every night, as she left the house, she joked that not one of her coworkers had figured out yet that she was a woman. I had a hard time imagining her doing the work she described: stacking pallets of ice cream, driving a forklift, loading delivery trucks. But she enjoyed it, and would have liked being there if it hadn't been because she *had* to be there, because Roman had lost what he called "the last job at the edge of the earth."

I hated how bad it was for her. She left work at midnight, exhausted, sweating the summer nights inside her polar pants, miserable, with no air-conditioning in her Dodge Valiant (Dutch had given her one of the "pre-owned" cars off the back of the OK lot).

She arrived home with her clothes wet from the icy mist that formed on her and then melted, her cheeks chafed by the ski mask, hands wrinkled from sweating inside the gloves. She earned enough to cover the bills, with nothing left over for what she called luxuries—first-run movies or hardcover books. We spent late nights staying up playing Boggle, watching TV movies, cooking stir-fry in the wok. Some nights Alison came over, a girl I was half dating, and she and Gladys would spend the evening reading each other's poetry while I listened and tried to look thoughtful. Days, I slept through my classes at Page High School. I took it as normal that neither of my parents ever seemed to care much about my attendance in summer school, Gladys because she believed that the math, woodshop, PE part of the curriculum stagnated the imagination and that a day spent daydreaming ("envisioning," she called it) was more valuable, and Roman because he thought school was altogether horseshit and would never lead to serious money. "Just look at me," he'd say, and sometimes I would and then panic for a month or two, collecting enough decent grades in those bursts to get me through.

Roman was living, for the time, in room 19 at the Journey's End Econo Stay. He'd lived there briefly, three years earlier, when he'd been set for a two-week swing through Tennessee selling corrugated cardboard boxes to local shipping firms and had gotten fired the day before he left after arguing with his boss about the best way to market empty boxes. So instead of leaving for Tennessee, he checked into the Journey's End and spent two weeks trying to scrounge and borrow enough money to convince Gladys that he'd been to Tennessee and done a competent job. Over the weekend, he'd driven the four hours across the state border and mailed home a batch of postcards, all of them the same, showing a pretend hillbilly family in long johns and boots, smoking corncob pipes and sleeping in one bed. The caption, written in a fake-illiterate scrawl of backward letters and misspellings, read *Family Togetherness*.

Gladys had bailed Roman out of jail with the three hundred dollars that she kept on top of the refrigerator in the ceramic pitcher she'd made in pottery class. She called Dutch two days later, after Roman moved out of the house and into the Econo Stay. I knew this only because I'd eavesdropped on her half of the phone conversation, most of which consisted of Gladys saying, "I don't know, I haven't thought that far ahead." Dutch was off to Japan for a meeting between Japanese carmakers and Plymouth executives, an honor he'd won by being Dealer of the Quarter in all of North Carolina. He wrote Gladys a postcard (the plain white kind, which he'd bought at the post office and taken with him) to tell her that he would "assess the situation" as soon as he arrived back home. At the bottom of the card he wrote, "Regrettably, there is little to eat here except for rice and fish."

So for those summer evenings I was left alone in the house while Gladys drove a forklift at United Dairy and Roman watched baseball games at the Econo Stay. He'd been gone six days with no word when finally I called to see how he was doing (the police had extracted from Gladys a promise not to let me drive anymore).

"Working on something huge, Gabe," he said. I could hear the announcer calling play by play in the background. "This will turn your mother around pronto." I knew that in his mind this meant some scheme for making big money, which seemed a little difficult given that he had no job and no prospects; having blown household products, it was as if he'd sunk through the floor, into the earth. There was nowhere left to go. I knew too he'd *better* turn her around; she seemed to be settling into the idea of having him gone.

"It might turn her around if you got a regular job," I said. "A store or something. If you brought home a paycheck every couple of weeks." I heard him sigh on the other end. He would likely complain to the school board, wondering where I'd picked up this kind of language.

"You're right, Gabe. Maybe Shakey's Pizza would take me on, give me a little paper hat, a neckerchief. Now we're talking."

"Roman, you know what I mean. And I'm serious, you better do something."

There was silence on his end, and I could picture him scratching his head. I wondered how much of his hair had grown back in a week.

"I don't know, son. A steady nine-to-five gig? Where would that put me?"

"It might be worth a try."

"Yeah, but where would it put me?" I had forgotten that for Roman there was no such thing as a rhetorical question; it was bad sales technique because it gave customers an open chance to ignore you, to erect what Roman called the little brick wall.

I shrugged, looking around at our empty house, the walls hung with macramé owls and rugs that Gladys had made, poems by Walt Whitman and Carl Sandburg which she had cut out of her books and framed. On the mantel sat Roman's bowling trophy from the year he'd worked at Foutch Enterprises, an actual company with a building and parking lot instead of just a PO box number. Roman had worked as one of a dozen sales reps under some middle-management team-player type. For a while he'd flirted with the idea of becoming a team player himself, paying into a retirement plan, hooking up with a lunchtime contract bridge group, acquiring dental insurance. He anchored the bowling team, a Tuesday-night group which called itself the Keggers and wore satin bowling shirts embroidered with their names inside foamy beer mugs, plus a tiny X on the breast pocket for each time one of them finished off the equivalent of a keg of beer. During his high school years in Medina, Ohio, Roman had a job as a pin-setter for the local alley, before that particular automation had reached the Midwest, and so he was good enough that the Keggers made him team captain, gave him the trophy for MVP. And he hated every minute of it. He'd told me about it the night before he turned in his resignation, nearly a month before he told Gladys.

"They keep *track,* Gabe. These old codgers finish a can of Bud, then take out their little ledger books and pencil in '12 ounces.'" He studied me to see if any of this was sinking in. "Every time, even if they're plastered, just so they can have another X on their fucking shirts."

His face was drawn as he told me this, his eyes bloodshot and bleary, and even though I was only twelve at the time, I knew this face had to do with more than bowling and ledger books. He'd seen himself in these men and it scared him.

I stared now at the dusty trophy on the mantel, the marble and plastic topped by a bowler frozen in mid-release, his gold shoe kicked back behind him, his gold arm lifted high. Along the bottom of his foot and up his back ran a seam where the plastic had been pressed in its mold. For a moment I imagined opening the gold seam like a zipper and freeing the tiny man trapped inside, letting him release the ball, make his strike, drink his beer, mark it down in his ledger book, and go back to work on Monday morning.

"I don't know where, Dad," I said. "Maybe it would put you back home."

"Wrong answer, son. It would put me straight down the next twenty-four years till retirement. Whoosh, there it went."

"Okay. Well, I'll let you go watch the game."

"This idea is a winner, Gabe, so don't worry."

Just before we hung up, I heard the noise of the TV crowd rise up in a faint static roar, the voice of the announcer escalate to shouts; someone, somewhere, had made the big play.

During those evenings alone at home my major concern was boredom. The wheel of high school friendships turned on involvement; it didn't really matter with what, and you could invent something if you wanted to, but it all ran on cliques, even down to the group of people united only in their hatred of cliques. I couldn't even qualify for that one; I wasn't an outcast so much as a kind of social libertarian. I auditioned with a few of the more fringe groups: the kids who blew things up, the kids who drew F-16s and machine guns on their schoolbooks, the kids who grafted personalities and hairstyles from rock bands, older kids who tooled up their cars with headers and mags and then spent Saturday nights circling the town, the kids who carried hip knives and thought suicide was cool, the Jesus kids, the Satan kids, the kids whose fathers had money. I didn't even attempt the more mainstream groups: the jocks, the brains, the year-book staff. None of them fit me and I didn't much care. I liked being alone, and never felt the need to escape my parents. By default I ended up occasionally hanging out with a loosely formed group of artsy types: boys who airbrushed their own T-shirts or sculpted clay Hobbit characters in art class, and girls who wrote weepy songs and kept poetry in spiral notebooks. I found them mostly because it kept Gladys happy in her belief that I was headed toward a life of artistic brilliance. They found me because Gladys let them drink beer, smoke their clove cigarettes, and play Emerson, Lake & Palmer full volume on the eight-track. She sometimes invited them for what she called an "exhibition," which meant that the guys would show off their lat-est T-shirts and posters, paintings of sunsets over beaches or doves carrying peace signs or sometimes skulls with dripping eyes, and the girls would read their anguished poetry, in whispers with their long hair hiding their faces, or in dramatic bursts filled with imaginary daggers thrust into their hearts. If they were asked by Gladys to explain "how they ever dreamed up such a thing," the boys would shrug and say they just thought it looked cool, and the girls would say that no one could possibly understand how much pain they had in their hearts. It seemed to me that this was their hobby: having pain in their hearts. Then it would be my turn to read.

"Gabe, let's hear from you," Gladys would say. "You've been quiet awhile."

"I'm working on something," I always said. "An idea, something big." For some reason this seemed to satisfy her; her faith in me was without question. Once, after two or three beers, I stood, cleared my throat, and opened my mouth, trusting the words to find their own way out. The only thing that would come to me as a first line was, "Everything in life is really shitty." This was the general theme of Alison's and Joanie's work, but rendered by them with more drama and lyricism.

I shook my head. "I'm not ready to share this," I said.

Gladys smiled, and told me that such work could not be forced. "It'll come," she said.

"It will," Alison said. "Just let yourself breathe." She said things like this to me all the time. We were dating off and on, mostly off, and she always said that our relationship was "spiritual," which meant that I was not allowed to touch her below her braided belt.

Those nights alone I wandered through the neighborhood whistling at dogs, chasing possums from trash cans, throwing gravel at the bats circling the streetlights. Sometimes I hopped on one of the orange Duke Power buses and rode it all over Greensboro, reading the newspapers that people left behind. Other nights I walked over to Alison's house, where we sat on her porch and I anguished over an invented writer's block, knowing this would lead to kissing and groping. At home I would dig out old copies of Roman's *Playboy* collection and look at the women and read about their turn-ons and turn-offs, calculating which category my own attributes fell into. If Miss January from 1972 happened to list "men with ponytails" as a turn-on, I would imagine her as my girlfriend at Page, taking her to bonfires and pep rallies and out behind the gym to drink beer and have sex. During most of those nights I made a concerted effort not to even touch the erection I invariably got, because in at least one or two pictures of every spread, the models wore lingerie much like that which Gladys kept hidden in the laundry basket, and the second I let myself make that connection I thought there existed some terrible psychological malady buried inside me, and that maybe I *would* end up a famous artist, a heroin addict obsessed with his mother, dead of suicide at age twenty-seven or so. While I read I would pour myself a glass of Roman's whiskey, fire up a cigar from his sock drawer, and wish sometimes that I had normal parents and that *Playboy* and liquor and cigars would be off-limits and that I could have the pleasure of sneaking them. But I never had to sneak anything. Gladys wanted to patiently endure my artistic temperament, and Roman wanted me to grow up a man. I felt stuck somewhere in that gray land between their wants where, I was certain, my own wants lay buried, whatever they might be.

When his money started running out, Roman brought the Chevy home, parked it in the garage, and covered it with a canvas tarp. He said he would hoof it awhile, and I knew this didn't bother him much. From his years of door-to-door, years carrying sample cases and vacuum cleaners, he could walk seemingly without ever stopping. Every year, just for fun, he trekked the March of Dimes Walkathon, all twenty miles in his suit and wing tips, selling bottles of lemonade from a cooler.

He came into the house to give me the keys. Gladys was at the community college or at Artists Space for some class or another: macramé, pottery, beginning ballet, yoga. Roman came in and looked around at the TV, his reclining chair, the things Gladys had hung on the wall. "So the old house hasn't changed much," he said.

I shrugged. "You've only been gone three weeks—what did you expect?" His hair looked like a Marine sergeant's.

He nodded. "Start it up once a week to keep the engine lubed. Wax it down once or twice. Check for leaks. Any questions?" he said.

"Does this count as a divorce, a trial separation, or domestic strife? We had to fill out a form about our home life in school the other day, and I didn't know what to put."

"School? What in hell for?"

"It's a segment of English class called 'Being Human.' The forms are supposed to be a basis for discussion."

His jaw stiffened. "What's the name of your principal?"

"Mr. Reeves," I said. Roman wrote down the name inside a matchbook cover and stuck it in his suitcoat pocket, where, I knew, it wouldn't be seen again until the dry cleaner found it.

"For now, if there's a blank that says 'pissed-off mother' you check that one."

"Why don't you come back here? You can't work things out from across town."

"That's a question for your mother, Gabe."

I shook my head. "She's not keeping you away. I mean, hell, she has to go work at the dairy every night." Even as I finished saying the words, I saw that they weren't true, that Roman and Gladys had talked, decided things, made arrangements, without my ever knowing it. She had thrown him out, didn't want him to come back. He stared at me, letting the realization sink in.

"I just don't get this," I said.

"Listen, son, there's a big difference in men and women."

"I've noticed," I said.

"Yeah, but there's a difference in how they get angry. That's all this amounts to. If you got a mountain to get rid of, you can blast it out with dynamite or you can let the wind and rain work on it for a few thousand years. That's the difference."

"Thank you, master," I said. I had been watching *Kung Fu* on TV.

Roman squinted at me. "What's this 'master' shit? How old are you now?"

"Sixteen."

He scratched his head. "I thought you were fifteen."

"I was, then time went by, and I turned sixteen."

He shrugged. "If you want to take the car out it's okay by me.

You wreck it and I garnish your wages until it's paid for. You dig?" Whenever he made these attempts to be hip, to use language he thought the kids were using, I knew that it meant he felt some separation between us, a distance he believed he could bridge as easily as he closed a deal: with the right words, carefully chosen.

I nodded. "Done deal," I said.

I began taking the car every night to visit Gladys at the dairy, to talk to her during her break. It was something to do. I felt bad thinking of her working there, and somehow I thought that a steady reminder to the both of them of my presence in this world would bring them back together. At times I felt like the only thing they had in common. Gladys was happy enough to see me that she didn't bother asking about my driving the car, even though I was prepared to lie and say I'd taken the bus. We met in the employee lounge, where they had a freezer filled with free Fudgsicles, Dixie cups, and ice cream sandwiches. Gladys took one for me every night while she drank coffee, ate ice cream, and smoked Marlboros, a habit she picked up from her supervisor, a tall Hispanic man everyone called Snowball for the clump of frozen sweat and condensation that perpetually hung from his goatee. Before I took the first bite of the Fudgsicle, I raised it in a toast to Gladys and said, "The only emperor is the emperor of ice cream." I'd recently learned the poem at school, and though I didn't have a clue what it meant, I liked how it sounded, and it made Gladys happy to hear me quote poetry.

Before she sat down with me, she'd spent a few minutes in the hot room, a wooden stall with an orange heat lamp inside like the kind fast food restaurants use to keep the french fries hot. I watched her stand under the light and peel off her frozen coat and gloves and ski mask, letting the warmth soak into her face and hands. Then she sat with me and drank and smoked and chewed, her hair damp, smelling of cigarettes and hard work. She showed me how her watch crystal had cracked after she left the freezer and walked too quickly into the hot room. I would have offered to take her job, or any job, but I knew she wouldn't hear of it. Roman had started work right out of high school, and had only gone back to junior college after they were married, when she signed him up for a course called "The Great Books." Every night, she told me, he sat in his recliner drinking Crown Royal and turning pages, saying over and over, "What's so great about *this?*" He lasted less than a semester.

Gladys offered me her cigarettes and I took one. "You've seen your father," she said. She lit my cigarette for me and another for herself.

"So have you," I said, alternating drags with bites of ice cream.

She shook her wet hair. "Just talked on the phone twice. How's he doing?"

"Well, his hair is growing back."

At this she smiled and shook her head again. I took the smile to mean that she was ready to forgive him, to count losing his fifth job in six months and having to fork over bail money plus a fine and court costs as some sort of kid's prank, just Roman being Roman.

"He's ready to come home," I said.

She stubbed out the cigarette and fanned herself with her hand, warm in the polar pants. Her mouth tightened. "There are a few conditions he'll have to meet."

"Like what?"

"Like get a steady job, for one. Has he done that? What's he do all day at that motel? Float in the pool?"

I thought of the sound of the baseball games over the phone during the afternoons, and other sounds I'd heard, music from *The Price Is Right* and *Hogan's Heroes* reruns, the crinkle of potato chip bags, the hiss of pull tabs being opened.

"He's looking for a job," I lied. "It's not easy right now. Times are tough." I knew it was probably difficult for her to take seriously my assessment of the economy when I had ice cream dripping down the front of my Doobie Brothers T-shirt.

She rolled her eyes. "I can guess what kind of job," she said. "He did this at a motel once when we were staying at Carolina Beach." She told me that this had happened years ago, during July, the last few days of vacation when the money ran short and they had to eat bologna sandwiches in their room at the Bee Hive Motel instead of going out for fried shrimp. Roman took the thirteen dollars they had left and cashed it in for quarters at the front desk, and late that night he climbed the short fence around the pool and emptied all the Cokes, Tabs, Grape Nehis, and Brownies out of the soda machine and into his Styrofoam cooler. The next day when the temperature climbed to ninety-two and the pool area was crowded with bathers who hit their fists against the empty machine, Roman sat in a chaise lounge and sold the drinks at fifty percent profit, making enough in two hours to spring for shrimp and hush puppies that night at Calabash.

I laughed. "That's great."

She shook her head. "It's not great, Gabe, that's the point. Why does everything have to be some big setup?"

I threw my cigarette on the concrete floor and stamped it out. "I bet you weren't complaining about it that night, stuffing yourself with shrimp."

Her eyes moved across my face. "Why are you taking sides in this?"

"Why are you *making* sides?"

She tossed her cigarette beside mine and stepped on it. "He almost got you put in jail, Gabe. I'm sick of it. I am. You should be too."

"Well, sorry, but I'm not."

"He has to settle some things with Dutch. Then maybe we can stop this ridiculousness."

"What does he have to settle?"

"He just has to listen to him, accept a little common sense for once."

"That's the condition?"

"That's it."

"Dutch has plenty of common sense," I said. "He has it the way other people have diarrhea."

Gladys's face reddened, as if she'd just stepped from the freezer. "Those are your father's words. Don't sit there acting like some ventriloquist dummy, Gabe."

"Who's a dummy?" I looked up as Snowball stepped into the break room and rooted around in the case for an ice cream sandwich. He walked over to us and took one of Gladys's cigarettes.

"My son is, sometimes," she said.

"So this is the Gladys progeny," he said. "I heard about you." He took a bite and then a drag, which seemed to be the in-house method of ice cream consumption.

"This is Gabriel," she said. The way that she said it, using my full name, I could tell she was angry with me.

He smiled. "The angel Gabriel from heaven came," he sang in a ragged baritone. Ice crystals glittered in his goatee and eyebrows, so much so that I couldn't tell if their natural color was gray or black or somewhere in between.

"So tell me, Gabriel, how you earn a dollar?"

I looked at Gladys. Whenever other adults asked about my plans or job prospects, she usually jumped in to explain my future as an artist, to tell them that I had talent but little discipline, had not yet found my form. At those times, I felt guilty for knowing that I had no talent of any kind, that my head was no torch of inspiration, aflame with artistic insight, but more like a dimestore flashlight, dependable enough, practical for small jobs, but of little brilliance. This time, though, Gladys was too angry to say anything.

"I'm a student at Page," I said.

"Hear there's big money in that these days," Snowball said. He laughed one of those big, harsh cigarette laughs, which made me instantly like him even though he stood there belittling me. Gladys had mentioned him, how he was always showing off pictures of his three kids, talking about the picnics they had taken, the camping trips together. It always sounded strange to me, all this regular family togetherness, like the hillbillies in the postcards Roman sent.

"I'm also going to be an artist," I said as a way of making up with Gladys.

"Artist?" he said with no contempt in his voice, only deep puzzlement, as if I'd said I planned to be a tree or a fish. "Okay, Rembrandt, your mother and me got to get back to work."

Her break over, Gladys stood and slipped on her parka, pulled on her gloves. Then she leaned over to kiss me on the cheek.

"Tell him I miss him," she whispered, her voice breaking on her own soft words.

I went to visit Roman at the Econo Stay, hoping to prepare him for the condition that Gladys had laid down, hoping to soften the blow. I knew how it would be when he heard he had to sit still for "common sense" from Dutch, especially since this particular application had to do with his marriage. With Gladys behind him, Dutch would deliver a bucketful of common sense, would dump it right over Roman's head and expect him to sit there and take it. I'd seen the effects of Dutch's doling out of common sense every year on the first Saturday in April, when he came by the house to do Roman's taxes. He volunteered every year, though looking back on it I'm sure this also came about by some suggestion from Gladys, combined with his desire to please her. He would arrive promptly at ten, wearing his white suit with the Ford Dealer and American flag pins neatly aligned on the lapel. By ten o'clock on any Saturday morning, Roman would be out on the front porch leaned back in his Supra-Webbing chaise lounge, sipping a Bloody Mary from a tall glass with a piece of limp celery sticking out. He wore for these mornings a red-and-white Ban-Lon shirt with the open collar turned up, a pair of burgundy swim trunks, leather house slippers, and sunglasses. He looked like some old-time Hollywood mogul, and I sometimes felt sorry for him that we didn't have a pool for him to lounge beside. Instead, he would sit on the porch and watch me complete the mowing and trimming, for which he paid me a dollar an hour (less than most jobs because the Priddy boys down the street would do it for the same price, and Roman always went for the low bid, all considerations of family aside). He watched me all morning long, as if the yard were our pool and me some starlet on a rubber raft. Occasionally he thumbed through the sports section, or Gladys would join him for a drink and they would lean in together to talk and laugh out loud, distracting me from my work while I tried to figure out what their conversation might be about, what jokes they shared, how their usual anger could give way to so much affection.

So on the first Saturday in April, Dutch would arrive and insist that they go inside where the noise of the mower would not distract them, and then tell Roman that he ought not to drink until after they'd finished their accounting. This suggestion seemed reasonable enough to me, but Roman would recount it later as if it were the most telling symptom of some horrible disease from which Dutch suffered.

They sat at the kitchen table drinking the coffee Gladys had made, and within fifteen minutes things would begin to fall apart, usually about the time they started going through Roman's receipts for the year. Every year, according to Dutch, Roman had a full array of tax deductions available to him, or, as he termed it, a "free lunch from Uncle Sugar." He said this and expected us to laugh, but only Gladys took him up on it. My father qualified as an independent subcontractor for the various firms he represented throughout the year, and the cost of every hotel room, every bowl of chili, every fixed flat or oil change, every dry-cleaning or hat blocking, every road map or box of Kleenex—all of it, if he bought it on the road—was deductible. The problem was documentation. Every year, Dutch insisted that Roman keep careful track of his receipts. The year before, he'd even bought Roman a spiral notebook with pockets labeled for different expenses, and had called every two months or so to make sure Roman was keeping records. Then, when he arrived on Saturday, Roman brought out the notebook, and Dutch opened it to find it contained three receipts for cigarettes, a broken toothpick, a postcard from Tweetsie Railroad, a handful of dinner mints, and a pair of novelty X-ray Specs.

"What in hell," Dutch said.

"Roman, you promised," Gladys said.

"Hey, these are for you, Gabe," Roman said, handing me the specs. "Picked them up in Myrtle Beach and then forgot all about it."

"Thanks, Dad," I said. I slipped on the X-ray Specs and watched the two of them. Dutch was thumbing through the blank pages of the notebook, his face scarlet; I didn't have to see through him to discern his mood.

"Roman, this is just shiftlessness. I'm sorry, Gladys, but how does anyone expect me to *tolerate* this? How?" Gladys's face colored.

Roman bit the stained celery from his drink. "I've got you there, Dutchy boy, because I did save everything. So I didn't use your little contraption here, so sue me."

"I think the federal government will take care of that."

"Just keep your garters up a minute." Roman walked down the hall while Dutch looked at Gladys and me, slowly shaking his head. I couldn't tell if he was doling out sympathy or expecting some. Roman brought back a giant Lakeland Amusement Park beer stein jammed full of receipts, most of them homemade, written on matchbook covers, cocktail napkins, or scraps of road map. Dutch remained silent until he came to a receipt near the bottom, $12.48 for "gas, beef jerky, 2 Zagnuts, decent haircut." The receipt was writ-

ten in Roman's hand on a brown paper towel. Dutch held it as if it
were a soiled diaper, then let it flutter to the floor. I stood there trying to imagine what kind of store might sell both gas and haircuts.
Dutch was silent as he gathered his pen and adding machine to leave,
then he told Gladys she deserved better, told me to try to steer clear
of the garden path, and told my father to have a good time in prison.

Things were worse than I expected at the Econo Stay. I noticed
immediately the three empty Crown Royal bottles which stood
lined up on the TV set. The only evidence of food was the scattered
plastic bags of vending machine chips. Roman was without his tie
or suitcoat, which he usually wore, loosened and rumpled, when he
wasn't dressed on Saturday mornings as a Hollywood mogul. His
shirttail had come untucked on one side, and he had cigarette burns
below the breast pocket. The brown holes, three of them, formed
a little surprised face, wide-eyed and open-mouthed, as if Roman
had arranged them that way.

"You gonna stand there all day?" he said. I'd been so preoccupied
with the tiny face on his shirt that I'd failed to notice the purple
Crown Royal bag arranged neatly across his shoulder.

"Just wanted to see how you're getting along," I said.

"Let's go ride, get out of this room. And I want to see how
you're treating the car."

I could tell that he was embarrassed by the condition of the
room, by the condition of himself. He quickly tucked in his shirt
and wet down at the sink what little hair he had. He grabbed his cigarettes, scratched his unshaven chin, looked at me, and shrugged.
Amazingly, though he'd glanced in the mirror twice, he hadn't seen
the Crown Royal bag on his shoulder. Either that, I thought, or else
he wanted it there, had put it there for a reason. I was afraid to ask,
afraid to hear the reason, because it would not make sense to anyone but him, no more than his reason for shaving his head or trying

to sell cleaning products to crazy Dr. Ballister. He grabbed a bottle and a folder stuffed with papers and we left.

He let me drive, which avoided my having to insist on it, and I headed west out I-40 toward Winston-Salem. I had no place to take him, and we rode for a long time without speaking, the radio buzzing, air conditioner blowing thin clouds of condensation. Roman smoked and looked out the window at the fields of cows and tobacco, at the off-ramp Howard Johnsons and BP stations. I had gotten way past any worry over not having a driver's license; it seemed a minor glitch that only interfered with my driving if I thought about it, like the Chevy's tendency to pull to the right. Every time I glanced over at Roman he was staring out the window, not with sadness or distraction, but with what appeared to be genuine interest. He didn't take any notice of me, and I ended up watching the tiny burned face below his breast pocket, the purple drawstring bag on his shoulder, trying to understand him by his collection of accidents and mistakes. I worried at how far we had gone, worried that we would ride in this manner all the way into Asheville and Knoxville and Nashville and then Arkansas, never stopping except for gas. Then I realized that for him this ride was nothing, a short hop for the man who had once driven into Tennessee to mail fake postcards, who had sometimes logged seven thousand miles a week behind the wheel. The thought relaxed me some.

"You burned holes in your shirt," I said. I was trying to think how to broach the subject of Dutch and his doling out of common sense.

Roman glanced at his shirt. "I got another one," he said. He looked over at me finally. "So what's new?"

I shrugged. "School's okay," I said, trying to remember how many days I'd missed in the last two weeks.

"What grade are you in now?"

"Eleventh. I'll finish up next year," I said, knowing that finishing up was only one of several possible scenarios regarding school.

"Jesus, that's hard to believe. I remember the day I dropped you off for first grade. You were bawling your eyes out like I was taking you to Sing Sing or something. Know what I did?"

"Told me that adversity is good for the soul?"

Roman turned and looked at me a full half minute. "Where do you get this stuff? Hell, no, I pulled your teacher aside, one of those draw-on-eyebrow, big-hair kind of women . . ."

"Mrs. Kenny."

"That's it. Pulled Mrs. Kenny aside, told her to keep an extra eye on you, and slipped her twenty bucks."

"What?" The car started to drift and I jerked it back. I wouldn't have been any more shocked if he'd told me he had slipped his hand inside her blouse.

"What did she do?" I said.

"What do you think? She took it. Worked, too. When I picked you up she had you standing right there at the curb, her arms wrapped around you like you were her own lost son."

I suddenly had the bottomless feeling that everyone that had ever been nice to me or shown an interest in me as a child had been bribed by my father. I didn't know what to say.

"How's your mother?" Roman said. He offered me one of his Pall Malls and I took it. I punched in the dash lighter and waited for it to click while I thought up the best way to say this.

"She's doing okay, but she hates her job at the dairy." I left out that she hated it mostly because the circumstances he'd created had put her there.

He shook his head. "What is that, minimum wage? All the cottage cheese you can eat?"

I took a drag and blew smoke out the window. Somewhere along these unfamiliar parts, I had gotten off I-40 and onto the old road toward Boone. We passed signs advertising the tourist attractions: Blowing Rock, Tweetsie Railroad, Unto These Hills, the Land of Oz.

This last one was a theme park based on the movie, where you could walk through a fake farmhouse that shook and rumbled, with the sound of tornado winds and a barking Toto played over the loud-speakers, and when you walked out the other side, the house sat tilt-ed and broken, with the stockinged feet of the Wicked Witch of the West stuck out from beneath. There were yellow-painted brick paths that wound through the woods, actors in costume, tree-trunk-mounted loudspeakers blaring "Over the Rainbow." Plaster statues of Munchkins and overgrown toadstools were scattered along the way. The main building was a souvenir shop and museum, where they had on display Dorothy's ruby slippers alongside Margaret Hamilton's bicycle, and where inexplicably I always came away with a rubber tomahawk and a cardboard Indian headdress as souvenirs.

Roman's territory for Moran Sprinkler Systems had once includ-ed this part of western North Carolina, and sometimes we would go with him and Gladys would take me to the Land of Oz. She never liked the other attractions as much. Tweetsie was too violent, with its fake cowboy-and-Indian shootout, and Blowing Rock was too dangerous to climb. Looking back, I think even then she had plans for my becoming an artist, and somehow thought the Land of Oz would inspire me. All I can remember caring about was the cheap crap in the souvenir shop—the coloring books and corncob pipes and rubber spears. Gladys must have noticed the tackiness of the place and chosen to ignore it. What brought her there may have been nothing more than that one song, "Over the Rainbow," piped through the woods, the beauty of Judy Garland's voice carried among the pines, across the parking lots and hot dog stands. With that core of almost accidental *feeling* at the center, Gladys could tol-erate the cheap crap. This must have been what kept her writing all that bad poetry, what kept her married. As we drove past, Roman pointed with his cigarette at the peeling Land of Oz billboard ("Experience the Magic!!" it read). He told me to pull off.

Though the parking lot still sat intact, the building that had once held the ticket booth and the souvenir shop stood rotting away, the roof all but caved in. We walked past tangled stacks of crumpled aluminum siding and two-by-fours, shattered window frames. Old air conditioners and a rusted refrigerator were scattered among boxes of Land of Oz bumper stickers faded with age. The paths still circled through the woods, and here and there as we walked along them we found yellow-painted bricks stacked off to the side, grown over with kudzu. The cement-block foundation of the tornado house held the remains of bonfires, old bags of beer cans and fast food wrappers. Most of the buildings were gone, the woods reclaiming any sign of them. Along the way I noticed a few remaining plaster toadstools, green with moss. We stopped along the path, sat on a pair of tree stumps, and passed the bottle of Crown Royal. The purple bag still sat folded across Roman's shoulder, and still he had not noticed it.

"Why did you want to come here?" I asked.

"Used to come here all the time," he said. "I'd get past Knoxville and want to stop for a piss and a smoke, bite to eat. You remember your mother used to bring you here."

I nodded, thought about this a moment. "Mom wants you to come back to the house."

Roman looked at me, his eyes puffy and dark. "She does?" His eyebrows went up. "That was easy. I was all set to put you to work, to soften her up. I guess we won't need this." He held up the loose sheaf of papers he carried stuffed inside a manila folder.

"What is that?"

"Doesn't matter now. Let's go home," he said.

"Well, not just yet," I said. I imagined the Cowardly Lion running along the dirt path, wondering where the hell everybody went.

"What do you mean, Gabe, not yet?"

"She wants you to do something first. A little thing, no biggie. Won't take you half an hour." I was, I realized, trying to sell him the idea.

"Clean up my act a little? Get a job? I know all that already. Nothing new there."

Though I wondered how he thought all of this could be done in half an hour, it did sound like plenty, and for a moment I was angry again at Gladys for wanting more, for wanting, I thought, to put his failure before him and make him look at it.

I kicked at a piece of gravel. "She wants you to talk to Dutch. Actually she wants you to listen to him."

He took a drink from the bottle. "Then I guess that deal's off, isn't it?"

"Dad, you need to settle this thing. It's been three weeks."

"*We* need to. Not Dutch. It's none of his damn business."

"You don't have to do anything he says, you don't have to talk to him. It won't be as bad as tax day even. Just a little listening, like I listen to you all the time. Why is that so hard?"

Roman paced up and down a little section of the yellow brick road. "I'll do it with one catch. If you can tell me what Dutch has to do with my marriage."

He stood there in the silence of the woods, the plaster toadstools slowly falling to dust around us, waiting for my answer: no rhetorical questions. And of course I had no answer to give. What did I know of the inner life of their marriage, or of any marriage? I shrugged.

"That's what I thought," Roman said.

"Then why don't you just pretend? Sit there and think about baseball stats, or try to say the alphabet backwards, and look at Dutch every few minutes and nod your head."

"Gabe, there's a principle involved here I think you're missing."

Here he was standing on principle, the man who had once applied a fake plaster cast to his own arm to convince his insurance customers how easily accidents could happen at home.

"I'm not missing much. I know this whole situation is bullshit," I said.

"Agreed."

"I don't even know what the problem *is*. It's like you both are arguing about wanting the same thing."

"It's complicated, son."

I felt like some high school football coach, wanting to get back to fundamentals, back to square one. "Do you love Mom?" I said.

"Love," he said, sitting beside me. "Love, love." He shook his head slowly, as if he'd just uttered some profound truth.

"I love a good bottle of whiskey," he said, and took a drink. "I love new upholstery in a car. I love women's voices echoing in a hotel lobby." He looked at me to see if any of this might register. I watched him, wanting it to.

"Okay, son. Picture one of these big, open-air fancy hotel lobbies with palm trees and couches, the women standing close together in the morning after breakfast, making plans, wearing sun hats." He smiled, as if at some memory.

"I love how happy a customer is after he's bought something, not because he *has* it, but because he *bought* it. I love to look out the window of the car when I don't know where the hell I am and see cows or golfers—same thing—standing in a field. I love jukeboxes where your quarter comes back but you get the credit anyway. I love it when you turn a corner and a bunch of kids scatter because they've been up to no good. I love big, blond-headed Texas women. Big up close, in their hands, their feet. Big lipstick. And you know why?"

I shook my head.

"Because they won't give the likes of me the goddamn time of day."

I felt confused, caught up in hearing him say to me more than he'd ever said, trying to get a feel for him as someone other than my father. I wanted to keep up, follow along. "Well, why should they?" I ventured.

He pointed at me. "That's it exactly. You got it."

"So what about Mom?"

"She's in there," he said, then noticed the look on my face. "Way up near the top," he said.

"Well that's something, anyway," I said.

"It is," he said, missing my sarcasm. "After twenty years, it's more than you think."

It had turned near the long-shadowed part of afternoon, and we headed toward the car to start back to Greensboro, walking along the path I'd walked all those times as a kid, when I'd wanted to believe the lies the theme park made, to give myself over to the costumes and giant mushrooms and plaster figurines, but couldn't. We were halfway to the car before I realized I hadn't asked where I fit into his list. I imagined myself squeezed in somewhere between . . . I don't know, canned meats and new shoes.

We rode along in silence, both of us full of enough whiskey to make us sleepy, the light of evening falling in hard slants across the road. Roman had his head turned toward the window, looking, I guessed, for golfers or cows. I noticed that the purple bag was missing from his shoulder, lost somewhere at the Land of Oz. As if we had never dropped the thread of our conversation, Roman said, "Your mother and I will work something out. You shouldn't worry about it."

"I'm not worried," I lied.

"Good. I have some ideas. Better than talking to Dutch."

"What ideas?"

He again held up the folder of papers he'd carried with him all afternoon. "This right here," he said. "Our secret weapon." When I asked again, Roman refused to tell me what was in the folder, saying he'd let me in on it soon enough, when the time was right. I tried to imagine what the papers might be, thinking of everything from multiple drafts of some fervent, soul-baring love letter to a mass of bonds, stock certificates, and promissory notes with which he meant to bribe his way back into her affections. Those and anything in between seemed possible.

Chapter 3

Two days later Roman dropped by the house and found me watching *Dialing for Dollars* and frantically dialing and redialing Shirley Beacham, the movie hostess, because I knew the count on the Win-Wheel, knew that the answer to the day's quiz was Chuck Connors, and knew that the jackpot stood at $150. As for Roman, he knew better than to look for me at school on a Friday afternoon. Gladys was off practicing with her madrigal singing group. Roman started in talking without as much as a hello.

"Dutch is back," he said. "Your mother called to tell me, so this means she's going to want to have this meeting soon."

"What did she say?"

"She left a message. I was out."

I tried to imagine where he had gone. He'd been two weeks now without the car, five weeks without a job. By this point, what he called his "field of prospects" must have looked like a scrub desert.

"Where'd you go?" I said, angry that he'd blown a chance to talk with her.

"No, I mean I was *out*." He mimed drinking from a bottle.

"Call her back."

"I will," he said, "but I need to work it out in my head first. If we'd followed my plan, we wouldn't need any of this shit. Now it's too late." He stopped pacing and looked at the TV screen, where Spencer Tracy was transforming from Dr. Jekyll into Mr. Hyde.

"Which of us you think is having a worse day?" Roman said.

I could tell he was nervous at the idea of talking to her. I liked this in him, that with things this bad, he could not bring himself to be slick with her, would not just try to sell her on himself the way he sold lightbulbs or omelet pans.

"I'll talk to her when she gets home," I said.

He nodded. We watched for a few more minutes in silence while Spencer Tracy slobbered about in bad makeup chasing young, virginal women through the streets of London. I waited for Shirley Beacham to come back on because the jackpot was up to $175 since the last commercial break. Then the phone rang and it was Gladys, calling from the community college.

"You're home," she said, with no surprise in her voice.

"I was working on some ideas. Some of this stuff is really fresh and challenging." These were words I used only because I'd seen them written on the grade sheets that Gladys's instructors at the community college gave her. If I could manage to take a few steps back from myself, I became appalled at how easily lies—whole fabrications—came into my mind and mouth. But mostly I just lied and didn't think about it. As long as she was happy.

"I shouldn't have interrupted, but I need you to talk to your father for me."

I glanced at him. "You want to set up the meeting with Dutch."

"I don't think 'meeting' is the right word. 'Family conference' is better."

"I'm included?"

"Of course you're included. I know you don't like the idea, but Dutch will help us, Gabe, give us a little objectivity on ourselves. Does that make sense to you?"

I said that it did make sense. Gladys set up the meeting for the next morning at the house. Roman stood in the doorway to the kitchen, listening as we finished the conversation.

I hung up the phone. "Ten o'clock tomorrow. She wants it to be friendly. We're having coffee and doughnuts."

"Good enough. I'll fix Bloody Marys."

I had forgotten that the next morning would be Saturday, that Roman would want to do his Hollywood mogul bit in the chaise lounge.

"Dad, that's a bad idea and you know it."

"My house," he said.

"Yeah," I said, "and if you want to live in it again you'd better act right tomorrow. All you have to do is *listen*." This sounded like a speech I heard parents giving their children.

He cupped his hand around his ear. "What did you say? I couldn't hear."

This didn't strike me as all that funny.

By the time I woke up, Gladys had brewed coffee and made a doughnut run down to Krispy Kreme. I found her in the kitchen, smoking, biting her nails. She wore the perfume and eye makeup that she used only when Roman took her to the occasional sales banquet. She stood to hug me, wearing a white, lacy dress I'd never seen before. On my way to the kitchen, I'd noticed what looked like half her wardrobe strewn across their bed—dresses and pants, shoe boxes, her lacy underwear tumbled on the floor. It didn't occur to me until I saw her, until she hugged me, that this family conference was anything to get nervous about. I'd assumed everything was what Roman liked to call a done deal, that they would sit, talk, laugh a little over how silly they'd been, and then Roman would bring in his suitcase and unpack in time for lunch. Gladys had tiny white blisters around her eyes, from the dairy, she said, caused by ice crystals freezing to her skin.

"Do they look bad?"

"You look fine," I told her. I had trouble believing that she could be so worried over this conference, following her insistence that it should happen. I had never much thought about it until I watched her sitting there nearly shaking with what seemed almost a kind of stage fright, throwing back cups of coffee, smoking cigarettes and stubbing them out in her half-eaten doughnut, but I realized then how hard it must have been for her just to *manage* the whole of Roman. I thought back to the list of things he'd named for me among the ruins of the Land of Oz, the world as he shaped it for himself, boundaried off by his own arbitrary set of likes and loves and hates. It was within these boundaries that Gladys lived her life, a life I understood for the first time as a series of shoves and pushes to keep her position, as Roman had said, "way up near the top," not to be knocked down, displaced by some new make of car or new brand of liquor.

Or woman, I thought, seeing some basic reasoning on her part behind the lace bras and underwear. I remember this moment in the kitchen as the first real insight I had into the two of them, or anyone else for that matter, like I'd dug at the surface of their marriage and unearthed a little fingerbone or a sliver of pottery.

I sat with Gladys and took a bite of doughnut as the doorbell rang.

"Everything's going to be fine," I said around my mouthful.

Dutch came in loaded with souvenir gifts from Japan. For Gladys he brought a long silk kimono which came wrapped in Japanese newsprint bound with twine. Gladys put the kimono on over her new dress and spun in a circle to model it for us, twirling the green and black and gold of it in folds that looked like flowing water.

"I love this," she said. "Thank you, Dutch."

"That's really . . . you look beautiful," Dutch said, blushing. He blushed more than any man I've ever met. Gladys smiled and twirled again.

The inside of the kimono was decorated with what looked to be hundreds of tiny pink flower buds connected by green vines. Gladys inspected the oily silk while we listened to Dutch retell the pitch he'd

gotten from the Japanese tradesman, how silkworms had been har-
vested by hand from the mountains and fed a diet of tiger's milk and
fish oil to make them produce the finest silk in the world, how the
spinning techniques had been invented by an order of monks over five
hundred years ago and passed down through thirteen wars. Dutch's
voice went up an octave as he recounted all this, and it looked like he
was close to tears, moved as he was by the plight of this particular
kimono. As I listened to him gush, I wondered how in hell he ever sold
a single car. Gladys ran the silk back and forth through her fingers,
inspecting the fine stitching along the seams, and then her head jerked
as she looked up at Dutch and quickly back to the cloth between her
fingers. I looked too and after a minute saw what she saw: that the
flower buds on the fabric were actually tiny, detailed drawings of men
and women entwined in various sexual positions. Between Gladys's
fingers, a tiny princess had her thighs wrapped around the shoulders
of the tiny prince. Gladys's jaw clenched as she glanced for a moment
at me, and I kept my gaze on Dutch and his story. He noticed the both
of us staring at him, the look of shock in Gladys's face.

"It's true," he said. "The glassblowers construct these little silk-
worm houses, all their own. Hard to believe, I know."

He didn't realize what it was he'd given her, and with the two
of us staring at him, knowing for ourselves, I felt sorry for him. This
same reaction to Dutch came at odd times, sneaking up behind a
cover of my vague dislike of him. He seemed too much at times like
the persona created for him by the TV advertisers, completely clue-
less, lost in the world and trying to understand how he'd come to
accumulate so much money and his Disneyland house and why even
those weren't enough to keep his Miss North Carolina from the
magnet pull of Las Vegas. I felt it when he walked in the door that
day, looking as he did any April at tax time, wearing his white suit
with the lapel pins neatly lined up, trying to smile as if someone had
pulled a gun on him and told him to act natural. He wore his hair
in whatever style the makeup people gave him on the days they shot

commercials, and in between commercials a cowlick rose up on the side of his head above his ear, and sometimes I'd see him, when he thought no one was watching, lick his fingers and try to smooth the cowlick back into place. It wouldn't stay.

He'd brought me a present from Japan as well, a toy puppet with spring-loaded arms, wearing boxing gloves. The box said "Punching Ghost." There were instructions written in English on the side:

> 1. Moving arms to make fighting.
> 2. Very scary toy.

"This thing's a lot of fun," Dutch said, wearing the puppet on his hand. He punched me in the nose with it, then gave it to me and made me punch him back.

"Thanks, Dutch," I said.

A moment later, Roman used his key to open the door. He came in wearing his best seersucker suit, one that Gladys had picked out for him, and he hadn't been drinking. The shirt he wore was the one with the tiny face of cigarette burns, but I was the only one that noticed, and it had apparently been cleaned and pressed. Gladys quickly removed and folded away the kimono.

"Dutch, how's business?" Roman asked, shaking his brother's hand. "Gladys, damn, it's good to see you."

She stepped to him and kissed him on the cheek, which struck me as peculiar; this had been exactly her greeting to Dutch.

"Your hair all came back," she said for something to say. "I heard sometimes it doesn't."

He shrugged. "No problem growing hair."

"All the Stricklands have good heads of hair," Dutch said.

"Yeah, just look at Abbie Hoffman over there." He pointed at me, and they all turned to look. I shrugged and laughed, wondering when the conversation might turn away from hair growth. I was glad to see, at least, that there could be areas of agreement between Roman and Dutch.

"How's your poetry going these days?" Roman asked Gladys. "You tearing off a few good ones here and there? I bet you are."

"I've written some. When there's time, with work and everything . . ." She let her voice trail off, but I could see she was as touched by Roman's asking about her poetry as I was surprised. He'd never before mentioned it except to ask how much poems were going for these days on the black market.

"Well, anyway," he said, "maybe you could read one to me sometime."

"I'd like that, Roman," she said, and smiled.

Dutch nodded. "If you had any poems that dealt with Ford cars or light utility vehicles, I maybe could make use of it, in a print ad or something."

"What's all this talk of my poetry all of a sudden?" Gladys said.

"I just think it's a good thing," Roman said, and glanced at me as if there were some secret between us I was supposed to keep quiet about. "I don't know too much about it," he said.

"Well," Gladys said. "Let's talk about what we came here to talk about."

We sat and she poured coffee for everyone. Dutch put ice cubes in his. Roman and I slid doughnuts onto our paper plates, but Dutch passed, saying all that grease was bad for the system. He withdrew from his jacket pocket a piece of paper on which he'd written "Household Budget."

Gladys spoke. "We all know that like any family we've had some problems and that we need to work those out and clear the air a little bit. The main problem *seems* to be money, but—"

"You nailed it," Roman said. "Not enough dough." He was chewing a mouthful of doughnut as he said this, and I laughed. They all looked at me.

"The real downfall here is responsibility," Dutch said. "Or lack of it."

There fell a moment of silence and I looked across the table at Roman, but he only sat, drinking from his coffee cup.

"We've all been a little irresponsible," Gladys said. I started to say "Not me," but then thought of all the days of school I'd missed, and kept quiet.

"So we agree the problem is money," Roman said, wiping his mouth with a napkin. "Dutch, if you just pry open your checkbook there, float me a little loan, five thousand, say—just a loan, I'll repay every dime with interest—then I've got a few things lined up and I'll get myself established again."

So this was it, the reason he had finally agreed to the family conference, had stopped drinking for a day, had put on a nice suit and combed his hair—not for *her*, not for our family, but because he thought to hit up Dutch for an easy loan. I clenched my fists against the tabletop. *Damn you, Roman*, I thought.

"Right, Roman," Dutch said. "I'm in the habit of throwing good money after bad. I'm a complete jackass."

"You get no argument from me," Roman said.

"Everyone just needs to listen instead of talking," Gladys said. "Roman, the problem is not lack of money. The problem is how we live. We're not *normal*."

"We have a house, a car, we pay our bills. What's not normal about that?"

She shook her head. "Every month men come in here and take away half our furniture, then two weeks later come and put it back. Three times last year the phone was cut off when I was in the middle of a conversation. We don't have any health insurance." Her cheeks had reddened, her face damp.

"You want to bet on yourself to get sick?" His voice rose. "Be my guest."

"I have a plan to solve most of this," Dutch said.

"Like I said," Roman answered, "five thousand would make my problems go away. That's plan enough."

"Dad, would you just fucking hear him *out?*" I said. Roman

looked across at me as if I'd just thrown my coffee in his face. My legs were shaking.

"This is hard on him," Gladys said.

"It's hard on everybody," I said. "Don't talk about me like I'm not here."

"My plan is a simple one, Roman," Dutch said calmly. "You come back to work for me at the lot. New cars this time, top of the line, and I'll pay you salary plus commission and full benefits. You temporarily turn over your finances to me, checking account, savings, whatever, and I'll show you how to manage it as we go along. In the meantime, I'll pay an allowance to Gladys for the household and an allowance to you for your car, with enough left over to take your charming wife out for some dinner once a week, and your son to a movie now and then. I'll even let you finance a new car through the company at more than fair rates, if you want."

For a moment this all sounded great: with salary plus commission Roman would soon be rolling in money. We could get new furniture, Roman would have new wheels, and, I thought, the Chevy would be mine to keep.

Gladys smiled at Roman. "And you thought we were here to gang up on you," she said.

Roman nodded, gazing at his empty plate. "Well, boss," he said to Dutch, "I already have a good idea for your next commercial. We'll hire some stunt driver, maybe even Evel Knievel himself. With me so far?"

"Sure," Dutch said. He glanced around, uncertain.

"Evel straps on his helmet, buckles himself in behind the wheel of one of your Plymouths. There's a drumroll. He guns the engine, pops the clutch, and drives that car square up your ass."

"Oh *God*, Roman," Gladys said. She looked close to slapping him.

"Come on, Dad," I said. "You promised you wouldn't do this."

He pointed at me. "You stay out of it."

"I can see my efforts here have been wasted," Dutch said, blushing again. He folded his papers and put them away.

"No, wait, Dutch," Gladys said. "Roman, please. Just please do right now what you're supposed to do. Just reach out and shake Dutch's hand and tell him thanks and then you can move back home and we can start being a family again." I knew that already all of this had happened in her mind. I also knew that this whole thing was done with.

"This is between us, Gladys," Roman said. "Dutch doesn't need to be here."

"I invited him."

"Uninvite him. See you, Dutch."

"No, instead I think I'll uninvite you," Gladys said.

"Fine then," he said. Before I could think of anything else to say, to somehow salvage some of this, he was out the front door. I kept waiting to hear the roar of the Chevy's engine, the squeal of its tires, as I had so many times before, but then I remembered that he was on foot, that he had walked the four miles in from the Econo Stay on Highway 6.

"I'm sorry, Gladys, Gabriel," Dutch said.

"It wasn't your fault," she said, and silently I agreed with her, it wasn't his fault. It seemed that as much as Gladys had expected and even visualized the outcome she'd described, Roman had seen the opposite and done what he could to make sure that it worked out that way. It was as if he enjoyed being away from us, living at the Econo Stay and eating Fritos for dinner, but I knew that wasn't true. I didn't understand it, understand *them*.

"I don't know how Roman's going to keep living at that place," Gladys said. "What's he doing for money?"

"He doesn't have any money," I said. "He's running up a bill, most likely." I didn't really know that he was out of money, but after saying it, I was sure.

"He can't go on like that," Gladys said. She bit her thumbnail.

Dutch poured himself another iced coffee, his third since we'd sat down. "Gladys, I'd offer you the same deal I offered Roman, but I don't think my customers would go for a pretty woman selling cars."

"I'll do it," I said. The words were out with no more thought than you'd give a sneeze.

Dutch looked at me and raised his eyebrows. He looked at Gladys. "You'd have to cut your hair, clean yourself up a bit."

"No," Gladys said. "I don't want you working there." She glanced at Dutch. "Or anywhere, I mean."

"I could put him on weekends," Dutch said. "Might be good for him."

She looked at me, her eyes tired. "You really want to do this?"

I really didn't, having had a minute to think about it, but decided that maybe if I made enough money, she could quit her job at the dairy. I thought of those TV movies where the estranged parents get back together over some malady involving the child, the kid hit by a car or struggling bravely with cancer. Working for Dutch seemed disaster enough. "It'd be great," I said.

She nodded. "We'll try it for a month. Then we'll see."

Dutch shook my hand, then mimed a pair of scissors with his fingers. "Snip, snip," he said, and smiled.

Gladys cut my hair for me and I put on a shirt and tie and a pair of corduroy pants, and I thought I looked like a game-show host. By this time I was driving the Chevy everywhere I went, and no one bothered or cared that as yet I had no license. My first Friday at the job, Dutch explained what he called "the realities of the situation."

"I'm not going to lose any sales with you, Gabe. Selling requires experience that you simply lack. But there is honest work to be done, and I'll pay you a fair salary."

The upshot of this little speech was that I got to do all the shit jobs that no one else wanted, and that Dutch would pay me minimum wage. Most of my work involved sitting in a closet office with a bare-bulb lamp, going down page after page of teletype printout filled with the vehicle identification numbers of all the used cars that came wholesale onto the OK lot. I had to check the VIN numbers, sometimes even calling the tax office in the city of origin to make sure that the cars had not been stolen or retagged. It wasn't terrible work, but it was tedious. Other days I worked in the parts department after it closed, cleaning and boxing returned parts—exhaust systems, headers, headlights, window mechanisms—and finding their place on the shelves. I spent those Fridays and Saturdays by myself, and only occasionally would the salesmen (old guys with pompadours, too much cologne, and gold pen and pencil sets clipped to their shirt pockets) allow me to go out and talk to a customer, and only then when the customer looked like a complete no-sale, teenage kids out for a joyride, very old people, poor people in dirty clothes. They also sent me out on the rare customer who came to look at cars in the rain. I was the worst salesman imaginable, and usually my pitch went like this: "You want to buy anything?" I knew if Roman heard it, he would punch me in the head, and probably sue the school board.

One Saturday I came home late, my good clothes covered with dust from my work in the parts room, and I found Gladys in her bedroom putting her own clothes in a suitcase.

"Sit down for a minute," she said.

I sat on the edge of her bed. "Going somewhere?"

"I talked to your father, and he needs to move back into the house. He has zero money, and the motel is going to kick him out."

I had talked to him once in the two weeks since the family conference, and he told me only that he was making plans, that he would need my help. I didn't tell him I was working for Dutch.

"And you can't stay here with him," I said.

She put her hand against my cheek. "You understand so much," she said, as though I should be proud of my grasp of the obvious.

"So where are you going?"

She took a deep breath, looked away from me. "For the time, I'm moving into Dutch's house." She had in her hand a bundle of her underwear, which she slipped underneath the other clothes.

I slid off the bed and stood. "What are you talking about?"

"Don't make anything out of this, Gabe. He has that huge house, almost all empty."

"What is the deal with you and Dutch?"

"There's no *deal,* Gabe."

"He likes you," I said. "He bought you that kimono, gave you a car. He always talks about how pretty you are, how charming you are."

"And you don't agree with him?"

"You know what I mean."

"Besides," she said, folding her jeans into the bag, "he's letting me stay for free."

"For no money, you mean."

She stopped and turned to me, her face red. "That's a tasteless comment. Dutch has been a good friend to me, Gabe."

"Now I know why."

"He's been a good friend to *us.* He gave you a job selling cars, didn't he?"

"You always said you didn't *want* me to sell." By this point, I was nearly shouting.

"Christ, Gabe, you're not selling them door to door. And I don't think a little responsibility is such a terrible thing."

I had not told Gladys the real nature of my job, how I was stuck away each Saturday in a dirty closet, checking VINs until my eyes watered. I let her imagine that I was out there every weekend taking people for test drives, presenting their offers to Dutch for approval. As for responsibility, I also neglected to tell her that in our basement I had stashed away a dozen exhaust pipes, carburetors, ball joint assemblies, and oil pans, returned parts that would not match up with the inventory list. Instead of searching for them through back lists, I simply stashed them in the trunk of the Chevy and then signed off on the list.

"Listen," she said, "if you're so worried, why don't you come live at the house too? Dutch invited you, and there's plenty of room."

"Just the same, I think I'll stay here."

She thought for a moment, then nodded. "That might be for the better," she said. "Your father is going to need some help readjusting."

"I don't think he'll adjust to this."

She snapped closed her suitcase and turned to face me. "For now, you are not to tell your father where I am. Tell him I'm staying with a friend, which is exactly the truth."

"He'll find out."

"He won't if you don't tell him."

Fifteen minutes later, I watched through the window as she drove away in her Valiant, toward the house that Roman always referred to as "Dutchland." I tried to picture the two of them there, swimming in the pool, taking the paddleboats across the lake. I thought of Gladys's lacy underwear, how it had always seemed like some secret to me, some unfulfilled promise, and I hoped that this—Dutch—was not the promise finally fulfilled.

Roman's readjustment to moving home consisted of borrowing twenty bucks from me, taking out the Chevy, and returning with a sack of greasy food from Bif Burger and a fresh bottle of Crown Royal.

"So you and I are baching it for a while," he said.

"Yeah, I guess so," I said. I considered each word before I spoke it, believing that I would somehow give away Gladys's secret without even realizing I was doing so.

"This works out good," he said. "You and me have plans to lay, not to mention women." He nudged me with his elbow and some of the whiskey sloshed down the front of my shirt. It was one of his sales-meeting jokes, and I had no response for it. We stood in the middle of the kitchen, digging burgers out of the sack and passing the bottle.

"Why'd you cut your hair?" he said.

"For work," I said without thinking. I cursed at myself, believing it would be better if he didn't know about my job with Dutch or anything at all about Dutch. I figured the Crown Royal was loosening my tongue, so I passed it back to Roman and poured myself a glass of Coke. "So," I said, "what plans are you talking about?"

"What work? You didn't go get a job on me, did you?"

My face burned, and I turned away from him. "No, just thinking about it. I thought I ought to cut my hair in case I had an interview or something."

"Appearance, number one," he said. "We have to work on those clothes of yours, but forget all that. As of right now, you're working for me."

I didn't ask how or what he planned to pay me, given that he still owed the Econo Stay three hundred dollars. Gladys had promised to send me fifty dollars a week so we could buy food. She would pay the utility bills herself, though I suspected Dutch had taken over that area of her life.

Instead I asked Roman what it was we would be working on together.

He drew me into the living room, opened his suitcase, and withdrew the same folder of papers he'd carried with him that day to the Land of Oz.

"This is going to put your mother right back here in this house, with us, guaranteed," he said. He handed me the folder, and I sat down with it on my lap. Inside was a small Xeroxed poster, with a picture of William Shakespeare surrounded by big dollar signs. Beneath that was writing, the letters like calligraphy:

Ye Olde Poetry Contest!!!
$500
HUGE CASH BONANZA!!!
Sendeth Thy Verse Today!!!
Don't Delay!!!
Or Thy Money Might Get Away!!!

At the bottom was a post office box number and a deadline of August 31. There was also notice of a five-dollar entry fee.

"What the hell is this?" I said.

"What does it look like, son?"

"But I mean, what does this have to do with Gladys?"

"I forget with you sometimes, Gabe, I have to spell out every little detail."

His plan was for us to advertise the contest all over the state, collect the entry fees, which he figured would total at least three thousand dollars, toss all the entries in the dumpster, and name Gladys the winner.

"She'll never know it's us," he said. "I mean, who would suspect?"

"What if she doesn't enter?"

"She always enters these things. The only ones she ever wins are the kind where they make her pay them. That cheap racket."

"Yeah, like this one," I said.

Roman shrugged. "It's for a good cause." He rubbed his chin with a paper napkin. "To be on the safe side, you'll make sure that she gets the word, and you can encourage her to enter."

"What if her poem isn't the best one?"

He looked at me. "Have you been paying attention to anything I've said in the last seventeen years?"

"Sixteen," I said. "I still don't see how this is going to get her back."

"After she wins, the first thing she's going to do is call you. She might even call me, but somehow I end up on the phone congratulating her, and she's beside herself, right? So I say, 'That's great, honey, how about I take you out to dinner and we celebrate?' We go out and have this knockout time because she's on the moon and I've got all this money from the contest. Enough to buy the best meal in Greensboro, and get myself staked with some other things I'm lining up. She's happy, I'm happy. Just like old times."

"I'm not sure about this," I said.

He rubbed his mouth. "We want her back here, son. That's what we both want. And what she wants, deep inside her."

I held up the poster again, read back over it, and thought that somehow this would work, that Roman could make it work. "What do you need me to do?" I said.

"First we get a couple thousand of these printed up. You have any money?"

I told him I did.

"Good, that's good. Of course, as soon as we set aside the prize money out of the entry fees, you start getting paid back with interest. Now, the next thing, you know where your mother is staying?"

I swallowed and bit the inside of my cheek. "She's staying with a friend," I said.

"Okay. Your first job is to take a poster to her, real casual, like you just happened to see it stapled to the lamppost."

By now the rest of the burgers in the sack had gone cold and congealed. Roman drank from the Crown Royal and passed the bottle to me and I allowed myself a good long swallow, having got past his question about Gladys's whereabouts. We sat for a minute not speaking, looking at the poster Roman had made, the picture of Shakespeare faintly smiling at us, as if he were in on the whole scam. I recognized the picture as having come from my old Authors card game, which I kept with other forgotten games in my bedroom closet.

"This thing's going to work, Gabe," Roman said. "I feel it."

I passed the bottle back to him. "I feel it too," I said.

Chapter 4

We started out the next morning with three reams of printed-up fliers, a roll of tape, and a pair of staple guns we bought at Fleet Plummer hardware. By midday we had covered all of Greensboro, Winston-Salem, and High Point with posters tacked to streetlight poles, taped to mailboxes and phone booths, hung in the windows of delis and coffee shops and bars. We hung posters at all the retirement villages, because Roman said that blue-haired old ladies wrote poetry all the time and had no other real use for their money. I suggested placing posters in local bookstores and libraries and on the bulletin board at Artists Space downtown. Roman was excited, having fun. By midafternoon my fingers were blistered, and we had worked through half our stack of posters. Not until late in the day did I realize that this was Saturday and that I'd missed work at Dutch's car lot.

By dark we had covered the little towns around us—Kernersville, Statesville, Asheboro, and Clemmons. Using my money, Roman bought me a big spaghetti dinner at Cellar Anton's, and he ordered wine and lit cigarettes for us both. While we sat there eating, a woman with a huge cascade of blond hair and equally plentiful breasts strolled around the room playing "Somewhere My Love" on her mother-of-pearl accordion. She wore a short skirt and a puffy peasant blouse. Roman watched her awhile, then tipped her five dollars of my money as she strolled past. She smiled and winked at both of us, and Roman winked back and smiled, flashing his gold tooth.

"This is it, Gabe," he said. "We're on a roll, and we just started. Tomorrow, I'll cover the mountains and the coast," he said, and I pictured it literally, the tourist brochure beauty of the North Carolina mountains and seashore papered over, every inch, with dollar signs and Shakespeare's faint, playing-card smile.

"But we'll split up," he said, "so that you can go to work on your mother."

The woman with the accordion strolled back through our room playing "Sunrise, Sunset." Roman tipped her another five and requested "Lady of Spain." Somewhere on his list of loves must have been "voluptuous women playing the accordion, taking tips, and flirting." As if his list could encompass any possibility he might happen across in this world. Sitting there with a full stomach and my head warm with wine, I had to admit that this one didn't seem all bad.

The next day, Sunday, Roman took enough of my remaining money to rent a car for his drive to the beach and the mountains while I drove the Chevy out to Dutch's place. I hadn't been to his house since the last Christmas that Dutch lived with Miss North Carolina, more than two years earlier.

He'd met Miss North Carolina when they worked together on a local telethon. Dutch stayed awake for twenty-nine hours wearing his tuxedo with a light-up bow tie (the idea of his advertising team), selling cars around the clock with part of the money going to help organizations battling teen pregnancy, which was Miss North Carolina's pet cause that year. By four in the morning (Gladys had insisted we watch the entire telethon, in shifts, to give Dutch "spiritual support"), Dutch was existing somewhere beyond fatigue and kept announcing to the live TV audience that he was doing all of this "to help out with teen pregnancy." He told us later that at every commercial break the assistant director would scream in his ear, "The *fight* against, the *fight* against." Miss North Carolina said that unlike most wealthy men, Dutch was a generous man, a hero and true role model, and for a short while, I think she believed it.

They were married in the middle of her reign and so she had to keep it quiet or else give up her crown, which, she said, they would have to pry from her cold, stiff fingers. A justice of the peace performed the ceremony one Friday evening at Dutch's old place, a three-room apartment down the street from his dealership, where he lived as frugally as is humanly possible. There were only five guests at the wedding, but Dutch had to buy three lawn chairs from Roman just so everyone would have a place to sit. After the marriage, Miss North Carolina continued the duties of her title, speaking at junior high schools and appearing at the ribbon-cuttings of shopping centers, doing thirty-second public service announcements on local TV. Her real name was Sandy Goforth (on her commercials, she urged pregnant teens to "go forth and be a winner!"), but no one, with the exception of Dutch, called her that except to her face; the rest of the time, she was simply called Miss North Carolina (Roman sometimes called her "Dutch's wet dream"). She was pretty, in a painted-up way that I think Roman actually appreciated. I seemed to be the only one in the family who liked her much, and that was only because when we visited them at their new place (Dutchland) on Memorial Day or the Fourth of July, she would sun herself beside the pool wearing a white crocheted string bikini and would untie the top when she lay on her stomach. This seemed to me as good a reason as any to form an attachment.

I drove through the open front security gates of the house, where two copper-green lions stood atop brick pillars. The drive wound through stands of oak trees which had been planted to overhang the road, but were still only saplings, less than ten feet tall; I imagined it would take a hundred years for them to over-hang the road. The house itself was three stories, red brick with ornately topped white columns lining the porch. Out across the yard stood a lawn jockey, boxwoods trimmed in the shape of dogs and armchairs, and lavish fountains with cherubs spouting water from their mouths or from their tiny marble penises. There was a pond stocked with rainbow trout that eventually found their way to the dinner table, and docked at the pier were three pastel-colored paddleboats and a two-person diesel-powered submarine that Dutch had ordered from a science cat-alog and given Miss North Carolina for her twenty-first birthday.

Looking back, I can never understand the odd mix of aesthetic influences that had put together that strange house. The roof, for example, was made from slate that had been imported from Italy, but the columns that upheld it were made of formed plastic set in place with silicone cement. I've always imagined the house as rep-resenting the battle going on inside it, between Dutch's excessive frugality and Sandy Goforth's heedless extravagance. But it had been around this house that the advertising men built their image of Dutch for the car-buying public—eccentric, anything-for-a-deal— and if it sold cars, he went along. Every Christmas, he had the house strung with 250,000 lights, and he stood at the gate dressed as Santa Claus, handing out candy canes and **Ford #1** buttons.

I rang the doorbell, which still played the pageant theme song "Miss North Carolina, You're Everything." I was surprised when Gladys opened the door, as if I hadn't really believed she was liv-ing there. She wore a terry-cloth bathrobe and a white towel around her neck; on her way to the pool, she told me. Dutch was off filming a new commercial and promos for *Twilight Theater*. There had been no servants living in the house since the days of Miss North Carolina, except for the woman who came by in the evenings to cook Dutch's meals, and the weekly cleanings of the janitorial service.

"I'm kind of surprised to see you here," Gladys said as I followed her through the entrance hall. "I've missed your visits at the dairy."

"I didn't think you'd be working there anymore," I said.

"Gabe, I know you think Dutch is *keeping* me, but all he's doing is letting me use the third floor of the house."

I nodded. "I just came by to see how you're doing." The Shakespeare poster was folded away in the back pocket of my jeans.

"Dutch said you missed work yesterday. He was concerned."

"He'll probably fire me," I said, hoping it might be true. We were standing in the kitchen, rows of copper cookware hanging from a rack above us.

"He won't fire you, Gabe. He said that maybe you needed a little more responsibility at the car lot."

"Dutch must be the national spokesman for responsibility," I said.

Gladys dropped her towel on the butcher-block table. "Why are you so hostile? Dutch is trying to *help* you. He wants you to have a better job, a more enjoyable job."

I wanted to say that nothing could be more enjoyable than drinking Crown Royal with my father while running all over three counties with a staple gun in hand, but instead I just nodded.

"By the way," I said. "I thought you'd want to see this, if you haven't already." I took the poster from my pocket and unfolded it. She laughed a little while she read it over, and for a moment I felt a wave of panic that the poster, the wording of it, could be no one else's but Roman's. She'll see right through this, I thought.

"That's a pretty big prize for a poetry contest," she said.

"It sure is," I said. "And you'll win it, too." She looked at me. "I mean, I'm sure you will. You're really good at poetry."

She handed back the flier. "Thanks for thinking of me, but I'm not really interested."

My stomach tightened. "What do you mean? You always enter these things."

"And I always lose. I'm not exactly blessed with abundant talents."

Of course this had always been true, of her as well as me, but we had never admitted to it before. It had always seemed part of some game that allowed her to reshape us into what she wanted us to be, a lie that we lived as if it were some secret code between us.

"I really have a feeling about this one, Gladys," I said. "I'll enter your poems for you."

"I'm not *lazy,* Gabe. It's just I'm busy at night with work, I've been helping Dutch with some of the housework around here, and he's been teaching me about investments. Do you realize I'll be retirement age in just over twenty years? Do you know how fast twenty years go by? No, of course you don't."

"So you win the five hundred, and then you invest it. Please, Gladys."

"Gabe, just drop it. I'm going for a swim before I leave for work. You want to come?"

I followed her out to the poolside I hadn't seen in two years, where during those patriotic holidays I sat in a chaise lounge eyeing Miss North Carolina, her tanned back fanned by brown hair, the white crescent of her breast curving out against her towel, while hiding my erection with a copy of *Mad* magazine. Sometimes when the others were inside fixing drinks and I thought she was asleep, I would make a sudden noise of a dog barking, hoping it would startle her into sitting bolt upright, forgetting her half-nakedness. Instead she would slowly turn her head toward me.

"You are the strangest young man," she'd say in her exaggerated drawl.

I sat now on the redwood deck beside the twisting pale blue slide which emptied into the pool. A gush of water ran endlessly down the slide. At the far end of the deck, outdoor stereo speakers made in the shape of balls were mounted on the noses of twin alabaster statues of seals. As always, Mantovani and 101 Strings played gently, the sound settling out over the pool like a light mist. Mounted on the fence were tiki torches, which at night burned citronella oil to keep away mosquitoes. A toy train ran on tracks around the perimeter of the pool, its cars used to deliver drinks to swimmers. I watched Gladys churn through her laps, sleek in her black one-piece, her arms browned and firm, knifing through the water with hardly a wake. Whenever she'd stop to catch her breath, I would pitch her again on the idea of the poetry contest, and again and again she refused. I thought of Roman, cruising North Carolina in his rented car, plastering the mountains and covering the seashore with the false promise of money while I sat here failing at the one simple job that was mine to do. My hands started shaking.

But I did have one more angle left. I waited until Gladys slid out of the pool and sat on the edge drying her legs.

"*I'll* enter this contest if you will," I said.

She looked at me and raised her eyebrows. "Have you written some poems, Gabe?"

"Well, I'm working on something," I said. "Something big."

"Can you show me, or tell me about it?"

"Not exactly," I said. The trickle of water ran down the slide. Neither of us spoke.

"Gabe, in all this time, have you ever really been working on anything? Are you pursuing any artistic or creative endeavor at all? *Anything?*"

She watched me, and I waited for some elaborate fabrication to form in my mind, a lie complete and whole and perfect. None would come.

"No," I said.

"That's what I thought," she answered quietly, without anger, as much as I would've liked to have *heard* anger in the place of her resignation. I stood up to leave, and left the flier for her on the redwood table at poolside. When I looked back, Gladys was slipping into her robe, and the flier had blown into the middle of Dutch's pool and was taking on water, collapsing in on itself, slowly sinking.

By the early part of the following week the post office box overflowed with entries for the contest, more than twenty of them the first day.

"I could make a career of this," Roman said. He pulled the trash can from the post office lobby over next to our box and one by one rifled through the entries, retrieved the five-dollar checks, and threw the poems away.

"None from your mother," he said. "She must be working up a good one." He chuckled.

"That must be it," I said. I'd told him nothing of my visit with her, other than I'd given her the flier and made sure that she knew the prize was five hundred dollars. I convinced Roman that we ought to at least take the poems home with us and hold on to them until after the contest was over. He told me that *now* I was starting to think, as if for sixteen years he'd been waiting around for this particular capacity to finally kick in.

That night, after Roman was asleep and snoring in his bed, I dumped the box of poems out on the living-room floor and read through them. My hope was that I'd find some good enough (but not *too* good) to show Gladys and convince her that I'd written them. But none of them were right; the subject matter would tip her off, they were too old for me, none of them *fit* me, which I knew she would see immediately. It was hopeless.

Every night that week I visited Gladys at the dairy, sitting in the break room eating ice cream sandwiches, smoking cigarettes I bummed from Snowball while he showed me photos of his kids. Gladys had quit smoking because, she said, she was swimming every day now and enjoying the feel of her new muscles. Besides, Dutch wouldn't allow it in the house. Each night I thought up a way to casually mention the poetry contest, and each morning Roman and I drove to the post office and brought home a paper sack of new entries.

"I don't understand this, Gabe," Roman said, later in the week. "You *did* talk to her?"

I told him that she was working on something and planned to turn it in near the deadline. This lie bought me some time, and Roman was happy enough waiting, since we were still a month away from the deadline, and already he'd collected nearly nine hundred dollars in entry fees. I kept myself awake with coffee and cigarettes late into the night, having decided I would sit and write my own poem, knowing it had to be good enough to look like a real effort. If I could show her something that even resembled serious talent, it would be for her like the fulfillment of some long-kept wish, and what I'd heard of resignation and responsibility from her at poolside would vanish in the time it took her to read what I'd written. It was up to me to restore her empty, foolish, long-held illusions.

I sat at the kitchen table with a ballpoint pen and a pad of legal paper, and dug in. After half a dozen tries, my best effort was this:

Time

Time is not our friend
He catches up in the end.
Near the end of your life
Through your toil and your strife,
You have nothing left to defend.

Time flies by so fast
The world, it cannot last
By the time that you're grown,
Everything that you own
Has been thrown over as ballast.

—Gabriel Strickland

I read it over for ten minutes (twice as long as it took me to write), then wadded it up and threw it in the trash. Then I remembered that Roman sometimes went through the trash, thinking he'd thrown away an envelope with money in it, and the last thing I needed was for him to catch me committing poetry. I retrieved that poem and the others like it from the trash and set fire to them in the bathroom sink, then flushed the ashes down the toilet. I knew from reading the entries that my poem was likely the worst one that had ever been written. It had the rhythm of some limerick on a gag birthday card. Writing poetry that sounded like any kind of greeting card was, according to Gladys, a sin that real poets considered equal to taking another life. But I couldn't help myself; every time I sat and tried another poem, it came out with exactly the same rhythm, only with different words. Sometime near three a.m. I decided that this tendency amounted to something approaching a birth defect.

I decided that there had to be *some* art form that would suit me, that would give me something to show Gladys, to let me passably fake possessing talent. I took from the closet Gladys's acrylic paint set and pad, knowing that this was even less likely to work than the poems. I tried to paint a mountain landscape, because I'd seen a man on Public TV who could paint a good one in about six or seven minutes. The results ended up as the poems had, in ashes, all my efforts toward creation and beauty washing along toward the county sewage treatment plant.

By the second week I was no closer to convincing Gladys to enter the contest, and in fact had given up on talking her into it, knowing if I pushed too hard she would get suspicious, if she hadn't already. During that week I tried calligraphy, short stories, and charcoal sketches, and all of it ended up flushed. One night I walked down the stairs to the basement where Gladys had stored some of her other art supplies—candlemaking, macramé, beadwork—and where Roman's Mr. America Body Sculpting kit sat rusted from what felt like a hundred years earlier. Hidden behind the steps were all the orphaned car parts I'd brought home from Dutch's dealership. I hadn't yet decided what to do with them; they were worth good money, and it seemed a waste to throw them away.

As I stood there staring at all that gleaming chrome, at the stamped and forged steel, trying to decide if I might sell the parts at a flea market or maybe even do the honest thing and try to sneak them back onto the parts shelves, I knew that I had found my answer. I knew, without having then the language to articulate it, that in my efforts at creating art my problem had been form, my adherence to representational work—my salvation lay in abstraction.

I'd seen such sculptures displayed downtown near the Wachovia building, sculptures made from crushed cars, from lengths of barbed wire welded together with parts from farm tools. These same works had even been on the local TV news recently because the city had spent ninety thousand dollars to commission them, and a group of citizens had picketed the square, carrying signs that said YOU CALL THIS ART? and OUR SCHOOL KIDS NEED THAT MONEY FOR MILK. One man they interviewed walked around with hot dogs sewn to his clothes, saying that the city ought to give *him* ninety thousand dollars for *his* art. One of the artists explained her work in language that made almost no sense to me, and as she spoke, Gladys nodded, her face knitted in concentration. Roman kept saying, "What a load of horse hockey," over and over, but smiled and shook his head because the woman had managed to grab her part of that ninety thousand from the city fathers. Gladys had insisted I go with her the next day to see the works. Her favorite sculpture depicted the skeleton of a rat trapped in a block of Lucite, with a photo of napalmed Vietnamese children held in the rat's teeth. She said the protesters were "philistines," whatever that meant.

I knew that the car parts ought to be welded together, but I had neither welding equipment nor know-how, and so started in with a roll of duct tape. I found a set of headers for a '73 Fury and bolted them upside down to a square of scrap plywood I found in the basement, then wove through the flared pipes with pieces of wiring harness and seat belt. I taped to that a carburetor, a rearview mirror, a horn ring, a main spring, and two dozen push rods. It formed a sort of odd, metallic octopus which swayed and clanked when I turned it. I found in a copy of Gladys's *National Geographic* pictures of yachts floating in the bay at Martha's Vineyard, and other pictures of Mandinka tribesmen in West Africa. I tore these out and taped them to the ends of the push rods. I stopped finally not with a feeling that it was finished, but because the entire thing had become too topheavy and threatened to fall over.

I stepped back and looked at it, deciding that at least it looked like *something*, like a piece of work intentionally put together. I tried to decide what to call it, remembering that the names of the works on the square downtown seemed as arbitrary as the works themselves; some had complicated titles, such as *A Focusing on the Material Relationship Between Man-Made Waste and the Space-Time Continuum*. Others were simply named, such as *3 no. 3*, and *Untitled X*. Thinking of this, I remembered too that every one of the works had beside it a placard on which the artist explained the meaning of the work, the theory or idea behind it. One of the works, a plastic tube cemented to a barstool, was accompanied by a long and vituperative essay on the way that men thought about women. I knew that a jumbled heap of car parts held together with duct tape wouldn't mean much without such a placard, that I'd have to write one and it would have to make sense and sound, if not smart, then at least passably like what Roman had called "horse hockey." This brought me back right where I'd started, having to write something good and not being able to. I was tempted to tear the whole thing apart, to go upstairs and wake Roman from out of his snores and tell him that I had failed, that Gladys was not going to enter the contest, that I had no means of convincing her. I did not sleep well that night.

Early the next morning Roman set off for a "business meeting" with someone he kept calling "Mr. Vic Comstock," as if "Mr." were the man's first name.

"Who's Mr. Vic Comstock?"

"An associate, Gabe. You'll meet him soon enough."

I wondered what kind of business my broke, unemployed father might find to have a meeting over, and where this Mr. Vic Comstock had come from. I knew the names of most of my father's friends, road men like himself who met occasionally at Hooray Harry's to commiserate over poor commissions or slow summer orders, but I'd never heard of any Mr. Vic Comstock.

Roman dressed for his meeting in the same seersucker suit he'd worn for the meeting with Gladys and Dutch, except that he'd bought a new shirt to replace the burned one, and a new fancy, patterned silk tie which he must have bought with poetry contest money. He seemed nervous, redoing both his hair and his Windsor knot several times. Then he took with him all the cash from the poetry contest and left in his rental car.

I drove the Chevy downtown and walked around studying the sculptures on display. They were as I remembered them, except for the one that had been built of plastic blocks that people were supposed to steal. One of the works was titled *Wax Impressions of the Knees of Five Housewives*. Another, *Various Plastics Separated by Layers of Grease, with Holes the Size of My Head and Waist*. For over an hour I walked around making notes, copying phrases off the placards, and coming up with my own phrases now and then, picking ones that sounded right. After that I spent time in the library, going through books on art criticism, lifting phrases from those as well. At home I sat in front of Gladys's typewriter and turned my attention to writing my own (albeit plagiarized) explanation for my sculpture, my own "vision and aesthetic." Here is what I wrote:

What we know of the automobile is really only our image of the Americanized automobile-icon as supplied to us by Madison Avenue. When the cat kills the mouse he abstracts the mouse, and in the

same vein Madison Avenue abstracts and distorts
our true experience of the automobile by serving it
up to us through false images we gratefully
devour. This piece attempts to abstract the reality
of the <u>actual</u> car (as real as yachts or West
Africans) and not the image of the <u>illusory</u> car,
and thus make real the abstraction for the viewer,
more real in the abstract than is the unabstract-
ed icon abstracted in the image.

I pasted the card to the wooden base of my sculpture and read
it through three or four times, immensely pleased with what I'd
written, though I didn't understand a word of it. I read it out loud,
made a little song of the words. I was proud of my sculpture, not as
a work of art but as a work of salesmanship, a work of bullshit, a
scam. It occurred to me that people know something is art because
they become convinced of it, in exactly the same way they become
convinced that buying a suction-cup radio for the shower is a good
idea. I had what I thought of as a flash of insight, that this is what
art *is,* what it consists of. I thought, *I can do this.*

"Gabe, I'm shocked and moved," Gladys said. "I can't believe this
is *you* that made this." She read the card again and moved slowly
around *AutoCratic,* as I had titled my work. After loading the sculpture in the trunk of the car and driving it over to Dutchland, I'd
found her in sitting at the kitchen table eating stir-fry vegetables,
looking over various prospectuses from investment companies and a
catalog from the community college. I heard Dutch down the hall in
the rec room, working out. I thought of Roman doing his bench
presses and preacher curls in his long pants, a cigarette in his mouth.
I kept glancing down the long hall, worried that Dutch would walk
out and see the sculpture and start asking about the car parts.

"Your use of space, the sense of textures and shadow . . . this is an advanced piece of work," Gladys said as she walked slowly around it again, shaking her head.

"Thanks," I said, feeling no shame.

"It's primitive in its way, the use of tape, the torn magazine pictures. But that only points up its ultimate meaning, which is about technology and perception, finally, isn't it?"

"Well, sure," I said. "I mean, of course it is."

"That's a subtle irony for someone your age." She smiled at me.

I shrugged. "Subtle irony is my middle name."

Suddenly Dutch walked into the kitchen drinking his iced coffee, his face flushed and sweaty. He shook my hand, saying he was pleased to see me, and for a moment seemed to take no notice of the jumble of car parts in his kitchen, parts stolen from his own stockroom. He wore white sneakers with no socks, madras shorts, and a yellow T-shirt. I realized for the first time how muscular he was, not thick and doughy as Roman had been during his Mr. Clean days, but cut and angled, his muscles hard and sinewy. I would learn that every morning he swam fifty laps in his pool, and on weekends rode his stationary bicycle and practiced yoga. He believed, he would later say, in keeping in shape physically, fiscally, and spiritually.

"Dutch," Gladys said, "Gabe made this sculpture." She beamed, her eyes wide.

I held my breath as he looked closely at it, bending down to read the card, lightly touching the carburetor and headers.

"Parts from the junkyard?" he said.

"That's right," I answered, amazed that he didn't recognize the parts from his own shelves.

"Well I think that's fine," he said. "It's very satisfying to do work with your hands." I couldn't believe that he was not going to ridicule the work, as I knew Roman would have.

"I want you to have it," I said to Gladys. "And I want you to keep writing your poetry, I want you to enter that contest." I finished my little speech using all the sincerity I had practiced up during the drive over. "I only did this sculpture because of you."

This was true enough, though not in the way I implied. If there was any shame in me at that moment, I didn't let myself feel it. Gladys nodded, and tears rimmed her eyes. She promised to get something together that afternoon and to send it in right away. I gave her another copy of the poster, which I'd brought with me, and she hugged me. Despite the fact that I had just successfully bull-shitted my mother, I felt better than I'd felt in weeks. She asked me to stay for dinner and I agreed. I was tired of food from Bif Burger.

All of the food at Dutch's table was fresh and good, cooked to what my own abused taste buds knew of perfection. We sat huddled at one end of the elaborately carved dining-room table while Dutch's cook served us dinner. Mrs. Loggins had the large, starched look of school cafeteria ladies. She said nothing, simply placed at the other end of the table her delicious summer fare—Caesar salad, steamed asparagus, corn on the cob, new potatoes, yeast rolls—and left. Dutch (and now Gladys, I discovered) ate no meat, and I didn't miss it. I ate triple servings of everything and drank the one glass of white wine Dutch allowed me, while Gladys asked me questions about the ideas behind my sculpture. I lied easily, emboldened by all the success I'd had thus far. She laughed when I told her I'd stayed up late at night to finish it, living those hours on coffee and cigarettes. "A true artist," she said. I noticed that she had not asked anything about Roman, but I assumed that Roman was still a sore subject with Dutch.

Dutch listened for a while before saying anything.

"You know," he said, "I have to admit that when I first saw Gabe's sculpture, I thought it was supposed to show an octopus trying to fix his car."

I blushed, remembering that at one point I had thought nearly the same thing. Gladys laughed loudly, thinking, I knew, that this was another example of Dutch's droll humor. In fact he did blush and laugh at himself a little when he saw that he'd made a joke.

"Either that," he said, "or one of those six-armed Indian goddesses doing a dance to please the Great Mechanic in the sky."

Gladys laughed until her face was red, and I laughed too, not at the lame joke itself, but at the idea that Dutch had *made* a joke, that by way of wine and high spirits a little bit of personality had bubbled to his surface.

That was the first of several times he would surprise me that evening. After we'd finished our slices of watermelon and toasted pound cake, we made our way through the elaborate house, through the few trappings left behind by Miss North Carolina, the blue glass lovebirds mounted in display cases, the tapestries and Persian rugs. In the rec room, bright pole lamps illuminated the billiard table and Dutch's exercise machine. Finally we ended up in the ballroom with its cathedral ceiling, yellow wood floors and amber chandelier, stereo equipment recessed in the walls. Dutch clicked on his reel-to-reel tape deck and the Tommy Dorsey band flooded the room, brassy and thumping. We took turns dancing with Gladys, me trampling her insteps in my Chuck Taylors, fingers pressed to the thin cotton of her summer skirt, my palm balanced along the sharp curve where her waist met her hip. I noticed, then quickly tried not to notice, that she was braless beneath her pale cotton blouse. Her movements were fluid, her body strong. In her face shone a high color, her eyes wet with drink and exertion. She could not quit smiling.

Dutch danced stiffly and mechanically and technically good, full of fancy swing twists and fox-trot dips he'd bought from some Arthur Murray instructor. He held her close as he moved her around the floor, his shoes clicking on the wood, hers squeaking. I saw him counting to himself, keeping time, careful against the loose-boned sloppiness that in my mind makes good dancing. Their movements together were so tightly choreographed that I knew watching them that they'd danced before, alone together in the big house.

Near midnight we finally tired ourselves with dancing, the yellow floor tracing the path of our scuff marks. Dutch directed us out back of the house, where we sat by the pool in Adirondack chairs. The rails of the model train gleamed like knives in the moonlight. The train sat unmoving, and I imagined a tiny engineer, off for the night, at home relaxing. The blue water in the pool, lit from below, lapped quietly at the edges of the concrete and threw wavy aqua light on our faces.

"So, Gabe," Gladys said, "are you working on more sculptures?"

"I've got a few ideas," I said.

"You should keep at it, not let up," Dutch said. "'Nothing recedes like success.' Ray Kroc said that, the founder of McDonald's."

"Slapping together Big Macs isn't quite the same as making art," I said. I tried to sound like I possessed fragile creative sensibilities capable of being bruised. The truth was I'd have gladly traded my sculpture for a Big Mac and a chocolate shake.

Gladys put her hand on my arm. "Dutch just means that he'd like to see your ideas come to fruition, instead of just remaining ideas."

"I've seen your mother doing her poems, her paintings. It's work, and you ought to approach it like a job," Dutch said. "Assign yourself a regular schedule. Specify particular techniques you're to learn and a deadline for doing so. That's exactly, for example, how I approach playing the guitar. It's a matter of——"

I looked at him. "You play guitar?" I thought of all the times I'd pretended to play, jumping on my bed in my underwear.

"Yes, I do," he said.

"Go get your guitar, Dutch," Gladys told him. "Play something for us."

Gladys and I sat in the light of the pool while Dutch disappeared up the walk and inside the brightly lit house. Above us in the lavender sky, bats flew in dips and cuts. There was the steady summer hum of cicadas, and the occasional zap of a mosquito killed by the bug lamp. I kept waiting for Gladys to ask about Roman, but she only sat taking in the night, smiling at me, her eyes reflecting the water. "You're going to enjoy this," she said.

When he returned, Dutch sat and withdrew from its case a battered Martin guitar, the fretboard slick with wear, the pick guard chipped and worn. There was a thick leather strap and a happy-face sticker pasted on at the base of the neck. Looking back, I can't remember exactly what I expected him to play as he tuned up the strings—probably some wimpy AM song by the Carpenters or America, or maybe his own jingle which played at the end of his *Twilight Theater* commercials ("Buy a Ford you can afford at Dutch Strickland's today!").

Instead he slipped deftly into a quick, bluesy run up the fretboard, flatpicking single notes, bending and pulling strings, then back down again through the blues scale, gliding into chords, then drawing out single notes that hummed off the Martin, meshed sounds weaving in the air out over the pool and up into the night. Three times he ran through the scale, slipping in chords to back himself, holding bent notes to the point of breaking before he started singing. His voice was at once shy and whispery and deeply melodic, a rich, hushed baritone perfect for blues, sounding broken-in and worn, ragged with living. If I closed my eyes, it was impossible to connect this voice to the Dutch I knew, the humorless man on TV who water-skied dressed as a fish, who drove a car filled with Jell-O, who lived in this ornately tacky house. He finished his song, the last note still resonating as he placed the guitar on the cement.

"'Believe I'll Make a Change' by Pinewood Tom," Dutch said. "He did it a little better than me."

Gladys clapped and whistled.

"God almighty, Dutch," I said. I didn't have any other words.

"This illustrates what I was talking about," he said. "Playing that guitar is basically no different than setting the timing on a Fairlane.

You learn to place your fingers where they're supposed to go, then do a particular set of movements in a certain order."

"You . . . you're really . . . you're damn good, Dutch," I said. I could not make myself say "talented." Dutch waved his hand, brushing away my praise.

"I'm adequate," he said. This was not modesty so much as his own reasoned assessment of himself.

I shook my head. "No, you really should be onstage somewhere. One of the clubs downtown. You ought to have a nickname, like Blind Dutch Strickland or something."

For the first time in memory, Dutch laughed out loud, let it expel from him in a burst, as if he'd saved it up for years. Gladys and I both laughed as well, more from surprise than anything else, and for the rest of that night we made a game of referring to Dutch as Blind Dutch, and he would laugh every time. It was not the name itself that pleased him so much, I think, as it was the idea that someone had *given* him a nickname. I imagined that for most of his life, growing up through elementary and high school, any nicknames he'd been given by the other kids would not have been ones he'd like to hear repeated. For the rest of that year, with everything else that came to happen, Dutch and I had this one area of common ground, where he would sometimes play songs for me and I would call him by his nickname. It was a way of getting along.

By two a.m. we were yawning, swatting mosquitoes, finishing the last of our drinks. Suddenly, Dutch sat forward in his chair.

"Listen, Gabe, I want to buy that sculpture from you."

I glanced at Gladys. "Why? I mean, I gave it to Gladys."

"But I want to pay you for it," he said. "I said that art is work, right? One gets paid for his work. A matter of principle." He withdrew his wallet and handed me forty bucks.

I looked again at Gladys, and she smiled. "I guess you're a professional artist now."

"If you're going to do this," Dutch said, "you ought to take it seriously." I could only nod and shake his hand, the money still held in my other hand.

"Tell you what," he said. "You find an art course you want to take at that place Gladys goes to, and I'll foot the bill. You can find out if you are really serious about this or not."

I looked at Gladys. "I have the catalog," she said. "This is a good opportunity for you."

Still suspicious of Dutch, I wondered if his motive was to make me fall on my face in the class, to convince me that I had no talent (as if I needed convincing) so that I would get this out of my system and settle down to real work, to a serious life. Whatever his reasons, I knew that keeping Gladys happy was the quickest way to make her forget her previous unhappiness, to get her back home with us again.

"Okay, then," I said.

I got up to leave, and Gladys went inside to the kitchen to wrap up some cake for me to take home. Dutch and I stood watching a Japanese beetle that had fallen into the pool and now struggled, making tiny dimples in the water. He touched my shoulder.

"You did a good thing here tonight, son," he said. "You made your mother as happy as I've seen her since all of this started."

I might have said the same to him. I remembered back to when I would watch Gladys standing in the basement, snapping laundry beneath her pink lightbulb, and wonder at who she was. It seemed tonight that *this* was who she was, this tanned, fit, dancing, laughing woman. She was, as Dutch said, as happy as she'd been since . . . since I could remember. She'd forsaken her edginess, the belief that at any minute things would go irretrievably wrong. Living in a house with the furniture permanently in place had probably helped. Maybe, I thought, all she had needed was a break from Roman, a little vacation away.

"I'll tell you one more thing," Dutch said. "You ever steal from me again, I'll nail your hide to the wall."

I looked at him for a second, then nodded. "Okay," I said.

I took my pound cake, climbed into the Chevy, and started away down the long drive with its puny trees, into the balmy August night. As I waved goodbye to the two of them they stood together in the yellow light shining through the doorway and spilling in a slant across the lawn. They waved back, as if they were my parents seeing me off to the prom, off into some new life. When I looked back in the rearview mirror they lingered there in the door, and before I drove out of sight of them, I saw Gladys lean back toward Dutch, resting her shoulders against him.

Chapter 5

"We're in business!" Roman shouted as he burst through the front door, waving a sheet of lavender notepaper. I recognized the paper Gladys saved for her poems, refusing to allow grocery lists or refrigerator notes to be written on it. Finally, here was her entry in the poetry contest. Roman tossed the paper on the table and withdrew from his jacket an envelope all ready for her, with a letter of congratulations and a cashier's check for five hundred dollars inside.

"Aren't you going to read her poem?" I asked.

He stared at me. "Let me guess. Maybe it's not good enough and so she loses the contest. Is that what you're thinking?"

"No. I mean, of course she wins, but you could at least read what she wrote."

He thought about this. "I never have much luck understanding her poems, Gabe. Help yourself, though."

"Maybe later." I took the envelope with the poem and stuffed it in my back pocket.

Roman withdrew his fountain pen. "Now all I need is her address."

"Her address?"

"Yeah, you know, son. The place where she lives. Should be on the envelope there. I forgot to check."

I withdrew the envelope and unfolded it as if it were a bomb I had to diffuse. I bit the inside of my cheek and looked at the return address, half expecting it to say "Dutchland," with a tiny picture of Gladys swimming in Dutch's pool while he played guitar alongside her. Instead, to my relief, there was a post office box number. I gave the number to Roman.

"Allow her two days, and if you haven't heard from her, you call her and just casually ask if she's heard anything from that contest." He smiled his full, gold-tooth smile. "I love it when things work out," he said. A new one for his list.

Later on, after we drove to the post office to mail the check, Roman took us to Belk's so that I could buy a new suit, a new Arrow shirt, and a tie that Roman picked out, wide, with a picture of fox hunters printed on it. I felt pleased that he wanted to go to so much trouble and effort for our dinner with Gladys, a dinner that had not yet even been planned, but then he told me we had other plans, a Friday-night business meeting with Mr. Vic Comstock.

"He specifically asked me to invite you, Gabe. He said he wants to shake the hand of Roman Strickland's son." Roman announced this as if I should be impressed by the generous spirit of this man I'd never met.

I nodded and said, "Okay," while the men's department clerk checked my inseam for fit. I stood with my hands at my sides in front of the three-way mirror and studied the various versions of myself and Roman reflected back.

Gladys called the next afternoon just as Roman had predicted, to tell me she had won. Her voice quavered as she told me, and I could tell she was near tears. She said the fact that things had worked out this way, my sculpture, her winning the contest, was "meaningful," and "portentous." I did my best to sound surprised and excited, and after a few minutes of talking with her I really *felt* excited, relieved that it had all happened the way we'd planned after all the lies and the miles of Shakespeare's face and the near misses with Gladys. After I'd talked to her for a while, Roman picked up the extension. For a few moments I heard his breathing as he said nothing, listening to her voice. Finally, he broke in.

"Congratulations, Gladys."

"Oh, Roman. Well, thank you. I'm very excited. Gabe inspired me, you know."

I heard him think about this one for a few moments.

"You ought to feel real proud of yourself," he said to her. "A great poem like that, big contest winner. From what Gabe says, this is hot stuff."

She laughed. "I don't know about that," she said.

Having gotten her to laugh, he went into the windup for his pitch. "Listen, with all this excitement, how about I take you out for dinner. Our favorite table at Cellar Anton's, some lasagna and wine. What do you say?"

"I don't think that would be a very good idea, Roman, but thank you for the offer."

"Did I mention I'm paying?"

She laughed. "Well, but no, Roman, really."

"I won't take no for an answer," he said. "I'll pick you up in the car. It'll be like we're dating. Who knows, I might even make a move on you."

I winced, knowing he was pushing too hard, talking too fast, starting to panic.

"We're not dating, Roman, and that whole idea makes me uncomfortable. I'm sorry."

"Gladys . . ."

"Roman, please."

I knew I had to step in quickly, or we would lose the whole thing.

"I have an idea," I said. "Why don't you come here for supper. I'll fix all your favorites, tacos, stuffed celery, homemade ice cream. Then you can read us your winning poem." For a few moments there was silence, and I thought she might have hung up.

"That sounds good, I guess," she said.

"Hey, it sounds fantastic," Roman said. "It sounds like the best idea I heard today."

Shut up, *shut up*, I thought.

"I'll even make homemade guacamole," I told her.

"Well . . . but remember, I don't eat meat anymore."

"I'll put beans in the tacos."

"What do you mean, you don't eat meat?" Roman said. "What else is there to eat?"

She ignored him. "I guess that sounds okay," she said. "It'll be nice to see you."

"I can't wait," Roman said. I heard the truth of this in his voice.

"Roman, please, if you would hang up for a minute, I need to talk to Gabe."

"How about tomorrow night, Thursday?" he said.

"Tomorrow's fine."

"This is going to be great," he said. He was silent another moment, and I pictured him trying to think of something else to say. Then he clicked off.

"Gladys?"

"Gabe, listen to me. I'm going to need your support tomorrow night. Whatever gets said, whatever happens, I want you to promise that you'll help me out. You're part of all this."

I figured that she needed me to do what I'd just done: run a little blocking for her so that Roman wouldn't knock her over with his eagerness to please. "Sure, Gladys," I said. "Whatever you say." Slowly, slowly, I was helping them to each other.

When I hung up and walked back into the kitchen, Roman wanted to know what else she had said. I told him she just wanted to make sure that everything went okay, that she was nervous.

"Well, who isn't?" he said, not looking at me.

"Dad, be careful when she's here. Don't say anything at all about money."

He ran his fingers through his hair. "What am I supposed to talk about then?"

"Ask her about her poems." I took the lavender envelope out of my back pocket. "Have you read the poem she sent us? Be ready to talk about it after she reads it."

"I don't know how to talk about that, Gabe. I never once understood a poem. And I don't mean just the words. I don't understand why people *write* poems, why they read them, why they buy books of poems, or teach them in school. I don't get what poems are supposed to *do*."

I shook my head and withdrew Gladys's poem from the envelope. This is what I found written there:

What Is Left

Awake at night, I try to hear
The spoilage of milk in the fridge,
Or the sound that absence leaves behind—
Squeak of mail slot, flutter
Of postcards dropped on the floor.

Instead whispers the noise of tires rolling,
The rotting of trees, the slow wearing out
Of world, of long frozen nights.

"Dad, this is about you."

"Let me see that." He took the paper and read it over, his face gathered in concentration.

"This is my exact point," he said. "You tell me it's about me, I read it, and not once does the name 'Roman Strickland' surface here, and neither does the word 'husband,' or anything even close to that. What do we get instead? 'Spoiled milk,' and 'mail slots,' and 'rotting trees.' So please don't try to tell me this is about me."

"You're probably right," I said, wondering how he could be so blind to her, blind to himself.

We spent the next day in preparation for Gladys's visit, cleaning and vacuuming, washing the floors, ironing our clothes, spraying Mountain Fresh Glade in all the rooms. Roman had never before done any housework, leaving the domestic chores to Gladys (or the maid during flush times) and the yardwork to me. I gave him a feather duster and directed him toward the living room, and he went about hitting the tables and chairs *whap! whap!* as if he might just scare away all the dust. A deliveryman brought the vase of yellow roses Roman had ordered, which he placed on the dresser in the bedroom. He kept coming into the kitchen while I was cooking up the beans, chopping lettuce and tomatoes, starting the ice cream in the electric freezer.

"Shouldn't we have steaks or something?" he said. He kept bouncing on his toes.

"You heard her, she doesn't eat meat anymore."

"Yeah, but *bean tacos*? Stuffed celery? I mean, Jesus, welcome to the Waldorf-Astoria."

I shrugged, spooning sour cream out of its plastic tub. "It's what she likes."

"Well, yeah, but . . ." I waited for him to say, "It's not good enough." For him, of course, nothing ever could be, but instead he ran his hand through his hair and walked away, still bouncing on his toes. I heard him in the den, whapping the TV with his feather duster.

Gladys knocked his eyes out. She wore a white eyelet sundress trimmed in lace, the dress made whiter still by her browned muscles, her shining dark hair. She wore no makeup, and I noticed that the ice-crystal burns around her eyes had healed, her eyelashes and eyebrows had lightened from the chlorine in Dutch's pool, the days spent in the sun. Silver earrings framed her face, a half-moon on one side, silver star on the other.

"Hello, Roman," she said. We stood together in the entrance hall. "You're looking nice, your hair all grown in. Gabe, I've never seen you like this."

I wore the suit and fox-hunter tie I'd bought two days before for my meeting with Mr. Vic Comstock. Roman wore his own new suit from Belk's, and it was only now I noticed how alike the suits looked, the only difference being the faint pinstripes in Roman's suit and his blue paisley tie.

"Holy shit, Gladys," Roman said. "Look at you."

She smiled. "Thank you."

"Well, come on in. I mean, hell, have a seat. You want a martini?"

"Just ice water," she said.

"Water? Come on. How about champagne? I was saving it for later, but what the hell, we could all get hit by a bus before then, right?"

For a moment I tried to figure out how that might happen, and then I saw Gladys pursing her lips. "Dad, I think she just wants water," I said. I tried to send telepathic messages to Roman: *Don't push it. Back off.* While Roman went into the kitchen for her water and his martini, she pulled me aside in the hallway.

"You look like Roman Junior," she said. "That's what he wanted to call you, if I hadn't put my foot down."

"We just wanted to look nice."

"I know, honey. It's sweet." She squeezed my arm. "I'm glad you're here tonight."

Roman walked out of the kitchen. "Knock, knock," he said as he handed her the glass.

She looked at me, and I shrugged. "Who's there?" she said.

"Gladys."

"Gladys who?"

He grinned. "I'm glad it's you!" He sipped his drink as his face reddened. This was an old joke of his. I thought of my basement lessons: if only you can make them laugh.

Gladys did laugh, politely, I thought. The way she laughed when . . . well, when salesmen came to the door with their jokes and running patter.

"A little ice-breaker," Roman said.

"Very creative," she said.

"Speaking of which, to you, for your big win," he said, lifting his glass. Gladys raised hers and they clinked, and since I didn't have one I raised my hand and said, "Clink clink." Roman glared at me. The last thing he wanted was for me to act like a kid, as if that might be the reason for Gladys's absence from our lives. I think that night I was nearly as nervous as he, believing along with him that somehow the working out of our poetry scam, a clean house, a vase of yellow roses, and bean tacos with homemade ice cream were enough to fix what it was that was wrong with our lives, could undo damage that stretched back further than my own life. I wanted to hope that a knock-knock joke could win her, that a fox-hunter tie could convince her, that selling her on ourselves would put our lives back together. I truly was, for that night, Roman Junior.

"Let's eat," I said.

Roman waved his arm in the air. "Yes, by God. Bean tacos all around!"

Gladys sat and ate heavy portions of all her favorites, though I noticed she kept twisting her napkin, tapping her fingers on her glass, looking around the room, and then settling her eyes on me. I thought back to how nervous she'd been the last time we'd all been together in this house, the Saturday that Dutch came around in his white suit and lapel pins, bringing with him his offers of steady work and steady income, a pension plan and accident insurance, offering a life in which all accidents of fate or fortune would be insured against. In short, Dutch offered Roman some version of his own life and what came with it, the stability that Gladys desired, the sameness that Roman hated.

"This was delicious, everything," Gladys said. "I'm glad we're all together like this."

"We're supposed to be together like this," Roman said. "We shouldn't have screwed it up."

"You're right," Gladys told him. "We shouldn't have. But we did."

There was a space of silence. "Who wants ice cream and coffee?" I said.

"I'd love some." Gladys smiled.

I poured coffee into our good cups and saucers. There followed the familiar sound of Roman stirring in his three sugars, Gladys her one cream, the years-old noise of any morning at our house. When I went to the freezer and removed the small silver bucket, I discovered that the ice cream had not formed up; I had not put in enough rock salt or ice, or there was too much cream, or I'd not let it turn long enough. For whatever reason, all I was left with was soup.

"I'm sorry," I said.

"That's okay," Gladys said. "I shouldn't be eating it anyway."

"I ought to watch it too, I guess," Roman said. He patted his stomach.

I stuck my finger in the ice cream soup and tasted it, then set it on the sink.

Roman cleared his throat. "Well, Gladys, what do you say you move your things back here tonight and we pick up right where we left off." He smiled. "I saved your place."

Their simple agreement that they should watch their weight was enough for Roman to convince himself that they were on even ground again, that everything between them had somehow realigned itself, that their problems, ignored, had gone away.

She shook her head. "Roman, I think you're missing something here," she said.

He looked around the room, as though he expected the refrigerator or the stove to be gone. "What are you talking about?"

She glanced at me, then looked at Roman. "I'm not coming back."

"What are you talking about?" he said again.

Gladys bit her lower lip. "For the first time in my life I'm start-ing to feel like a whole person. I'm in the best shape I've ever been in, I'm going back to school in the fall, and now I won this poetry contest after all those years of rejection. Like everything I ever wanted to be is coming together, and I'm not about to start fight-ing it. That's what I'm talking about. I know you don't understand."

I thought of the night I left Dutchland and how in the yellow light of the house I'd seen Gladys lean back against Dutch, hugging herself. I knew that I should feel awful about this, that she wasn't coming back, that she was leaving us. But, sitting there at the table with her brown skin and taut muscles, her smile framed by the stars and the moon, she seemed like some culmination of herself, the way all those artists I'd read up on had talked about there being a form of the fin-ished work buried in the block of granite, a shape for them to dis-cover and reveal. That is how I thought of Gladys that night—she'd found the real shape of her life and had to chisel us away to get at it.

Roman's face looked stung. He didn't say anything.

Gladys blushed and kept her gaze on the placemat before her. The steam from our cups of coffee rose like smoke signals from three miniature fires.

"I've spoken to a lawyer," she said quietly. "He's going to arrange a trial separation. That's what he called it."

"The poetry contest," Roman said. "Winning that goddamn con-test is part of this new you, am I right? The new you that decides to toss twenty years of marriage on the garbage heap."

"Dad," I said.

"Roman, I am not going to be bullied over this, and yes, win-ning the poetry contest came at just the right time." She shrugged. "It's like a validation of everything I'm trying to do."

Roman looked at me like he was close to laughing. "A dog," he said. "Even a damn dog knows not to take a shit right next to his supper dish, you see what I'm saying, Gabe?"

"What does that mean, Roman?" Gladys asked him.

"Nothing," I said. "It doesn't mean anything."

"It means I'm sitting here like the cat that ate the fucking canary. Or even better, canary and bean tacos," Roman said. Within that one moment he was willing to throw away everything, to leave Gladys with no affection for him, hating everything about him including the years she had at his side. I'd seen this before, when he knew a customer had broken, no chance for a sale, and would say anything in the way of insult or scorn that might happen into his head. It was nothing more than pride, I think, stupid in the way most acts of pride are.

I shook my head. "Don't say anything else," I told him.

Already Gladys was angry. "No, Roman, if you have something you'd like to say, then why don't you say it and we can end this little game you're inventing."

He nodded, his face set hard. "I would like to."

"Don't, Roman," I said.

"What?" Gladys asked.

"I'd like to ask a question." He looked up toward the ceiling. "'Awake at night, I try to hear the spoilage of milk.' Now, that's not really about me, is it?"

Her face froze for a second, then she looked at me. "But how . . ."

"Just the same," Roman said, "I thought it deserved to win."

It took a minute for the meaning of this to settle out in her mind. Once or twice she tried to form a question, hers lips opening and closing, her wide eyes shifting between me and Roman. Then, like a lost memory, it came to her.

"You bastard," she whispered.

He wouldn't look at her, embarrassed, as always, by his own capacity for meanness.

Gladys turned her gaze on me. "You *knew* about this. You were in on it. That's why you wanted me to enter so bad. That's why you gave me the sculpture."

I shook my head, my stomach knotted with bean tacos and misery. "Not entirely," I lied. "I really liked making the sculpture."

She closed her eyes. "I'm leaving. I can't stand this."

"No, you stay here," Roman said. He pushed back from the table. "You and Gabe drink your ice cream. I'm going." He walked into the entrance hall and turned toward the bedroom for his wallet and jacket, then stopped. The yellow roses still bloomed in the bedroom; he had arranged fresh sheets on the bed. He avoided these and went out the front door without a word. I heard the familiar squeal of his car tires on the pavement.

We sat a few minutes in silence, Gladys crying. "I'm sorry," I said. "We just wanted you back."

"So this is how you decided to make it happen, by tricking me, lying to me."

I bent my knuckles back until they popped. "I never thought you would know."

"I would have known, even if it hadn't come out, Gabe. Don't you see that?"

I nodded, twisted my napkin.

"You need to learn one thing your father never did, Gabe. That if you love somebody, the best, the *only* thing you can do is be honest with them. It counts more than anything."

"We thought you'd be so happy about winning that you'd come back here to live with us."

She shook her head. "That's a stupid plan, Gabe. It doesn't really make sense to me."

I shrugged. "When the only plan you have is stupid, that's the one you go with."

At this she let herself laugh a little. "No more plans, okay?"

I said okay, and she took my hand. "It was still a good poem," she said.

"The best in the batch," I told her, though I'd only read three or four of them.

"I still care about my work, even if it's not much good."

"And I really am sorry," I said.

She nodded. "The offer stands for you to come live at Dutch's house. He really likes you, Gabe."

I almost said, "I really like me too," but this was an old joke of Roman's and I let it pass. Instead I told her I would think about it.

Later we sat outside in the dark on the front steps. We drank coffee and watched cars pass by on the street, the neighborhood families walking past the lighted squares of their windows.

"Do you think Roman is all right?" she said.

"Probably drive around half the night, then come home and drink until he falls asleep." Somehow, in the space of a month, I had become the expert on Roman's habits and moods, as if she had only a passing acquaintance with him. We were quiet a moment.

"There's a dozen yellow roses in the bedroom," I told her.

"Oh, no." She blinked away her tears. "Damn him," she said. Somewhere, a dog barked, setting off all the others in the neighborhood.

"So you dropped the A-bomb tonight," I said.

She smiled a little. "The A but not the H," she said.

"Dutch?"

She nodded.

"I knew it," I said. "I knew something was going on there."

"Well, heavens, Gabe, you're not blind. And let's not be naive about it. It's only recently, not the whole time I've been gone."

I watched a man bicycle past in the dark, tiny red lights attached to his head and legs.

"What I'd like to know is when things turned wrong for us," I said.

"It started before you were born, I guess. And *you* were never the problem. The kind of marriage your father and I have—had—turns pretty quickly into a competition. Like Ping-Pong, when you have to win by two but the game stretches into twenty-one to twenty, twenty-seven to twenty-six. Your father and I are up to, I don't know, ten thousand eighty-four to ten thousand eighty-three. It's always money, or how he's supposed to love me. I just got tired of the game."

I felt like this would be a good point to say something reassuring, or to pat her hand, put my arm around her shoulders. But she said all of this without sadness or self-pity, only a kind of resignation and small anger, as if her car had finally quit on her and now she had to find a way to get a new one. A new car, a new life. Easy.

"You really should keep making sculpture," she said. "You have an eye."

I nodded. "Okay. You should keep writing poetry. You have an ear."

"Actually, this whole stupid thing did get me writing again."

"And you *did* win. Five hundred bucks."

She gave a slight smile. "That's true," she said, then linked her arm through mine. "We're going to be okay with all of this. Maybe it's too much right now, but in time things will seem normal. A new normal you're just not used to yet. You'll see."

"Sure," I said, thinking not of her words of sympathy for me but of her Ping-Pong marriage with Roman. She had walked away, put her paddle down on the table. This was her analogy, a way of explaining it to herself. But I had *played* Ping-Pong, hours of it in the basements of people I knew from high school, and my experience of playing on those rainy afternoons told me this: there is *always* another game.

Chapter 6

All during the drive to Vic Comstock's house, Roman made me practice giving myself a firm handshake. "How do you do, sir?" I kept asking myself.

"Speak forcefully," Roman said.

"Who the hell *is* this guy?" I said. "You act like we're going on a blind date." I was wearing my new clothes, with the fox-hunter tie, and tassel loafers that Roman had made me shine at the kitchen table using a vegetable brush and his can of Kiwi polish.

"This 'guy' happens to be the man who's going to end all our money troubles."

"He's giving you a job?" I asked. It was too much to hope for.

"I told you, Gabe, we're business partners. Think of yourself as a junior partner."

"Junior partner in what?"

He smiled as he turned into the driveway. "You'll see."

We walked along the curving flagstone path, then Roman took two deep breaths before he knocked. Mr. Vic Comstock opened the door of his sprawling brick rancher, looking exactly like someone Roman would choose for a business partner. I could have picked him out of a lineup. He wore a pale salmon-pink suit, double-breasted, with a beige shirt and matching salmon ascot. A gold ID bracelet glinted on his wrist, a gold zodiac medallion around his neck. His white shoes seemed designed to match his thick pompadour of white hair. His tan looked as though it had come from a bottle, the creases in his face paler than the skin surrounding them. His even, dentured smile flashed beneath a thin white mustache.

"My friend, it's fine to see you again," he said, shaking Roman's hand with both of his hands, his pinkie rings glittering. His voice was as heavily drawled as I remembered Miss North Carolina's, though it was low-pitched and whispery. The house was decorated for a party, with crepe paper streamers dangling over bowls of snack foods and tables of liquor. A TV set flashed noiselessly in the living room, another in the kitchen where he had us sit. He poured us each a bourbon.

"This young man is Gabriel," he said, as if he'd figured out the answer to a puzzle. "Are you giving the young ladies a run for their money?"

I shrugged as he clapped my shoulder, the smell of his cologne enveloping me. "Not really," I said. I looked around at the kitchen, all burnt orange and Formica.

"Think if we were his age again, Roman," he said, though he must have been twenty years older than my father. "The way women are now. Hardly bother with hellos or underwear."

Roman laughed and cut his eyes at me, and I laughed also, like a trained circus dog.

"Roman, have you let our friend here in on our plans?"

Roman shook his head as he sipped his drink. "Not yet I haven't."

"That's fine. Tell me, Gabriel, what do you think the American public is most willing to hand over their hard-earned money to merely observe, assuming we can charge them just for looking? Not owning, just an exchange of money for a simple viewing. The average man."

I shrugged again, remembering Roman's lessons during our basement weight-lifting sessions. "I don't know, Mr. Vic Comstock—"

The words, his full name as I'd come to know it, spilled out of my mouth before I could stop myself. Roman winced.

"Vic will suffice," he said, smiling with his even teeth. "Tell me."

"Something new and different?"

"Good, that's good," he said. "But be specific."

Roman nodded at me, and I knew he'd been through this same set of questions. I tried to think of how he would answer.

"Sex," I said.

"Excellent!" Vic rattled the ice in his glass. "Look no further than game shows with their busty prize hostesses and their shiny machinery, the cars, boats, motorcycles. What if you combined that environment with violence? Or scandal? Death maybe?"

"Then you'd have a first-class, no-lose winner," Roman said.

"Don't answer for him," Vic said, raising his hand. Roman was silent.

"I'd pay for that," I said. "Sex and death and violence, I mean, who wouldn't?"

Vic patted my arm with his bony hand. "First-rate, Gabe," he said. "And of course the morality of such an exchange is relative. Rod McKuen said, 'There is no right side or wrong side.'" Vic Comstock's brow was furrowed, as though he'd given this question considerable thought.

"What is all this about?" I asked. Roman looked at Vic, waiting for him to answer.

Vic ignored me now and turned to Roman. "If you're ready to sign, we'll be in business." He drew papers from inside his suit and flattened them against the table.

"Dad?"

Roman winked at me, signed at the bottom, and handed Vic an envelope I recognized as the one he'd used to keep the money from the poetry contest.

"Roman, what are you doing?" I said. I tried to kick him under the table. I heard the slam of car doors outside, the first of the party guests arriving.

Vic Comstock pocketed the thick envelope of money, smiled, and looked at us both. He stood and hoisted his glass of bourbon. "Welcome, friends, to the Starship *Enterprise*."

Somewhere near midnight, as I walked past the gold-etched mirrored tiles lining the halls of Vic's house, I saw myself disheveled and drunk in my wrinkled suit and fox-hunter tie, and wondered if Vic might have once worked as the social director on some perverse, hellbound cruise ship. Above the grind of four blenders whirling out daiquiris and margaritas in the kitchen, the click of the pornographic View-Masters which some of the men were enjoying in the living room, and the shouts of human bowling (beer kegs rolled at a group of businessmen and showgirls) from the driveway, I heard Vic Comstock singing: *"Jack be nimble, Jack be quick, Jack go underneath the stick."* He sang in a shaky alto that despite his affinity for rock and roll and novelty party songs somehow made him sound like a member of the Lawrence Welk family crooning show tunes. I remembered earlier in the evening hearing him sing "Jumping Jack Flash," and decided there, watching my own open mouth in the mirror, that he was for some reason partial to songs with the word "jack" in the lyrics. (Near unconsciousness, I was able to confirm this an hour later when I heard him belting out "Hit the Road, Jack.") In the den I found Roman with a shot glass balanced on his head, doing the limbo beneath an eight-foot summer sausage held by two middle-aged women in silver lamé dresses. He looked like a contestant on some grotesque game show.

"Gabe, my only one and only son of mine," he said. As he straightened to shake my hand, the shot glass dropped and skittered across the floor. He was sweating, his face red and puffy. I'd never seen him this plastered. He was celebrating, he'd told me, and would soon explain why he'd handed over all our money to Vic. I didn't like seeing him this

way, though I'd seen much the same reflected in Vic Comstock's mirrored hallways. Roman drank often, but he'd never in his life been a
drunk. I'd always thought of him as the imbibing equivalent of those
who gorge on Twinkies and buttered rolls without ever gaining a stray
pound. Roman never stumbled or fell when he drank, never got sick
or suffered a hangover or said things he later regretted. I'd rarely seen
his hair out of place when he drank, or his shirttail out, his shoes
scuffed up, spots on his tie. He always smelled like his Tiger Rose hair
tonic or his Old Spice. A neat appearance, he'd told me during our
basement sessions, goes without saying. Now he smelled like taco
chips and looked like the victim of a recent mugging.

There were at least fifteen men at the party that night and probably twice that in women. They all looked as though they'd been
ordered from the same catalog: the men in suits either too dark or
too light, with pocket handkerchiefs, alligator belts, gold nugget
watches and signet rings, men's hose instead of socks. After a few
drinks they allowed themselves to loosen their ties. The odor of hair
tonic drifted through the rooms, enveloping women of a type who
would mistake the smell for that of money. They were, I suppose,
"cheap" women, though that night they looked to me both bright
and expensive. They wore tight pastel halter dresses cut low over
heavy bosoms, their skin freckled where the makeup stopped. Their
faces shone with orange lipstick and blue eye shadow. Buoyant platinum hair billowed out around their faces, stiff and light as
meringue. Their hands flashed with mood rings, their necks with
rhinestone medallions and choker necklaces. Their mouths opened
with shouts of laughing, shiny with drink. To me that night those
women looked edible, like sugar confections that later might cause
cavities and stomachaches. I couldn't imagine where Vic Comstock
had found these women, and so many of them. I'd never seen anything like it in my life.

Roman came back from the kitchen with two glasses of some
drink called the Valley of the Shadow of Death, which smelled like

a mixture of pineapple juice and lacquer thinner. He handed me one and together we stood watching Vic dance a fox-trot to the tune of "Tumbling Dice," a cigarillo dangling from his mouth.

"You're having a good time, aren't you?" Roman said.

I shrugged and said that I guessed I was. Roman nodded and straightened my tie.

"Listen," he said. "I don't want you with your guts in a knot over this thing with your mother. You know how the world works. Just one of those things."

"So what do you have planned?" I asked. This was the first time all day he'd even referred to what had happened at dinner the night before. I figured he'd been planning for hours how he would win her back, how he'd get big money, send her a hundred yellow roses, drag a string quartet to her window and serenade her—anything that involved money and love.

He looked at me, his eyes glazed and heavy. "Planned?" he said.

"You know. I mean, what's next for getting her back? What are we going to do?"

He looked away from me and shook his head, then turned back to me. "Were you there last night or was that a cardboard cutout of you? Weren't you listening?"

My face burned. "Yeah, I heard everything everyone said, and I've heard it about four hundred times before too. So now, all of a sudden, this is final, *this* is the one that counts." As I said this, the first of many swells of nausea I was due for that night ran through me.

He put his hand on my shoulder. "Let's say you're out selling, I don't know, twelve-packs of Roach-Pruf, and some woman—"

I shrugged away his hand. "I don't need to hear another one of your bullshit examples. I want you to tell me how you're going to get Gladys back. If you even care."

He raised his hands. "Hey now, calm yourself down, son."

I tried to calm myself, watching Vic Comstock in his expansive living room direct a game of Pin the Tail on the Donkey, only the donkey was a poster-size photo of George McGovern and the tail was a raccoon tail of the type that boys once hung from bicycle handlebars. Every time some blindfolded player managed to pin the tail to George McGovern's crotch, the room exploded with laughter, the women doubling over and spilling their drinks on the shag carpet. I thought of what Gladys must have been doing that night, sitting by the pool watching the tiny train circle the water, listening to Dutch, with all his technical expertise, play "Can't Hold Back the Tears" or "Just to Be with You," while she breathed the chlorinated air, relieved with what she'd told us, that she'd gotten through it. I wondered if it occurred to her for even one instant that she'd done the wrong thing, that good or bad she could not make a life without us in it. I looked at Roman.

"Roach-Pruf," he said calmly. "I knock on the door, pitch the hell out of her, and she smirks a little, scratches her head, says, 'I don't think so. Sorry.' What am I going to do?"

Roman waited for an answer, and I thought again of Gladys during our basement sessions of weight lifting and Roman's school of hard knocks. I wanted her there for this, to look at me and roll her eyes and smile.

"You're going to walk," I said. "She's not interested."

"Hoo boy," he said. "Rule number one, 'I don't think so' means yes. Sure as I'm barely standing here. A shrug means yes. 'Maybe next time' means yes. 'I'm not sure' means yes."

Some of the other salesmen had stopped to listen to Roman, pausing to sip their drinks and nod their heads in agreement. "That's right," some muttered. "Man knows his stuff."

" 'Soon' means yes," he continued, gesturing with his hand. "The least little hesitation means yes—'Come back tomorrow.'" By this time his voice was loud enough to carry over the music. "What does it mean, boys?"

And the circled men shouted back, "Yes!"

" 'Let me think about it' means yes," Roman shouted. " 'Let me

ask my husband' means yes. Half a goddamn *smile* means yes." He
wiped his mouth with his sleeve.

"But a door, son," he said, leaning in toward me. "A door in your
face, that means no. Just no. Not anything else."

"Amen," the salesmen yelled, eyes red with drink.

"Last night was not a door in your face," I said.

"You don't know your mother the way I do."

"So you're giving up? Just like that?"

"A man stands and beats on a slammed door, I'd be willing to
call him a fool. I'm no fool, son. Remember that."

I watched him head off into the kitchen, throwing his arm
around Vic's shoulder, tossing back his drink. He was right, I didn't
know Gladys the way he did; in many ways I knew her better, knew
the part of her that most loved and most distrusted Roman, the
part of her he would not admit to because of how complicated it
seemed. In his version of her, things were simple: she loved him
because of the money he provided, and the more he provided, the
more she loved. He'd blown door-to-door on household goods, the
last job at the edge of the earth, and she in turn had cut off herself
to him, the way the power company shuts off the electricity when
the bill is not paid, her love for him just another utility, taken for
granted until it's gone.

But at our dinner the night before, I *had* seen in Gladys what
Roman had called the "least little hesitation." The way her eyes held
him when he spoke, gesturing with his hands, cursing the bean
tacos. The looks she directed at me, those covert smiles and rolls of
the eyes I'd missed those weeks. I thought then of telling him what
twenty-four hours earlier Gladys had sworn me not to tell, not yet:
that she was living—sharing a bed, ballroom dances, and midnight
swims—with Dutch. I thought at least this would make him angry
enough that he would not cave in so quickly, that he would go after
her with all the crazed determination with which he'd stood on the
hood of his Chevy. If there were a thousand ways to make ten thou-

sand dollars, as his books promised, there must be at least that many ways to keep a marriage together.

But then I thought better of telling him about Dutch. I *had* promised Gladys, and it might have seemed to Roman perfect proof of his version of Gladys: Dutch had more money, so he got the greater portion of her love. For the time, I decided to keep my mouth shut, and at least make the attempt to enjoy myself.

I walked downstairs toward the sound of a billiards game. The rec room slowly throbbed with light from twin lava lamps at opposite ends of the Naugahyde bar, and from the traffic light mounted in the corner of the room. Along the bar were miniature toilet ashtrays with the inscription PUT YOUR BUTTS HERE. I had found at least one TV so far in every room of the house, most of them large console models, others built into the wall. Two men in pinstripe suits stood at the bar lining up shots of bourbon and then downing them in quick succession. No one at this party was using drugs—no marijuana smoke drifting through the rooms, no cocaine mirrors or tabs of acid. Instead, everyone drank Manhattans, old fashioneds, martinis, Rusty Nails. The women threw back champagne cocktails and Pink Ladies. They were, all of them here, Roman's counterparts— stuck in Mr. America world, full of old life, nostalgic not for some bygone era, but for what their own pasts had been, dragged along behind them like some battered steamer trunk. They believed in money, in the power of a fat roll of money carried in your front pocket, or the force of a new Cadillac with leather seats and a V-8 engine. They were desperate in wanting to think that they had not lost currency in the changing world, that in a country where door-to-door salesmen were quickly going the way of milkmen and ice-houses, there would still be a way for them to get by, that there would remain the promise of the good scam, the big score.

That night, I saw what Roman must have seen: Vic Comstock *was* that promise. Compared to the rest of them, with his zodiac medallions, turtleneck shirts, and Rolling Stones music, he must have seemed thoroughly modern, a space-age savior sharing their own taste for quick money, with a ready feel for what the world had become, which they all, Roman especially, lacked. In the face of this, they must have looked to Vic Comstock to intercede between them and the end of the twentieth century. They could come to the party, dressed as they were. My father, naturally, had gotten in on the ground floor.

Beyond the bar loomed a large pool table covered in red felt, lit by a hanging lamp that advertised Seagram's 7. The table had come out of some bar (probably one of Vic Comstock's failed enterprises) and still had a sliding metal coin slot. A plump woman in a short white dress, high-heel sandals, and orange eye shadow circled the table, eyeing the lay of the balls, a Virginia Slim dangling from her bright lips, a martini glass balanced on the rail. She looked as if she'd come with the table from out of the same forgotten bar. Every time she bent and shot, she missed, the balls sometimes leaping the rail and skittering across the shag carpet.

"Oh, no," she'd say when this happened. I walked up beside the table and stood there awkwardly in my rumpled suit, my wide print tie, like a scale model of the older men at the party. I drank my Valley of the Shadow, clucked my tongue every time she missed, and retrieved the balls for her when they jumped ship. Neither of us spoke. I enjoyed the predictability of her misses, and the genuine surprise it was when a shot went in.

Eventually she managed to get all the balls into the pockets, and the table lay empty. I lit a cigarette and politely applauded.

"Croquet, now there's a game," she said, finally looking at me. Her eyes were startlingly blue, and against the background of orange eye shadow resembled a pair of tropical fish darting in a tank. I tried to picture her in her white dress and sandals on someone's lawn, playing croquet on some lazy summer Sunday. But she was one of those women, it was hard to imagine her in daylight.

"I like lawn darts," I said. "You have family fun and the threat of death all at the same time."

She nodded. "That's good, you're a funny one. I like that," she said. She told me that her name was Kami Sue Hightower, and that I should call her Kami Sue even though her friends called her Kamikaze only because she used to drink them all the time, only now she didn't and had never much liked the nickname anyhow. When I told her my name was Gabriel, she said it sounded like I ought to have monks following me around, chanting such a name. I told her I would try to arrange it, and got to watch her laugh again, her eyes wrinkling at the corners.

While I stood there waiting for something else funny to come to me, I looked at Kami Sue. She must have been as old as if not a few years older than Gladys, but I felt drawn toward her in a way I'd never felt with any of Gladys's friends. Despite her plump middle, the wrinkled skin around her neckline, the bargain-basement party clothes and makeup, the platinum tumble of hair, she managed to give off, like radar waves, the promise of sex. She was the type of woman that caused boys to sneak into X-rated movies, or to stay up nights with binoculars trained on the neighbor's lighted windows. Something in her manner of dress, a voice made of too much cigarette smoke, the expensive—not cheap—smelling perfume she wore: all of it, taken together, seemed not so much tacky or gaudy but simply *misplaced,* a misplaced loyalty to styles that had passed, to an outdated idea of women. Neglected and forgotten everywhere but in this house, with my own father and the men like him. All at once, I felt grateful for her presence in this place, for there being a place where what she was still mattered for something.

"What do you do for a living?" I said. *Oh man,* I thought. Maybe Roman was right, a Dale Carnegie course wouldn't do me any harm.

She laughed and touched the lipstick at the corner of her mouth.

"I work for Champagne Escort Service," she said. "Most of the other girls are here too. We're not supposed to mention it."

"I won't say anything," I told her. This seemed to fit, that Vic wanted to be seen as the kind of man who could crowd his party with women, but not as the type who would have to pay to do it.

"And it's strictly escort, nothing else. I once went to the Governor's Ball in Raleigh. I also manage my own investments—money markets, a few penny stocks just for play, T-bills."

"That's impressive," I said, meaning it.

"Between that and my couponing I have it worked out to retire at fifty-five with a hundred and eighty thousand invested. Enough for a nice house and a couple vacations a year. Oh, and I used to be an underwear model for Sears catalog. What do you do?"

I didn't really have an answer for this one, and as soon as she said it I realized that tomorrow was the first of September and Tuesday morning the first day of school. I had given no thought to going. The entire country was gearing up for the Bicentennial the coming year, and here I was shirking my part in the American dream, not even pursuing my education. In a little less than two years I would be an adult in the eyes of the law, and I had no plans beyond throwing in with whatever Roman had concocted with Vic Comstock, no idea of what I would become. All of a sudden I felt like Cinderella at the ball, waiting for the clock to strike twelve against all my possible selves. I thought of Gladys telling me that had she not put her foot down, I would have gone through life with the name Roman Junior. Now Gladys had gone, taking all her influence with her, and I stood here in my pinstripe suit and fox-hunter tie. Somewhere, some jeweler was forging the pinkie ring that one day would be mine.

"I'm partner in a business deal with Mr. Comstock and Mr. Strickland," I said.

"The young executive."

"Something like that."

"You're also a Strickland," she said.

I told her that Roman was my older brother, and she seemed too drunk to tally the difference between the years on my face and the years on his. She just nodded, and asked what kind of business venture we were embarking on.

"You'll have to wait till later to see," I told her, trying to make this sound as if I were one of those men for whom power and control equals sex; actually though, this was my answer because it had been Roman's answer to the same question when I asked it earlier. All I knew was it had to do with the floodlit expanse of Vic Comstock's backyard. Through the bay windows in the dining room I had seen several acres of yard, and three large shapes covered by white sheets. It was obvious that the shapes beneath the sheets were cars; I had the thought that this was Roman's plan, to transform himself into some version of Dutch, to open his own used car lot in Vic Comstock's backyard.

"Let's peek," Kami Sue said. She took my hand, the warmth of her own hand spiked with rings and painted fingernails, her palm dusted with talc from the pool cue. I followed her through the back part of the basement, past the water heater and furnace, stepping over a dusty assemblage of old cat toys out through the back door into the yard.

The ankle-deep grass gave off the summer smell of wild onions, though a few yellowed maple leaves, hinting of fall, lay scattered at our feet. She led me through them, dew wetting our shoes, her perfume trailing behind her. I began to get an erection, following her with it. The light from Vic Comstock's house spilled in yellow slants across the yard, the entire house a hive of music and laughing and conversational buzz. We came to the first sheet, covering some large American car, maybe a Lincoln or a Cadillac, its tail fins slicing upward underneath. Kami Sue lifted up the sheet by the corner, and the first things we saw were a flat, crumbling tire and a bent fender powdered with rust. I thought that if this was how Roman planned his big score, sinking his money into restoring these traps, he'd finally lost his mind completely.

We pushed up under the sheet, fumbling in the dark for the door handle. If anyone from the house had looked outside right then, they would have seen what looked like some Halloween ghost attempting grand theft auto. Finally Kami Sue found the handle and popped open the back door. We ducked inside and closed it behind us. Inside, the dome light did not work, and we sat in what thin light made it from the house and diffused through the sheet, as if we were sitting inside a lampshade on a bedside table somewhere. The interior threatened to choke us with its dust, the roof rumpled and partly crushed, headliner sagging, the leather upholstery brittle and cracking. I leaned across and saw the front seats scattered with bits of windshield glass.

"Nice wheels," Kami Sue said. She held her nose.

"Driven by a little old lady every Sunday to the demolition derby," I answered. Kami Sue laughed at this, and I got to feel clever and witty again.

She sighed as her laughing subsided, and together we sat there in the pale-gray-colored darkness with the sound of our breathing.

"You know, when I was in high school and business school way back in medieval times this used to be the thing for girls, to get laid your first time in the back of some big, expensive car," she said, words spilling out of her. "As if the more money the guy shelled out for his car, the better the sex would be. Only I missed all of that, never much cared about it, and my first time ended up being in a church parlor about fifteen minutes after my wedding in Carrington, South Carolina. The little table radio was playing 'Ragg Mopp,' I'll never forget that."

I needed for something to happen then—the car to roar to life and drive off with us inside, the sudden shine of a policeman's flashlight, thunder and lightning crashing around us—something to derail us from the path we'd started down, a path boundaried by the blooming of her perfume in the close car, her knee resting against mine, the erection bumping the loose change in my pocket, all this talk of sex. But nothing else *was* happening, and so I told her that her story was interesting, that I'd never been to South Carolina except for Myrtle Beach, and that I'd never heard the song "Ragg Mopp" though I liked Led Zeppelin and Foghat pretty well, and all the while I looked over at the freckled deep fold of her cleavage and the shimmer of her stockings, the soft bulge of her stomach inside the dress. I had a cramp in my calf muscle.

"How about you?" she said. "Your first?" She said this with the quiet strain of nostalgia in her voice, as if she believed that I, like her, would have to dig deep through reminiscence to locate this particular memory. It must have been the suit, or the Tiger Rose hair tonic Roman insisted I wear that night, that threw her off; either that, or her own drunkenness. How could I tell her that my "first" existed only on some plane of possibility? I took a deep breath and let my hand settle against her thigh, taut in its nylon stocking.

"I think it was in a backseat," I said as if I'd had a lifetime of recollecting what had not yet happened. "Old car with tail fins, leather upholstery."

I leaned over to kiss her, leaning through my own drunkenness and disbelief, nearly searing my face on the cigarette she'd just lifted toward her mouth. She pulled the cigarette away, put her hand across the back of my neck. She let me kiss her, and kissed back, grunting a little, and my hand lifted and resettled itself on the undercurve of her breast, and I traced with my fingers its complicated bolstering of underwire and strap and hook. It was the most *muscular* kiss of my experience, before or since, her hand pulling at the back of my neck, her mouth and tongue pulsing against mine, moving thickly in my mouth. Then she held my face in her hand and kissed my cheek, breathing in my ear.

"That's a sweet kiss," she said. "You're sweet."

Though "sweet" would not have been my first choice of compliments, I decided it could be worse, and hoped that she meant it and that it was not just a whispered nothing drawn from some list on page 43 of the *Champagne Escort Service Employee Handbook*. I had no response except to push my hand deep inside her freckled cleavage. Her flesh there was softer than I could imagine flesh capable of being, and my fingers slipped easily inside the fabric of her bra, tracing the raised edges of her nipple. She kissed me again and shifted in her seat, stirring the thick dust out of the upholstery, grunting again in little chirps. Her other hand came up beside my face minus the cigarette, and for a moment I worried over what had become of it, knowing that this dried-up upholstery would go up like tinder, imagining the fire marshal finding our remains with my skeletal hand still lodged deep inside her charred cleavage. Then she moved her hand down and settled it over the distension in my pants, and all images of doom went away. I settled back, the sagging headliner brushing my hair and dropping bits of fluff over my face, Kami Sue tracing me with her fingers, leaning into me and closing her eyes. I noticed the tiny veins of orange eye shadow that had settled in the folds of her eyelids. She began to whisper again as she gripped and rubbed me through my pinstripes, telling me how sweet I was, slurring her words.

"You're both such sweet, handsome men," she said. "You and your brother."

This stopped me a moment, my brain briefly disengaged from my lust. *My brother?* My sense of being an only child was long entrenched in my concept of family hierarchy. Then the lie I'd earlier let off the leash came running back: *Roman.* At once, as I realized this, the closeness of the car—the cellophane light, the mask of her perfume, the softness of her breast—all of it opened up, folded, and fell back to the dark and distant horizon. I thought: This is *this* woman, of the world of Vic Comstock, of Champagne Escorts, of billiard games, money markets, and "Ragg Mopp." The world of sex, the world of commerce, the world of my father, all right there in the car with us. It was too much. I felt my erection retreating, as if on horseback. I swallowed, took a breath, and started to push her away.

"What's wrong?" she said.

"Nothing. It's just . . . I don't know."

She patted the empty folds of my pants. "Oh, sugar, that's okay. It's probably all the dust in here."

My face burned. I didn't know what to say to her. I knew that if my sudden impotence was caused by the dust in the car, this likely qualified as the oddest allergy in medical history. I thought instead that I must have some disease, its origins either physical or mental— it didn't matter. I would never have children, I decided, never satisfy a woman. I would never be a part of this or any other world that lay in the future; my only belonging was in back of me, and it, in the space of three weeks, had been wiped out. I felt close to tears.

"We'll just sit and chat awhile," she said.

"I'm sorry," I told her, and ducked out my door, fighting my way through the sheet.

Back inside the house, a conga line snaked its way down the mirrored hall and through the guest and master bedrooms. I found Roman and Vic in the kitchen drinking cognac and looking over a notebook calendar spread open across the butcher-block table.

"Dad, I need to tell you something," I said. "It's about Dutch." I heard myself slurring words, felt a faint dampness and ache in my groin.

"Dutch? He got wind of what we're doing and he's first in line for a loan, right?"

At this Vic Comstock laughed, then wrote in the name *Fayetteville*, a military town in southeast North Carolina, on the October 22 page and drew three dollar signs beside it.

"The head, Roman," he said. "The head and the tits will make us rich in Fayetteville alone. All those GIs."

"Dad, you don't want to hear this, but I need to tell you."

"I don't want to hear it and it's about Dutch. You know, Gabe, that's one hell of a pitch."

"Dad . . ."

"Listen, it'll wait, whatever it is. We need to get you in the inner circle here, junior partner."

I thought of Kami Sue calling me junior executive, of Gladys calling me Roman Junior. I was everyone's derivative.

Before I could say anything else, Roman and Vic walked into the living room and through the house, rounding up everyone, shutting down the stereo and whooping like cattle drivers, herding the whole gathering into the backyard where the cars sat parked and covered with sheets. Vic Comstock fired a portable generator and banks of floodlights burned into the summer night. Vic stood beside the first car, where not ten minutes before I'd sat feeling up a woman my father's age. Roman stood beside me at the front of the circled gathering, smiling, his arms folded across his chest. Vic Comstock spoke through a bullhorn.

"From the time of the ancient gladiators the general populace has paid for the privilege of proximity to death. I invite you to consider what television programming we are provided, how purveyors of soap, soup, and soda bring us through the airwaves a nightly buffet of carnage, cop shows, murder movies, and such atrocities as Vietnam. Bought and sold. This, friends, is not social commentary on my part so much as it is mere observation on the nature of commerce as it reflects the human soul. We shell out for a glimpse of tragedy. We *are* our spending." His words echoed across the grass.

"Get the hell on with it," Roman whispered.

Vic shielded his eyes against the floodlamps.

"On the foggy night of June 29, 1967, along the road to New Orleans, a 1966 Buick Electra 225 collided with a quarter-ton truck, killing instantly the driver, club owner Ron Harrison, and one Mr. Sam Brody. The car's most famous passenger, Hollywood superstar Miss Jayne Mansfield, was decapitated."

Roman nudged me with his elbow. "This is going to knock you on your ass," he said.

"That very car sits before you even now," Vic shouted. He gripped a corner of the sheet covering the car and whipped it off into the lit-up night air, allowing it to billow out behind him like a matador's cape. I half expected to see Kami Sue still sitting in the back wondering where her young executive had disappeared to. A chorus of murmurs rose up from the gathered crowd.

Vic struck the trunk lid with the butt of the bullhorn. "Miss Mansfield's fair head bounced once here, then here—" he slapped the rear bumper— "and ended its roll fifty yards away, her buxom torso lodged there, in the front seat, next to the remains of her pet Chihuahua. Her bloodstains are yet visible, her memory yet viable."

He whispered this last sentence, working the crowd, which edged closer, the women standing on tiptoe, leaning on the men's shoulders for a better look. Roman nudged me again and pointed at them with a nod of his head. "Money," he said.

I looked at him. "You're going to sell a wrecked Buick, and somebody's going to buy it because of what's-her-name? That's what you did with all our cash?"

"Just be quiet a minute, you might learn something," he said. I didn't tell him that I'd already learned plenty that night; it was *he* who needed to learn something: about his wife, about his brother.

"Please, there's more," Vic shouted through the bullhorn. His words carried in small electric waves that seemed to rush along the ground into the trees. We followed him through the dewy grass toward the next covered car, this one half the size of the first. As we moved farther away from the bank of floodlights our shadows lengthened, and people drew into small groups, talking about Jayne Mansfield and the movies she'd made, her media battles with Jane Russell and Marilyn Monroe, her death in the car. Some of them paused to touch the car, approaching it cautiously, as if it were Jayne Mansfield's casket and she were laid out in a funeral parlor. I had never heard of Jayne Mansfield, had never watched any of her movies. In my mind the car was now more famous as the place where I'd blown my first and possibly last chance at a sexual encounter, where I'd understood my world as unraveling under my fingers.

Farther out in Vic Comstock's backyard we stopped and stood half-circled around another sheet-covered car. Vic raised his bullhorn.

"On September 30, 1955, a young man passing through Bakersfield, California, decides to exercise the racing engine in his silver Porsche 550 Spyder, a young man filled with the twin intoxicants of youth and fame, drunk not with alcohol but with his very self. He takes the little car up to speeds in excess of one hundred and thirty miles per hour, then slams head-on into Mr. Donald Turnipseed's 1950 Ford Tudor. Mr. Turnipseed walks away, but—" Vic whipped away the sheet—"young rebel James Dean breaks his neck and dies in an eyeblink." There were more gasps and murmurs, and three of the Champagne Escort women started singing "Dead Man's Curve," until those around them shushed them. Before us lay the twisted car, ringed by its own scaly rust, its black racing numbers faded and peeling.

All together there were three cars out there under the false moonlight of the floodlamps, including Bonnie and Clyde's tan 1934 V-8 Ford ("One hundred and seven bullet holes, each the size of your little finger," Vic shouted through the bullhorn).

By the end of our tour, the partygoers looked as if they themselves had been in car crashes. Some had grown sullen in that drunken way that seems to border on despair. Others scrutinized the wrecked cars with a kind of bright-eyed, drooling curiosity, as if the wrecks had only just happened and broken bodies lay scattered about bleeding. They passed around the publicity stills Vic had of the stars leaning against their shining cars, bathed in flashbulb light. Many of the men shook their heads and clicked their tongues over the fact of James Dean's death, as if the news, after twenty years, had not yet sunk in. Some of the women were crying; none of them, the men or the women, would pull themselves away from the cars and back into the vast, modern house with its lava lamps and TVs. I knew little of the tragic and famous—Marilyn Monroe and James Dean were to me only occasional names on the *Dialing for Dollars* movie—but for all of those people my father's age, it was as if they were walking around surveying the wreckage of promise, trying to figure out how their own lives, hurtling happily along through the fifties and early sixties, had wiped out on some Dead Man's Curve of a changing world.

Whatever it was that kept them out there in that yard until dawn, I knew that Roman's instincts had been right: people would pay to feel what they'd once felt, for the emotions of twenty years before. His plan ("marketing strategy," he called it) was for him and Vic to haul the cars all around the South, to fairgrounds and craft shows, to the openings of shopping centers, to tractor pulls, car shows, swap meets, flea markets. Anywhere, he said, where people walked around with money in their pockets. They would take turns delivering some version of the pitch that Vic had given that night, and charge four bucks a pop to let people touch the cars and sit in the driver's seats. He figured that after expenses—twenty-five cents per mile, hotels, meals—they would pull in close to two thousand dollars a day, and could cover maybe four shows a week. He told me this while we stood together in the new wetness of morning, feeling our drunkenness becoming the first painful fuzz of hangover, watching the last remnants of the party leave. Kami Sue waved to me as she left, and I felt my face burn, imagining for a moment that the car would be on display not at county fairs and flea markets, but at some Museum of Sexual Dysfunction, a wax figure of me propped up in the backseat. Kami Sue looked older, as if the light of day had added back years that nostalgia and drunkenness had taken away. I waved goodbye.

"Friend of yours?" Roman said.

"Sort of."

He nodded and looked around. "Nothing like a few death cars to spoil a party."

I smiled. "They bummed everybody out."

"Yeah, but they couldn't get enough of them, you notice that?"

I told him that I had noticed.

"So the poetry contest money paid for the cars?" I asked.

He laughed. "About one bumper and one tire, maybe. Vic put up seventy-five percent, I chipped in twenty-five. He lined up the car

collectors, and I put in the marketing, setting up where we're going
with these things, doing the research."

He stopped long enough to light a cigarette. He had his tie loosened, hat tipped back on his head.

"And it wasn't just the three g's from the contest either, son."

"No?"

He wouldn't look at me, in the same way he once would not look
at Gladys. "I took a second mortgage on the house, cashed in an old
insurance policy I had, sold a lot of that shit out of the basement to
the junk dealer. I came up with it, though, nobody has to carry me."

"God, Roman. This could wipe you out."

"It could but it won't. This is a shot, Gabe. *My* shot. The real
thing this time, no bullshit, no bosses, no commission. Just money,
a sure thing."

"But, Dad . . ."

"And you. You're part of this, like I said. We need somebody to
help drive, help set up signs, so on. Vic's a good man but he's not
exactly spry."

"School starts—" I looked over toward the rising sun—"well,
three days from now."

"School," he said evenly, as if he'd forgotten not just my own sta-
tus as student, but the very fact of a national system of secondary
education.

"Yes. I'm supposed to be there."

He shrugged. "We'll write a note to get you out. Not like we
haven't done it before."

"Out for how long?"

"I don't know. A year, maybe?"

I thought about that, a year without people my own age, without
my life progressing along what most would think of as a normal
course, a year in the company of middle-aged men spent hauling
around the broken and wrecked past of other middle-aged men,

charging them to see it. This was *his* shot, a chance at having a life that no longer included Gladys, and I realized in that moment that their marriage was a done deal, a dissolved partnership, and dissolved with it my own past and all I had ever known of forging out a life, not understanding its strangeness for being immersed in it. What did not sit right in my mind was the fact of this big change coming about by way of *Roman*, my father, the man who in that early fall of 1975 still wore the same hair tonic, button suspenders, and diamond stick pins that had been the fashion during the years of World War II, the time of his growing up, the man whose very soul seemed tattooed with the past, a product of Mr. America world. He would now take that world and offer it up at four bucks a pop, under the direction of Mr. Vic Comstock, the man with plastic furniture, with rock and roll music, the man who drank strawberry wine, who wore Libra on a gold chain around his neck. I wondered then what had happened to Vic's past, how a man older than my father had come to live this way, and realized that he'd sold all of it, his own past, and had convinced Roman that he should do the same, that there was big money in it. But it was not just the past of James Dean or Jayne Mansfield that he was prepared to sell, but *our* past—his, mine, and Gladys's—thrown in with the second mortgage and the insurance policy: a marriage, a history, a family. I thought about this while my hangover began its hard rain inside me, throbbing away. I felt nothing so strong as the compulsion to stop him. I would go with him whether he'd wanted me to or not, whether I wanted to, just to keep him from selling out everything of himself.

"Dad," I said, and waited till he looked at me. "It's about Gladys—Mom. She's not staying with a friend."

"No?"

I took a breath, looked out over the expanse of ruined cars. "No. She's living with Dutch."

Chapter 7

As the Chevy eased up the curved asphalt drive of Dutchland, through the tunnel of emaciated trees and past the trout pond, I saw Dutch standing on his dock untying the algae-stained paddleboats, the four of them colored like Easter eggs, and shoving them with his wing tip out into the middle of the pond. He was huffing and spitting, failing or else choosing not to notice my arrival. At the time, with so much on my own mind, I didn't note the strangeness of what he was doing: there would be no way to retrieve the boats short of swimming out into the pond and dragging them back like drowning victims.

At the house Gladys stood leaning against the doorframe with her arms folded, the way I'd seen her in the rearview mirror that night I'd driven away from the house. Only this time she was visibly agitated, rubbing her arms, biting her lips.

"Gabe, your timing couldn't be better," she said. "Did you see him along the road?"

"Dutch? Yeah, looks like he's freeing the paddleboats." I thought about it for a second. "What's wrong with him?"

She rolled her eyes, the gesture I had missed so much in all my recent dealings with Roman. "You ever doubt your father and Dutch are brothers," she said, "just get them angry. They might as well be twins."

"What is going on?"

"Well, we have a visitor."

For a second I felt my stomach drop, thinking that Roman had somehow beaten me here, but that was impossible; I'd just left him sitting in Vic Comstock's burnt-orange kitchen wearing his underwear and hat. It had been twelve hours since the sun had risen on Vic's party, the sun that had pushed all the guests home, that had pulled from me with a force like evaporation the truth about Dutch and Gladys. After I told him, Roman stood staring off over the tops of the pines where the white morning sun sat like a golf ball lost in the trees.

"We need a little clarification here, son," he'd said, and pulled me along by a fistful of my jacket sleeve toward the back part of Vic Comstock's yard, where sat the wreck of the Porsche Spyder shining with dew. There was no one out there with us. He spun me around to face him, took off his hat, and dropped it on the ground.

"Now," he said. "Tell me."

"I just told you." He was going to make me *say* it.

"You mean your mother and Dutch . . . you mean she's not just renting a goddamn room or just staying there as some favor he's doing for her or cooling her heels or any of that. You mean she's . . ." He looked off to the trees behind us. "You mean *everything.*"

I swallowed and cut my eyes away, watched a red ant crawl across the band of his hat. "Everything," I said.

He paced in a small circle, hands in his pockets. "And you've known about this for exactly how long, Gabe?"

I looked away again, my throat knotting. Across the cowling of James Dean's ruined hood were painted in script the words "Little Bastard." It seemed like an accusation. I felt a sudden nostalgia for the time when lies formed in me as easily as thoughts, but somehow the events of the last three weeks had wiped that away.

"Since the start, I knew she was there with him. But it was a while before . . . before everything else got started." As I spoke, my tongue thickened in my mouth.

He nodded, chewing his upper lip. "Dutch," he said slowly. "God damn." He shook his head with a mixture of defeat and wonder, like some high-priced criminal admiring the ingenuity of the government sting operation that will send him away for a hundred years.

"I didn't want to tell you because I thought she'd never come back if you blew up about it," I said. "And you would have."

He nodded and wouldn't speak, still pacing in slow, small circles. He remained quiet for the rest of the day. What worried me most about his reaction was his refusal to drink, his rejection of even one short hair of the dog, which usually, after a commanding drunk, he required in clumps and tufts. He sat at the kitchen table, refusing to dress beyond his boxers, T-shirt, and hat, typing out our first week's itinerary with the cars, chewing his lip until it turned purple. Near the end of the day he told me that I should go see Gladys to let her know I was going away with him, to tell her I would miss a year of school. I wasn't sure how she would react to this last part, and I went prepared with an off-the-rack speech about what a great opportunity it was for an artist to travel, to meet different kinds of people, to live unconventionally. I didn't know if she would buy this anymore.

As I left, Roman looked up from Vic's electric typewriter. "One more thing, son," he said. "Tell your mother that I know."

"You know what?"

"I *know*," he said. "Let's blow a little smoke in the beehive."

"Why don't you tell her?"

"You're in this, Gabe. Like it or not."

Earlier that day, Roman had typed out and mailed a note to the school principal, saying that I would be out indefinitely because of a long-term illness in the family. As I walked out the door, I began to think that this diagnosis was not far from the truth.

The visitor to Dutchland turned out to be none other than Sandy Goforth, former Miss North Carolina of 1970. Gladys walked me through the house into the kitchen and we sat together

in the breakfast nook, talking. I thought of all my visits to her at
United Dairy, only now instead of coffee, cigarettes, and ice cream,
we shared herbal tea and tiny crackers made from kelp. *The new
Gladys*, I thought. Through the bay window of the nook we watched
Sandy Goforth sunning herself in a chaise lounge beside Dutch's
pool, lying there with her straps untied as if she had been plucked
straight from my memory. Beside her chair leaned the rattan shoulder bag she'd carried since I'd known her, with **MISS NORTH
CAROLINA 1970** embroidered on the side in bright red. Later
on, closer examination would reveal that the bag now looked as if
it had been chewed by a dog, and the red embroidery spelled out
MISS NO   ROLI   7, with the other letters long since unraveled.

"She came banging at the door at eleven o'clock last night,"
Gladys said. She put her hand up partially covering her mouth. "You
should have seen Dutch, like he's seeing Mrs. Usher at the top of
the stairs. She waltzes in doing her pitiful lambie-pie bit, crying and
saying how Las Vegas didn't *agree* with her, and Dutch stares at me
like I'm head bouncer and I'm supposed to toss her out the door."

She laughed. Already this had become one of the stories she
would tell about Dutch, rounding off the details as she told it, the
same as she had once told stories about Roman. The time he sold
Girl Scout cookies, the time he sold body parts off their car to pay
for gas as they drove it back across country. I knew those by rote,
and now would have to learn these new ones. Accumulate enough of
them and you can cement a pair of lives for a decade or two.

"What does she want?" I asked.

"My first thought was money, but Dutch had an agreement
when they got married, and she signed off on the divorce. He
reminded her of this about five minutes after 'Hello.'"

"So?"

"She wants to stay here awhile, to 'locate her center,' she says.
Woman has two university degrees and she can't find a *job*." Gladys
flushed and looked away. "I should talk."

"And the shock made Dutch lose his mind."

"What do you mean?"

"He's trying to kill the paddleboats. Drown them, I think."

Gladys laughed again. "For him those boats are *her,* I think. I mean, can you imagine Dutch buying those for himself?"

I tried and could not even picture Dutch out on the pond *pedaling* one of those Easter-egg boats. Where was the practicality? They didn't take you anywhere and were not much exercise. In that moment, trying to imagine Dutch floating around in all his white suited rigidity, I thought that maybe what Gladys did for him, what need she saw there, was to allow him a chance at some *fun.* Maybe that was the extent of it—for Gladys to teach him that dancing did not have to proceed as if choreographed by engineers, that blues guitar music could be just something to float you through a summer night instead of an exercise in chord progression and fingering technique. Maybe she had been right in seeing something during his late-night commercials that neither I nor Roman saw: the Dutch beyond the Dutch, I thought of it then.

I looked out the window at Sandy Goforth sleeping in the sun, her mouth open, a transistor radio beside her ear. Her hair was longer than I remembered, and she'd grown so tan she looked bronzed, like a pair of baby shoes.

"How is Roman?" Gladys asked. "It feels like two years since Thursday night."

He's sitting in Vic Comstock's kitchen in his underwear, chewing his lip, planning to make money by selling death. This is what I wanted to say, but instead said, "He's fine."

"Really? I mean, I worry about him. Constantly. I just want to know he's okay."

"He has a big plan in the works that's supposed to make him rich."

"There's a news flash," she said, with more sarcasm than I wanted to hear; Dutch was teaching *her,* too.

"He swears this is the real thing," I told her, and she smiled that same pitying smile I used to see on housewives when I accompanied Roman door to door. *And it's not for you this time,* I almost said, but didn't.

We heard the front and back door open together, and both Dutch and Sandy Goforth came into the house, as if three years of marriage had put them forever on identical wavelengths. Dutch walked into the kitchen first, his pants legs wet above the ankles. Down through the winding halls we heard Sandy Goforth whistling "Love Will Keep Us Together." She had an uncommon talent for whistling, for fancy trills, glissandos, and multiple octaves, so much so that she had whistled "The Maple Leaf Rag" for the talent portion of the Miss North Carolina Contest, and during her reign had been invited to whistle *Peter and the Wolf* with the local symphony orchestra during a Pops in the Park concert.

Gladys winced, shook her head. "How did you tolerate that for three years? It's like living with some overgrown canary."

"And just listen *what* she's whistling," Dutch said, his face nearly scarlet. "She's trying everything she can to aggravate me."

If this was her plan, she'd succeeded beyond all expectation. I'd never seen him like this.

"I'm throwing her out of here *today*," he said. His lapel pins were crooked. "The law is on my side in this."

Gladys shook her head and stood up for more herbal tea. "You can't throw her out, Dutch. She has no money, no place to go." Everyone was speaking in stage whispers.

I held up my hand as if I were sitting in history class. "I thought you said she's not here for money."

"*Right. Sure,*" Dutch said. "She just came here to *whistle*."

"I know, I *know*," Gladys said, as if they'd argued this twenty-five times in the day that Sandy Goforth had been there, "but still, we can't—"

Just then Sandy whistled her way into the kitchen, where the three of us sat looking at her as though we'd been plotting her assas-

sination. Her mouth held its pucker, her eyes shifting beneath the
bill of an Elon College Fighting Christians baseball cap. She'd been
Miss Elon College on her way to the Miss North Carolina title. She
wore the same white terry-cloth bathrobe that Gladys had worn on
my first visit. Her ponytail, about the same length as my old one
(this is how I thought of it, as if I'd put it away in a closet), stuck
out the back of the cap, and her toenails were painted pink. She was
the most effortlessly sexual woman I'd ever seen, without the heavy
makeup or sprayed hairdos of the girls my age, and without the
striving, worn-out glamour of the Champagne Escort women. I
decided it was well within the realm of possibility that my pubes-
cent lust had evolved into a pure, unalloyed love.

"Hi," I said.

She nodded and smiled, her pale green eyes framed by slight
crow's-feet, a swipe of freckles across her nose. I'd forgotten these
details about her or else had never seen them, having studied only
that white curve of her breast flattened against the chaise lounge.

"How do you do," she said formally, then a slow recognition
washed across her face. "You! The Roman Strickland doll, all grown
up full-size!"

I blushed as she crossed the room to hug me. She smelled of
chlorine and cigarettes.

"I never thought I'd see you again," I said, because it was the
truth. For those first ten minutes in her presence, I felt perpetually surprised.

"That's just wishful thinking you caught from your uncle, hon,"
she said. She looked at Dutch and winked.

"Las Vegas just called," Dutch said. "They want you to rush right
back. They're sorry."

"We'll all have dinner together," Gladys said, practiced at the
role of peacemaker. "Then we'll discuss . . . arrangements." Gladys
had recently let go Mrs. Loggins, Dutch's cook, and spent afternoons cooking, finally making a home out of Dutch's house.

"Tonight *I* will do dinner," Sandy said. "Nobody has to lift a finger."

Dutch snorted. "Including *you*. House of Wong still delivers, Sandy. Just call them up and say 'The usual.' They'll find us."

"Dutch . . ." Gladys said.

Sandy winked at me. "Some little weasel must've crawled up inside your uncle," she said.

"Must have," I said.

"Gabe, just try to stay out of this," Gladys said. But I saw already that I wouldn't be able to stay out; it was like some constantly evolving game, and I wanted to play.

Sandy fixed herself a rum and Coke, and dropped a handful of cocktail peanuts in the glass, moving about the kitchen as if she'd never stopped living there. She told me she wanted a look around "the old homestead," and asked if I would join her. Dutch and Gladys seemed relieved for the chance to talk in private. Sandy took my elbow and we started off down the hall toward the ballroom. Her hand was warm, her fingers long, and I felt the faint stirring of my old poolside erections. As we left I heard Dutch muttering, "Don't steal anything," and Gladys shushing him. I couldn't decide if he'd meant me or Sandy.

In getting to know her, I discovered that a dozen years in the pageant system had left her with something akin to the posttraumatic stress syndrome that returning vets brought back with them from Vietnam. She had the habit of speaking in euphemisms, as swearing did not uphold the "standards of Ladyship" outlined by the Miss North Carolina Pageant Bylaws. When she got angry, often as not what emitted from her pretty mouth was something along the lines of "Fudge you!" or "Bull sticks!" It was her most annoying, least endearing habit, and I would later take it on myself to break her of it. She'd made some progress on her own, had acquired a smoking habit, would drink beer out of the bottle, and had stopped wearing makeup to the grocery store. She'd done away with hairspray altogether, and had taken to wearing cutoff jeans and sweatshirts most of the time, along with her Fighting Christians baseball cap.

As we walked along through the elaborate house Dutch had built for her, she told me about her life in Las Vegas, how she'd worked as a "product enhancement model" at trade shows in convention centers and exhibition halls. Her job was to stand around wearing anything from a bikini to a sequined ball gown with satin gloves and be part of the display of products that manufacturers were attempting to wholesale to distributors. In one memorable week, she'd helped sell hunting knives, glow-in-the-dark lingerie, beekeeping equipment, electric toothbrushes, and Huey helicopters.

"I mean enough's enough," she said. "To H-E-you-know-what with that."

We made our way into the ballroom, where she noted the absence of the brass lions that had once occupied each corner of the room. All through the house she commented on such absences, the presence of Gladys's Early American furniture and macramé hangings in place of her own elaborate tapestries and jade statues, as if the loss of these objects added up to her own absence from this earlier life. With all the scholarships she'd won from pageants, Sandy had gone to school long enough to earn double degrees in finance and interior design. Her plan had been to earn big money designing hotel rooms, bars, and lounges in Las Vegas, invest the money, and retire at forty-five. I thought of Kami Sue Hightower and all her squirreled-away escort money. Everyone, it seemed, desired an early exit from daily living. Sandy told me that somehow along the way she'd taken a wrong turn, down a moneyless path that led straight to beehives and electric toothbrushes.

In the master bedroom, she seemed for the first time dejected to find part of her old life missing: the teak water bed that she'd designed herself and had built by a local cabinetmaker. In its place stood a queen-size four-poster with a blue quilt thrown across it— the very bed that the repossessors had carried to and from our house at least a dozen times over the years. Now, I thought, through adoption it had found a permanent home.

"What is *that* piece of shit?" Sandy yelled. As I thought to congratulate her on her avoidance of euphemism, I turned and saw sitting in the corner of the room my sculpture, *AutoCratic*, as if it had hidden itself there just to jump out and scare me.

"You don't like it?" I said.

"No, it's great if you're a rodent looking for a home," she said. "Did your mother make that?"

"I don't think so." I looked at the bends of exhaust pipe, wiring harness, duct tape, carburetor parts. She was right, it was at best a pile of vaguely interesting junk; the placard I'd written only made it pretentious junk, and I prayed she wouldn't read it—my signature was at the bottom. Looking at my sculpture I thought of the tumble of scrap metal that had been James Dean's Porsche Spyder, now rusting in Vic Comstock's backyard, of the speech that Vic had made, the Champagne Escort women singing "Dead Man's Curve" and those nearby shushing them. His tear-jerking speech now seemed more artful than anything I'd written on that placard, than anything written on the placards for the sculptures downtown. I thought of all those drunk, nostalgic people lingering till dawn in the wash of memory and lost promise that Vic Comstock had wrung from a pile of rusty metal. That was not just bullshit, I decided. Or else it was, and bullshit is what we sometimes need to help us believe that we are still among the living.

"Your mama has good taste," Sandy said. "Maybe that's the exception that proves the rule."

"Ha," I said.

"But she does go for the *conventional*, doesn't she?"

At this, I really did laugh. "You must not know my father."

"Oh, I *know* your father all right," she said. "That's why I think this Dutch thing might be good for her. Conventional."

Since the night that Dutch had played the guitar for me, I had turned over the same possibility: that he might be good for Gladys, like medicine, that she was better off without Roman for the pain he caused her. But something in the logic of this bothered me—like someone with an arthritic arm one day deciding he might as well have it lopped off.

"Here's my favorite Dutch story," she said. She sat on the bed and patted it for me to sit beside her.

"After I had the ballroom all finished, just gorgeous with my lions there and everything, Dutch *informs* me that he has no intention of dancing, that he thinks it's a waste of time and poor exercise. So fine, I hire this nice, handsome instructor, an older man, and he comes every Tuesday and we have a big old time of it. So Dutch puts on his Mr. Possessive act and *informs* me he's fired the instructor and from now on he'll be my partner. So he gets this kit with the cutouts of the feet, all numbered? Except instead of taping those to the floor he has them *painted* there, like these bunny tracks all around in a big circle, numbered one to two hundred and fifty-three. A fox-trot. Ruined my nice floor." She frowned.

"So what happened?"

"Well, one day I go in there with lacquer thinner and erase about half the footprints, just any which way, and renumber most of the rest. This is about two weeks into him learning it, so we go in that night, put on some nice Henry Mancini, and Dutch throws out his lower back trying to follow those footprints, stepping on my *shins*, and saying 'What in the . . . I don't understand the . . .' I could not stop laughing."

She laughed again now.

"Dutch and me, we were wrong from the starting gun," she said. "But your mother, I think that's a different story."

As it turned out, Sandy provided dinner for us as Dutch had predicted, by calling the House of Wong and ordering up moo goo gai pan for four, plus extra "hot stuff" and fortune cookies. ("The fortunes better be good," she said before she hung up.)

"You know," Dutch announced to no one in particular, "Sandy used to phone some of the very best restaurants in North Carolina."

"And not one would deliver corn dogs," she said. "Dutch pouted his little head off."

"Now, children," Gladys said, meaning everyone but me.

The food was delivered, and at Sandy's insistence we pushed back the sectional couches and rolled up the rug inside the conversation pit, lit a gas fire in the fireplace (the temperature outside was still in the middle eighties), threw down a couple stadium blankets, and had a picnic, passing the little white boxes with their wire handles.

"So Monday's Labor Day," Sandy said. "What's everybody planning to do?"

"Labor," Dutch said. "You know that's a major sale day for me."

Sandy began counting on her fingers. "Hail sale, Christmas in July sale, Moonlight Madness sale, We're Blowing Up Prices sale . . ." She stopped her list and smiled. "How'd I ever forget this big, important one?"

At this, Gladys laughed. She and Sandy had always gotten along well, though they'd never become close friends. One Fourth of July, after hamburgers, bottle rockets, and too many beers, Sandy retrieved her Miss North Carolina tiara from her bedroom closet and wore it to play tether ball in the backyard. Gladys suggested loudly that the entire pageant system was degrading to women, and she offered up Sandy as Exhibit A. After that night, it was as if they possessed the capacity for friendship but were always embarrassed by their mutual performances that night, the things they'd shouted at one another, and this embarrassment slowly hardened into a wall between them. But on more than one occasion during that short marriage, Gladys told Roman that Sandy was the best thing that had ever happened to Dutch. That someone had finally cracked his shell. Roman always said, "So we agree that Dutch is cracked?" This joke, for a time, became part of the fabric of their marriage.

"Tell me, Sandra," Dutch said. "What are your plans after you leave here tomorrow?"

Using chopsticks, she lifted a clump of rice to her mouth. "Who mentioned leaving? I mean, can't I just *crash* here for a few days?"

Dutch tried to use the chopsticks, then put them down and lifted his fork. "Crash. Interesting descriptive term, but I don't think we want to be responsible for cleaning up your wreckage, meaning, of course, your life in general."

His words reminded me of the reason I'd come here in the first place. All at once, I had a stomachache, the moo goo gai pan burning in my chest. I looked over at Sandy as something like genuine hurt flashed across her face, then vanished.

"What *do* you want to do now, Sandy?" Gladys asked.

She shrugged. "I don't know, grad school maybe. Go back to Carolina Beach and get my old job back at Snow's Ice Cream. It was good enough when I was fifteen, right?"

Dutch started to say something, then changed his mind. Sandy patted my knee.

"Maybe I'll marry this one. Still have the old monogrammed Strickland towels." She and Gladys laughed.

"I'm growing a mustache," I announced, a decision I made as the words left my mouth. I liked the way they looked on some of Vic Comstock's and Roman's friends, and on Vic himself. Among those men there was an understood code of facial hair: no sideburns, no goatees, no hippie beards or walrus mustaches. It had to be of proper length and trim; it had to look good above a cigarette: *dapper* was the word.

"First the ponytail, now this," Dutch said. "You may have noticed, Gabe, that most youngsters today are going for the clean-cut look." I think he was glad to have someone other than Sandy to pick on for a few minutes.

"When did you come by this decision?" Gladys said.

"Recently."

Sandy rubbed my upper lip with the back of her finger. "*Real* recently," she said. "Anyway, I think you'll look handsome. You already have your mother's looks."

I smiled, my face warm.

"And what did you get from your daddy?" Sandy asked, lowering her voice as if this were the most lascivious thing anyone could ever think of to ask another person.

Dutch snorted. "His sense of responsibility."

"What is that supposed to mean?" I said.

"Yes, Dutch." Gladys put down her fork. "What does that mean?" There was a hint of edge in her voice.

"Ask him. Ask him about the job I go out of my way to *create,* and then he shows up twice and that's it."

I think I was as surprised as Gladys to hear that I hadn't been showing up at the dealership. During everything with Gladys, the poetry contest, Vic Comstock, and Roman, I had somewhere forgotten the idea that I was expected to come to work.

"You should at least give notice, Gabe," Gladys said.

I shrugged. "Sorry," I said. I was grateful enough that he hadn't told her about the stolen car parts assembled in their bedroom. Dutch shook his head as if the future of America had depended on me and I'd blown it. He muttered something about genetics.

"Oh, lighten up, Dutch," Sandy said. "So he didn't want to help sell your stupid cars. We should consider that a sign of intelligence."

"Gabe," Gladys said, "you know, Dutch is trying to help you adjust. I'm trying. You have to let us."

"That's right, son," Dutch said. "We all have to adjust." I had a long, if vicarious, history of feeling annoyed with Dutch, but having this feeling for Gladys was something new. Something I did not like.

"Adjust to what? My mother shacking up with my uncle? Happens all the time, I bet."

Trying to think of what to say, Dutch jabbed his finger in the air at me, like the punching ghost toy he'd brought me from Japan. Gladys looked at me, her mouth set.

"You're angry at me, Gabe, but it won't help anything if we go around swiping at each other. Don't act like your father."

She and Dutch held hands as they spoke to me, their united front, I realized, already planned out and rehearsed. What I could not swallow was what Sandy had suggested earlier: that somehow all this was good for Gladys, that this had made her happier than I could remember ever seeing her, that contentment with her life had replaced the day-to-day dread that she'd once worn like an old T-shirt.

Dutch wiped his mouth. "The upshot, son, is that your mother and I have discussed some changes for you."

"What changes?"

"Well, number one, you move in here with us. I'll let you have your old job back, and we'll pay to enroll you in Greensboro Day School."

He paused long enough to smile at me.

"Next, we assign you a set of chores here at the house, which you'll do as a matter of just carrying your part of the load around here. Nothing better for the soul than a little responsibility. And finally—this is the best part, Gabe—we get you enrolled in some college accounting courses and start preparing you to one day take over full ownership of Strickland Motors."

He and Gladys were nearly shaking with the pleasure of their generosity, as if for Christmas they'd just given me the gift of immortality and endless wealth.

"What are you saying?" I asked.

"Lord, it's the mummy's curse, Gabe," Sandy said. "Run for your life."

Gladys patted my arm. "Your Uncle Dutch is offering you a stable, rewarding life's work, Gabe. You ought to be grateful."

"Just *hold* it a second," I said, thinking of the last day we'd all been together, when Dutch had offered a similar deal and Roman in turn had offered to have Evel Knievel drive a car up Dutch's ass. I remembered most of all how angry I'd been at Roman for passing it up.

"This isn't what you want," I said to Gladys. "You want me to be an artist, a sculptor or painter or something, not some car salesman."

She looked at me, biting her lip, and for a moment I felt a pang of fear that she would admit to what we'd always known, that I had no talent of any kind beyond building elaborate lies. Instead, she smiled.

"That poet you're always quoting, Wallace Stevens? Dutch did a little research and found out Mr. Stevens was an insurance man *and* a poet."

"Big-time, too," Dutch said. "Vice president of the company. And that's not the half of it."

He withdrew from his pocket a piece of his green ledger paper and started reading from his notes written across the back of it.

"Anton Chekhov—very famous writer—was a medical doctor. T. S. Eliot was another poet like our friend Mr. Stevens, and he worked in a bank. Composer Charles Ives also worked in a bank. O. Henry, the only one on the list I'd ever heard of, frankly, worked in a drugstore and then a bank. Of course, he went to prison, so he's not the best example, but you get the idea."

Sandy licked rice off her fingers. "It's amazing how many famous people weren't car dealers."

"The point is, Gabe," Gladys said, "you can have a stable life, without the kinds of worries that . . . well, that we've always had, and that stability will give you the freedom to pursue any other kind of creative endeavor you want. You can do both."

"Poetry, sculpture, they make fine hobbies, something to do on the side," Dutch said. "I keenly enjoy playing guitar, but would hate it if I had to make my living by it, if I had to sit on some street corner or in a smoky bar playing for tips."

"You really should think about it, Gabe," Sandy said. "You'd look great in a chicken suit, up there on a big billboard. Or a tuxedo with swim fins? That always gets me hot. Or maybe—"

"Last year, after taxes," Dutch broke in, his cheeks red, "I brought in somewhere in the neighborhood of one point eight million dollars, and that's only the dealerships, never mind investments. Forgive me for being so crass, but my point is made, I think."

So it was. Even Sandy had lost her smirk, and all of them looked to me expectantly while the gas flames curled noiselessly in the fireplace. Up until that day, I would have thought this to be the point where Gladys would interrupt to tell me that money was not important and that I should not dedicate my life to chasing it. But I saw then, in her face, in her fingers intertwined with Dutch's, in her easy presence in this house, that it was precisely that—the chase—which made it all so bad. The endless pursuit of money, the lifelong commitment that Roman (and I, she feared) had made to figuring out the acquisition of it as if figuring out some great riddle, an unanswerable koan. I saw the logic of her new way of thinking, that money was not what ruined a life so much as the obsession with it, and here was the proof: Dutch, a man who for the first ten years of his success had happily existed in a three-room apartment with a hot plate and a black-and-white TV. She wanted me to *have* money so that I would not ever think I *needed* it.

Sandy had passed around fortune cookies and I cracked mine open, expecting the fortune to tell me that money and luck would find me or that I would begin an important journey. Instead, it said, "Some think you handsome, others not." I frowned at it and stood up.

"I just came here to tell you that I'm leaving tomorrow with Roman and a friend of his. We're going out to make some real money."

Dutch snorted so that a piece of his cookie flew out of his mouth. Gladys stood and said, "Leaving where? What are you talking about, Gabe?"

Dutch got up to stand beside her while Sandy stayed on the floor eating crumbs from the eggroll wrappers. I told them about our plans, leaving out as much as I could and still have a coherent explanation. We were touring carnivals and county fairs with a proven attraction, I told them, one that would make us good money in a short time.

Gladys was shaking her head before I even finished my sentence. "Gabe, you know I won't allow this."

"What kind of attraction?" Dutch asked.

"He and his daddy are going to be sideshow freaks," Sandy said. "Identical twins born twenty-five years apart."

"Shut up, Sandy," Gladys said.

"You can't stop me from going," I said. "You left *us,* remember?"

Gladys turned away and looked at the fire. Dutch let out a sigh.

"I don't believe you're doing this, acting this way," Gladys said.

"You've dropped kind of a big load on us here, Gabe," Dutch said. "Why don't you give us a few minutes to talk things over in private."

I walked back through the entrance hall and out the front doors into the yard, and stood beside a boxwood that had once been cut in the shape of an armchair. I lit a cigarette and would have climbed into the Chevy and driven off except for the grating feeling that I'd forgotten something. I cut across the yard, past the marble fountains and statues of cherubs, toward the pond. It was darker there, the light of dusk cut off by stands of pine trees, the sky overhead a dark pink. On the opposite bank the four paddleboats eddied and bumped into one another, sending deep thumping sounds across the water. I sat with my legs dangling, letting the toe of my shoe dimple the water. Beside me, tethered to the dock with a fraying shock cord, was the miniature submarine, its top slick with algae and spattered white with bird shit. The submarine bobbed in the water, a thin rainbow of oil around it. No matter how hard I tried, I could not see Gladys belonging here. The dock behind me clattered with footsteps, and I turned expecting to see her. Instead it was Sandy.

"The weird thing about that old sub was it had a little CO_2 torpedo tube made to shoot—get this—those little frozen dinner rolls you get from the grocery store. I guess they figure no kid's gonna kill anybody with a dinner roll."

"Unless you shoot it down their windpipe."

She nodded. "One New Year's your uncle and I were out there drunk as Spaniards—"

"Dutch was drunk?"

"Yes—and I got his underpants off him, shoved them in the tube, and fired them out into the middle of the pond. We watched it through the windshield, they way they unfurled, then dropped past where the headlight shined. Looked like one of those jellyfish. Dutch got so mad he wouldn't put his pants back on and walk to his own house until I went up there first and got him some fresh underwear."

Sandy sat down beside me and held out two fingers for a cigarette. I lit it for her.

"All the way back down the hill I'm staggering along with these Fruit of the Looms in my hand, crying my eyes out because I knew already the marriage was a goner."

I nudged the submarine with my toe. "You never let me go inside this thing. I mean, even tied up to the dock."

"That was Dutch too. Convinced that somebody would get killed and that if it was you Gladys would never forgive him and Roman would sue his a-double-s halfway till Tuesday. He's a very careful man, Gabe. I think Gladys wants to try out being careful for a while too. Dutch is showing her how."

I shook my head, flicked my cigarette into the water. "You should have let me get in it anyway. You should have told Dutch to go screw himself."

"Oh, I did eventually, honey," she said. "Believe me I did." She pointed at the sub. "Be my guest."

Inside the sub was dark and cramped. The battery was long since dead and none of the controls or lights worked. The engine would not run. We crawled inside and shut the hatch, then I lit a match so we could see our way to the two metal seats that took up most of the inside. I sat, banging my knees on the steering stick, wondering how Sandy and Dutch had ever managed to undress themselves in here. With nothing working, the sub was an isolation tank, rocking noiselessly in the surrounding blackness.

"So this is what I was missing," I said.

"It's a little better when it works. Not much, though."

"Why did you want this thing? I mean, it seems so dumb."

"Boy, Gabe, you're a subtle one." I heard her sigh. "I don't know. Back then it seemed like something I could show off. The most wasteful thing I could think of to buy and expensive too, and he would buy it for me. This, that big, gaudy house, a little white convertible, you name it. See how much he loves me, world? How important I am?"

"You and Roman would have made a good match. Except anything he bought would get repossessed the next week."

She laughed. "Your daddy and I would not be a good match. Too much alike. And anyway, I got over that way of thinking. I came back here not for one red dime, but just to see, I don't know, if Dutch maybe still loved me? That's not quite it. I don't love him anymore, but if it was anything I wanted out of him, it was that. Just to know I'd left a mark."

"So did you?" I asked. The sub bumped against the dock.

"Ha. I think the day I left he put my stuff on the curb for trash, and with it any feelings he had for me. You couldn't bruise his heart with a jackhammer."

I lit two cigarettes for us and in the flash of match saw her green eyes, wide and searching.

"You know the plan, don't you?" Sandy said. In the dark, the glowing tip of the cigarette seemed to be the source of her voice.

"What plan?"

"Dutch psychology. They'll let you run off with your daddy, thinking he'll fall on his face and you'll come crawling back to tell

Dutch he was right about everything. I got the same when I first made noise about Las Vegas. He's talking her into it right now."

"I don't need anybody's permission," I said.

"No, but even with it you'll worry about your mother, about her worrying over you."

"She seems happy enough here without me."

"Boo hoo hoo," Sandy said. "You sound like a little boy sent off to camp, missing the little ketchup-and-mustard smiley face his mama used to put on his hamburger. Young men your age have fought in wars, Gabe."

I felt the warmth of my face as I blushed there in the dark. I wanted to tell her that it was not family life I missed, because we'd never had that anyway. The problem was my sense that this person, this new, happy Gladys, was not the Gladys I knew, was some shined-up, knock-off imitation of my mother. The idea seemed like the height of selfishness, that I might wish on her all her old unhappiness just so I could know her again, but it was more than that. Whenever I pictured the new, Dutchland version of her—dancing across the yellow wood floors, swimming laps in the pool—it was like one of those elaborate drawings where five things are wrong and you have to look hard to find them. I hadn't found them yet.

"Don't be all mad at me, Gabe," Sandy said. "I didn't mean anything."

"I'm not mad," I said. "I was just wondering what you're going to do now that you've come back and figured out that Dutch still hates your guts."

She was silent a moment, drawing on her cigarette. "You are Strickland through and through," she said. She dropped the glowing butt and for a moment it startled me, as if she herself had dropped to the floor. "I don't know what I'm going to do. Just waiting for the next whatever to come along."

"It better come soon," I said. "I don't think you'll be staying here very long."

"I think you're right."

"How are you set for money?"

She laughed. "Money is no problem. I don't have any."

"So what's your plan?"

She thought about this for a minute. "This thing your daddy has cooked up," Sandy said. "Is it any good, or just more of his bullshit?"

"It seems good to me, but then I was a big fan of the moon-landing lawn chairs."

She laughed. "Is it the kind of thing where you might could use an extra hand?"

"It's the kinda thing nobody has ever done before, so I can't say."

"Is it hard work?"

"Probably no harder than dropping hints all over the place," I said. "Why don't you come by tomorrow and I'll show you what we're doing."

"And what would Roman say about that, Gabe?"

I hadn't thought of this. "I don't know. Show up and find out."

She was quiet a minute. "I just might take you up on that," she said.

All at once I felt better than I had all day, like I really was a partner in Roman's venture and could sign on someone else if I wanted to. Besides, she'd made a profession of drawing people in to look at things and spend their money; if she could sell a Huey helicopter, then Jayne Mansfield's death car would be a piece of cake. As I told myself this I was also silently rehearsing telling it to Roman, and I knew he would go for it. I knew I could sell him on her.

"Welcome aboard, Miss Goforth," I said.

"Thank you, Mr. Strickland."

I held out my hand, groping for hers, and accidentally touched her breast.

"Sorry," I said. I heard her stand and turn the handle on the hatch. The cool night air drew into the submarine, carried in with moths and light from the moon.

She crawled out and reached back to give me a hand up. "If that's how y'all conclude business meetings, I'm in for a strange time."

Back at the house, everything went as Sandy had predicted it would, with Dutch giving a sermon about allowing young people the chance to stretch their wings, about the grass always being greener, the world is not like a movie or TV but young people need to find that out for themselves, experience is, after all, the best teacher. The speech sounded like one dredged up during a slow day at the Toastmasters Club. Through all of it Gladys stood at his side, nodding her head though unable to look at me. I couldn't decide if she was ashamed of me or Dutch. I kept waiting for her to interrupt his little litany of bullshit, at least roll her eyes, but she just kept nodding, looking away, until I felt the impulse to ask her, "Who are you?" as I had before, in our basement, when she hid away her lacy black underwear.

Above us we heard Sandy Goforth sliding closed the closet door, emptying the last wispy traces of herself from out of this house put up in her name, built around an infatuation that no longer existed. Everything she brought with her fit into one small suitcase and her dog-eared **MISS NO   ROLI   7** bag. I went upstairs to get her, telling Dutch and Gladys I planned to drop her at the Amtrak station. Before we left, I remembered that one thing that had nagged me, the snag in my memory, and went into Gladys and Dutch's room, found her poetry journal on the nightstand, turned to an empty page beyond the last entry, and wrote:

Gladys—Roman knows about everything. I'm sorry he had to find out. Get better.

Love, Gabe

Sandy watched over my shoulder as I finished the note and signed it.

"Get better? She's not sick, Gabe. She looks healthier than I've ever seen her."

I read over my note, nodded, and crossed out the part telling her to get better. I left the journal on their bed.

After our quick and awkward goodbyes, as we drove out down the long driveway, Sandy put her feet up on the dash and whistled "Leaving on a Jet Plane" as floridly as she could, as if the song had been written by Beethoven instead of John Denver. I looked back in my rearview mirror, expecting to see Dutch and Gladys leaning in the doorway, but instead saw the door closed and the lights downstairs going off one at a time—the kitchen, the ballroom, the den—until the whole bottom half of the house was dark.

Chapter 8

Our first night out, on some unlit and empty two-lane road that carried us through North Carolina and into South Carolina, Roman broke a ten-mile silence by shouting, "Hey, watch this!" and then clicking off the headlights. I dragged myself out from under sleep and an itchy blanket to find us hurtling along under stars through a night as black as ink.

"What are you doing?" I said. I leaned up, resting my elbows on the front seat. "We're going to end up in our own show."

"Not likely," Roman said, turning fully around in his seat to grin at me. "'Death Cars of the Complete Nobodies'? Don't think that would fly, son."

"This involves a problem of logic as well," Vic said. "Who'd showcase our fatal remains should we have such an accident? Rod McKuen said——"

"Turn the lights *on,* Dad," I yelled. I could see nothing of the blacktop ahead of us, and wondered how he kept the Chevy on the road. By feel, I guessed, all those years and miles he'd driven. Wind whistled at the top of my window, competing with Sandy beside me in the backseat, who, it turned out, whistled even in her sleep— lightly, as she snored. I heard the other squeaks and rattles a ten-year-old car will make, and the noise and scrape of the Death Car bodies roped down on the trailer behind us.

"We're on the road six hours and already you three are starting to bore me," Roman said. "I'm just trying to liven things up a little bit."

He meant to kick us out of the depression that had settled on us with the discovery that we had missed our first gig at the fairgrounds outside Randleman, pulling in to find only muddy tire ruts littered with discarded popcorn boxes and paper cotton-candy cones. Vic rechecked the dates on his itinerary, shook his head, muttered that there must have been a snafu in the works somewhere. Our next gig was ten hours away, in Valdosta, Georgia.

"It's good to start right off with a fuckup," Roman had said. "Get it out of our systems."

We had assembled early that morning in Vic Comstock's backyard, where the Death Cars sat glistening with dew. We attached a trailer hitch to the bumper of the Chevy, checked the oil and coolant and tires. Earlier, at the house, we'd closed the venetian blinds, unplugged the appliances, and set the thermostat at fifty. We rigged up a gadget Roman had once sold door to door, which would click alternate lamps on and off to make the house look occupied. Roman had already taken care of details I didn't think of until days later—having the mail and newspaper stopped, hiring a neighbor boy to mow the yard through September. The finality of it all made me feel the way Gladys must have felt the night of our dinner with her, when she had gathered up the last of her things, put her hair rollers in the front seat of her Valiant, taken the photo albums away in a shoe box. With one exception: we planned someday to return.

Beneath the front wheels of the Chevy something made a loud thump, muffled like a stomach punch. Roman clicked the headlights back on, the green dash lights illuminating his face.

"We hit somebody," I said.

"I don't think it was some*body,* Gabe," Roman said. "Some*thing* more likely. Unless it was a dwarf."

I smiled. "Or a Munchkin. With the Land of Oz out of business, they're just drifting around the countryside."

"Trying to find themselves," Roman said, and we both laughed.

"I'll venture another guess and say rabbit," Vic said.

Roman shook his head. "Rabbits don't hit right in the front, usually from the side, either trying to get out of the way or jumping *at* the damn car. Not too bright."

"A skunk," I said, knowing there was no way to know for sure, and that at the rate we were traveling it was a mile back by now.

"Skunk would be wafting up through the air vents by now," Roman said. "You'd have that window down fast and damn the cold."

"Dog or a cat," I said.

"I've never hit one at night."

"Opossum then," Vic said.

"Strong possibility there," Roman said. He shook loose a Pall Mall and punched the dashboard lighter.

"Those things will kill you, Roman," Vic said. Recently he'd given up his cigarillos. "Coffin nails," he said.

Roman shrugged. "Better than being hit by a car with no headlights. Next guess, Gabe?"

"A mongoose," I said.

Vic wheezed with what sounded like an asthma attack, until I realized that for the first time I was hearing him laugh.

"A spider monkey," he said. "Or perhaps, my young friend, a duck-billed platypus."

I started to like him a little bit. "Mr. Comstock, a man of your position ought to realize that *had* to be a sea lion."

Vic wheezed a few more times and I laughed with him, giddy in the early-morning hours, while Sandy snored and whistled beside me, her thigh pressed against mine. Behind us, the Death Cars rattled over potholes, the road ahead unwinding in the headlights. Roman drank black coffee spiked with Crown Royal, which he said would keep you awake and you wouldn't much mind *being* awake.

"There is a right answer," Roman said. "I know what we hit."

"Bullshit," Vic said.

Roman shook his head. "Wrong again, Vic. Any more guesses?"

"It was a great big old blacksnake stretched out across the road." This came from Sandy, who smiled, her eyes still closed beneath her Fighting Christians ball cap.

"You were going around that curve, pretty sharp one, too," she said, "and hit him first on the left wheel, then the right. Two thumps, one right after the other."

Roman smiled back over his shoulder while Vic tuned the radio, angry not to have thought of this. I was too amazed to be angry.

"A minute ago you were sleeping," I said.

She shrugged. "Doesn't mean I wasn't paying attention." With her fingernail she poked my thigh, still pressed to hers.

"The snake," Roman said. "Alive or dead when we plastered him?"

"Dead already."

"How so?"

She smiled again. "Snakes don't sun themselves at night, last time I checked."

"She's got you, boys," Roman said. "Got you by the short hairs. I knew we brought her for some good reason."

Actually, I had spent the first fifty miles of our trip trying to figure out why Roman *had* allowed her along. She'd shown up that morning carrying her suitcase and a pale blue bag of golf clubs she'd retrieved from her motel room. (The previous night, she told me that she had checked into the motel as soon as she stepped off the

bus, knowing ahead of time that Dutch would not let her stay.)
Roman, Vic, and I had been up since dawn, loading the cars on the
trailer. The cars were only rolling shells, no engines or drivetrains,
and using the hand-cranked winch attached to the trailer and all our
breath and muscle, we managed to load the Jayne Mansfield car. The
other two were smaller and lighter, though by the time we finished
Roman was gulping air, his hands on his knees. As we stood catching our breath, Sandy came strutting from around the side of the
house, whistling. We straightened up and clapped the rust from our
hands. Roman looked up at Sandy, who stood leaning on her golf
bag, smiling. She had her hair piled up on top of her head and wore
dark corduroy pants and a white Baltimore Colts sweatshirt. The
sleeves fell down past her hands.

"I'll be damned," Roman said.

"Well, that's old news by now," she said. "Hello, Roman." Her
voice did not sound the same as the day before, and I realized this
was what Gladys had called her lambie-pie bit.

"What in the name of Jupiter are you doing here?" Roman
asked, too shocked by her to have figured it out. She cocked her
head and widened her eyes at me.

"Ga-abe," she said. "You were supposed to—you know."

"Son?"

"We haven't been introduced," Vic said, starting toward her with
his hand extended. "I'm Vic Comstock and you are, may I say, love-
ly." His zodiac medallion glimmered in the sun, and his white
turtleneck was flecked with rust and dirt. I saw her shy away from
him a little, nearly wincing as he pumped and then kissed her hand.
Pale in the light of early morning, he looked vaguely like some
space-age funeral director.

"What's this all about, Gabe?" Roman said. "You seem to hold
the answer to all of life's little mysteries these days."

I swallowed. "I invited her along." All at once I saw how easy it would be for Roman to simply say no, and that would be the end of it.

"Wonderful notion," Vic said, probably pleased that for once he did not have to contract for female companionship. Roman stared at me. I stepped over to him, out of earshot.

"She was at Dutch's and he wanted her out. She didn't have anywhere else to go."

"You," Roman said. "You made this executive decision all by yourself."

"Well, yeah."

"You going to make a habit of picking up strays this whole trip?"

I smiled. "Only former relatives."

"Darn you, Gabe," Sandy shouted, her hands on her hips. "You told me it was okay."

"But I thought—"

"It is okay," Roman shouted back, still looking at me.

"It is?" I started breathing again.

"Only one suitcase," he said, turning to her. "And lose the clubs."

She pulled her cap from her back pocket and snugged it down on her head. "I only have one suitcase, and the clubs go with me," she said. "They're therapy."

Roman chewed his lip, looking at her as if she'd just raised him fifty dollars in a poker game. Sandy pulled an iron from the bag and chipped an acorn over our heads.

"All right, shove 'em in the trunk," Roman said, nodding at the Chevy.

Now she slept again beside me, snoring and whistling, her thighs splayed, taking up most of the backseat. I still could not figure out why Roman had allowed her to come along. Maybe he felt that being on the receiving end of Dutch's disapproval joined them together in some loose association, a club. Three members now, I thought. In the front seat Vic slept, his head lolling from side to side. I curled up in the corner, watching out the window the white stripe along the side of the road, the occasional mileage signs for Waycross and Lakeland. When he thought everyone was asleep, Roman began softly singing to himself, first "Smile," and then "Good Golly, Miss Molly," then "Show Me the Way to Go Home." The end of one song triggered the start of another, a half-drunken *Hit Parade.* He sang in a slight, sighing warble, the way you sing a baby to sleep, and I prayed he would not sing himself to sleep. I listened to him sing, listened to Vic and Sandy with their dueling snores, listened to the rattle of our fortunes behind us, trailing us, never quite catching up. And then I slept.

In Valdosta, the Lions Club Carnival was five hours away from opening. We were to set up in the parking lot of the Food King, where all around us the carnies were hammering up their game booths, shouting to one another, or lying asleep on the asphalt. Vic consulted his leather notebook.

"We need to locate a gentleman by the name of Harris Pettigrew. He runs the show here."

We left the car and trailer parked, and walked around looking for Harris Pettigrew. The carnies were hard at work, sweating in the still-hot south Georgia late summer, drinking beer, listening to eight-track tapes of CCR and Jimi Hendrix. Most of them were young guys with ponytails, some old with heavy beards or heavy wrinkles, fading tattoos on their arms or chests. We saw only a handful of women, and as we walked past, some of the men stopped their work to ogle Sandy, offering suggestions of things for her to do with them. I kept expecting her to break down and run crying back to the car, but she only smiled at them or stuck out her tongue when they said something disgusting. Once or twice she flipped them the finger.

"Just some good, clean family fun around here," she said.

Roman paused to take off his suitcoat. "We better make some money in this rat hole."

"This rat hole is exactly the kind of place where we'll make money," Vic said. "Three days from now you'll love Valdosta so much you'll want to get married and settle down here."

Roman nodded. "We'll see," he said.

Harris Pettigrew managed the E. Browning Lovell Attractions, a small-time amusements company which did shows in Georgia and Florida. He wore a black shirt and a bolo tie, had a thick Midwestern accent. A gun handle stuck out the front of his pants, and he spoke into a walkie-talkie to his assistants scattered around the lot. He carried a clipboard.

"I don't give a rat's ass," he was shouting when we found him. "If it slopes it slopes. Work around it." He noticed us and held up his finger, asking us to wait a minute. He popped a sunflower seed into his mouth and spat out the shell. "I don't care. You do what I said and if it don't work, then you make your own decision. Have a nice day." He clicked a switch on the walkie-talkie and looked at us, then his clipboard.

"Hanky-pank or grab joint?" he said.

We looked at one another.

"*Habla ingles?*" Roman said.

"What are you runnin'?" Harris said. "Do *not* waste my time."

"We have the cars of famous people who got killed," I said. "In the cars."

"Oh, hell yeah," Harris said. "The blood fest. You must be Comstock." He shook my hand, nearly breaking it.

"I'm Vic Comstock," Vic said, annoyance edging his voice. "These are my partners."

"I couldn't be happier for you, bub," Harris said. "Set up over there, northwest corner, next to the kootch. You need anything?"

"A drink," Roman said.

"Around here? Close your eyes, reach out, and grab something. Chances are it's a bottle." He ran his finger down his clipboard, then took a pencil from behind his ear and drew a line across the page. "We don't run tickets here except the gate. Charge whatever you can get, but don't go overboard. You from these parts?"

"Not exactly," Sandy said.

"They're poor fuckers, corn and pig farmers. We're here to take their last few bucks, but, believe me, it's only a few. But we'll have twenty thousand through the gate first day, so you'll do a good take. Have a nice day."

We pulled the trailer around to the northwest corner of the lot, next to Rusty's All-Star Venus Revue, which was a canvas tent surrounding a stage where in a few hours, I figured, women would be dancing half naked. While the three of them stretched and found the Porta Pottis, I took a look around. The carnival-lot sawdust lay in swirls and clumps interwoven by miles of orange extension cords. Generators hummed, cut by the buzz of circular saws, the pounding of hammers, shouts and curses. The air swarmed with the smells of cut wood and diesel fumes and, from somewhere, hot dogs and onion rings. Back behind us, not a hundred yards off, was another world entirely. Women in curlers and scarves dragged their kids into the Food King; boys in green aprons rounded up stray carts; stacks of watermelon sat rotting in the heat; dogs stuck their noses out of car windows, where a hundred windshields reflected the sun. I thought about all the kids my age back home, going to classes, eating in the cafeteria.

"Thinking up some more big executive decisions?" Roman said, shattering my thoughts. He had his sleeves rolled up, set to take the cars off the trailer.

"This is all weird," I said. "I mean us being here, doing this. All my friends are sitting on the third floor of Thompson Hall right now, learning about the Spanish-American War or something."

He lit a cigarette. "You don't have any friends. You said so your-self when we left town."

"You know what I mean. It's still weird."

He shrugged, tossed his match to the ground. "Your weird is these guys' normal." He swept his hand around to indicate the car-nival lot. "Weird just means you aren't used to it yet. And believe me, son, you get used to everything if you go through it long enough."

"What about Gladys?"

He thought a minute, rubbing the back of his neck. "You have me on that one. In hindsight I'd have to say she never got used to me, I guess. Still weird in her book."

I watched a stockboy muscle a snaking line of carts toward the store. "I didn't mean that. I meant you getting used to her being gone, being . . . you know, with Dutch."

He tipped his hat back. "Your mother seems to have adjusted to the idea without too much turmoil."

"I'm asking about you."

He smiled. "Still loitering around in the weird area. Leave it at that."

Vic and Sandy walked up carrying cardboard trays of Cokes and hot dogs, and we dug into them as if we'd already done a hard day's labor.

"So, what's next?" Sandy said, chewing dainty bites of her hot dog. "Not that this isn't heaps of fun."

"We unload the cars, arrange them in some pleasing pattern, open our wallets," Vic said.

"We need a sign," Roman said. "Every game and concession around here has a big, bright sign. What do we have? Nothing."

"I can make one, but it won't be much," I said.

Roman lit a mangled cigarette, crumpled the empty pack, and

threw it to the ground. "Just something to let the deaf ones know we're here."

Together the four of us muscled and winched the cars off the trailer and placed them side by side in the sawdust. Then we took the lengths of cord we'd used to tie the cars down, swiped a few orange cones, and roped off a circle around the cars, leaving an opening where the gawkers would walk in to sit in the cars and finger the bloodstains, where I would sit to take their money. Sandy's job would be to walk around the fairgrounds handing out the fliers Vic had printed up, advertising the cars. When we'd finished setting up we stood there looking at one another, standing back to look at the cars, moving them a few feet right or left. It felt like there should still be more work left to do. All around us, the wooden stands and rides were only half up. Hammers continued to echo across the grounds. Many of the carnies were seriously drunk by now, and they got into little pushing, falling-down fights that lasted about half a minute.

We unhooked the trailer from the Chevy. After some discussion, we decided that Vic and Roman would drive into town and find a place to stay, while Sandy and I went into Food King to buy materials for our sign. Vic and Roman drove off waving out the window, honking the horn.

"Like two boys on a shoplifting spree," Sandy said.

"They're excited about making money," I said.

"Who isn't? I mean, if we make any."

"You don't think we will?"

"Would you pay four bucks to look at some busted-up cars?" she asked me.

I looked over the rusted heaps, twisted scraps of metal in the sawdust.

"It's not the cars, exactly," I said. "It's the pitch."

"The pitch, huh?"

"That's right. Say you're in Las Vegas for the weekend, are you all that interested in electric toothbrushes? No, but you'll stop by to see the good-looking woman in the bikini."

She smiled. "You're a charmer, Gabe. Almost as bad as Roman."

We started off in the direction of the Food King, passing by our neighbors at the carnival, the big canvas tent patched in places with duct tape, with the big sign out front for Rusty's All-Star Venus Revue.

"What is that?" Sandy asked.

"Naked women dancing around on a stage. They call it a kootch show."

"You know a lot about kootch shows, Gabe?" She jabbed my ribs with her elbow.

I shrugged, my ears warming. "Never seen one, if that's what you mean. I heard the carpenters talking about it. They'll start lining up while they're pounding the last nail, from the sound of it."

"Are they really, you know, *naked*? Completely?" I knew that her thinking of this—naked women parading around a stage—likely set off every one of her Miss North Carolina alarms. During her reign she'd written a guest editorial in the Charlotte paper defending the swimsuit competition against the feminists who had been writing letters to the editor denouncing the practice. One woman had written a letter comparing Sandy to a country ham hanging in a butcher's window, both the victims of men's taste for meat. I sat by the pool while she composed her response, shaking her head and muttering to herself. She preferred to keep a low profile—talking at elementary schools, cutting ribbons—for fear that the pageant officials would find out about her marriage to Dutch, but the country ham comment was just too much. I don't remember the editorial itself, only that she'd defended the swimsuit competition as a tasteful display of athletic conditioning and posture, and said that

the woman who had mentioned the country ham had likely thought
of this while looking at her own thighs in the bathroom mirror.
Dutch made her take this last part out.

"They probably wear G-strings and, you know, things," I said.

"Things."

"Yeah."

"It sounds almost quaint. I get a picture of Mae West or something. Gypsy Rose Lee."

As she said it, we rounded the corner behind the tent and came
upon a small turquoise trailer with a ripped awning, and beneath
the awning, sitting on a beach chair, was one of Rusty's All-Star
women.

She was unmistakable, this woman: a handful of years past middle age, thick ringlets of brassy-white hair, long red nails. Her
unnaturally heavy bosom pushed out of the top of her long green
kimono (I thought of the gift Dutch had brought Gladys from
Japan). She wore no makeup, though you could tell her face was
accustomed to it; she looked somehow stricken without it. She had
on one false eyelash, which made that eye seem swollen and
bruised. I imagined her as a Champagne Escort Service dropout. A
little transistor radio on the table next to her played "I Get a Kick
out of You." She was smoking, drinking coffee, and reading a tattered paperback copy of *Future Shock*, shaking her head and grimacing as she struggled with this glimpse of the future, a future, I
assumed, that did not include kootch shows. She looked up at us,
blowing smoke from her nostrils.

"Looks like we're neighbors," she said, surprising both of us
with her British accent.

"Looks like," I said.

"I hope we'll have the chance to get acquainted."

"We'll be around," I said.

"Yes," Sandy said. "I'm sure we'll see more of you later."

We said our goodbyes and kept walking across the lot toward Food King.

"Very funny," I said.

"What?"

"See *more* of you?"

"I didn't mean *that*, Gabe." She rolled her eyes. "Anyway, I don't think we should be right next to the kootch show."

"Why?"

"Who's going to pay to see the cars? Men, right? So you have a bunch of men walking toward our corner of the lot, and what do you think they'll want to see most, smashed cars or naked women?"

"Tough call," I said.

"And besides, you have those same men walking out of there, all charged up with sex, and what will we give them? Blood and death. If it were me, I'd say, 'No thanks. Think I'll go buy a corn dog instead.'"

"That would be the first thing I'd think of."

"Well. But you see what I'm saying?"

"I do, but you haven't heard the pitch."

"What pitch?"

"For the cars. Vic *sells* those cars, the whole idea of death. Men and women will be crying, he makes it so sad."

"So we're charging people to make them sad?"

I nodded, held open the Food King door for her. "Just like every other movie that comes along."

She shrugged. "I'll take your word for it."

We steered our cart up and down the aisles of dog food and vegetables and canned goods. Sandy insisted on buying a box of Oreos and a six-pack of Brownie chocolate soda along with the poster board and Magic Markers I picked up for the sign. As we rolled through the store, elderly couples would smile at us, thinking, I knew, that we were some young couple just starting out, newlyweds stocking the pantry of their little fixer-upper on the outskirts of town. For a few moments the idea appealed to me, and once, while Sandy was trying to decide between Mallomars and Oreos, a middle-aged man wearing a golf hat and carrying a shopping list walked past us with his wife, and I smiled at him, rolled my eyes, and clucked my tongue. He smiled back and winked, the two of us sharing a joke over how indecisive the wife could be once you let her loose in the store. I thought of Gladys, enjoying such small worries as what cookies to buy after twenty years of much larger, more frightening worries. On the way out the door I swiped a postcard from the metal rack and bought a stamp from the vending machine. I borrowed a pen from Sandy, thinking of all the postcards Roman had sent us from the road over the years. Another part of the secret conspiracy Gladys and I once shared was the fact that on all of the postcards, hundreds of them going back twenty years, Roman always repeated the same message. Now I wrote the same thing, *Going gangbusters. Miss you. Talk soon*, and signed my name at the bottom. I copied Dutch's address from the slip in my wallet and dropped the card in the mailbox. Only after the lid banged shut did it occur to me that this might only upset Gladys—Roman Junior, on the road.

We walked out of the cool, pale light of the Food King back into heat and punishing sun. Workers were walking the tracks of the kiddie roller coaster, tightening belt drives beneath the teacup ride, setting up a PA system on the stage. Through all of this activity, I saw Vic and Roman sitting on the hood of the Chevy, leaned back against the windshield, their feet sticking up and their bare white legs visible above their socks, passing a pint bottle and shucking peanuts out of a paper bag. They didn't look to be hurtling toward anything, either immediately or in the future. They looked like old men in the park, waiting for the pigeons. Sandy nudged me.

"Look at the financial geniuses," she said.

I nodded and laughed, but felt the same pang of uncertainty that she had felt earlier. It couldn't be this easy to just drive into town, do a ten-minute setup, and wait for money to walk up and hand itself over. All the other carnies were pounding nails and painting, soldering wires, drinking and sweating in the sun, their faces etched by all those other days of hard work and sweat. We were eating cookies, smoking cigarettes, sitting around.

Sandy stopped, reached in the bag, and drew out a Brownie. She opened it and drank.

"Later on, after we close up," she said, "I want to go to that show."

"What show?"

"The *show*."

"The kootch show?"

"You catch on quick, Gabe."

"You don't want to do that," I told her.

"You sound like your uncle. I want to go see. I just . . . I'm curious."

I looked at her, and she blushed a little. "I don't get it," I said.

"*Now* you sound like your father. It's like you wanting for two years to get inside that crummy little submarine and ride around Dutch's duckpond. Dumb, but you wanted to do it. You begged me. So that's it, that's all. For as long as this little trip lasts, I want to feel like I've seen a little bit of what the world is like."

"What do you mean? You lived in Las Vegas, you—"

"—had a cramped little efficiency with a hot plate, Gabe. I went home from the exhibition halls, fixed a peanut butter sandwich, watched Tom Snyder on this tiny black-and-white TV, then cried myself to sleep thinking I'd ruined my life. I wanted to have a drinking problem but I couldn't afford it."

I shrugged and looked at her, her eyes wide with some mixture of sincerity and bravado, like a teenager playing chicken.

I shrugged. "We'll go to the show," I said.

The carnival would open in half an hour. Somehow, out of that drunken swirl of hammering, sawing, and painting, the rides and games had emerged ready to go, as if they'd been there for years. The four of us leaned on the hood of the car, studying the blank poster board like a group of generals planning a ground attack.

"So write in big letters, Gabe," Roman said. "'Celebrities' Death Cars,' and put two bucks admission. I think four bucks is a little optimistic."

"My friend," Vic said, putting his hand on Roman's shoulder, "I agree on the price, but I have to say, among your many gifts we cannot count an aptitude for the written word."

Roman flinched. "What the hell does that mean?"

"Your wording. It sounds as though the cars *belong* to the celebrities, as if they are the collectors instead of us."

"So what's your suggestion?"

"'Death Cars of the Celebrities.' Short, succinct, to the point."

"Wrong," I said, only because I wanted to get back at him for Roman. "That 'the' makes it sound as if we have a death car for *every* celebrity instead of just some. False advertising."

"Maybe 'Movie Stars' Death Cars,'" Roman said. "It even rhymes."

Vic shook his head. "Bonnie and Clyde were not movie stars."

Sandy said, "How about 'Famous Dead People's Cars'?"

It was Roman's turn to shake his head. "King Tut is a famous dead person. These nuts were famous for being alive."

Vic clucked his tongue, and I grinned at Roman. "How about 'Cars of Once-Famous Living People, Now Dead Because of Those Same Cars'?" I said.

Roman acted as if he were deep in thought. "We'll need a bigger poster," he said.

"This is ridiculous," Vic said. "The show opens in fifteen minutes."

"I've got it," Sandy said. "'Death Cars of Famous People.'" She smiled.

"And what's another word for 'famous people'?" Vic said. His face was red by now.

"I think 'celebrities' might work," Roman said.

"Hey, yeah," Sandy said.

"'Death Cars of Celebrities,'" I said. "Just take out that 'the' and we're set. Dad, that's one hell of an aptitude for the written word you have there."

"Thanks, son."

Vic shook his head. "Perhaps 'Annoying Shitheads from North Carolina' would be more appropriate."

Roman frowned. "Don't think it'd sell, Vic."

By the time the gates opened I was sitting at a card table beside the opening in the ropes, my cashbox full of change, the freshly lettered sign propped in front, the photos of Jayne Mansfield and James Dean taped to the front of the table. I looked like a kid operating a lemonade stand in a junkyard. Vic walked around outside the ropes with his bullhorn while Roman stood beside the cars, ready to showcase the dark stains we figured were blood, the scrap of cloth we thought must have been torn from James Dean's shirt. Sandy was off passing out fliers. Roman had made me wear my shirt and fox-hunter tie even though most of the other carnies were wearing rock band T-shirts and cutoff blue jeans.

Slowly the grounds filled up with young families, teenagers in packs or in couples, a few old ladies carrying cardboard fans, there to win blue ribbons for their quilts and canned goods. The air throbbed with rock music played over the PA system, the shouts of the barkers selling their games, the screams from the Hell House ride, with the green and yellow neon twirling through the sky, the smell of greasy food. Nighttime came slowly; the Food King was dark, closed for the evening. I looked over at Roman and he gave me a thumbs-up sign, the same way he had years ago when I used to drive his car and follow him through the neighborhoods while Gladys waited for us at home. I smiled back at him, for that one moment feeling nearly torn in two by how much I missed our old life, how much I missed her, missed the times when I would mow the grass on a day such as this one, and the two of them would sit on the porch drinking highballs, whispering and laughing together, Roman in his Hollywood mogul getup and Gladys in her yellow sundress, both of them watching me as if I were the most fascinating thing on the planet. When I would finish and shut off the mower, Roman was always ready with the old joke, which he'd adopted for his own: "I love hard work; I can sit and watch it all day."

The first small crowd gathered outside the ropes, and Vic launched into his pitch, his voice heavy as he talked about that fateful day in September 1955, about Dead Man's Curve and the young star hurtling from out of the firmament, cut down in his prime. Soon he had gathered around him a good crowd of fifty or more, and the first few walked up to me to pay their two dollars. From there Roman took over, putting his hands on the men's shoulders, steering them around the wrecks, pointing in through the windows, inviting them to sit in the driver's seats, put their hands on the wheel. It looked strange, as if he were a salesman on a lot, trying to get them to test-drive a pile of debris. I took the first dollar we made and stuck it away inside my pocket, because Vic had insisted that we frame it.

By now Vic had worked up to a fever, shouting like a Pentecostal preacher, pacing back and forth. The crowd grew, people craning their necks to see the source of the commotion, pointing at the cars. A few more paid to come in, and I saw Roman help a young woman into Bonnie and Clyde's backseat so that her boyfriend could snap her picture. Sandy walked past, her mouth red from candied apple. She smiled and kept going, passing out fliers as she went.

But something was wrong. Although the crowd was by now over a hundred (even the off-duty cops had shown up), only seven people had paid to see the cars up close. Fourteen dollars in the first half hour. Vic noticed this about the same time I did. He broke off in the middle of a sentence about the bloody, bullet-riddled passion of Bonnie and Clyde. He looked at me and then at the crowd. They waited, blinking at him like sheep. Roman, who was snapping a picture of the young woman and her boyfriend kissing in the back of Bonnie and Clyde's Ford, failed to notice any of this. He was enjoying himself.

"All right now, ladies and gents," Vic said through his bullhorn. "You've heard all about it, now see it up close, get the whole story, the gory details, touch the very bloodstains themselves. Only two dollars, to your right, pay the boy."

He stumbled over this last part, his voice faltering, as if he'd lost the script he carried in his head. He loved weaving his stories about the famous dead, but was not comfortable asking for money. He could sell, I thought, but couldn't close. Here was where Roman needed to take over. The people gathered around us pressed up next to the rope, whispered in one another's ears, finishing the story he had stopped. Vic looked tired, though he kept raising his bullhorn and asking for money.

"Only two paltry dollars," he said. "Best show on the midway. You might as well spend it here as anywhere else." This got Roman's attention like a kick to the head. He looked at Vic and then me, and I shrugged at him. Slowly, when it came to them that the show was over, the people started to disperse. Vic's bullhorn made a popping noise when he clicked it off.

Roman stormed away from the cars and jumped over the knee-high rope. It was the first time in my life I'd seen him jump, one of the few times I'd seen him this angry.

"What the fuck was that, Vic?" he said.

Vic shrugged, avoiding Roman's gaze. "They don't want to see the cars, that's their problem. I don't know, Roman, perhaps we're overcharging them."

"Two dollars," Roman said. He looked at me, hands on his hips.

"Two fucking dollars. You can sell somebody a bag of *dirt* for two dollars. Look at this." He bent over and picked up a chunk of gravel, waved it at Vic. "I could walk out into this crowd and sell *this* for two dollars. You can sell *anything* for two dollars."

I was thinking of Gladys's stories: Roman selling the Girl Scout cookies, Roman selling the sodas out of the machine, Roman selling body parts off his car to pay for gas. Vic nodded like a schoolboy who had been caught cheating. Sandy walked up, her fliers gone, hands busy with a bag of caramel corn.

"Uh-oh," she said.

"Son, how much did we take in so far?" Roman said.

I opened the box. "Eighteen dollars."

"Divided by two and spread over a couple hours. Jesus, Vic we're burning it up. Four and a half an hour, minus what we pay these two. Hell, let's go sign on at the goddamn Burger Palace; I think we're due a raise, don't you, partner?"

"I understand the source of your anger, Roman—"

"Listen," Roman broke in, "don't start this feel-good shit with me. *You* are the source of my anger. You had a hundred prospects out here and didn't sell a quarter of them. It's the old joke about skydiving, Vic, you only have to worry about those last couple of inches. Same thing in selling this show: you worry about that last few seconds, when the money leaves the pocket. That's where you live and die."

Vic tugged on his earlobe and studied the pile of sawdust at his feet. For the first time since I'd met him, he seemed old, and I felt sorry for him. We stood there for a moment in embarrassed silence.

"I won a framed picture of Three Dog Night," Sandy said. "But I gave it to some kid."

"Roman, I'm just not the salesman that you are," Vic said. "Never have been. My arena is more investments, generating capital."

"Dad, you take the bullhorn," I said.

He shook his head. "We need Vic out there getting all teary and weepy over what's-his-name. That's what's drawing 'em in. I can't do that."

I looked across Roman's shoulder to next door, where Rusty's All-Star Venus Revue had them lined up, doubled back three times through a series of ropes. The man who stood outside Rusty's—a fat red-haired man holding a microphone—did no more selling than running through the women's names ("Peaches Fontana, Mimi Chantal, Starr La Beau"), then punctuating his list with the repeated words "Naked! Naked! Naked!" Every so often, one of the women would walk out in her bathrobe onto the small stage and take the microphone, promising all the "red-blooded American males out there" that they would "see what they don't see at home." I thought it strange that they assumed the men had never seen their own wives naked. The men—farmers in long-sleeves and pants, young men in muscle shirts—stood silently in line, mute and serious with their two dollars in hand. From inside the tent came whoops and shouts and whistles, the tinny sounds of recorded music.

"What are we going to do?" Sandy asked. She was chewing a piece of saltwater taffy.

Roman lifted his hat to scratch his head. "Tonight we might as well close down, do a little creative thinking, see what we can do tomorrow. First rule, once you've hit a wall, don't keep banging your head against it, and second, there's always tomorrow."

We made our way back to the hotel in town, pulling the empty trailer behind us, leaving the cars on the carnival lot. For the rest of the evening Vic was contrite, silent. He bought us all a dinner of ribs and baked potatoes, and picked up bottles of rum and Coke along the way. The hotel rooms were decorated with green shag carpet, green-striped wallpaper, and big paintings of matadors. It was ugly, Roman said, but away from the highway and traffic noise. We made our drinks and sat in folding chairs around the pool, which despite the still-warm weather had been emptied for the season. Roman chain-smoked his Pall Malls, throwing the butts into the foot of greenish water that remained in the kiddie pool.

"Handful of nights like this and we'll be home before the World Series," Roman said.

"I apologized about as much as I can," Vic said. He was drunk after one long drink. A shock of his silver hair drifted down out of his pompadour and across his eyes. He had changed out of his white bucks and into leather bedroom slippers.

"It's not you," Roman said. "I took off on you because . . . because I'm a shit sometimes, Vic." Roman threw out this assessment of himself offhandedly. No one bothered to object, and I thought, Why should they? It was true, sometimes.

"What we have is a product," Roman said, "not unlike a rug shampooer."

"That's the first thing I thought of when I saw them," Sandy said.

Roman regarded her for a moment, taking her in as if in that instant he resigned himself to a lifetime of female torment.

"A shampooer," he continued, "is easy to pitch. It's a gadget, does neat things, comes with ten attachments. A toy, really. Easy to pitch but hard as hell to sell. Fun to look at, but pay my blessed money for the thing? No thank you. Same with the cars. Fun to hear about 'em, especially the way ol' Vic here puts body and soul into it."

Vic looked up and smiled, tears forming in his eyes. He was not a good drunk.

"What we have to figure is how to close the sale, get them through the ropes."

"Let Vic pitch the cars, then hand you the bullhorn for the close," I said.

"You're thinking, son, thinking like a salesman. How old are you now?"

"Sixteen."

He nodded. "That's good, you're on track. But it won't work."

"Why?"

"Breaks the bubble. He hands me the horn, we might as well hang up a sign that says, 'We're going to take your money now.' Like a pitcher opening his glove too much. They see it coming and they're gone."

"I've been thinking about those women at the kootch show," Sandy said, glancing at me.

"That's funny," Roman said, "so have I."

"Let's attend to the business," Vic said, pushing his hair off his face. His head briefly lolled on his chest. He snapped to attention. "At hand," he said.

"This *is* business," Sandy said.

I looked at her. "Sandy . . ."

"You all brought me along, I'm here, I'm going to speak. Now, it seems to me I can't remember even once all those women parading naked around the front of the stage."

"Too bad about that," Roman said. "Might have taken my mind off of bankruptcy."

She looked at him and smirked. "But," she said, "I do seem to recall a couple hundred men in line just waiting to see them." She looked at us as if expecting cartoon lightbulbs to appear over our heads. She rolled her eyes.

"They are paying to get *inside*," she said. "If the women were *outside*, with a little rope around them, there wouldn't be anything to pay for. We've got the doggone—"

"'Damn,'" I corrected her.

"—the damn cars sitting out for everyone to see. What's left to pay for? A close-up view, right, or sitting in the cars? Is that worth two bucks, when a good long look is free?"

Roman and I looked at each other. He shook his head. "This would go a long way toward proving how smart she is if it weren't such perfect evidence of the godforsaken idiots we are."

"You're right," I said. "She's right." I looked at Sandy, and she smiled.

"It's the old free milk and a cow business," Roman said.

"That particular maxim pertains to sexual matters, my friend," Vic said in a brief moment of lucidity.

Roman shrugged. "Sex, money, whatever." He clapped his hands together and leaned forward to pour us all a drink. "We're back in business," he said.

"I don't want to rain on any parades here," I said. "But where are we supposed to get a tent?"

"Doesn't have to be a tent," Roman said. "Am I right on this, Sandy? Just block them off somehow, run a curtain around the whole thing." He looked at me. "You'll think of something."

"Me?"

"Well, hell, Gabe. You did such a good job with our sign."

Sandy laughed. "I have some other ideas, if you want to hear."

"Better hold them till later," Roman said, tilting his head toward Vic, who was passed out completely, chin on his chest, the chain of his zodiac medallion pressing into his jaw.

"I'm about tired, anyway," Sandy said. "One genius idea a day is pretty much my limit."

She stood, stretched, yawned, slipping her feet back into her clogs. Roman stood up, stepped across, and hugged Sandy. "Thank you," I heard him say. She looked across his shoulder at me, wide-eyed, but she could not have been any more surprised than I was.

For the next few minutes after Sandy left we sat together smoking and sipping our drinks, watching the skimmers on the kiddie pool skirt around the cigarette butts floating there. Vic snored fitfully, sometimes sounding as if his breathing stopped for a few seconds. He looked like some old man in a wheelchair, wasting away one more day in the solarium room of a nursing home. Roman must have seen this too.

"It's hell getting old," he said. He pointed at Vic. "That's me in twenty years."

"No way," I said, though I had no real reason to doubt him.

"My problem is I've always been impatient. Like tonight." He shook his head. "I get pissed off, pack it in, and hurt everybody's feelings instead of just sitting down and trying to see the obvious."

"You didn't hurt my feelings."

He smiled. "Genetics," he said. "You inherited your mother's thick skin. Takes about twenty years to wear away completely. Should happen about the time I'm getting to be a real pain in the ass."

I studied the side of his face as he watched the pool, then I looked away. In the brief history of our extended conversations, such personal revelation could occur only if we weren't looking at each other. If we didn't break the bubble.

"She misses you," I said out into the air. Vic muttered in his sleep. "She asks about you every time I see her."

He was silent a moment. "She's better off where she is," he said.

A fast, hard knot formed in my stomach. "If you're so goddamn impatient," I said, "then why aren't you impatient to get her back?"

He thought about this. "When you were little, I don't know . . . five, eleven, something, you'd want to get on one of those little merry-go-rounds outside the grocery store, and of course your mother always insisted that you have your ride. She used to tell me that the artistic impulse is bound up in play, whatever that means."

He stopped to light another cigarette. "I suspect it doesn't mean anything."

"Not really," I said, thinking of my sorry attempt at sculpture.

"Anyhow," Roman said, "you'd be sitting there smiling, riding around and around and around, the damn machine playing these songs, 'Daisy, Daisy,' and 'She'll Be Comin' Around the Mountain.' Old crap. I'd wait until Gladys wasn't looking and you had curved on past me, and I'd reach back and pull the plug on the ride."

I looked at him.

"'Oops, the ride's over,' I'd say. Did that for three years, and neither of you ever noticed, not once." He shook his head. "I think about that sometimes, not giving a little kid his full quarter's worth of ride. Not wanting to hear another song, see you go around again. It's that kind of impatience gets you fired from fifty jobs."

"You were just trying to get ahead," I said, though I could not shake from my mind the picture of my father pulling the plug on my fun. It seemed hideous, as if he'd pulled the plug on my life support system.

"Look how far ahead I am," he said. "Blew right past everybody."

"We'll do all right," I said.

He nodded. "You know what I think your mother wanted out of her life, Gabe? It's so simple, even we can figure this one out."

"What?"

"She wanted her full quarter's worth of ride." He made a motion with his hand like pulling a plug. "Pop," he said.

"She's the one that left," I said. "And don't forget, I always got back on next week, didn't I? For another ride, I mean?"

He smiled. "Nobody ever said you were a genius, Gabe. Except your mother, of course. She's smarter than both of us put together."

I looked at his watch, surprised to see it was only ten o'clock. Usually such conversations were the type that carried you through until the early hours of morning.

"I'm tired," he said, standing. I thought for a moment he meant to leave Vic there all night, let the dew settle over him in the morning.

"Where am I sleeping?" I said.

"Vic decided earlier that the 'children' should share a room. In the interest of propriety, he said." Roman handed me a key for room 104. "Just don't forget she's still sort of your aunt. More or less."

Fifteen minutes later I lay under the cheap motel blanket, letting the smell of ashtrays and Lysol bring me toward sleep. Sandy lay in the other bed with her back to me, her entire head nearly covered by the sheet. I fell into half-dreams, pictures of Roman and Gladys and me in the basement, or on trips to the grocery store, or in the backyard playing lawn darts. Sleep settled over me in slow ebbs, until something shook me, by the shoulder, out of it. I opened my eyes and Sandy stood over me, pulling her T-shirt down to cover her thighs.

"Get your butt up, Gabe," she said. "We've got a show to see."

Chapter 9

As I looked back across the audience seated on the wooden bleach-
ers, I was happy to see at least that Sandy was not the only woman
in the audience. There were two others, out of a crowd of more
than a hundred, everyone talking in whispers, as if in church waiting for the plate to pass. I saw a good number of the men making
conscious effort to avoid eye contact with anyone around them—
toeing the sawdust, studying their boots.

"I think most of the show will be up there, Gabe," Sandy said,
breaking my reverie. She took my elbow and turned me toward the
stage.

"You looked like you'd gone into a trance," she said.

Just as I opened my mouth to answer, the tall black PA speakers
at either end of the makeshift stage blasted out a charge of the
thumping, jangling disco music we'd heard earlier. The fluorescent
light fixtures strung on wires above us went out, and the floodlamps that were nailed to the tent poles lit up the stage. The front
of the stage was adorned, strangely enough, with flags from different countries.

The yellowed curtains parted and out stepped Rusty, the red-
haired man we had seen outside shouting "Naked!" across the car-

nival grounds. He took up his microphone now as the music temporarily abated, asking if we were ready, promising us the show of our lives. The music cranked up again as Rusty shouted out the name of the first dancer, Mimi Chantal.

"She must be French," I said into Sandy's ear.

She pulled back to look at me, smiling. "I imagine that's a made-up name, Gabe," she said. I felt like a little kid who misses the punchline to a dirty joke.

Mimi slipped through the curtains wearing a long, brown, shiny slip-dress, stained down the front, with matching gloves and spike heels made from clear plastic. She wore a red wig, and her face in the harsh light looked startled, coursed with wrinkles this close up (we had, at Sandy's insistence, sat down front, near the exit). Sandy watched, open-mouthed, though a little disappointed, I could tell. I think she had expected Mimi Chantal to slink around in a sequined dress with a feather boa and fans, or have doves flying off with layers of scarves. She wanted some show biz, something cheaply elegant instead of just cheap.

Mimi Chantal pulled off her gloves and dropped them on the stage. None of this so far seemed to excite the crowd of men, who sat with TV faces, watching blankly, although I noticed a good dozen of them crowded, elbowing each other, leaning at the far end of the stage. With no break the music shifted from one generic tune to the next. Most of the men puffed on cigarettes, the smoke hanging in thick tatters around the floodlamps. Moths flew around the lights, throwing weighty shadows on the stage. Mimi Chantal looked bored by all of it, until finally she remembered to smile, as if remembering some fact she'd memorized for a test. When she did smile, I realized this was the woman we had seen sitting outside earlier that day, reading *Future Shock*. I hadn't recognized her beneath the red curls. I remembered how polite she had been, how mannerly. Just as I started to tell Sandy, Mimi hooked her thumbs into the thin straps of her dress and let it fall to the stage floor in a tumble.

"No G-string," I said, without looking at Sandy.

"Or things," she said.

Mimi stood naked before us, lazily gyrating, her breasts low, moving horizontally, nipples colored with the same bright rouge she wore on her cheeks, her stomach etched with a thin white scar. She was thick-waisted, lined with stretch marks. I watched as she began to touch between her thighs, and felt my face burn, for Mimi Chantal more than myself. Without wanting to, I also felt a faint stirring in my jeans. I couldn't look at Sandy, as if she occupied some blind spot in my field of vision. All the men remained for the most part quiet, though a few of them hooted at Mimi and some clapped. The crowd of men leaning at the far end of the stage had increased, though from where they stood it must have been hard to see; I couldn't figure this out. Then Mimi stepped, not bothering even to dance, over toward the crowd, who began to whoop and slap their palms on the stage, pushing one another aside. They seemed to know something the rest of us didn't. Mimi stood touching herself with one free hand, using the other to wave to individual men she apparently knew. Rusty made this big, leering face and shouted to Mimi through his microphone, asking what she had in mind for his audience.

"You don't think . . ." I heard Sandy say, more to herself than me. Just as I tried to figure out what Sandy might be thinking, Mimi walked downstage and crouched before the men, pushing out her thighs until her legs were splayed. I kept expecting someone— Rusty, a couple of bouncers, security guards—to step up and push the men away, but instead Rusty shouted though his microphone, telling the men to "get their two dollars' worth." Inside my chest and throat rose the nervous thump of my own blood, my heart like rushing water in my ears. I couldn't see much of what was happening, only Mimi's still slightly bored face above all those reaching arms, the heart-shaped darkness between her legs disappearing under a terrible flurry of hands and fingers.

All at once I felt Sandy's hand gripping my arm, pulling at my shirtsleeve. I looked at her.

"Oh my God, Gabe," she said. I turned to her just as I heard the crowd of men around the stage send up a cheer. Sandy's face looked stricken, as if we'd just watched someone get mangled in an accident.

"Let's get out of here," I said, pulling Sandy by her arm. The music was dying down and Mimi stood to take her bow. We ran out of the tent just as Rusty asked for a round of applause and invited tips to be thrown for Mimi. The last sound I heard as the tent flap closed behind me was the metallic rain of pocket change hitting the stage.

We ran as if being chased, out across the sawdust expanse of the carnival grounds and into the darkened lot of the Food King. We reached the front doors and stood panting in the light from the Coke machine. I leaned against the newspaper rack.

"It's okay," I said between breaths. "I think we lost them." I tried to laugh a little, to show how silly we'd been. Sandy wasn't laughing.

"Lord have mercy," she said, shaking her head. "Lord God, Gabe. That was just *sick*. I mean . . . it's just . . . it's not *decent*." Watching her, I suddenly felt as if indecency were the worst of crimes against humanity.

I nodded. "It's not what I expected," I said.

She sat on the sidewalk, her back against the Coke machine. "That kind of . . . whatever you call it. Why would she *do* that?"

"For the money, I guess," I said.

She shook her head. "It's just not right."

I worried that this episode might backslide her fully into Miss

North Carolina mode, that she would trade her beer-drinking, ball-cap-wearing, and cursing for the propriety of manicured nails, a garden club membership, and a can of Final Net. I was sure it *could* happen, the way in war movies the shell-shocked vet loses it when a taxi innocently backfires.

"We shouldn't've gone in the first place," I said.

"And that was only the *opening* act. Imagine what came after."

I tried and failed to imagine what came after. In my mind I saw only Mimi Chantal at the edge of the stage, crouching, spreading her legs. I felt the same faint stirrings I'd felt before, with all manner of guilt and shame attached.

"What is *wrong* with men?" Sandy asked. "What is it, Gabe? I mean, *you* didn't like that show, so what's wrong with the rest of them? What is it with sex and men?"

I wasn't too comfortable being designated national spokesman for male degeneracy. I shrugged, though I knew she could not see me in the dark.

"You *didn't* like it, did you? I'm not wrong on that?" she said.

I shrugged again, my face warming. "No, I didn't, exactly," I said. "But I still watched it, and I would probably go back and watch now."

Sandy shook her head, mentally throwing me on the top of the compost pile with the rest of my gender. "At least you're honest. I just wish I understood it."

"It's like . . . I don't know . . . a bad car wreck or something, you just watch it," I tried to explain. "You rubberneck."

"Oh, Lord, so that's the big secret. Men see intimacy with women as a bad car wreck."

I thought of my failure with Kami Sue Hightower, an episode that had managed to involve both intimacy *and* a bad car wreck. I shook my head.

"Intimacy . . ." I thought about the word. "Being close with somebody. That's *this*, two people talking together. What's going on in that tent down there is not closeness." I swallowed. "That tent is only about money."

She was silent a moment. "Well, at least you're smarter than most of them, Gabe."

"Thank you."

"Of course, you're young still."

"Only six years younger than you," I said. I saw her turn toward me, silhouetted in the red fluorescent glow.

"Yeah, you're catching up."

I nodded, not really hearing her. I was thinking of Mimi Chantal, opening herself to the fingers of strangers for nothing more than the promise of a few dimes and nickels, and of Vic, passing off the bought women from Champagne Escort as his own conquests. I thought of my own lies to Kami Sue Hightower, telling her anything while I tried to slip my hand between her breasts, my artsy posing for Alison, and of the other lies I'd told, for Gladys during her first days shacked up at Dutchland, and for Roman the hundred or so times during my growing up when he'd pulled me into the buy-and-sell shadows where he lived his life and said to me, "Don't tell your mother." Sex stood at the middle of it all, menacing and sneaky, ordering everybody around, barking out commands, while intimacy, like some frail, four-eyed first cousin, stood shaking against the wall, waiting for things to quiet down.

"It kills me," I said. "It's like everything to do with sex has to involve cheating somebody, or keeping some secret." I jiggled the handle on the empty newspaper rack. "Usually both at once."

"Well, see, you are growing up. Gaining insight every day."

I laughed. "You are the most cynical naive person I ever met."

She sighed and let her head rest against the Coke machine. "I'll tell you one thing, though, I never slept with anybody I didn't love," she said.

I nodded, then shrugged. "So?"

"So I just like to think that romance is not dead if you don't want it to be." I could just make out her eyes, sad and liquid.

For half a moment I had the impulse to lean down and kiss her, to show her that indeed romance was not dead, not if you didn't let it be. Then my brain reminded me, as Roman had, that she was still my aunt, more or less. But she was getting to me, in a way that had nothing to do with the poolside erections I'd gotten watching her sunbathe at Dutchland, when I'd barked at her hoping for a glimpse of breasts, my lap hidden by a copy of *Mad* magazine. Or not *nothing* to do with it, exactly. Something new made up of old stirrings and new stirrings together—the same mix, I thought, that had pulled Gladys out of our lives. Whatever it was, I didn't trust it. I felt sex back in behind it all, sneaky, roping me in with everyone else.

"Your little saying would make a nice needlepoint sampler," I told her. "People could frame it and hang it in their bedrooms."

She sighed and looked away from me. "Don't be an asshole, Gabe, and don't be your father. You haven't earned the right to any real meanness."

"Not yet," I said.

"Did you ever?" she said. "Sleep with someone you didn't love?"

I didn't answer for a minute, my mind running through a list of possible lies, rejecting them all. "I think the real question is did I ever. Period. I'm the most naive cynical person *you* ever met."

"You mean you *never?*"

"No. A few post-date gropes," I said, thinking of my poetry sessions with Alison. "There was this one girl, but it never got all that far, just touching and kissing. She said we had a spiritual relationship."

Sandy laughed. "Just what you're looking for, all those nights when you feel like your body is going to explode. Who else?"

"Nobody really. There's been this huge lack of opportunity."

"How old are you again?" she said.

I told her my age.

"I keep forgetting you're that young," she said. Between her and Roman, I considered having my forehead tattooed to read I'M SIX-TEEN.

"I remember those post-date gropes," she said. "Coed wrestling in the frustration Olympics."

I laughed. "That's about right."

She stood and, I was glad to see, did not bother to dust off her pants. "I'm tired," she said, the awkwardness buzzing between us.

"Well after a hard day of thinking up genius ideas, why should-n't you be?" I said.

She leaned back her head as if to look at the stars. Above us was the metal Food King awning, laced throughout with bird nests. Sandy yawned and stretched, then, before I could react, put her hands on my face and kissed me. Her lips just brushed mine, for an instant, then I leaned into her and let my tongue touch the edges of her lips, my arms still at my sides. The smell of baby shampoo and a sweet, honeyed perfume rose from her with the heat of her skin. My hands moved as if dangling from balloons, and my fingertips reached under the bridge formed between us to trace the small, gentle arc at the side of her breast, my hand slow, learning slowly her contours. She brought her own hand to mine then, to move it away, I thought, but instead she held it there, not letting it move. Her other hand curved around my neck, and I felt the warmth of her mouth beside my ear.

"We're letting this moment be, Gabe," she whispered. "We are letting it be and I want you to remember it. For all your life when you are after women and you are wanting women and they are wanting you, and it's not spiritual but physical, I want you to remember this and know that it is not cheap and it is not a car wreck or some crappy show. It is this, and this is how it is supposed to feel, always." I heard her breath.

"I'll remember," I said, and she held me a minute longer as I closed my eyes and let the moment repeat and repeat inside me, then she pulled my hand away from her, stepping back. We looked at one another. I could smell the wetness of her mouth on my lips.

"See there?" she said, breaking our silence. "Romantic as hell, if you want it to be."

"You're right," I said, finding my voice.

She brushed my hair off my forehead. "What did they used to say in high school? 'Stay sweet, don't ever change,'" she said.

"Nobody ever said that to me."

"You haven't been in school enough to hear it, from what I've heard tell of you."

I smiled. "That part's true."

"Well, don't," she said. She took my arm and we started back toward the Chevy at the edge of the lot. "Ever change, I mean. At least, for the worse if you can help it."

I nodded. "I'll work on it."

The next morning we all had breakfast at the Red Bird Cafe next to the hotel. Roman had only a glass of buttermilk, saying that his heartburn was acting up again. All my life he'd drunk buttermilk for most any ailment; it was not hard to imagine him pouring a quart of it on a fractured leg. While Sandy and I had been out watching Mimi Chantal, Roman had been up making a rough sketch on hotel stationery of his design for cloaking off the Death Cars. Vic had already been out to the shopping center early that morning, knocked on the trailer door, and awakened Harris Pettigrew, convincing him to put up four galvanized metal fence posts at the corners of our assigned area on the carnival lot. This was the best he could do, Harris said, this late in the game. He'd used up all the

chain-link fencing, so posts were it. Vic shook his head as he related all of this to us.

"He was less than cordial," Vic said. "I suppose I called too early.
He was in his underwear, with a woman in the trailer."

Roman tossed me a hundred-dollar bill. "Gabe, somehow—I
don't care about the particulars—you get a fence up between those
posts, around those cars. Nobody sees so much as a lug nut unless
they pay up, right, Sandy?"

"That's the idea," she said, smiling at her newfound importance
in this endeavor.

"Me and Vic are off into town with—"

He stopped in midsentence, gesturing at Sandy as though he
couldn't remember her name. Usually when he referred to anyone
who had recently turned up what he thought was a good idea, he
called them "Einstein." I could see him searching his brain for the
name of one famous *female* genius. When I opened my mouth, only
one name surfaced in my own brain. I *had* missed too much school.

"How about Emily Dickinson?" I said. She had been the topic the
last full week I'd attended summer school, back in June.

"What are you talking about, Gabe?" Sandy said.

Roman looked at me and blinked.

"'I heard a fly buzz when I died,'" I said.

He squinted. "What does that mean?"

"It's a poem. She wrote it."

"Well, that's fucking brilliant. I mean, what's it about? They have
flies in heaven? That's something to look forward to."

"There's more to it," I said. "I forget."

Vic raised his hand, as if in school. "I myself am partial to Rod
McKuen," he said. "'Never be afraid to say, What is it.'"

"What is it?" Sandy said.

"A line from 'Fields of Wonder.' A recent work."

"Is there something wrong with me?" Roman said. "Does everyone walk around with the names of famous poets right at their fingertips? Are you supposed to recite a couple times a day, like brushing your teeth?"

"You mean you *don't?*" Sandy said. "Roman, your life is so empty."

"Not as empty as my pockets. Son, do your job. Me, Moneybags, and Emily Dickinson here will head uptown to see what other ideas we stumble across."

Without a car, my shopping choices were limited to the Food King and its neighbor, King Mart. I decided my best bet was King Mart. Just inside the front doors, shoppers stood beneath a flashing light, picking up for a dollar each large bags of plain, cheese, and caramel popcorn stored in tins made to look like NFL football helmets. It was a perfect item to sell, perfect in its uselessness. This place, the King Mart and the others like it, was what was becoming of all the door-to-door men, the energy of a hundred thousand salesmen—the peddlers, field men, drummers—not evaporating but condensing into these fluorescent-lit aisles, into Muzak and blue-light specials. Here they sold twenty-five styles of shirts, car deodorizers, plastic ficus trees. All perfectly useless. But there was a coldness about it all, a lack of desire; if *you* don't want to buy, the dozen in line behind you will. No one was on commission here. The only people who presumably cared if you bought, the store managers with their framed, smiling pictures by the entrance, were hidden out of sight, tucked away in offices instead of out pounding pavement, lugging sample cases, getting caught in downpours. The ones you *did* see, the counter-leaners and checkout girls in green smocks, didn't give a damn if you left empty-handed, yawned as they rang you up. There were no sympathy sales here, no one to make you feel good for having spent your money, for having *bought*. There was money in it, gray metal boxes full, but no love. It seemed to me then that Roman and his type—*me*, I thought—didn't stand a chance. I shook the idea from my head.

There was not really anything made to do what we wanted. In the sporting goods department I found only one tarp on the shelf. After a half hour of searching and some quick math I settled on two hundred feet of clothesline and thirty-five shower curtains. The girl at the checkout kept staring at me as she rang up my purchase, pondering my selection with some mix of boredom and confusion, chewing her purple bubble gum like cud.

"For my new house," I told her. "Thirty-five bathrooms."

"That must be some place."

I nodded. "I do a lot of entertaining."

She nodded.

"And laundry," I said.

She stopped nodding, bored with me. "Thank you for shopping King Mart."

"Don't mention it."

I had just enough rope to stretch around the four fence posts that Harris Pettigrew had installed for us. I pulled it as tight as I could and then put in place all 350 plastic rings for my shower curtains, and then, finally, snapped the curtains in place and taped them together with duct tape.

I stepped back. The whole thing looked ridiculous, the curtains alternating white, beige, and pastel colors, some of them printed with pictures of seashells or mallard ducks or flowers—like kids' drawings hung in a classroom. Still, they did what they were meant to do; I could not see the cars at all, not one lug nut. The other carnies were stirring from underneath their hangovers, stumbling out of their trailers shirtless, scratching, stretching, drinking from Mountain Dew bottles. Our British kootch show neighbor was back outside on her folding chair, still smoking and reading *Future Shock*. Her red wig was gone. She looked over and waved.

"What then, is it wash day?" she said, laughing. I waved back and looked at her for a minute, trying to see what it was in her that could push her out on that stage every night to open her legs to strangers. Behind her, the kootch show tent, outdoor stage, and ticket booth sat quiet and stark, like someone's living room the morning after a party has gotten out of hand. I walked over to prop up my lemonade-stand sign outside the curtains, then parted them to step through. The pale pink light filtered through the shower curtains gave the cars a strange glow, like old tinted photographs. Cut off from the surrounding noise and jump of the carnival, the broken cars seemed to be waiting for something, like ghosts, not realizing they'd been wrecked. I thought of the sunrise in Vic Comstock's backyard the morning we first saw the cars, the morning the women sang "Dead Man's Curve" and all those middle-aged salesmen cried. Now we had packaged that morning in the yard, and I knew we could sell it to anyone.

I had a few bucks in my pocket and decided to buy lunch, though the only place open was the funnel cake stand. I ate two of them and drank a large lemonade, and still the others had not returned. At the edge of the lot was a phone booth, and with no planning or thought of what I might say, I swung shut the door, dropped in all the change I had, and had the operator connect me to Dutchland.

The phone rang and rang and I let it, imagining the rings echoing empty in the big house, reverberating out across the pool, past the tiny drink train that surrounded it, imagined it rattling the bones of my sorry sculpture, probably by now starting to rust. I enjoyed this reverie, this little parade of homes I was conducting, so much so that I nearly did not register the electric rattle on the other end and Dutch's tight voice saying, "Hello? Hello? Is this a prank of some sort?"

"It's not a prank, Dutch."

"Gerald? Are those ads set to run?"

"It's not Gerald, Dutch. It's Gabe. I'm in south Georgia."

"Well, Gabe, that's just fine. South Georgia is fine, Gabe." His cordiality sounded as if he'd been practicing it in front of a mirror.

"It's hot here, but the show is going well. We're doing great money so far. Couldn't be better." I bit the inside of my cheek.

"Glad to hear it, Gabe. Of course, not much has changed here. I've been working on a new ad. The boys have me—get this—driving a brand-new Plymouth Volare into this large mound of ice cream. Actually, between you and me and the lamppost, it's some sort of chemical foam, so it doesn't melt between takes. They cover the car with chocolate syrup and I'm wearing this giant cherry on top of my head, and I plow right into the middle."

"Wow," I said.

"This is to promote our 'Month of Sundays Sale.' Every car on the lot going at five percent over invoice for four Sundays in a row in October. So, of course, Sunday and sundae. But, I don't know . . ."

"Sounds great, Dutch," I said. Actually I was surprised to hear him talk to me this much, with no gloating, no disapproval. Either he was handing me more rope or, as Gladys insisted, he somehow genuinely liked me.

"You think so?" he said.

"Sure. I mean, what's the problem?"

"I'm afraid the Styrofoam cherry is a bit beyond the pale. I feel . . . I fear this whole thing might tend to make me look a little foolish, Gabe," he said.

For half a moment I stood in stunned silence, my eyes wandering over the phone booth graffiti, the offers of cheap sex and little drawings of Kilroy. *That's the whole point*, I wanted to say. It had been the point for the entire ten years of these commercials: a man this foolish, this stupid, could not possibly be anything other than honest, could be no more cagey or deceptive than a barnyard turkey. How could it be that he had not ever known this? Once again, in a sneak attack, my sympathy for Dutch hit me full in the chest.

"I don't think so, Dutch," I said. "I think everybody likes a good sport."

"That's my thinking exactly, Gabe. I appreciate your opinion."

"Well," I said.

"Yes. Well. Your mother is nearly done drying her hair. I'll just call her down. Our celebration ran a little late last night, I'm afraid."

It seemed an odd thing to celebrate another of Dutch's *Twilight Theater* commercials. I would have thought they'd be old hat by now, as much a regular part of his business as payroll deductions. I heard some muffled confusion on the other end of the line, hushed voices, the phone dropped.

"Gabe? Where are you? Are you coming home?" Gladys said this as if I'd been kidnapped, which in her mind I probably had been.

"I told Dutch, we're in south Georgia. Doing business. Going like gangbusters."

"Where have I heard that before," she said. I imagined her listening to me and rolling her eyes at Dutch.

"We're doing fine, really. You should see Roman, like a little kid trading baseball cards."

"I guess Dutch spilled the beans. I'm sorry not to tell you myself. Are you mad?"

"What beans?"

"I heard him telling you about our celebration."

"The new commercial? No, I'm not mad. He can make all the commercials he wants. Gladys—what are you talking about?"

"Oh, no. He didn't . . . Gabe—"

"Gladys?"

"Dutch and I . . . we're . . . Okay, here it is: we're going to be married, Gabe."

I looked back at Kilroy, as if he might explain this latest development to me. I blinked a couple of times.

"You're already married," I said.

"Yes, Gabe, and you understand that that's over now."

"No, I don't understand."

"Be happy for me, Gabe. Dutch gave me a brand-new Bonneville with this big red bow around it last night, and while we're out riding around, he asks me. I know it's corny . . ."

"You sure it wasn't a commercial? Camera crews secretly filming you?"

She was quiet a moment. I felt my face warming. "So this is your response," she said. "You make a joke out of my happiness."

"No," I said. "The June Bride Sale. Nothing down. Elope with great savings. I like it."

There was a rap on the glass of the phone booth, and I turned to see a short, freckled man I recognized as Bosco the Clown from the dunking booth on the midway. He was swaying, drinking some clear liquid out of a Coke bottle. Bits of glue were stuck here and there to his leathery face, to his hairline. He rapped his knuckles on the glass again and mimed dialing a phone, as if this were part of his act.

"Get off the damn phone, kid," he said.

"I'm not going to have that, Gabe," Gladys said. "I just won't have it. Dutch was half-right, apparently—you'd get away and see for the first time what Roman's life is like, out there in the world. Only you were supposed to turn from it, not embrace it."

I turned my back on Bosco. "So that was the big plan? Sorry I screwed it up by liking my father, but one of us had to."

"I gotta call my probation officer," Bosco said. He pointed to his empty left wrist, then knocked the bottle against the door so the clear liquid sloshed down the glass, cleaning it in a thin swipe. "Off," he said.

"Gabe, you are not five years old. Your father and I are not going to stay together for the sake of the child."

"So you don't love Roman anymore? That's completely gone? And in the place of that broken-down old love you got this nice, new, shiny one with Dutch. You just traded up. Am I getting all this right, Gladys?"

"Gabe. What do you have to be bitter about? Toward me?"

I held the phone, mouthing silent attempts at some answer. None would come. I suppose I had started to think that for all those years of my growing up she *had* stayed only for the benefit of the child. I thought of my father's story about bribing Mrs. Kenny in the first grade so that she would be nice to me and how well it worked—every day, she walked me out to the curb and waited with me for Roman to pick me up, her sweatered arms steady against my shoulders. Security bought and paid for, under the table. I wondered now if the whole of my time growing up with Gladys's love and attention had been only something extorted thorough the blackmail of guilt, or bought off with easy sentiment. Now I was grown; all bets were off.

Bosco kicked the door. "Off," he said, as if confirming my thoughts.

"Hold on," I said into the phone, and let it dangle by its wire. I pulled open the door and grabbed Bosco's shirt collar. He was a good three inches shorter than me.

"Listen, asshole," I said. He held his bottle with both hands, as if his only fear were that I might grab it away. His eyes were rheumy and yellowed. I saw up close that despite his thick shank of dark hair, he was an old man. I let him go. "Just wait your turn," I said.

"Hey, you want me to get throwed in jail 'cause I miss one appointment?" He looked like he might cry. He drank from his bottle and picked at the dried glue on his face.

"No. I don't want that."

I lifted the receiver.

"Gladys? Tell me this one thing, yes or no: do you love Roman anymore?"

She hesitated. "Gabe, I just . . . I can't say right now."

I knew that Dutch was there with her, in the room. "Yes or no. Dutch won't know what you're talking about."

"It's a complicated answer, Gabe," she said.

"Then it's not no," I said. "No is an easy answer."

"Not yes either. There's a lot to explain."

"I have to go."

"What do you mean? You can't ask a question like that and then just—"

"If I don't," I said, "some clown's going to get thrown in jail."

Bosco pointed the mouth of his bottle at me and smiled. "Good one, Ace," he said.

When they returned from town, Sandy drew out from the backseat a pair of big cardboard boxes filled with clothes.

"Nice job," she said, pointing at the curtained-off cars. "Step right up here, folks. See the world's largest outdoor shower stall."

"Hey, you can't see the cars, can you?"

"He's got you there, missy," Roman said. He drank from a pint carton of buttermilk.

Sandy smirked and lifted a box. "I'm going to change," she said, and stepped behind the curtains. We were an hour away from four, when the gates would open. Vic borrowed the keys from Roman and left in the Chevy, heading down the road back into town.

"What's going on?" I asked.

Roman shrugged. "Beats the hell out of me."

We stood for a moment, watching the men who ran the midway rides emerge from their trailers, blinking their bloodshot eyes in the sun, smoking, blowing their noses with their fingers.

"Good job there, with the curtains," Roman said.

I nodded. "Thanks," I said. "I talked to Gladys."

He turned toward me. "She's here?"

"Telephone."

He nodded and laughed at himself. "She sound okay? Did you tell her I said hello?"

"Well, yeah," I lied. "Nothing new, really." *Except that you'll be served papers the second you hit the state line.* "Dutch is filming a new commercial."

"I guess he needs more money. His mattress is getting a little thin."

I laughed.

"But this is our week for money, right?" he said. I gave some combination of a shrug and a nod.

Roman spat on the sawdust. "It damn well better be or we'll be home in about five days, circling the want ads."

The curtains parted and Sandy stepped out wearing a curly platinum-blond wig, bright-red lipstick, and a long silver lamé dress. The most startling transformation, though, had happened with her breasts. She wore what must have been an old Jane Russell–style torpedo brassiere, size huge, stuffed full. Her false breasts were giant, like cartoon drawings of breasts.

"Guess who I am," she said in a husky, throaty voice.

"Mimi Chantal's sister," I said. She smirked at me.

Roman was smiling and nodding. "She's Jayne Mansfield, Gabe," he said. "And she's going to double our ticket sales." By now some of the carnies had shaken off their hangovers enough to notice her, and a chorus of catcalls and whistles careened around the lot, like dogs barking at night.

"Put these on," she said. She tossed her cardboard box to me. Inside were a leather jacket and wraparound sunglasses. "You're

James Dean," she said. I picked up the jacket, then leaned down while Sandy spread Dippity-Do into my hair and combed it back, her oversized breasts buffeting my face. I tried on the jacket, which fit but was the wrong design. I needed a *biker* jacket; the one she'd found was long, with large pockets, cut from tan Naugahyde. She slipped the glasses onto my face.

"I look like a pimp on *Kojak*," I said.

"Well, the jacket's not right, but it'll do until we get some money. You need to shave the mustache." By now, my attempt at growing the mustache I counted as a failed experiment. I nodded.

Roman circled me, looking me up and down. "Try to act the part, anyway," he said.

"Too bad Mr. Clean never killed himself in a car wreck," I said.

Sandy smiled. "We have other plans for Roman."

Before I got a chance to hear about those plans, Vic returned in the Chevy, honking the horn and smiling his level, dentured smile. He exited the driver's side, his eyes full of Sandy in her new getup.

"I'm picturing you in a bubble bath," he said. "Pure glamour."

Sandy smiled with the attention, and I could tell she was going through a Miss North Carolina Pageant flashback.

"Young friend, I'll need your assistance," Vic said to me. He waved me over, his diamond pinkie ring flashing.

From the back of the Chevy we lifted out the broken remains of a Harley Davidson motorcycle, the front fork bent and twisted, the gas tank caved in, rear wheel missing.

"That's going to be a little tough to ride," Sandy said.

"What is this, Vic?" Roman said.

"This," he said, "in the fictionalized account we'll offer up, is Evel Knievel's motorcycle." I smiled, thinking of Roman's offer to Dutch.

"Funny you'd find it here in south Georgia," Roman said.

Vic nodded. "Without my associates, I have no way of purchasing another legitimate collectible, so this will have to do for now. But," he said, "we won't charge for this one. We'll place it outside the tent, along the lines of our voluptuous neighbors venturing outside in their bathrobes."

Roman thought about this. "A little teaser, something to get them inside for the real thing. Sort of like a free sample."

Vic nodded. "Exactly. And so now we have two little teasers here," he said. He ogled Sandy.

"Dad, I don't know about this," I said. "The whole thing is bullshit. Some guy might walk past here tonight and that's *his* motorcycle."

"Getting ripped off at the county fair," Sandy said. "There's a new idea."

"We won't charge anyone for this one, Gabe," Roman said. "What do you think?"

I thought about this, then nodded. "Okay."

"That's settled, then," Roman said. "But we have to sell it. Gabe, make up another sign. Vic will give you the words. Gates open in ten minutes."

I sat at my card table and carefully wrote out Vic's heavily embellished story of Evel Knievel and his jump at Caesars Palace in which he cleared the towering fountains but fractured fourteen bones in his body. He gave me words to describe our motorcycle, linking it to those splintered bones, to a body torn apart without even the comfort of a quick death. I kept staring at the rusted parts, thinking of that moment in Evel Knievel's jump when some small thing went horribly wrong, then reminding myself: The story's not true, we're just making it up as we go.

By ten o'clock that night, I had over eighteen hundred dollars in my cashbox. People gathered around the motorcycle were busy inventing their own accounts, finding spots of blood on the seat, threads of Evel Knievel's torn clothing. Vic orbited the curtains, his voice choking with emotion, his words carrying up into the night. Sometimes Vic would take over the cashbox duties, and I would go inside the curtains to lean against my ruined Porsche, letting a cigarette dangle from my lips, the collar of my leather jacket turned up. The flash of Roman's new Polaroid camera threw shadows against the plastic curtains, shadows of the twisted cars, the people moving around them. He sold the photos of people sitting in the cars, two bucks a pop. Middle-aged men had their pictures taken with Sandy on their laps, leaving big red lipstick smudges on their cheeks. Some of the women kissed me, as if I had stepped straight from the big screen into the heat of a south Georgia night. Every half hour or so Roman stuck his head out through the curtains to see how we were doing. Sandy had bought for him a tan belted trench coat and a brown fedora, so that he looked like some black-and-white-movie detective examining the scene of the tragedies. Vic's clothes were already enough of a costume, I figured, and Sandy hadn't tried to change him. His wavery, amplified baritone reached new heights as the night wore on. Many of the people Roman's age who left the show did so with tears in their eyes, clutching their two-dollar Polaroids as if it were the only documentation of their memory, as if it gave their nostalgia some meaning. And we were raking it in.

After leaving Valdosta, we made our way up the East Coast through Georgia and into South Carolina, following an itinerary of county fairs, automobile shows, demolition derbies, and shopping center openings. On off days we made side trips to find flea markets and set up in the parking lot to make a quick couple of hundred. We had veered away from Florida right at its border, saving it, Roman said, for the winter. The next couple of weeks we ate in steakhouses and Italian restaurants. On Vic's birthday we were in

Savannah, and we went to a Greek restaurant where Vic drank ouzo and made a fool of himself dancing during the floor show. At every stop we made a minimum of a thousand dollars a night, and some nights saw three times that. At Roman's insistence we plowed some of the money back into the business, as he called it, and we bought professionally lettered signs, discarding my homemade ones. Sandy got to buy herself several gold and silver lamé dresses and a pair of platinum wigs. I was outfitted with a real leather jacket and threw my Naugahyde one into a trash barrel.

I bought straight-leg jeans and motorcycle boots, plain white T-shirts, and a bottle of Vitalis, which Sandy used to comb my hair back into something resembling James Dean's DA. (I had a hard time imagining James Dean using Dippity-Do.) I liked these clothes so much that I took to wearing them all the time, even on our days off. Though we could have bought a tent like the other exhibitors, instead we kept our shower curtains, which we put up using tent poles. It seemed like some kind of collective superstition that we not change too much of what had brought us so much sudden luck. I wanted, as I knew Roman did, for Gladys to be there and see how well we were doing. I tried to explain it in postcards, but knew they didn't mean much. She had seen too many of them before, with the same words. It felt, finally, like Roman had made it, the way he had always dreamed. But all of this success, the ease with which we swept into small town after small town and back out again a couple of thousand dollars richer, bothered me. I was not used to unalloyed prosperity, and had trouble believing it now. There were no repossessors to take away our belongings, no Gladys for Roman to blow things with, no sinkhole through which all our money might disappear. Something, I felt sure, had to go wrong, but as I was fast becoming Roman Junior, enamored of steak dinners and easy money, it was impossible for me to tell what that something might be.

Chapter 10

We arrived in Carolina Beach the same day that the rain did, the kind of low-pressure cell that settled in along the coast as if it, like anyone else, had come there for a well-deserved vacation. It rained three straight days, washing out the Shagger's Jam, which was an off-season beach music festival meant to wring out a final few tourist dollars before the place shut down for winter. Vic knew all about the shaggers, old college frat and sorority types, preppy throwbacks in penny loafers and oxford-cloth shirts. They were men and women who danced a lot, drank beer as often as possible, and bought and traded whole sections of the state. They were rich, drunk, and nostalgic for the old days, and we would have picked them clean. But the rain settled in, the shaggers stayed away, and the four of us passed those days shuttling back and forth between the Surf-Bee Motel and the Waffle Hut, where we drank coffee and smoked and got weather bulletins from a waitress named Ida.

"Still rainin'," she'd say, and we'd nod, work the crossword puzzle, deal out hands of gin.

Sandy would look out the big plate-glass window and say, "You know, she's right again. That's uncanny."

It was hard, in that weather, to feel anything past lethargy, even though Roman and Vic made repeated efforts to get angry about the money we were losing. After blowing five games of gin, Roman tossed his cards on the table and stood up to stare out the window, leaning on the cigarette machine.

"This would've beat Charleston," he said. "Three thousand the first day, without breaking a sweat."

Vic nodded as he studied the jukebox selections, frowning at George Jones and Tammy Wynette, at the Captain & Tennille. "Regrettable in the extreme, my friend," he said. "We would have emptied their madras pockets." He punched in "Come and Get Your Love" and "Jive Talkin'." The volume was low, the record scratchy.

Roman nodded, thinking, I knew, of the metal filebox in the spare-tire well of the Chevy. The box contained our first four weeks of profits: twenty-two thousand dollars.

The boredom that washed in with the rain was multiplied by an unforeseen screwup in our itinerary. Carolina Beach was to have been our last big show before the close of the season, and we had planned to take a couple of weeks off before heading to Florida and the Gulf Coast for winter. Now we had three weeks off, three weeks' worth of money we would not get our hands on. And it was more than that we missed, I think. I gave up my James Dean clothes in the interim, as Sandy had traded her silver lamé for her Fighting Christians ball cap, her gray sweatshirts and jeans. Everything was packed away, back in its Goodwill boxes. We were back to just being us. This seemed like a comedown.

The Bee Gees stopped singing, and the only sound that remained was the wet hiss of water poured on the grill and Bill, the short-order cook, scraping away grease with his spatula. Roman still stood peering out at the rain, his hat tipped back on his head.

"You sorry sacks of mud better cheer up," he said. "You're going to spoil the party."

"Boy, that little pep talk really did the trick," Sandy said.

"My thinking is that to salvage something of this week we might make the drive up to Raleigh, find a couple of flea markets this weekend," Vic said. He withdrew his itinerary book from his pocket.

"Sorry, Vic, with you in charge of ice and music, I don't think you'll have time for it."

"What ice?" I said.

"I told you. For the party."

I looked at the others and we exchanged shrugs. "What party?"

He smiled. "The party we're having Saturday night."

"Ooh, fun," Sandy said. "The four of us sitting around with little fireman hats on our heads. If you three decide to play Spin the Bottle, count me out."

"She has a point, Dad. I mean, party with who?"

Roman dropped his hat on the table. "Hey, Ida. You free for a party Saturday night? We're paying for everything. In a house right by the ocean."

"What house?" I said.

Ida was free, as it turned out, and she even promised Roman the first two dances. Bill was also free, though he said he'd have to come right from work.

Sandy leaned over to whisper in my ear. "Maybe Bill can whip up some waffles and Ida can serve them to us."

"Let Roman have his fun," I told her. "He's never been this far ahead before."

After conferring in the hotel room together, Roman and Vic took off in the Chevy, leaving the trailer of Death Cars covered in blue tarps, and leaving Sandy and me to plan the details of the party: what kinds and how much food and liquor to buy, ways to "fancy it up a little," as Roman said. He also said, as he closed the door behind him, that money was no object.

After a couple of moments, Sandy looked at me. "Interesting philosophical concept," she said. "If money is no object, and we define object to mean something with tangible properties, then it doesn't exist. With me so far? So what we're out here chasing around in the rain and all these washed-out back roads is only an *idea* of cash that we use to bolster our empty lives, the same way we believe in free will or love. Or Santa Claus." She smiled at me.

I thought of Roman's basement education of me. "So *that's* what you did in Las Vegas, you studied with all the famous philosophers out there."

She shook her head. "I minored in it at Elon. And you ought to be glad I'm trying to throw a little knowledge your way, since you're a high school dropout and all."

"What about the party?" I opened the little desk drawer in between the twin beds and took out the hotel pen and notepaper. For good measure, I also took out the Gideon Bible.

"Good thinking," Sandy said. "We should pray over the party: 'Dear God, let the party be fun. Let Bill the fry cook not hit on me, and Ida the waitress not hit on Gabe. Amen.' There, I guess we're finished with our part of this."

"I don't think God wants to hear about wild parties."

She lay back on the bed, talking up to the ceiling. "Why not? I mean, he invented dancing, right? Music? Snack mix? Beer? So far, he's doing better than Thomas Edison."

I laughed. "But he'd ask you to leave, and if you looked back on the way out the door, he'd turn you into a condiment."

"I wouldn't mind being a bottle of catsup." She sat up. "See how we're advancing your education? First philosophy, now religion."

"And now the party," I said.

She sat next to me on the bed so that our shoulders leaned together. I licked the pencil theatrically and wrote a big **1.** on the paper.

"There, *now* we're getting somewhere," I said. It was her turn to laugh. She nudged me with her shoulder, and I thought of the night, a few weeks prior, when she'd kissed me, when my fingers had

touched her breast. It seemed now like something I'd only imagined happening. And I knew enough to realize that it was not a *real*
kiss, that what was behind her kiss was simple affection, which by
itself did not involve enough sneakiness or potential for real mess
to ever count as a reason for falling in love with someone. I wondered why affection couldn't be enough. You find someone you
like, get along with? Marry her.

"I think arranged marriages are not such a bad idea," I said.

She nodded. "And you're considering this as the theme of the
party?"

"It just occurred to me."

She nodded again. "You're a strange one, Gabe."

When Roman and Vic got back, we all left together in the
Chevy, towing the Death Cars to our newly rented house on the
beach. Along the way we stopped for cases of liquor and beer, chips
and dip, cheese blocks, crackers, date-nut bread and cream cheese,
and toothpicks with colored plastic frills on the tip. Sandy protest-
ed the whole time, wanting us, she said, to buy some food with a
little more class—Brie and smoked salmon—but Roman told her
he would gladly trade a little class for edible food.

The beach house was exactly that, a house right on the beach,
not back in among the row of worn-down hotels and bars that surrounded it. It looked as if it weren't supposed to be there, as if a
lifeguard might come along and order us to move it. The house was
octagonal, propped on stilts, the exterior of rough, unpainted
boards. The screens were torn, some of the windowpanes cracked.
On the front door someone had nailed a wooden plaque with the
name of the house burned in with a soldering iron: *The Seaworthy*.
From the looks of things, in a few more years the house would be
forced to live up to its name.

The front lawn of Bermuda grass had browned already, though

the days were still warm. It was surrounded by a rusty chain-link fence low enough to step over, the gate hinges wired together with pieces of coat hanger. Around back, the rotting remains of a fishing pier ran halfway to the ocean and quit. I pictured some silent-movie comedian diving off the end of it into the sand. Down the street from us was a topless bar named Hunny Bares, and across the street was a VFW post that advertised bingo every Saturday night. It was something to look forward to.

Inside the house was no better. The floor was mostly covered by a green, sand-filled rug, and the ceiling had a chandelier with light-bulbs made to flicker like tiny orange flames. All the furniture looked to be rejects from Howard Johnson's, the chairs construct-ed from wood-look plastic and blue-green vinyl. The window-unit air conditioner had left a green stripe of mildew down one wall.

"I glad we didn't buy the Brie," Sandy said. "It would have run right out of here."

"It has a few problems," Roman said. He shrugged. "Okay, a few dozen. But look."

He stepped across the living room and grabbed the edge of a curtain hung hospital-room-style on a metal runner. With a quick yank he threw it open, and there it was: the wide expanse of the Atlantic Ocean.

"Not another view like it in town," Roman said.

"And any real estate man will tell you location is the name of the game," Vic said.

"Our job, for the next three days, is to fix the place up. Get ready for this party. Make this house look like something."

At this, Sandy perked up. "Fix it up? You mean everything?"

"As much as we can get done before Saturday night."

She nodded, walking around the room, sizing it up. "And our budget is what?"

"Big," Roman said.

"Wait a minute," I said. "Why are *we* fixing it up? I thought that was the landlord's job."

"Exactly right," Roman said. "We're the landlords. Well, I am."

"You *bought* this place? What are you—I mean, why?"

"An investment," Vic said.

"Old Vic here is lending me the balance at a more-than-fair rate. Put a little work in, and this is prime beachfront property."

"We decided, mutually, that carrying the money around in a steel box might not be our best opportunity for return on a dollar," Vic said. He smiled, his dentures even and white.

"First thing is get rid of the stupid name of the place," Roman said. "'The Seaworthy.' What kind of name is that for a house?"

"Let's name it 'Burt Lancaster,'" Sandy said. "He's famous for lolling around on the beach."

"Not quite what I had in mind," Roman said. "Look at this."

He tore a scrap of paper from a shopping bag and leaned on the little Formica kitchen table to write. He held up his sign: *The Roamin' Paradise.*

"Get it?" he said.

Sandy and I nodded, looking at each other, while Roman attached his sign to the door.

"There is a lot to work with here," she said. "I'll give you that much."

Roman smiled. "Then let's work," he said.

The problem, we discovered by late afternoon, was that none of us had ever really done this kind of work before. Sandy, with her degree in interior design, knew how everything ought to look, but no one knew how to get it to that point. I'd never seen Roman do any work that involved tools. After our trip to Sears for supplies, he walked out of the bathroom wearing starchy blue jeans and a blue workshirt, looking as if he'd been dressed by vandals as some sort of prank. Vic wore his usual turtleneck and Libra medallion, and I'd retrieved my James Dean clothes. The four of us stood around looking at our pile of lumber, nails, sandpaper, paint, and caulking.

"Let's start with the obvious," Sandy said. "That rug has to be put out of its misery." This seemed like a simple enough way to start, with little chance for injury. We rolled it up, the three of us, and carried it out to the curb. Inside, Sandy was sweeping up the accumulated years of sand, dust, and dead bugs.

"Oak floors underneath," she said. "You got lucky." I started to feel better already, and I could tell Roman did too. We'd been working five minutes and had already gotten lucky, and Sandy sounded like she had at least a vague idea of what we were doing. She next set Vic and Roman on the task of sanding away all the mildew and curling paint from the inside walls, while she began to scrub down the kitchen with Mr. Clean, which I knew she'd bought for my benefit. I was sent outside with four cans of eggshell-white latex, a pack of rollers, and a paint tray. By now the rain had stopped, though it still threatened, and I kept urging the paint to dry quickly. I liked the easy repetition of the work, the fact that progress happened so quickly, and so undeniably. There was a surety to white paint.

Soon I heard from inside the banging of three hammers making a strange, short song, the only lyrics Roman's occasional shouts of *"Damnation!"* I had never done work before that produced such immediate improvement, that didn't involve waiting for some payoff. I knew Roman hadn't either. Soon enough I had a thin first coat covering all those rough boards, and I looked around for something else to do while it dried. Under a crawl space at the back of the house I found an old push mower and a few rusting garden tools, and I dragged them around to the front. I straightened up the downspout and the front gate, chopped away the honeysuckle growing along the fence, mowed the heavy thatch of grass on the front lawn. I stood in the parking lot of the VFW to admire my work. Already, after a few hours, the place at least looked like someone lived there.

Inside, Vic stood in the middle of the room with his thumb sticking out, wrapped in an old dish towel, while Sandy and Roman worked to replace panes of window glass in the kitchen.

"I'm the first casualty, I'm afraid," he said.

Somehow I had thought it would be Roman who would drop out of this effort early. This was too much like real work, which, as he used to tell me on those long-ago Saturday mornings, he could sit and watch all day. And this was work for no pay, which I would have thought amounted to blasphemy in his way of believing. But there he was on his dusty knees, his Sears workshirt wet at the armpits and along his back, small cuts on the backs of his hands, puttying windowpanes. He looked happy during this day and those that followed as we slowly knocked the house into shape, as we cleaned the floors, unloaded new furniture and a console stereo, painted the kitchen and the two bedrooms, patched the roof, planted cactus in the yard. I knew that at any time our work on the house might come to nothing, might wash away into the ocean, as had any other success he'd ever enjoyed. But this way of living, scrambling after paychecks, grabbing at luck, seemed to me to beat the hell out of the stance taken by Dutch and Ray Kroc and any number of other successful men: nervously hoarding away their money, suspicious of their own good fortune, waiting for the day to come, finally, when all their success would recede.

By Thursday afternoon we had everything ready for the party. Vic and Roman had walked across the street that evening to the VFW and found a dozen ready-made guests and their wives. Vic told us he had invited (I took this to mean "paid") a handful of girls from Hunny Bares to join us. Sandy and I did our part and invited the guy from the paint store, who we'd seen half a dozen times in those four days. Though he wore a name tag on his alligator shirt, the first day we met him he introduced himself formally, shaking our hands like a politician.

"I'm John Kornegey," he said. He smiled at Sandy. "Call me Skip." Within a few minutes he made a point of impressing on us that selling wallpaper paste and exterior latex was not his life's calling, that in fact his real work was that of filmmaker. Sandy found this exciting to no end, and while I wandered off and began dealing myself poker hands of paint sample cards, she questioned him at length about his ideas and the movies he was working on. He'd had only one produced so far, a local industrial safety film entitled *Hydraulic Press Safety: What You Should Know.*

"Yeah, I think Burt Reynolds was in that," I said to Sandy later as we sat on the ruined pier, watching the sun set over the Inland Waterway. "And Barbra Streisand sang, 'The World Is My Hydraulic Press.' Remember?"

Sandy smirked at me. "Don't be so jealous, Gabe. Just because you have no talent and some other people do." A week earlier, during some late motor-lodge night, I had admitted to her that the sculpture in her old bedroom was mine. She had not yet let a day go by without reminding me of it.

I grinned at her. "You know he's working on the sequel? *Hydraulic Press Two: What You Don't Know Can Cost You a Thumb.*"

She rolled her eyes and stood to walk back into the house, the boards of the pier creaking beneath her. For a moment I thought I really had insulted her; after all, she had been going back to see Skip even when there was no need. Once she went back to get all of us free painter's caps, about an hour after we'd finished painting.

A few minutes later, though, she returned, carrying her bag of golf clubs, which had been in the back of the Chevy for so long I'd forgotten she'd brought it along.

"Are you any good at that?" I asked her.

"I co-captained the team at Elon," she said. She withdrew a driver and pulled off the headsock, which had been hand-knitted to look like a dog, droopy felt ears hanging down.

"A golfing philosopher who knows interior decorating," I said. "You're every man's dream girl."

She shot me the finger. "Like you would know. Besides, it relaxes me."

She walked past me to the end of the pier, pushed a tee into the soft, damp board at her feet, and balanced a ball on top. She waggled the club a few times, then twisted and unleashed a hard, solid drive, the ball arcing, then disappearing against the dark blue sky.

"Nice shot," I said. "Can I have a try?"

She shrugged and handed over the club, along with a new ball and tee. As I set the ball into place, I noticed a tiny face drawn on it with marker pen: eyes, glasses, slight frown.

"Let me guess," I said. "If you lose it, it calls out your name until you find it."

"Not even close," she said. "That's Dutch I drew on there. A few in the bottom of the bag are Randy Perabo, who was my boyfriend before Dutch. It's fun sometimes. Tee 'em up and cream the shit out of them. Screw ten million years of evolution—put 'em back on the ocean floor where they belong."

I shrugged. "Cheap therapy, I guess." I looked at the tiny drawing of Dutch, his dimpled, disapproving face. I couldn't think of anybody I wanted to cream the shit out of. The only cheap therapy I needed had to do with Roman and Gladys, with everything already behind me.

"It would be hard to draw my whole life on there," I said. "Kinda like those guys who can write the Lord's Prayer on a pinhead."

She reached and pulled the back of my neck, lowering the top of my head toward her. "I don't see the Lord's Prayer," she said. "You kill me, Gabe. Most people your age are worried about how their futures are going to turn out. You're the only one I know who's worried about how his past is going to turn out."

I felt myself blush. These occasional upbraidings were painful reminders of the difference in our ages.

"You never know, maybe it's not too late to change it," I said.

"Just keep telling yourself that. Life doesn't make any sense looking backward or forward, only right now, today, is your tiny window when it all means something. And that's only a trick you play on yourself to make it from breakfast to supper with what seems like a real plan."

"So that's the answer I've been looking for: Life makes no sense. Well, thank you, Sandy. What are you supposed to do once you realize that?"

"You're supposed to tee up a golf ball and knock it into the ocean. See? Now that random act makes as much sense as anything else. It's self-validating. So do it."

I waggled the club a couple of times the way she had done. I had never in my life hit a golf ball. By now it was nearly too dark to see. I coiled backward, swung hard, and topped the ball. It gave a hollow *tock* and splashed right at the edge of the ocean, where the breakers unfurled on the shadowy beach.

"Full of symbolism and I screw it up," I said.

Sandy put her arm around my shoulder. Her sudden warmth next to me made me realize how chilly an evening it was. "The tide's coming in, so don't worry about it. It'll get where it's going one way or another."

Late that night, I sat on the front porch with Roman, nailing down loose boards. Our hammers echoed down the narrow blacktop road, sounding sometimes in unison, sometimes not. Across the street three cars sat parked at the VFW. Inside we could see two men and a woman around the tiny yellow-pine bar, talking and drinking beer. As I finished nailing the last board, Roman went inside and returned with two cold, sweaty beers. He was careful to pocket the caps rather than throw them out into his lawn.

"You talked to your mother lately?" he asked.

I took the beer from him and drank. "Called her a couple of nights ago."

"She's getting along all right? I mean . . . well, you know."

"Gladys is fine. She sounds fine, I mean. She asked about you," I lied. Every conversation I had with her lately had to do with her plans for a new life. She and Dutch would build a new house; she would go to school for a four-year degree; they would travel to Costa Rica in the spring.

Roman looked up from his bottle. "Really? What did she ask?"

I shrugged. "Usual, how are you, so on."

He was quiet a minute. "Well, here's the plan, son. You need to call her up tomorrow and convince her to be here this weekend for the party."

"What—are you kidding? She's not coming here."

"She will for you."

I shook my head. "I don't think so. Anyway, why?"

He took a long pull from his beer. "I'm giving her this house, Gabe."

He looked at me, waiting for the brilliance of his plan to wash over me. I had to stop myself from saying, *As a wedding gift?*

I looked at him a moment. "Why?"

"She comes for the party, we drink, dance a little to our old songs, then I hand over the keys, the deed, and the new doormat. It's all hers. We start over right here, on the beach."

"I thought you gave up."

He lit a cigarette. "Sometimes I wish it was in me to give up."

I shook my head. "It's not going to work, Roman. She doesn't care about houses."

"Refresh my memory, son. She's living, where is it now? Oh yeah, the mansion with the swimming pool and the ballroom and the gold fixtures in the master bathroom. That's the place."

"It's not the place. That's not the reason."

"Then it's Dutch? True, he always was a lady-killer. In high school, he must have had, Jesus, two or three dates. No stopping him."

"He's nice to her," I said.

"And I'm not?"

I shook my head. "Not always."

He nodded and grew quiet a minute. "You're right about that, son. That's the painful truth. But I think a new house on the beach makes up a little ground, don't you?"

"No, Dad, I don't. You can't just buy her back. She doesn't have a price."

"Everyone has a price, Gabe. You mean her price might not be money. Fine. We won't pitch it that way then. What I'm giving to her, what I'm offering, is this."

He held out his hands, blistered to the point of bleeding from his three days of work. "That's my blood, son. Sweat—you see where I'm going with this? Tears? Why not. We're talking heart and soul. Meaningful gestures. Name me a woman who can resist it."

"Right, except you mean bullshit gestures. Why does it always have to be some big scheme with you?"

He shrugged, lit another Pall Mall from the first one. "I'm doing it for her, am I not? Besides, whose side are you on in this thing, anyway?"

It was my turn to shrug. I wasn't sure. As Sandy had said, I was still worried about how my past was going to turn out, but not sure anymore that I wanted to do anything to alter it, especially if it meant ripping Gladys out of her current happiness, imagined or otherwise. But I knew Roman could do it, could sell her on himself and his meaningful gestures, bought and paid for. He'd done it before.

"Listen, Gabe, this is a cakewalk next to the poetry contest. She *does* want to see you. Or if not—if you've pissed her off somehow the way you're pissing me off—then make something up. Tell her you've been crushed beneath the wheels of a train."

"And so as my life bleeds away I'm calling her up to tell her this? How is that supposed to make sense?"

He smiled, blew sawdust off his forearm. "I have faith in you, son."

Getting her to agree to come was easier than I'd thought. All I had to do was destroy Roman's weekend.

She said no, at first, for all the reasons I'd predicted to myself: she was busy helping out at the dealership, she was taking a class at UNC-G, the four-hour trip was too long. I sat on a leather stool in the VFW bar, where I'd gone to make the phone call.

"But I really want to see you," I said. "It's been six weeks."

"I want to see you too, honey, but this weekend is bad for me."

"Roman wants to see you," I said.

"The answer's no, Gabe. And you know that's not a good idea, if—"

"And Dutch," I said quickly, pouring gasoline on all of Roman's plans.

"What about Dutch?"

"Well, I mean, we really want to see him."

"'We?' You, Sandy . . . you both want to see Dutch?" She sounded not so much disbelieving as sadly hopeful.

"Absolutely. We all feel nostalgic for Dutch." I watched the woman tending bar wipe down glasses with a dirty rag.

"Gabe . . ."

"I really do mean it. We were saying how nice it would be to see both of you again."

"And Roman . . . he was in on this conversation?"

"I think he said it first," I said. Once you got past the first lie, I knew from experience, the rest came easily. "He feels bad about the way he's acted in the past. He wants to make it up to you both."

"This is . . . I don't know, more than I hoped," she said. "Once you think you have him figured out, he—well, whatever."

"You'll come then?"

"Well, Gabe . . ." She grew silent a moment. On the TV above the bar, Mike Douglas was singing with James Brown.

"Okay. We will come. I do want to see you." She sounded almost relieved.

"Hey, great. That's just great."

"You haven't told him? About the marriage, I mean?"

"That's not my job," I said.

"No, of course not. But he needs to know, Gabe."

I sighed. Mike Douglas gave James Brown five. They were smiling and hugging. "Do whatever you need to do," I said. "Leave me out of it."

"Well, I'm glad you'll be there," she told me.

After giving her all the details and directions, I hung up. On the bar sat a near-empty pack of Salems, and I took one from it and lit it. I drew the smoke in deep and let it go slowly, my hands shaking a little. My best plan, I decided, was to say nothing, to pretend to Roman that it had been her idea to bring Dutch along.

"You want something, hon?" the bar lady said.

I smiled at her. "A time machine," I told her.

"You goin' forward or backward?" she asked.

I shrugged and stamped out the Salem. "Good question," I said.

By the morning of the day of the party, the house looked as good as it would ever look. We had new carpets, lighting fixtures, ceiling fans, two coats of paint on everything, new furniture from the discount store, and a brand-new console stereo with a stack of records still in the plastic. The refrigerator was stocked with all the food we'd bought, plus mixers and bags of ice in the freezer. On the back porch sat three washtubs of beer iced down and a charcoal grill ready to fire up. We were nervous, the four of us, like some bizarre version of a newlywed couple planning their first house-warming party. We spent an hour in the front yard arranging the Death Cars, covering them with tarps. It was planned as part of the evening's entertainment that Vic would repeat the show he'd given at his own party, a couple months earlier. We all wore our costumes (which for me didn't seem like a costume anymore). Vic had bought a new baby-blue turtleneck for the occasion. Roman bought four-dollar cigars. Sandy refused to wear her wig.

By seven o'clock the first guests started arriving. Bill and Ida from the Waffle Hut came in, popped a beer, and with hardly a word slipped a Doobie Brothers album on the console and started dancing. I imagined fry cooks and waitresses all over the world spending their off hours frantically dancing before they had to go back for their next shift. Sandy pulled me out to the floor for "Long Train Runnin'," and I got to watch her long hair, free of its ball cap, bounce around her face. She smiled at me, waving her arms in the air and whooping. I was in love with her completely, and knew that that love was stalled out in its tracks, that it would never get any-where past where it was right now. I wondered if that was what became of all love eventually: out of gas, or else plenty of gas and nowhere to go.

By eight o'clock we had twenty people in the house, most of them from the VFW. Skip Kornegey arrived, and I spent a long time next to the sink talking to him. He told me all about his lat-est script, which he said was "in development." Apparently, this was code for "unfinished." It was a horror story about a mad movie projectionist who kills the sex-crazed teen audience members who show up at his gothic movie house to watch revival runs of all the old classics. The working title, Skip told me, was *The Wizard of Ooze*. He seemed proud of his idea—smiling beneath his blond mustache—and so I didn't have the heart to ask him why sex-crazed teens would go running off to watch classic movies, or why they would continue going back after the second or third murder. Sandy kept opening beers for him, telling him she'd once played the part of the Woman Plagued by Mildew at a trade show in Las Vegas; he told her he was sure he could write a part for her into the movie.

During all this Roman kept checking his reflection in the toaster oven, tapping his watch and then listening to it, and walking to the front room to look out through the curtains.

"Gabe? She's coming, right? She should have been here already."

"It's a long drive. I probably gave half-assed directions. They— she'll be here."

"Listen," Roman said, "you two don't let me drink much tonight."

Sandy reached and took away his whiskey sour, poured it down the sink.

"Anything else?" she said.

Roman missed the joke entirely. "Talk to her, son. Put in a word for me tonight. You too, Sandy."

"A traitor to my own sex," she said. Roman didn't hear. He was almost pale with nervousness. Every once in a while I would look across the room and see him standing off by himself, his lips moving, and I knew he was rehearsing what he would say to her.

Finally, near ten o'clock, when Vic had just started his usual conga line through the kitchen, the knocker on the front door sounded. Ida opened the door to let in Dutch and Gladys. Somebody behind me said, "Hey, it's that guy from the commercials." Gladys rushed over to give me a hug, and Dutch looked around for someplace to hang his overcoat. Roman patted Gladys's shoulder as she hugged me.

"Look at you," she said. She touched my Vitalised hair, my leather jacket. "What is all this, Gabe?"

"A costume party, sort of. You'll see."

"Hi, Gladys," Roman said. He stood behind her like someone waiting to cut in at a dance. He still had his back to Dutch.

"Hi," she said, and gave him a kind of half-hug.

"God Almighty, you look good," Roman said.

"Well, thank you, Roman." She did look good. Her hair had grown out and she wore it all pulled to one side, across her shoulder. She wore a short, black summery dress, and her shoulders were tanned a deep brown. Dutch slipped up beside her, curving his hand around her waist, moving into Roman's field of vision.

"Gabe, you must be the rebel without applause," he said. Some of the VFW guys laughed at this, accustomed as they were to bad bar jokes. I shook his hand and glanced at Roman, who looked as if he'd been smacked in the face with a shovel.

"Roman, quite a little setup you have here."

Roman nodded. "Eleven hundred square feet is not that little for prime beachfront property," he said.

"Well, of course I didn't mean—"

"Roman, it was so nice of you to invite both of us. A really sweet gesture on your part," Gladys said.

He cut his eyes at me as if just deciding, after years of thinking about it, that he could murder me and get away with it. He forced his lips into a smile.

"Don't mention it."

We brought everyone into the kitchen for drinks, where Sandy hugged Dutch and Gladys, and introduced Skip to everyone, telling them he was a writer for the movies.

"Any movies we'd know?" Dutch said.

"You catch *any* hydraulic press movie and it's got his name all over it," I said. Skip laughed out loud at this, which made me like him despite the fact that he kept putting his hand in the small of Sandy's back, where but by the crappy luck of birth and bad timing my own hand might have been.

Roman poured Gladys a brandy with bitters and handed it to her, then asked in a loud voice, "How about you, Dutch? Still slugging back those Shirley Temples? A Pink Lady maybe?"

A few of the VFW guys standing around the refrigerator laughed, and Dutch's ears went red. "Make it a bourbon," he said. He threw down his first two drinks in quick succession, making a big show of sliding his glass back across the counter to Roman. I half expected him to challenge someone to a shootout in the street. I'd never seen him drunk before, but I didn't have to wait too long. Gladys kept giving him stern looks.

An hour later the party hummed along on automatic pilot, everyone finding little pockets of dancing or talking or smoking, looking through the stacks of records, nibbling at the cheese plate. Once I walked outside to bring in another case of beer and found Sandy and Skip at the edge of the pier, kissing. I decided to wait until later before I allowed this to depress me. The most interesting part of the night was the effect of drink on Dutch: he kept forgetting words in the middle of sentences. It wasn't that he allowed his sentences to trail off or meander as any good drunk does, but he simply forgot individual whole words, like little potholes in his brain.

He walked over to me and slapped my back. "This is great," he said. "This is really some . . . what do you call it?"

"Party?"

"Like party, but not quite."

"Shindig?

"No."

I scratched my head. "Affair?"

By now, some of those standing around us heard what was happening and they joined in to help.

"To-do?"

"How about wingding?"

"Not exactly." Dutch shook his head.

"Fête?"

"Brouhaha?"

Bill the fry cook raised his hand as if in class. "Soirée?"

"That's it!" Dutch said. He shook Bill's hand as we all cheered. This became the game of the evening: Fill in the Blank in Dutch's Memory.

After a while I noticed that Roman and Gladys were missing. Dutch of course was too drunk to have noticed; he was across the room near the stereo, and the people around him were trying to help him remember what brand of automobiles he sold. Vic was singing "Let's Get It On" along with Marvin Gaye on the stereo. He was a big hit with the VFW wives. The two Hunny Bares girls who had shown up stayed in the kitchen, making a meal of the free food.

I looked around outside the house without finding Roman and Gladys, then walked out on the pier. In the quiet, away from the party, I noticed how drunk I was. Back inside, I found them—heard the low rumble of their voices—behind the almost-closed door of the back bedroom. I peeked in through the crack of light. I couldn't make out their words for the noise behind me, and I watched them smiling, talking, Roman pacing the room. Then Marvin Gaye and Vic ended their singing.

"Just read it before you say anything," Roman was saying. He handed Gladys a bundle of papers. She sat on the edge of the bed, her back to me.

"This is the deed to a house," Gladys said.

"The deed to *this* house," Roman told her. He sat beside her on the bed.

"So you bought a house. Congratulations, Roman. What do you plan to do with our old place?"

"Live there. This is a summer place. We'll come here weekends."

"We?"

"You and me. I bought this for you, Gladys. I fixed it up for you. I did all the work myself. Look at this." He stretched out to her his callused, cut hands.

She held his hands. "Roman . . . why did you do this?"

He took off his fedora and set it on the bed. He still wore his detective trench coat. This was the pitch he'd been practicing for her all week.

"I want us to be *us* again. I want to patch things back together, the way I patched this house together. It can be done. It's hard work, is all. I learned that. Hard work and sweat and caring enough about it. I care enough about it. Have the house, Gladys. Have me back too."

She sat with her head bent, still awkwardly holding his hand and the wrinkled papers, like things she'd gathered up to throw away. She did not speak, and I knew she was crying. I swallowed and rested my head against the door. *Don't tell him*, I whispered, hoping my words were just loud enough to soak into her subconscious. *Not now*. Her crying made him awkward, and as I looked back through the crack he picked up his hat and began shaping it.

"Roman, I . . . this is all so very touching, it really is. I'm still so moved by you. . . ."

"Tell me this, Gladys," he said. "You still love me, don't you, or is that gone?"

"Oh, Roman, this is hard. I mean . . . I do love you, I always do. But it's like it's not enough anymore. Maybe when you're young it's plenty, just starting out, the way if you don't have furniture you can cuddle up together on the floor. But later, it's different. You want a bed, you want furniture."

"I'm making enough now to get all new furniture," he said. "And nobody will take it away this time. I know, Gladys, that was never any good for you. I won't let it happen anymore."

She shook her head. "That was only a metaphor."

He smiled, looking at the floor. "Well, you know what I always said when you took those writing classes: What's a metaphor? It's for grazing cows."

She laughed with him a little.

"I'm just talking about a level of comfort, Roman. Crazy love gets old after a while."

"This house is plenty comfortable."

She shook her head. "You don't understand."

Roman shrugged. "I understand from what's been said that we love each other. I want us to be together. It's no complicated thing. Is this about Dutch? Is he the roadblock here? Do you love him?"

"I appreciate Dutch—"

"And you love me."

"But I just . . . I don't . . ." She shook her head, looking away from him. I wanted to step into the room and explain them to each other, but I couldn't. I was not some outside observer.

"Listen, now," Roman said. "Here I am throwing all this at you at once. It's a lot, I know, so you just don't worry about answering right off."

This was part of his pitch, backing out before the word "no" could come. There was always a follow-up visit if you get out before "no," he used to tell me.

"Well, this is a lot to think about," she said gently.

"But hey, we'll talk again," he said. "No doubt of that."

"We will. Roman, tell me, how do you think Gabe is with all this?"

"Us? Seems fine. He's having fun with his old man, earning good money."

"I don't know," she said. "He's too young to be living this way. He needs to finish school."

"He will . . ."

Just then the stereo started back up with Grand Funk singing "American Band," and their voices faded out of hearing. I moved away from the door.

In the living room Dutch was dancing with Sandy, which I knew meant that both of them were far drunker than they should have been. Skip Kornegey sat on the couch scribbling in the little notebook he carried in his shirt pocket, where he kept his ideas for new movies.

"What's this one about?" I asked, sitting beside him.

He held up one finger for me to be quiet until he finished. Then he snapped closed the book and put it away. "Horror story. This bloodthirsty National Guardsman terrorizes the Southern town that rejected and mocked him. Eventually he leads the local down-trodden migrant workers in a cannibalistic revolt. His name is Sherman March, get it? The movie's called *Goon with the Wind*. Really, you hit on a good title, the rest kinda writes itself."

I finished my beer. "That title sucks, though."

He smiled good-naturedly. "Hey, in this game, it's a decent title, Gabe. The point is not art, not making a *film*. The point is drawing carloads of teenagers to the drive-in. It's a popcorn-and-beer title, that's all."

Soon Gladys and Roman reemerged from the bedroom, and Dutch stopped dancing.

"There you are," he said, throwing his arm around Gladys. He was swaying, sloshing his drink on the floor.

"This is a . . ." he said, then shook his head, letting go his idea.

Some of those standing around tried to help.

"A great night?"

"Lot of fun?"

"Never mind," Dutch said. "It's okay."

"Dutch, you always knew how to hold your drink," Roman said.

"True," he said, trying to stand up straight. "Almost as well as you hold a . . . um."

"A job?" Bill the fry cook said.

Dutch snapped his fingers and pointed at Bill. It was uncanny how Bill seemed locked into Dutch's wavelength somehow. All night he'd been the one to complete Dutch's sentences.

Gladys shrugged out from under his arm. "This is not appealing, Dutch. I'm not impressed with this display."

"Have we told little brother here the news?" Dutch said.

"What news?" Roman asked.

I stepped in beside them. "Let's eat something," I said. "Let's drop this."

"Tell him," Dutch said.

"Dutch . . ." Gladys shook her head at him. "This is not the time."

"Nonsense, Gladys, this is reason to . . . um . . ."

"Celebrate," Bill said.

"Yes," Dutch said. "And if you don't tell him, I will."

"Tell me what?" Roman said quietly. "Go ahead, Dutch. I can't wait to hear it."

"Well, my brother. Gladys and I are . . . um . . ."

"Leaving," I said. "They have a long drive ahead."

"That's right," Gladys said. She took Dutch's arm.

"We're . . . *shit*," Dutch said.

"Glad you came?" Ida said.

"What?" Roman said. He took off his hat.

"Don't say it, Dutch," I said. But it wasn't Dutch I should have worried about. Behind me, Bill quietly said, "Getting married?"

"Yes! Bingo! But that other word, old-fashioned," Dutch said.

"Betrothed," Bill said. "That's the word you want."

"The very one, yes. Thank you, . . .um."

Gladys and I looked at each other, then at Roman.

"She's my wife, Dutch," he said. "You forget that little detail?"

"Divorce," Bill said, before Dutch had a chance to get stuck.

We all got quiet then. Gladys's face flushed. "We'll talk about this outside. Please," she said. She started out through the back toward the deck and the pier, and Dutch and Roman followed behind like two boys being led to the principal's office. I started out with them, and Sandy grabbed my arm.

"Whoa, horsie," she said. "This is the part where the children get sent from the room. You've got a lot to learn about family fights." She was joking, but at the same time she rubbed my shoulder and gave it a little squeeze.

"Come dance with me, sweetie."

"Skip might murder me in his sleep he'll get so jealous."

She eyed me. "Yeah, he might. That jealousy bug is an airborne disease."

I laughed.

"Are you doing okay?" she asked. It seemed to be the question of the night.

"I don't know what I am," I said. "I've never seen Dutch like this, though."

"He's nervous. He feels like the big bad wolf here tonight, the homewrecker. Is that what you think?"

I shrugged. "That wolf was pretty bad, the way I remember it. Then again, the pig did build a straw house."

She smiled. "Well, he tried."

"Yeah, a lot of work behind a bad idea."

On the console stereo, War sang "The World Is a Ghetto." I felt inclined to agree with them. Sandy shimmied and twisted, her eyes closed, brown hair in her face. At some point she'd changed out of her silver lamé into a red minidress. She took up my hands, pulling me along with her, inventing a kind of drunken dance where we both swayed toward and then away from one another. Her face shone with drink and the heat of dancing, and I thought that never again would a woman look this beautiful to me, and the fact that she would never be mine, that the whole idea was impossible, made me want to quit the world of women forever right then. Skip sat on the couch scribbling notes into his book of horrors, and it seemed grossly unfair that, for a while at least, Sandy would be with him. More and more I liked Roman's idea that love was just another commodity to be bought and sold and traded and bargained for. It beat the usual system of dumb luck and blind chance, which seemed akin to hatching a plan for buying food and shelter with money you might win from the lottery. At least in Roman's world of money and love, you had a chance of actually hitting on something, of getting the payoff you wanted.

Twice I made excuses to go to the kitchen for beer, taking the opportunity to look out through the kitchen window. I was glad to see Roman, Gladys, and Dutch sitting around the glass table on the deck, sipping their drinks and talking (mostly it was Gladys talking, the two of them listening). She had, apparently, calmed them down. In the living room Vic found me and suggested that in a few minutes we should start the show. Behind us, the two strippers from Hunny Bares were auditioning for Skip, taking turns showing off their bloodcurdling screams, which were called for, I guessed, a couple dozen times in any of his scripts. He had promised Sandy one of the plum nonscreaming parts. I agreed with Vic that we should start soon. Enough talk of death might end the party; my head was already trying on tomorrow's headache.

Just as Vic and I began the task of herding the guests out into the yard, Bill the fry cook ran in the front door shouting, "Fight, fight!" Several of us ran behind him out to the yard, where I figured two of the VFW boys had started in some pathetic, half-drunken slugfest, perhaps mistaking one another for Germans. Instead we chased Bill all the way around to the back, beneath the deck at the edge of the beach, where Dutch and Roman had each other in a headlock and were kicking plumes of sand in the air, grappling for leverage.

Gladys stood halfway down the deck stairs, her hand over her mouth. Roman puffed, spraying spit out into the light from the deck floodlamps, while Dutch swung his fist wildly, hitting air. "Take it *back*, Roman," he said, his shouts muffled by Roman's trench coat. Together they fell into the sand as the VFW men circled around yelling, a few at the edge of the circle waving dollar bills, making quick bets.

Sandy walked up beside me then. "Oh my Lord," she said.

"Gabe, please," Gladys shouted to me. "Do something."

"Break them up now and they'll go right back at each other," Sandy said. Skip stood behind her, writing in his notebook.

Though my first impulse was to break them up, they were not doing each other much harm. Roman was tired, Dutch at a severe weight disadvantage. His tie had pulled loose of his collar, and between swings of his fist he kept reaching up to straighten it.

"Take it back, Roman," he sputtered again.

Roman held firm in his headlock, his legs splayed before him in the sand, Dutch half carried under his arm, as if he were nothing more than a beach bag full of beer and paperback novels. Dutch's headlock had slipped so that his arm loosely draped across Roman's back. Roman looked to be merely resting, catching his breath, and I thought that if someone had offered him a whiskey sour, he likely would have taken it.

Gladys had come down from the deck into the sand. She was angry now, her lips pressed together. It felt like nostalgia to me, to see her angry with Roman. She moved beside me, elbowing the VFW men out of the way.

"*Gabe,*" she said.

I shrugged. "Dad . . ."

"Hi, son."

"This is stupid, Roman," I said.

"Tell *him*." He pointed at the top of Dutch's head under his arm.

"Dutch, stop it," I said.

Roman shook his head. "Don't fight my fights for me, son." I didn't bother to point out that so far this only loosely fit the definition of a fight.

"Take it back," Dutch said again.

"What did Roman *say?*" I asked Gladys.

She rolled her eyes. "Roman said that I didn't love Dutch, Sandy never loved Dutch, none of his friends loved Dutch. That they only tolerate him because he has money."

I nodded. "Dutch didn't like this idea, I take it?"

"It was mean to say. He worries about that very thing. It's a raw nerve Roman touched."

Just then, his arm apparently grown tired, Roman shifted his lock on Dutch's head, and quick as a garter snake Dutch found his feet beneath him and rolled backward and away from Roman as he grabbed up Roman's hand in both of his own. This was, I suddenly understood, judo. For as long as I could remember, Dutch had been practicing martial arts to keep himself fit. But it startled me to see that he could actually use it. He stood, Roman's arm rising up with him as he twisted, bending the palm down toward the wrist. I had seen the same thing on weekly episodes of *Starsky and Hutch*, and knew that at least as far as the pimps and street hustlers of TV were concerned, this hurt like hell. Roman soon confirmed this for me.

"Shit, *damn,* Dutch," he screamed. He bent forward toward his own splayed legs, away from the pain. Dutch held him there, swaying with drunkenness.

"Okay then, now," Dutch said, as if he were ready to begin some ceremony. "I'd like you to take it back."

Roman laughed, then winced. "Fine, Dutch, I take it back. Everyone loves you, it's nothing to do with the pile of dough you're sitting on. I'm a good example: you're the richest guy I know, and I hate you. Feel better?"

Dutch let the words soak into his pickled brain, trying to decide if they constituted an apology.

"Let him go, Dutch," Gladys said.

Instead he increased the pressure on Roman's wrist. "*Damn* it, Dutch," Roman shouted. His face reddened. The VFW boys began paying off their bets.

"That's the end of it, Dutch," I said. "He took it back."

"No, I don't think so. Roman, I want you, nice and loud, to say . . . um . . ." Confusion slowly clouded his face. "Say . . ."

Roman started laughing. "Bill, don't you fucking help him this time. Nobody help him."

Dutch studied the sand at his feet, looking for his lost memory. "I won the fight, so you have to say . . . um . . ."

Roman laughed out loud. "The Pledge of Allegiance, Dutch?"

The VFW boys laughed and quickly got in on the game.

"Say the Preamble to the Constitution."

"Say the alphabet backwards, Roman."

"And say a little prayer for me."

"Say good night, Gracie."

"Say it ain't so, Joe."

Despite his pain, Roman was loving this. I stood watching, amazed; *he* was the one beaten, on his butt in the wet sand, his trench coat twisted around him and hat mashed beneath him, but somehow it had worked out for Dutch to end up looking foolish. Even Gladys had her hand over her mouth, trying not to laugh.

"We should just leave them out here," Sandy said. "Let the tide take them."

"As if the tide would want them," Gladys said.

"Dutch, are you going to let me up?" Roman asked.

"Not till you say that word."

"What word?"

"That . . . the one you say . . . when you lose a fight. Don't play dumb, Roman."

"Okay, here goes: 'ouch.'" Everyone laughed.

"No no no. I want you to say . . . um . . ."

By now, Dutch's face was flushed red, and he would not make eye contact with any of us. All at once I felt for him that familiar sting of sympathy, like a fishhook stuck in my heart.

"'Uncle,' Dutch," I said.

"Gabe." Sandy slapped me on the shoulder.

"Gabe, you shut your mouth," Roman said.

"Yes, Gabe, what is it?" Dutch said.

It was my turn to laugh. "Nothing. Skip it."

"What?" Skip said.

"Say it, Roman," Dutch said. He twisted Roman's hand farther back, and a flinch of fear shot across Roman's face.

"Dutch, you *stop* this now." Gladys walked over and pulled at his coat sleeve. I noticed his pins were missing from his lapel, lost somewhere in the sand.

"I'm not saying shit, Dutch," Roman said.

As I moved to pry Dutch's hand away, he gave up the effort and let go. Roman rubbed his wrist and got slowly to his feet. He leaned up in Dutch's face.

"The word is 'uncle,' asshole, and I'll never say it to you. Not in your whole fucking life."

By now Dutch was embarrassed enough to be sober, and mortification settled over him like fever; you could see it in his face. All the VFW boys pounded Roman on the back as if he'd just gone ten rounds and won by knockout. Gladys stomped off into the house, her arms wrapped around herself.

"That was better than our show," Sandy said. "We ought to trade."

In the morning I found Skip and Sandy asleep together on the couch, still in their clothes, huddled under her bathrobe. I was the first one up, and I put the coffee on, then checked outside that the cars were still there, unharmed. They were, though I found two of the VFW guys sleeping in Jayne Mansfield's car. In the backseat of the Ford I found one of the girls from Hunny Bares. It was like an Easter egg hunt.

"Wake up, sleepy bear," I said, as if we'd just spent the night together.

"Fuck off," she said back.

By now the others were awake, stirring around inside the house, making morning noises. Gladys came out showered and dressed to have a cup of coffee with me.

"I'm sorry about last night," she said.

"Last night wasn't so bad. Brothers fight, or so I hear."

"But I was the cause of this. It's me they're fighting over."

"They weren't exactly pals before, Gladys."

She drank her steaming cup, looking out over the pier to the calm ocean.

"Tell me, Gabe. Be honest. Would you be happier in your life if your father and I were back together?"

"Don't put it on me. It's not my choice."

"But if it were?"

"Broken homes are supposed to be bad, it's supposed to damage me. That's what they say at school. But I guess I just feel like I'm just living my life like anybody."

"Good speech. Now can you answer the question?"

"I'll be gone in a couple of years, college or whatever. The rest of those years are yours. I want you back together because I think you love each other."

"That's true."

"I think you don't love Dutch."

She sighed. "That's true in a way, I guess. I need Dutch right now, even if I don't love him the way you think. None of this is very easy, Gabe."

"No, I guess not. So don't go by me. Do what you feel like."

"If you said the word, I would go back with Roman. If you need an intact family behind you. I can't live with letting you down, Gabe."

"My word?"

"Yes."

"You would do that?"

"You know I would."

"Well, sorry, but it isn't going to be that easy either."

She nodded and smiled at me. "Never is."

Just then Dutch came in the back door, panting and sweaty in gym shorts and sneakers, done with his morning jog.

"I've apologized to your mother ten times now," he said to me. He bent over to catch his breath. "Now I owe you one."

"It wasn't my hand you almost broke."

He nodded. "In time I'll make my amends to Roman." He glanced at Gladys. "But you should never have had to see that display last night, Gabe."

I shrugged. "It was either that or charades."

Gladys patted my back. "He's trying to apologize, Gabe."

"Fine. Forget it, Dutch. All's forgiven."

"Let's talk outside for a minute."

He turned and headed out the front door, and Gladys pushed me to follow him. I found him sitting on the front porch, on the boards I'd painted just a couple days before.

"What?" I said.

"I always feared you'd grow up thinking badly of me, and this seals it, I'm afraid."

I didn't say anything.

"We're family, Gabe."

"So?"

"So don't think that doesn't count for something, even if it occasionally fails you. I do love your mother, and I'll do what I can to see she's happy. That, I know, means something to you. Am I right?"

As much as I did not want to admit anything to him, in this he was right. She was happier without love, because love cared nothing for the sufficiency she needed now. Love sneered at stability. Dutch was, if nothing else, sufficient and stable, like an economy car.

"Don't screw her over," I said. I looked at him. "Whatever else, be nice. Don't take her for granted."

"I never would, Gabe."

We were quiet a few moments. From inside the house came noises of cabinet doors opening, the refrigerator door squeaking, the smell of bacon and eggs. I heard Skip talking in a low voice, and Sandy laughing. Over all of it, almost subliminal, was the wash of the ocean. I thought of Sandy with her golf balls, and silently hoped she would never have reason or hurt enough to draw Skip's face on one of them. Or mine.

"Interesting little exhibition you have here," Dutch said. He motioned at the cars.

"Thanks. It's better with the costumes. We meant to do the whole thing last night."

He nodded. "Nothing like a good show. The James Dean car is especially accurate, from what I know."

"Accurate?"

"Well, the upholstery for one, the paint."

"What are you talking about, Dutch?"

"The color is about right," he said.

I looked at him. "How could the color be wrong?"

He stared at me a moment.

"Gabe, you know how to check the ID numbers. Have you?"

"No. Why?"

"Well, the cars aren't *real*. That is an old Porsche, but not a '54, I'm sure. The Buick is pieced together from three different model years. The Ford looks like an old hot rod put back the way it was. Good job on those bullet holes, though."

"Oh, God," I said, tilting my head back.

"You didn't know?"

"Nobody knows." I thought suddenly of Vic and his junkyard Evel Knievel motorcycle. "Almost no one."

"Well, listen, Gabe. I owe Roman something from last night, so I won't say anything. Besides, he wouldn't appreciate hearing it from me. But in your own time, your own way, you let him know. But remember, it's fraud, Gabe. He could go to jail."

Somewhere far off in the house, between the noise of the ocean and the noise of breakfast, I heard Roman's deep and steady snoring. Keep sleeping, I thought. When you wake up, everything you love will be gone.

Chapter 11

A week later we headed to northern Florida for a show at the Hot Rodders Association annual convention. Vic had set up the show as the first of our push through Florida, which was meant to last us the winter. We had spent the week making final improvements to the house, and trying to find someone to rent it for the winter. Finally, Skip agreed to move in, more I think because it gave him at least a tenuous connection to Sandy. He arrived the day before we pulled out, bringing with him a set of concrete-block-and-board bookshelves which he filled with copies of scripts and movie magazines, a director's chair with his name stenciled on the back, and posters of Clark Gable, Marilyn Monroe, and Boris Karloff. I began to think that his affection for Sandy was based only on having seen her in her Jayne Mansfield costume. They spent a long time on the front lawn kissing each other goodbye, and Sandy did not speak much all the way through South Carolina, would stare out the window quietly whistling sad songs. Trying to cheer her up, I invented another car game, which we had played an endless succession of since our first night out when we hit the snake. This one involved counting animals on my side of the car versus discarded items of clothing on her side. The goal was to have the highest number after twenty miles. She didn't want to play, would barely answer when I asked her, and Vic and Roman never did, preferring to treat us like two oversized kids in the backseat. So all the way into Charleston, I had to keep score for both sides, hoping she might get caught up in this newest version of our foolishness. After the first round I'd found fourteen animals and five hats and a sock.

"Fourteen to six," I said. "I'm killing myself."

"Well, do it quietly," Roman said. After a few miles of Vic, he was tired of conversation, and I knew his mind was filled with thoughts of Gladys and Dutch.

"And who knew there were so many dead animals?" I said to no one. "This new game is educational."

"You can't count the dead ones," Roman said.

"'Purgatory at the very least,'" Vic said, "'should await the driver driving over a beast.' Rod McKuen said that."

"Why?" I asked.

"The game's not fair," Sandy said. "There will always be more animals." She looked up from under her cap.

"She's alive!" I said, in my best drive-in-movie mad-doctor voice.

"My edification of you is just not sticking, Gabe. You need to handicap the right side of the car."

"How?"

"Well, obviously you can't include all animals. There're too many."

"Just cows, then?"

"That's fine, if you want to be boring about it." Slowly, she let herself be pulled into the game, forgetting, I hoped, Skip Kornegey. The distraction was for myself as much as her. All week, while we worked on the house, I tried to think of ways to tell Roman about the trailer full of fake cars that rattled behind us, the cars, I thought, that would eventually push us all into prison for fraud, the way Dutch said. The cars were Roman's ticket. He'd finally made it: drawing good money, selling an idea for cold cash, not working for someone else. It was better than the downtown artists I'd tried to imitate, bilking the city of thousands. It was, besides Gladys, the only real thing he'd ever wanted. Only it was not real.

"You think up something, then," I told Sandy.

She made the game more elaborate. I was to look for spotted horses, cows in full run, or sheep eating grass with their heads pushed through a fence. These would be matched up against mate-less shoes, feed caps, and socks. I got five bonus points for any dead animal not counting roadkill, and she got five for a pair of pants. By the time we reached Atlanta she was ahead twenty-seven to twenty, but I zoomed past her as we drove by the Tote-Em-In petting zoo. In one pass, I counted twelve sheep with their heads through the steel fencing.

"I just kicked your butt," I said.

She pinched me on the thigh. "Watch your mouth. And zoos aren't fair."

"You said nothing about zoos."

"I forgot. But it's definitely in the rule book."

"Bull. Thirty-two twenty-seven, I win."

"You cheated, if that's how you want to win."

"Would you two be quiet?" Roman said across his shoulder.

"There were twelve sheep and I saw them. That's cheating?"

"What if I saw an overturned Goodwill box? Think I would have counted all the socks and shirts and pants?"

"Yes."

She turned away from me, and I was shocked to see that she was really angry. "You think so little of me, Gabe," she said.

I didn't know what else to say or exactly where I had gone wrong, so I said nothing, turning to look out my window. We rode through south Georgia in silence, passing gas stations and used car lots and water tanks painted like giant peaches. The road rippled beneath us, the cars shaking behind us.

"This is great," Roman said. "We should have gotten you two pissed at each other a month ago."

The Hot Rodders Association Southeast Convention lasted for three days, and they were easy customers, lining up even before Sandy walked around handing out the fliers. They loved the cars, cried when Vic made his speeches. The women kissed me on the cheek for their Polaroids so many times that I told Sandy I felt like we were at a convention of great-aunts. She smiled, but not enough to let me think I was forgiven. It seemed impossible that anyone could stay angry over a chance sighting of a dozen sheep, but she was making a good stab at it. I knew that the real problem was her missing Skip back at Carolina Beach. Our first night in Lakeland she stayed up late talking to him on the phone, and once, at his urging, I knew, she did for him her best movie scream, which jolted me up out of my sleep as though I'd been electrocuted. She had her Jayne Mansfield act down after seeing *The Girl Can't Help It* one night on the Late Movie, and her fake breasts had grown substantially as she discovered their size was proportionally linked to the tips she received from all the old retired men after they had their pictures taken. I reminded her constantly that if that was her strategy, she might as well take a job with Rusty's All-Star Venus Revue. I never got any tips for being James Dean, though one woman did tell me that she would give me a discount on a haircut.

During all of this I ran through my mind again and again every possible scenario for telling Roman about Vic Comstock and our trailerload of fake Death Cars. But in all of them I was incapable of seeing the end of it, what Roman would do to Vic or to me or to himself for the rest of his life. I was continually tortured by perfect opportunities. During a lull one cloudless afternoon, Roman came and sat beside me on the grass, leaning back into the thin shade of the Bonnie and Clyde car. The wind blew the flaps of his trench coat against his chin. He cupped his hands to light a pair of cigarettes, then handed me one of them. I took a deep drag and held it in, my eyes closed, my stomach beginning its slow ache. I wanted Gladys here to help me with this.

He looked around at our patch of ground, corralled off by the shower curtains. "This is not bad," he said, his highest praise for anything. He took off his fedora and looked at it, his hair mashed in a ring around his head. I nodded.

"I think this is just what we need, a little Florida. We should head for Miami or some beach somewhere. Your mother would like that. She always liked the beach, the water, beach food, all that."

He said the same thing about every small town we passed through, talked about what he would have shown her, what she would have wanted to see. It seemed as though what pleasure he took in anything was only an extension of what he thought she would like. I imagined that all those times that now bothered her so—selling the parts off the car, selling the Girl Scout cookies— had been only gestures he'd made for her, that at the time she had enjoyed it, enjoyed the two of them for their foolishness and hopefulness together, but Roman never understood that what once worked would not always. He kept his wants for her the way he kept his seersucker suits and brown fedoras, pleased that he had never outgrown them.

I looked over at the fake cars, the pile of junkyard scrap in which abided the whole of what he'd wanted for himself. He flipped up the wide collar of his trench coat, replaced his hat, then lit another Pall Mall. The cars seemed almost to be waiting for something, patient with their own ruin, their own wearing out, and for a minute I felt sorry that they were not really what we pretended they were. I wanted that for them. My next thought was to wonder if it even mattered. I felt confused by it all and looked at him. He smiled and blew a pair of smoke rings, a trick that had amused me all through my childhood. I waved them away, knowing that I could not say a word to him about the cars. *Not now*, I told myself.

The second morning of the show (the same people came by all three days, wearing, I thought, the same clothes), low, dark clouds moved in over us and stayed there. There was no rain, but no sun either. The wind blew in cool gusts, rippling our shower curtains and throwing gray shadows across our Death Cars. People were somber walking into the show, as they had been that first morning at Vic's party. They moved slowly around the rusting bodies, touching the peeled paint, peering inside the broken windows, speaking in whispers. In the heavy air, Vic's megaphoned voice gave off low echoes that seemed to carry along the ground. On any such days we all felt it, the sense that our little made world inside the shower curtains was haunted by the deaths we were peddling, that the cars carried with them the ghosts of their pasts. I was tempted to think now that these cars had no past, but that too I realized was wrong; they just had ordinary pasts instead of celebrated ones, had their own unknown deaths and lives carried with them, that past decaying now as surely as their flaking quarter panels. We moved quietly among the cars on such days, pensive in our costumes, not smiling for the Polaroids, staying inside the curtains as much as we could, venturing outside only for lunch or bathroom breaks. Sandy kept her wig on during the breaks and we didn't look at each other much, as if we were ashamed of what we were doing. I didn't much like such days, and I knew Roman hated them, going around making bad jokes, laughing too much, trying to distract himself and everyone else. The only one he would ever manage to distract was himself, and that only because he loved so much what we were doing, loved this life he had shaped. He made us love it. Roman had no desire to be anywhere but inside those shower curtains, his hands dotted with the rust of the cars, the money of strangers in the cashbox. During lulls the four of us would sit with our backs against the cars and cardboard boxes of concession-stand food in our laps, silently wiping our mouths and sipping lemonade spiked with Crown Royal, then Roman would start telling stories about being on the road selling Bibles, or about the radio preacher he'd heard the night before while we all slept in the car.

"You won't believe what he said," Roman would tell us. Sandy and I would cut our eyes at each other and grin. This was by now a running gag. We always bit for Roman, could not resist biting. He would make a long speech, imitating the preacher, about tithing, about God's love, about the redemption of the world, about sinners going to their eternal demise. He let his voice rise, filling the still gray air.

"And you won't believe what he said," Roman repeated. By now we would be smiling, our fingers sticky with cotton candy or chocolate. This went on as long as he could stretch it out, until even Vic was smiling.

"What'd he say?" I'd ask.

"Oh it's bad, son. Bad news."

"Tell us."

"He said all of us are going to hell. Named us by name."

"How simply awful," Sandy would say.

"Soon?" I would ask. "We better spend this money."

This afternoon we finished our call and response with Roman, letting him pull weak smiles from us, and still no one was there to see the cars as the rain threatened overhead. I sat with Vic and Roman in the pink shade of the shower curtains. We had made our money for the day already; we had nowhere to go. Sandy paced around the fairgrounds. The rest of us smoked cigarettes and chewed the ice at the bottoms of our cups. I kept looking at Vic, trying to see the deception in his face, his desire to cheat us and the rest of the world. He offered me a Hershey bar and I took it. Roman picked up Vic's megaphone.

"PAGING SANDY GOFORTH," he said, his voice altered and compressed. "PLEASE MEET YOUR PARTY AT THE MONEY TENT."

He laughed at his own joke, and from somewhere I heard Sandy shout for him to shut up and not act so rude. He laughed again, and Vic started in telling us about some of the past ideas he had invested in. Roman told me once that Vic could have made a killing if he'd put his money in conservative stocks, or even a savings account, but instead he had blown most of it on risky inventions and on ideas that were way ahead of their time. I translated this to mean stupid ideas. Vic was still wealthy, Roman told me, but small-time wealthy. His money had run out through a funnel of misguided vision and basement inventors. Somehow, Roman admired him for this.

"The really big one," Vic was saying, "was the restaurant. The Doggone Diner. You'd sit and order delicious fare, expertly prepared, and the thing of it was, Gabe"—he turned to me—"your dog, the family pet, could sit right up there at the table with you. A special booster seat we designed, little napkin around his neck, same plates as the people, built-in water bowls, fire hydrant designs on the wallpaper."

"It's genius," Roman said.

"We pulled in ten thousand our first week. Lines down the block. We made the wire services, then the health department shut us down."

"That figures," Roman said, as if he'd had a lifetime of harassment from the health department.

"The sign outside showed this cartoon dog with a brush and can, painting through the word 'gone.' That was so cute, I thought." He sighed, seeming suddenly old and failed, and as much as I tried, I could not hate him. I liked him, I couldn't help but think, for the same reasons Roman did. I said nothing about the cars. We would just have to take our chances.

At our next show, out of nothing more than boredom, Vic suggested we shake things up a little bit. He wanted to wear the trench coat and hat and play detective for a while, and let Roman take over the megaphone duties. Sandy liked the idea, and suggested that I would look divine in silver lamé and a platinum wig.

I shook my head. "You aren't cool enough to be James Dean."

"Ha. You've never seen me sulk."

"Only for about half the trip," I told her. She looked at me. "I'm sorry I made you mad," I said.

She shook her head. "It's not you. It's not even Skip, really. It's just, I don't know . . . having a life."

Roman looked at Vic. "I don't like this whole idea, switching things around."

"Why?" Sandy said. "What man wouldn't want to see his oldest son looking glamorous?"

"I'm his *only* son."

"Not that," Roman said. "Well, yes that. But I mean we shouldn't tamper. What we have works. I say leave it alone."

It was Vic's turn to sulk, which made him look aged and worn in his white turtleneck and quilted paisley Nehru jacket. The Nehru jacket was a new addition to his wardrobe, picked up somewhere along the coast of Florida. Roman had told him it made him look like the couch in his grandmother's house. We were sitting around a picnic table in the snack area of the Tallahassee Exhibition Hall, under the bluish light of fluorescent fixtures. All around us gleamed the new paint and high gloss of the Four State Auto Show, with expensive sports cars revolving on carpeted turntables, exotic prototypes shining under stacks of lights.

"Just one day," Vic said. "That's all I'm requesting." Roman frowned. Behind us, a man and a woman were setting up a booth for Triple Miracle Car Wax, which the posters advertised was impervious to open flame and sulfuric acid. I thought this would be a great thing to have in case you accidentally drove your car into the middle of an industrial accident. On several of the revolving turntables stood young blond women with flannel shirts thrown over their bikinis, practicing their gestures and presentations. It seemed to me that if the exhibitors wanted to attract attention to some new car, the last thing they should plant beside it was a bikinied woman. Sandy noticed several of the women sitting behind us, eating pizza.

"I'm having all kinds of déjà vu here," she said.

"You're not even blond," I said. "How'd you fit in?" Roman picked up the megaphone and looked it over. Vic tried on Roman's fedora, which fell down over his ears, making him look like some old vaudeville comedian.

"I think I was an experimental brunette."

"Just today, Vic," Roman said. "If it screws things up, we admit that and change back."

The idea of Roman admitting to screwups seemed like another experiment, something new he might try, like the night he told me about pulling the plug on my merry-go-round rides. He gave in to Vic, I think, only because we were without our shower curtains during the Four State Auto Show, and our exhibit, like all the others, was covered by the price of admission. We had been prepaid, a fixed rate. Roman hated fixed rates, and was in a bad mood already.

Roman clicked the trigger on the megaphone. "HELLO, GABE," he said through it, making me jump. Sandy laughed at me.

"Would you quit that?" I said.

"QUIT WHAT?" This was starting to cheer him up.

"Don't put your mouth so close to the grille," Vic said.

"The first thing they teach at short-order-cook school," Sandy said.

"THAT'S A GOOD ONE, SANDY," Roman said. By now the girls in their flannel shirts were looking at us, laughing.

"HELLO, LADIES. NICE DAY FOR A CAR SHOW." He waved at them, smiling behind the megaphone.

"Oh Lord," Sandy said. "Modern technology has found a way to amplify your annoyingness. Wonderful."

"I don't think 'annoyingness' is a word," I told her.

"What is it then?"

Roman clicked off the megaphone. "Okay, Vic, you got a deal. We're already paid, money in the pocket, so what could go wrong?"

We spent the afternoon wandering around the exhibition hall before the opening of the show, looking at the displays and the shiny cars with their turbocharged engines, hopped-up stereos, power windows, alarm systems. One of the cars revolved fully upside down, the exhaust and suspension made from stainless steel. Roman didn't like any of the cars, primarily because they were new, I thought. We walked out to the parking lot, where collectors from area auto clubs were having a judged show for their restored vintage cars. All around us were flawless Thunderbirds, DeSotos, Bel Airs, and Packards, all with hoods up and shining engines exposed, signs posted asking viewers not to touch. Roman touched them anyway, rubbing the glossy paint, leaning in the windows to sniff the interiors. They were the cars he had grown up with, dreamed of owning, sitting now as if their assembly lines were still rolling. He moved among them the way our customers moved among the Death Cars, quiet and watching, as though disturbing those cars might unsettle the past. He shook his head, looking over the whole of them. "There is nothing like it, Gabe," he said. "Nice car, money in your pocket, a pretty woman in the passenger seat."

"So we reached the top of the list?" I said, thinking of his speech from the Land of Oz.

He bent down to eye the paint job. "What list?"

"Never mind," I told him. It was not the cars or the money or the women, I think now, but what they all had in common: a potentiality, a longing, a place where desire could endure. *That* was the top of the list. The problem with the years moving forward was simply that things lost their promise, wore out, failed. Cars, jobs, marriages, love. For Dutch, I knew, this was simple depreciation; for Roman, slow death.

Near the edge of the lot were the daily drivers, cars people had fixed up in their own backyards and garages, for a hobby. They were not the shining machines up for judging, not perfect, but they had seen hard work and they ran. The owners swapped parts over long folding tables; they had grease under their nails and wore satin baseball jackets with the makes and models of their cars embroidered on the back. Most of the fifties hot rods had fuzzy dice hanging from the rearview mirrors, some of them jacked up with wide racing tires and flames painted down the fenders. I liked these better than the fussy perfection of the other cars.

Roman grabbed my arm as if I were about to step into an elevator shaft. "Look," he said. "Would you look at that."

I looked, but didn't see much other than a man in a MoPar hat and sunglasses worrying a huge lump of tobacco in his cheek. He leaned against what looked like a funeral car, nodding his head in time with the car radio blaring out the Big Bopper, who sang "Chantilly Lace."

"Son," Roman said, loud enough for the man to hear, "you are looking at a 1968 Lincoln Continental Mark III triple black with suicide doors, hardtop, and opera lights. You are looking at perfection."

The man in the hat smiled and spat into a coffee mug. "Man knows his cars," he said.

"I know *that* car," Roman said. "Can you let me have a chew? I'm fresh out."

I stood watching while the man handed Roman the pouch of Red Man and Roman dipped his fingers in to pull out a clump. I tried in vain to catch his eye, but knew better than to say anything. Roman worked the tobacco in his mouth and spat on the sawdust. I kept waiting for him to gag or vomit, but he looked as if he'd been chewing every day of his life.

"I used to have a '62 convertible. Wife didn't much like what it did to her hair, though," Roman said. He and the man laughed and spat, and I saw then what was coming.

"Haven't owned a Lincoln since," Roman said, "but I would sure like to acquire this one."

"I can understand that, but I'm sorry to tell you it ain't for sale," the man told him. He grinned, his teeth small and browned. The Big Bopper was saying, "But . . . but . . . but . . . but."

For the first time, Roman looked at me. "Not for sale, huh? Well, I have to say, that's a shame." He smiled at me, just lifting the corners of his mouth, and I saw how happy he was right then, with an obstacle before him. There was, of course, no such thing as "not for sale."

Fifteen minutes later we were walking back toward the exhibition hall, the title and keys to the Lincoln in Roman's front pocket. He kept coughing and spitting, trying to rid his mouth of the taste of the tobacco.

"Okay, I admit that was the wide path," he said. "But I'm rusty one-on-one and I wanted him to say yes. Jesus, that tastes like horseshit." He spat again.

"Well, you did get him to say yes. One little thing, though."

"What?" He rubbed his teeth with his finger.

"You own that car now."

"Of course I *own* the car, and only eight hundred too. He could've got a thousand for it easily."

"What are you going to do with it?"

"Three guesses, Gabe. Here's a hint: it's a car."

"I know that, but you *have* a car already."

He was quiet a moment as we walked inside. I spotted Sandy across the hall, up on one of the empty carpeted podiums showing the flannel-shirt girls the proper way to gesture. Roman and I sat in a pair of folding chairs beside our Death Cars, still covered by tarps.

"Your mother loves riding around in a fancy car, Gabe. Steady money with our show, then the beach house, now this fine automobile. Things accumulate, Gabe. You wait and see, I'm wearing her down."

I wondered how to say to him that it was the wearing down of her over twenty years that had sent her away in the first place. I watched him take the keys for the Lincoln from their temporary paper clip and hook them onto his key ring. He jangled them, listening to the slight music they made against all the old keys: our house, the Chevy, empty sales offices left behind, forgotten padlocks and doors.

"Sounds like the key of G," he said, as if reading my thoughts. "As in 'Gee, that's one hell of a sweet car you got there.'" He smiled, flashing his gold tooth at me. I wanted to look him in his face and tell him you can add a new key, but the song is no different, the same wearing tune played over and over and over. I was tired of it. I tried to look at him, but he kept studying the keys in his hand. Across the way, Sandy was conducting a seminar in smiling, using her fingers to push at the corners of her mouth. The two girls were listening and nodding.

"So you did this for Gladys?" I said.

"Well, don't think I don't like a nice car, but sure, I think she'll like it."

I shook my head, took a breath. "Dad—"

"I won't let it happen, Gabe." He looked at me a moment, his chair creaking as he leaned back. His eyes searched my face. "If I bought the idea of it, maybe, even with that son of a bitch." He shook his head. "But I *don't* buy it. It's not her. It's just not."

"I don't think this is the way to make it not happen," I said.

He nodded. "I have twenty-five years of figuring her out, Gabe, so trust me a little bit."

I shrugged. Sandy and the girls kept smiling, gesturing at the empty air.

"Let me ask you," Roman said. "Do you buy it?"

The answer to that question felt like one of those relay races from Fun Day in the first grade, when you have to carry a teaspoon of water fifty yards to the finish line without spilling, and empty it into a bucket. If I could just keep all my thoughts about Gladys and Dutch and Roman in my head and move with them from one day to the next without any stray emotion spilling over, I might know the answer. But like the teaspoon race, it was all but impossible unless you went slow, and if you went slow, you lost. I would have the answer, I figured, right around Gladys and Dutch's tenth anniversary. *She's happier now*, I kept telling myself, though I really didn't buy it, but maybe only because that happiness meant that I would not be allowed to recognize her anymore. Roman sat watching me while my brain churned through all of this again. I was too much his son not to equivocate.

"I think it doesn't matter much what we think, if she's going to go ahead and do what she wants to do. And she wants to marry Dutch."

Roman flinched a little. "Well, that's fine, Gabe. And I'm going to do what I know to do to set things right. I won't let that son of a bitch win this."

I nodded, and Roman smiled at me. He slipped the keys into his pocket. "At least you're on my side in this thing," he said.

The show was an easy one, since there was no real pressure to sell it. We had fun, Roman walking around us with his bullhorn, making announcements like the red-haired man from Rusty's All-Star Venus Revue.

"JAMES DEAN, BONNIE AND CLYDE, JAYNE MANS-FIELD," he shouted. "LEARN THE TRUTH! SEE THE HORRIBLE WRECKAGE! IMAGINE THEIR LAST MOMENTS OF LIFE!"

Next door to us a couple of young guys in suits were selling discount accident insurance, and they regarded us as if we were angels sent to intercede on their behalf. On the other side, a woman in cutoffs and a Lynyrd Skynyrd T-shirt operated a small booth where she airbrushed T-shirts and license plates, most often with a picture of some enthusiast's beloved car. She kept asking Roman to turn down the volume on the bullhorn, though she smiled when she asked. Most of the time she sat listening to a police scanner and filing her nails. Sandy posed for pictures with all the middle-aged men and their teenage sons. She had added a Jayne Mansfield song to her act, "Promise Her Anything." I decided it could be Roman's new theme song. Vic had given up on wearing Roman's trench coat and fedora, which made him look like a little kid playing dress-up, and instead wore his own turtleneck and Nehru jacket. Most of the day I held my breath, waiting for one of the expert judges from outside to come by our show and spot the fake cars in the amount of time it took to glance at them.

"Would you relax?" Sandy said. She punched one of her fake breasts with her knuckles, knocking it into shape. "What is your problem? Stage fright?" With her nails she gently combed through my Vitalised hair. "What's wrong, Gabe?"

I looked into her green eyes, and wanted to tell her all of it. What I felt, I thought to say, was the opposite of stage fright; my fear was of pushing all of us *off* this stage and back into our small, ordinary lives. I imagined Dutch setting out a nameplate with my name on it, on a tiny desk beside his where I would sit and mirror his every movement. Even in my daydreams, things were not going well.

Just then a couple of men waved their camera at Sandy, and she went to have her picture taken with them. That left me standing alone with Vic, waiting for new customers.

"Quite a setup," he said to me. We still were not accustomed to one another, and usually we wound our way to talking about the cars or past failed ventures of his.

I smiled at him, looking hard at his face. "Yes, it is."

"And next spring I think I have a line on some additional memorabilia. Buddy Holly's guitar is one possibility, as is a hat that JFK wore in Dallas on that fateful day. Not exactly fitting our theme here, but certainly related."

My stomach knotted. "Where do you find these things, Vic?" I said. "Flea markets?"

He flashed his dentured grin. "I have a few associates who are collectors."

I could feel my face warming. "You know, Vic, I've learned a lot about James Dean," I said. "His movies, his life. And his car." This was true enough; following Sandy's example, I had learned all I could from a couple of library books and a few old magazines, most of it from our customers. It helped with the show to throw out a little scrap of trivia now and then.

"Body and soul into the effort," Vic said. "I like that, Gabe. An enterprising young man." He smiled again and clapped my shoulder. Goddammit, he liked me.

"For example," I said. "I know that a guy named Rolf Weuthrerich was riding in the car with James Dean, and he walked away from the accident with hardly a cut."

Vic nodded. "Very good, Gabe. Irony is part and parcel of what we are selling here."

"You're right, Vic," I said. "Irony is the word, all right."

Just then, two girls walked over toward us, both with lollipop sticks protruding from their mouths. They were about my age, one with straight blond hair, sandals, and toe socks, the other a pimply redhead wearing a T-shirt printed to look like a tuxedo.

"Oh, you wrecked your little car," the blond one said to me. "Are you hurt? You look like you have brain damage." They giggled together. The redhead chewed the ends of her hair.

I smirked at them and turned away. "Another example. I was thinking how ironic it is that James Dean got killed in a 1954 Spyder."

He looked at me and raised his eyebrows. "Where's the irony, Gabe? I'm not following."

"Who are you supposed to be?" the blonde asked me.

"I'm James Dean," I said. "I got killed in a Spyder." I tried to look tragically handsome. They were annoying, but the blonde was pretty. She pulled the Tootsie Roll pop from her mouth to check her progress toward the center.

"Oh, like that song," the redhead said. She held her Tootsie Roll pop like a microphone and started singing. *"James Dean, James Dean, I know just what you mean."* She shook her curly hair. The blonde joined in, singing into her Tootsie Roll pop, both of them off-key.

I looked back at Vic. "The irony is he was killed in a '54 Spyder, and this one here . . ." I patted the fender of the Porsche. "This one is probably a '57, built a couple years after he died."

I felt my heart thumping along the back of my neck. The girls put their arms around each other's shoulders, singing and giggling. *"James Dean, James Dean, you bought it sight unseen. You were too fast to live, too young to die, bye bye."* They rocked together, their hair swaying.

Vic looked stricken, as if I had just smacked him in the face. "Is there some problem with the car, Gabe?"

"The car's a fake, Vic, so cut the shit, okay?"

"Hey," the blonde said. She tugged Vic's sleeve. "Who are you? Dr. Spock?"

"There's some mistake, Gabe."

"Are you Dr. Spock or not? Which car did he die in?"

I looked at her, then Vic. He was wearing a baby-blue Nehru jacket and white turtleneck, his Libra medallion shining on his thin chest. "I think you mean *Mr.* Spock. Dr. Spock is a baby doctor."

"Gabe?" Vic looked afraid of me. He tried to smile.

"Just don't bullshit me, Vic, the way you've bullshitted Roman."

"What car did Mr. Spock die in?" the redhead asked. Together, they tried to contort their fingers into a Vulcan salute. "Live long and prosper," the redhead said to us.

"Vic, just tell me the goddamn truth. Please."

He shook his head. "Gabe, I want you to listen to me. Hear me out."

"Is Mr. Spock still alive?" the redhead said.

"Ladies, here you are," Vic said. He took out his gold money clip and handed them each five dollars. "Treat yourselves to some popcorn. And some manners." This was a first, I thought, his paying women for their absence.

"Oh, cool," they said. "Bye, James Dean and Dr. Spock." They walked off, still singing that I was too fast to live and too young to die. I wondered if those were the only two choices.

"I won't bullshit you, Gabe. I hold you in too high a favor for that."

I nodded. "So they are fake?"

"You seem to have deduced so already. You are smarter than most, Gabe. I didn't learn that they were counterfeit until some time after I paid eight thousand dollars for them."

I looked at him, trying to decide if this was another lie or not. I decided that it wasn't, only because by now I liked him.

"It's fraud though, Vic. We could go to jail. Unless we *say* they're fakes, and then who the hell would want to see them?"

He nodded. The show was nearing closing time, and the exhibition hall was clearing out. I looked over where Sandy and Roman were standing together, smoking cigarettes and laughing.

"Gabe, we will only go to jail if we're discovered in our duplicity. Thus far we haven't been. The cars look the part."

This had occurred to me as well. How many people could spot the difference between a '54 Spyder and a '57?

"I don't know, Vic. You should have fucking told us."

He combed his mustache with his fingertip, then looked at me.

"Fifteen years ago, when I was still a young man, I invested nearly twenty thousand dollars in an invention I thought could not miss. This was during the time when artificial Christmas trees were first the rage. Firs, cedars, Scotch pines, each more realistic than the next."

I nodded. "We have a fake tree. I mean, we did."

He smiled. "Many at the time came with aerosol cans of spray, to make one's house redolent of natural pine. To heighten the illusion of reality. Well, we took it one step further."

"We?"

"My young inventor and myself. In addition to the aerosol, our tree came with replacement snap-in branches full of browned needles. As the holidays wore on, you would replace the green branches with the browned ones. Plus, we included twenty glassine packets of brown plastic needles which you would sprinkle on the floor beneath the tree. The illusion of reality was complete."

"So what happened?"

"Total bomb. I think we sold ten of them in two years. I lost over twenty thousand dollars."

"I'm sorry to hear it, Vic, but still—"

"Where's the harm in fooling our customers, Gabe? They get exactly what they paid for, which is their emotional experience. Too much reality would be a bad thing, as it was with those trees, as it often is. Bad for our customers, bad for our pocketbooks."

He put his hand on my shoulder. The smell of cologne and Brylcreem enfolded me.

"From what I hear, Gabe," he said in a low voice, "too much reality was bad for your mother. As it would be for your father. He's finally made it, son. Don't take it away from him."

If nothing else, I decided then, Vic was sincere. He was the type of person I could imagine delivering a eulogy and making everyone in the funeral parlor cry as he talked about the dearly departed playing golf in heaven, hitting perfect drives against cloudless skies, drinking his favorite scotch at God's nineteenth hole. And he would believe every word of it. He might be full of shit, but at least he didn't *know* he was full of shit.

I nodded. "I already decided not to tell him. For now, anyway, so don't worry."

Vic smiled. "You truly are one of us, Gabe," he said. I halfway flinched. Most of the rows of fluorescent lights had gone out by now, and the girls in bikinis had donned their flannel shirts. Two workers were up on ladders taking down the big **WELCOME KNIGHTS OF COLUMBUS** banner that hung above the door. With the music and noise of the exhibits shutting down, I could hear the tiny hiss from our neighbor with the spray gun at the T-shirt booth. A young couple were watching her finish up work on their matching T-shirts. I walked over to watch with them. On each shirt, the woman had painted a fancy pink-and-red heart held aloft by a cherub with wings. The names of the couple, Randy and Melissa, were intertwined inside the heart, and beneath that was written "Love Angels." Except there was one problem. The woman had made a mistake on the shirts, so that both read "Randy and Melissa, Love Angles." I opened my mouth to say something, before they shelled out fourteen bucks on defective shirts, then thought better of it. They stood arm in arm, smiling at one another, waiting for the completion of the shirts that would forever seal their love in Day-Glo pink. They seemed happy enough to be each other's love angle. I didn't say anything. Sometimes, I repeated to myself, too much reality *is* a bad thing. I watched them hand over their money and slip on their matching shirts, still smiling.

The woman in the cutoff jeans waved at me as she packed away her painting supplies. I waved back, then turned to find the others so we could go for dinner. I saw them across the way, sitting at the picnic tables drinking from paper cups, Sandy with her wig in her lap, Roman trying to toss his fedora so it landed on her head, Vic checking his itinerary. They looked happy together, like some bizarre little family. As I started toward them, I saw the two girls—the blonde and the redhead—moving toward the exit. They waved at me. Above them, the workers were erecting the banner for the last day of the show, welcoming another of several groups who came in chartered buses at a special fare. The banner was folded over so I could not read the words, the two guys on their ladders pulling on opposite ends of the ropes that held it. The girls walked toward me.

"Bye, James Dean." They waved and smiled. I lifted my hand to wave to them as the banner opened up and my heart froze. Next to the logos for Coca-Cola were big black letters spelling out **WELCOME FRATERNAL ORDER OF POLICE**.

The girls started in their reprise. *"I know my life would look all right if I could see it on the silver screen."* They giggled and waved while I stood looking up at the banner, watching until the men were climbing down their ladders and I could hear Roman calling my name.

Tomorrow, I told myself, this place will be filled with cops.

Chapter 12

At a little past midnight, after looking at the *Travelhost* magazine drink coupons, restaurant ads, and area maps, and clicking through test patterns on the motel TV, I sat on the edge of the bed in my underwear reading passages from the Gideon Bible. I could not sleep, my mind full of the **WELCOME FRATERNAL ORDER OF POLICE** sign. I knew that everyone in the Bible was always on the lookout for signs of one kind or another, and though a plastic Coca-Cola banner hung in an exhibition hall seemed slightly less ominous than a burning bush, it still had managed to lodge in me a deep, gnawing fear. Knowing too that people often turned to scripture for comfort, I closed my eyes and opened to a random passage, turning the pages in the quiet hum of the room heater. Sandy slept in the next bed, her nose whistling and her brown thighs exposed. I lowered my fingertip and read a few verses in Second Kings, an episode when the prophet Elisha is teased by small children for his baldness, and he responds by calling a pair of she-bears out of the woods to devour them all. Somehow I did not draw much comfort from this.

 I closed the Bible, coughed, let the nightstand drawer bang shut, and sighed heavily a few times, hoping that Sandy would wake up and talk to me. Each noise I made prompted only a slight stirring, a long sigh, a tug at the covers. I had no more luck than four years prior, when I tried barking to raise her from her poolside naps. I looked at her, the tangle of hair around her soft face. "Welcome, Fraternal Order of Police," I said to her. I said it again, the words blending into some tuneless song I could not shake from my head. As I quietly sang it to Sandy, I knew it was not jail I feared for us— it would not come to that. What kept me awake through the TV national anthem and the magazine steakhouse ads and the wrath of an angry God was knowing that what we all had together would soon end. Possibly within the next twelve hours. The cars would go back to their junkyards, Vic to his poor investments, Sandy to her effort to find herself, Roman to the last job at the edge of the earth. I would be back in the beige halls and cramped desks of Page High School, learning algorithms and the dates of battles and treaties. All of us back into the fold of the ordinary. Gladys and Dutch would be so happy to see me, I thought.

I slipped my jeans and shoes on and walked out to the parking lot for a cigarette. The asphalt sparkled with broken glass, rainbow puddles of oil scattered across the surface like mirrors reflecting the arc lamps. Across the lot sat a couple in a car with the doors open and the dome light on, the car radio faintly playing "Sympathy for the Devil." Just as Mick Jagger asked if he could please introduce himself, I heard the motel door click closed and looked around to find Roman behind me.

"Hi, son. Looks like we're on a wavelength." He lit a cigarette, the flare of the match illuminating the T-shirt he wore, his navy-blue suspenders down around his hips, hat angled back on his head.

"Can't sleep either?" I said.

"Didn't even try," he said. "What I did try was calling your mother." I looked at him. Across the lot, the couple in the car rolled their beer bottles across the pavement.

"What did she say?"

He shook his head, blew smoke from the side of his mouth. "Didn't talk to her. I was all set to tell her about the new Lincoln, ask if I could take her for a drive sometime. She would have said yes, Gabe."

He looked at me as though this were a question, so I nodded.

"What happened?"

Roman shook his handkerchief from his pants pocket and dusted the hood of the Lincoln. He wouldn't look at me. "Dutch answered the phone, the sorry son of a bitch."

I shrugged. "It's his house, Roman. Real good possibility that he'd answer."

"It just seems fucked up that she's there. Of all the places she might be."

"But you *know* she's there."

He nodded, bent over to eye the surface of the paint. "Used to be this place in the mountains, up near the Land of Oz, remember? Place called Mystery Hill."

"Never heard of it," I said. Mick Jagger wanted to know who killed the Kennedys.

"Thing was, you'd park your car at the bottom of this hill, going up. You could look up at the top of it, Gabe. Put your car in neutral, release the brake, and damned if the car didn't roll up the hill. Tennis ball would roll up the hill, a marble, anything. We'd take the new guys out there and sucker them for half their money."

I laughed. "You should show me it sometime."

"You got a deal," he said. He took the Lincoln keys from his pocket. "The point is, that's how I feel about your mother over . . . you know . . . over at Dutch's. And now she's gonna *marry* him? It's against nature. It's the goddamnedest thing. I see it and can't believe it."

"It's like the opposite of faith," I said without thinking.

"What?" He stopped, cigarette held in his teeth, and looked at me.

"Well, I was just reading the Bible in the room, and faith is like when you can't see it but you believe it, right? I just said that what you said was the opposite." I shrugged.

"You got that right, Gabe. I have the opposite of faith that your mother ought to be with Dutch. That's exactly it." Mick Jagger stopped singing. The couple in the car closed their doors and the engine started, taillights coloring the haze of exhaust.

"You want to take a ride?" I said. "I still haven't really seen your car."

"Sure thing," Roman said. He lit another Pall Mall. "This night is lost anyway."

I walked around to the passenger side and opened the door, the inside glowing a soft dark red from the carpeting and headliner. Roman held up his hand.

"Sit in the back," he said. "I want you to see the work I did back there." I nodded, closed the door, and swung open the back suicide door. I knew that for the last day or so Roman had been working in the car, but I figured he was only cleaning it out, brushing the carpets with his whisk broom, cleaning the seats and dash. The rear seat was spacious, warm with the deep smell of leather, the tiny opera lights glowing a buttery yellow.

"What do you think?" Roman asked. Between the front seats, in the space for the armrests, he had wedged a tiny five-inch TV, with a cord running to the cigarette lighter. "Picked it up at an RV store. Runs on twelve volts. And look."

He reached around and swung open the door of a small wooden box mounted to the back of his seat. Inside the box looked like a spice rack, lined with tiny airline bottles of gin and bourbon and vodka, along with a pair of shot glasses. The lid of the door was held parallel to the floor by thin brass chains, forming a shaky tabletop.

"Built the whole thing myself," he said. "Almost like some fancy limo, you think?" I could see where the box was mounted to the seat back with screws, the whole thing slightly off-center, the varnish on the wood streaked with dark drips.

"It's really something," I said.

Roman started the engine and backed out, then rolled into the dark street, past the closed T-shirt shops and curb markets, past a plasma center and a public tennis court where a man stood hitting a yellow tennis ball against a wall. I clicked on the tiny TV and turned through the channels, finding nothing but snow and hiss.

"Still have to figure out how to hook an antenna to that thing," Roman said. The opera lights in the backseat still faintly glowed, and I could see my own face reflected in the rearview mirror. I turned off the TV and reached in the thin light for two airline bottles of Jim Beam, opened them both, passed one to Roman. We rode along in silence for a while.

"So," Roman said. "You been reading the Bible."

I leaned forward against the back of the empty passenger seat. "Bits and pieces. I read about some old guy who makes two bears devour this whole shitload of little kids. I don't remember getting that story in Sunday school."

"That's Elisha," Roman said. "Second Kings, Chapter Two, Verse something."

I turned and stared at the side of his face. He grinned, looking ahead at the empty streets. "I sold Bibles for six years, Gabe. You knew that. Most times, it was all *I* had to read, some late night or another in a thousand motel rooms."

I crawled over the back of the seat and sat on the passenger side, the wind tugging my hair at the top of the window.

"Not exactly a happy story," I said. "Few of them are, I guess."

"You mean in the Bible or in life? There're a few happy ones in both. Not that many, though."

"Like Noah's ark. I read that as a kid, in that book Gladys bought me? I think it was the *Golden Treasury of Bible Stories*, something like that."

Roman smiled. "She wanted you to 'grow spiritually.' I used to tell her the world made you do that anyway eventually. She used me as proof this wasn't necessarily so."

I laughed, but wondered if she might be right. "You read Noah's ark, all the cute little pandas and chipmunks in pairs, and all I could ever think about was the families and kids out there drowning in a mile of water."

Roman shrugged and tossed his cigarette out the window. "Everybody needs a do-over every now and then. Even God."

Even Gladys? I wanted to ask him, but didn't. Out the window I saw a man pedaling a bike one-handed, holding a grocery sack in the other hand. Roman turned the corner, headed down a street lit up with neon bar signs, the heavy thumps of music spilling out of doorways.

"About this other character, Elisha," Roman said. He seemed in the mood to talk. "He was really a fuckup if you think about it. The deal was he was this prophet in training, right?"

I smiled at him. "An apprentice, first-year man? Did he have an area manager?"

Roman laughed. "Well, that would be Elijah, I suppose. I bet Elisha got docked a week's pay for the she-bear incident. Thing was, he had all this authority, and he abused it."

"You don't think God wanted the kids to buy it?"

"Not a bit. I think Elisha gets his power, misused it. I think we're supposed to read it as a warning."

"If God likes you, don't let it go to your head?"

"Something like that."

I pulled two more Jim Beam bottles out of the makeshift bar and opened them. Roman drank his in tiny sips. I opened up the glove box, half expecting to see Roman's usual Crown Royal bottle and crumpled cigarette packs. Instead I found an old road map refolded so many times it felt like cotton, a travel pack of Kleenex, and a bag of sunflower seeds. I dug under those and found, strangely enough, a tiny rubber Pogo doll, dressed in an orange felt vest.

"Look at this," I said. "From the comics."

Roman took it from me and held it. Attached to the feet were two pieces of sticky foam. " 'We have met the enemy and he is us,' " Roman said. He stuck it to the top of the dash. "I found that stuff in there and just left it. It went with the car somehow."

I nodded and looked at Pogo. This seemed to be the whole of Roman's approach: that things should remain, no matter how much change you had to fight to make them do so. He wasn't much of one for do-overs.

"We need to talk," I said.

He drank, the tiny bottle hidden in his fist. "We are talking, son."

"Maybe we should stop awhile," I said.

"Sounds serious," he said. He swung the car into the parking lot of a miniature golf course, brightly lit with floodlamps shining down on the plaster elephants and windmills. The course was peopled by families, little kids up past their bedtimes, chasing green and red golf balls, knots of teenagers laughing. I thought for a moment about Sandy, and wondered if she might want to come here and send Dutch into the mouth of the big plaster lion.

"So, what is the big talk we need to have?" Roman said.

The talk itself didn't seem so big. I could tell him in ten seconds' time that the cars were fakes, that Vic had taken him, that the whole thing was over. The big part was in the years of fallout that came after. And that seemed to me huge, more than I could carry.

"Wanna go hit a round?" I gestured at the miniature golf course.

"What the hell is this about, Gabe?"

"Come on. You used to pull the plug on my merry-go-round rides, you owe me."

I got out of the car and headed toward the little orange hut. I heard Roman behind me, muttering as he followed.

I picked the blue ball and Roman the red, both of us outfitted with too-small putters, their rubber grips starting to split. At the first hole we had to hit through the legs of a big plaster gorilla, his dark face chipped, his body covered with scratchings of graffiti. Above us, bats flew in and out of the cones of white light from the floodlamps, and speakers mounted on the tall poles played tinny beach songs, first "Surfin' Safari," then "Yellow Polka-Dot Bikini." Roman still wore his T-shirt with his suspenders hanging down in loops, hat tipped back on his head. I noticed a few people looking at us. I checked my watch; it was one a.m. I hit my ball through the legs of the gorilla and watched it bounce along the green carpet, hopping over tiny ruts made by cigarette burns. My shot lipped out of the hole and I scored a two with the tap-in.

"Tough break," Roman said. He set his ball on the rubber mat and with no preparation or thought hit it. His shot bounced off the foot of the gorilla, glanced off one of the sideboards, and rolled into the hole.

"Hey, hey!" he shouted. He smiled at me, arms and putter raised in the air, and I thought that I had never seen him happier than in that small moment, and I knew then that this was what I loved in Roman, that he could find such complete happiness out of tiny chunks of time, in whatever success the next minute might bring him. It was what kept him out there for those years banging on doors, seeing most of them closed in his face, what kept him in the rain and in his marriage and in love with Gladys. Deep inside, he gave no more thought to the future than he needed to sustain the knowledge that there would always be another such moment, if not in this hour, then in the next, or the next. He loved the possibility of next moments.

"I'm kicking your ass, Gabe," he said. "Wanna lay a little wager on the game?"

"I don't have any money. I work for you, remember? If I had some, I might think about a wager."

He looked at me evenly as he pulled out his money clip and handed me a hundred. I looked down at Ben Franklin's knowing face. Roman dropped his ball on the rubber mat for hole number two and positioned it with his foot. On this hole we were required to roll the ball across a tiny carpeted bridge between two pale blue troughs of water guarded by grinning concrete alligators.

"Okay, now. Bet you ten bucks I win this hole," Roman said.

"Well," I told him, "I considered it like I said, and I decided against wagering." I grinned at him and pocketed the hundred.

"You little shit," he said. I could tell he was pleased with me.

"Hit the ball," I told him. He lined up his putt, and as he brought the putter back to hit, I shouted, "Stop!" Roman jumped and looked at me wide-eyed. People turned to stare at us.

"What?"

"Twenty bucks you don't ace it," I said.

A wide grin spread across Roman's face. "You're on." He lined up again, eyeing the grinning alligators.

"Stop!" I yelled again.

"Dammit, *what?*"

I grinned at him. "Good luck," I said.

He lined up a third time and hit quickly before I could yell again. His ball rolled left, into the pool of water.

"I think you missed," I said.

"Double or nothing," he said, "that *you* don't make a hole in one either."

"Sorry," I said. "I think there's a bigger future for me betting on your screwups."

He laughed out loud and handed me the twenty. Roman started

assessing the next hole while I rolled my ball past the alligators. On the next one, the ball had to roll through a tunnel in a little windmill house. I could hear the gears of the motor that drove the orange-painted blades, hear them lightly scraping the carpet. Roman wiped his golf ball with his handkerchief.

"Hey," he said. "That's your song they're playing. Five bucks says you can't name the singers." I listened over the scrape and whir of the windmill, over the shouts of children and teenagers, the rustle of wind in the palm trees, and heard Jan & Dean singing "*. . . won't come back from Dead Man's Curve . . .*"

"Isn't that where you got killed?" Roman said.

I looked at him, watched him as he stood watching me, bouncing the red ball on the blade of his putter, loving the son who would stay up through the night with him, half drunk and taking bets against the next perfect moment. A moment that refused to last. The song faded out.

"Hey, James Dean, hit the goddamn ball. I want to get my money back."

I shook my head. "The cars, Roman," I said. "It's the cars."

"What?"

"Dad," I said. "It's the cars. They aren't real."

"What cars?" He looked out across the lit-up parking lot.

"Our cars. James Dean, Jayne Mansfield. They're fake." I gripped the handle of the putter, my heart pulsing in the palms of my hands.

He smiled at me, blinked. "What is this, Gabe?"

"I mean it, Roman. They aren't for real." The smile dropped from his face as his ball skipped off the blade of his putter and disappeared under a bush. Behind us, a family lined up, waiting their turn.

"That's bullshit, Gabe. Who told you that?"

I thought a second. "I just know it's true. All of them came out of some junkyard somewhere."

Roman shook his head, rapidly blinking his eyes.

The man from the family behind us stepped up to us. "Do you mind if we play through?" he said. Behind him, his wife and two small kids patiently waited.

"Go ahead," I said. Roman stood muttering, turning the blade of the putter around in his fingers.

"Well," the man said, "you'll have to move, if you don't mind." He smiled, his face deeply tanned.

"Roman? We have to get out of the way."

He nodded without looking at me, and began walking diagonally across the course, cutting through the bushes, stepping over the carpeted holes, moving toward the car. I followed. When he reached the car he drew one of the tiny airline bottles from the seat back and sucked down the bourbon in two swallows, then skittered the bottle across the lot.

"Let's work through this from the start, Gabe," he said. "You seem to be the man with all the secrets these days."

I nodded. "I'd just as soon not have this one."

He held up his hand. "We don't know yet that you're right." He spoke slowly. "Tell me, son, how you think you know that the cars are fake."

I felt my eyes burning. "They're fake, Roman. I know they are."

He pointed his putter at me. "But we have those pictures, James Dean sitting in that very car. You have no proof of what you're saying."

"Vic," I said. "Vic told me."

Roman wiped his mouth with his hand. "So Vic just volunteers this information to you but not me. Mind telling me why?"

"He didn't volunteer. I made him admit it. He just confirmed what I already knew."

Roman nodded quickly, drawing deep, heavy breaths through his nose. "Okay. Now, son, don't bullshit me here, this is important. How do *you* know?"

I look around for the right way to say this. Pogo stood staring at us through the windshield of the car. Behind Roman's shoulder, the man who had played through our hole was bent over his little girl, helping her putt through the windmill. I looked into Roman's face.

"Dutch told me."

Roman's gaze held mine a moment, searching out the truth of my words. Then he raised the putter over his head and smashed it down in the center of the Lincoln's hood. The deep, echoing *thunk* ripped through me, and I shoved my shaking hands into the pockets of my jeans. Roman flung the putter far out across the road, where it noiselessly slid and bounced out onto the asphalt. I heard the guy in the tiny orange booth shout, "Hey!"

"Get in the goddamn car," Roman said.

I tossed my own putter gently across the orange railing into the bushes, then slipped into the passenger seat. Roman drove carefully out of the lot, as if easing around the next damage he might cause, and we headed toward the traffic light and the U-turn that would bring us back to the motel. As we turned, we passed over Roman's mangled putter, then merged into traffic. His hands were white on the steering wheel. We rode in silence. Roman turned into the lit-up parking lot of an all-night convenience store and cut the engine. We sat in the quiet, his key ring swaying from the ignition .

"I'm not mad at you," he said without turning to look at me.

"I know."

He walked inside the store and I saw him through the big front window pulling a pint of buttermilk from the dairy case, then asking the clerk for a pack of cigarettes. The clerk said something to him, probably offering matches, and I watched Roman shake his head and speak and laugh, and the clerk throw back his head and laugh with him. No matter how dark his mood, Roman could not help it, selling himself on everyone. In the car he still did not speak, instead sat punching the radio buttons while the car idled until he found a station playing dentist-office music. He downed the buttermilk in two swallows, grimaced, rubbed his stomach, tossed the carton out the window. We lit cigarettes from the orange coil of the dash lighter after unplugging the tiny TV. He kept circling the block, and I counted nine times we passed his mangled putter, as if it were some atomic clock marking the seconds of his growing despair. Roman kept shaking his head and occasionally saying "goddamn" under his breath, while I watched the dent in the shiny black hood of the Lincoln. As we moved through the city blocks, the reflections from the streetlamps and traffic signals made a slow, runny slide up the black lacquer, until they reached the dent, where they would swirl into colored circles and eddy around it before disappearing, the next sliding in behind it. I watched it for a long time, thinking about one time in ninth-grade science class, when Mr. Koontz brought in what looked like a small pool table, only the surface was full of curved depressions. When he pushed the cue ball across the felt, the ball would roll around and around the depressions, funneling toward the center. The model was meant to make us understand Einstein's general theory of relativity, showing the curves of space, the way light would be trapped by the gravitational pull of a black hole. I wondered if we were trapped now in some similar way, Roman deciding to forever move in circles, as if he had given up on any next moment by spending the rest of his life avoiding them. Finally, on our tenth pass, I noticed that the putter was gone, had been picked up or bumped into the ditch.

"What are you—we—going to do?" I said.

"I never was a cheater, Gabe. Not ever," he said. "Sure, I would pitch the hell out of most anything, and likely sell it too, but still and all, no matter what your pitch, a lawn chair is still a lawn chair, and a Bible is still a Bible."

I nodded. "So?"

"So, I'll tell you what. I'm not giving up this thing. None of it. I'm going to cheat, Gabe. I hate it with everything inside me, but I'll get over it. I'm going into the hall tomorrow and sell that show just like I always have. Nothing changed."

I sighed, tossed my cigarette out the window, and watched its tiny shower of sparks in my side mirror. "I have to tell you something else," I said.

"Damn, son, what else could it be? Have you seen X-rays of me or something?"

"Welcome, Fraternal Order of Police," I said.

"What is that supposed to mean?"

"Our guests tomorrow at the hall. About fifty cops. A whole busload."

Finally, he looked over at me, taking me in with his tired eyes. His gaze moved over my face for a moment, and then he started laughing. He shook with laughing, so that the ash broke from his cigarette and fell across his T-shirt.

"How much worse can it get, Gabe?" he said. "Huh? Okay, let me guess. The next sentence out of your mouth is to tell me that Dutch just made captain of the Tallahassee police department. He's driving the bus tomorrow."

I laughed with him as he elbowed me. "No, wait, wait," he said. "What you meant to say is that the cars are wired to explode the first time I tell a lie."

"Not even close," I said. "But the blood tests do show that Sandy is your illegitimate daughter. You owe her thirty thousand dollars in back allowance."

He laughed out loud, wiping his eyes with his thumb. He turned the wheel to steer us into the motel parking lot, then turned the key so the engine fell silent. "I nearly forgot to tell you, son," he said with mock seriousness. "I got us both jobs working for Dutch. We're his new butlers."

"No money," I said. "But all the free judo lessons we want." We sat in the deep red of the interior, giddy and laughing in all the darkness and quiet that surrounded us. Roman put his hand on my shoulder.

"I know one thing. If we sell this show tomorrow, son, you'll have something to tell your grandkids about."

"How come off-duty cops all dress like golfers?" Sandy asked me. "Except for the guns." I watched the crowds starting to form as we sat together in costume, eating pizza slices for breakfast. The cars were still under their tarps, and I tried to think of an excuse for just leaving them there. The show opened in ten minutes. Sandy kept her plate balanced on her lap, her hands busy with combing out her platinum wig. The busload of cops was there already, and Sandy was right, most of them wore plaid Sansabelt slacks or ironed blue jeans, with pastel-colored knit shirts, their badges pinned to their breast pockets, guns exposed in belt or shoulder holsters.

"It's a new version of golf," I said. "Your opponent gets a forty-yard head start, then you can fire at will."

"Ooh, want to play?"

"Sure. I'll even give you fifty yards."

She smiled. "What a dreamboat you are."

I didn't feel any real nervousness until I saw Roman come out of the bathroom wearing his trench coat and fedora, carrying his bullhorn. He had decided that morning to extend Vic's trade of duties, thinking, I was certain, that by his amplified words alone he could get us through this day. I watched Sandy tug her wig onto her head, her own brown hair wound into a tight knot. She smiled at me and began softly singing "Promise Her Anything," warming up for the show. Her voice sounded low and whispery, slightly off-key. She adjusted her fake breasts, waved to Roman across the hall. She finished the last verse of the song.

"What would you promise me?" she said. She looked at me, slightly tilted her head.

I shrugged. "What do you want me to promise?"

"Well, let's see. For starters, you already promised you wouldn't change and that you would remember what desire is supposed to feel like. Do you remember those?"

"Yeah, I do."

"Now I want you to promise that when something is really bothering you, you will come and tell me. Like, say . . . oh, now for instance." Her green eyes gathered me into their gaze.

Right then, I wanted to tell her more than I wanted anything. But I couldn't. All her life, she had been let down by things not being what they seemed. Dutch, marriage, Las Vegas. I knew it was only a matter of time before she figured out that Skip Kornegey was only some guy selling cans of paint in a small town. She still carried with her the **MISS NO   ROLI   7** bag, as if her five-year-old title still held sway, still meant something to someone. I remembered her golfing philosophy, how she tried to convince me (and herself, I thought now) that nothing had any meaning except the here and now. How could I take that away from her?

I smiled. "The song says 'promise her anything,' " I said to her. "Not 'promise her *every*thing.' "

"So you aren't going to tell me."

"Nope."

She looked evenly at me. "But you're admitting that there is something to tell?"

I looked closely into her eyes, and she into mine, both of us staring until we started to grin. I let the moment pass. "Nothing to tell," I said. "Everything's fine."

She looked at me a moment longer. "I don't know if I believe you," she said.

"Well, Miss Goforth, it's time to start the show." She adjusted her wig a final time and told me we would talk later.

By now the display women had stashed their flannel shirts, donned their high heels, and stood posing beside the various cars. The hiss from the spray booth had started up, and I heard small pops as Roman nervously clicked the bullhorn on and off. That morning he'd refused breakfast and instead stood outside the Tast-T-Cup diner, chain-smoking and pacing in tiny circles, grimacing, rubbing his stomach, drinking the bottles out of the back of the Lincoln. I'd sat pushing eggs around my plate, my own stomach twisting in knots while Sandy and Vic downed their pancakes and coffee. Now whenever I looked at Roman, he gave me a thumbs-up, his face white. I helped Vic pull the tarps from the cars and fold them away, while he babbled on and on about Ponce de León and the fountain of youth. I wasn't listening. Already, several of the cops stood looking at the cars, some with their kids in tow. They seemed to have a natural affinity for wrecked cars.

"STEP RIGHT ON UP, HAVE A GOOD, LONG LOOK," Roman shouted through the bullhorn. This was not his usual pitch. "SEE THE . . . UM . . . THE FINAL DESTRUCTION OF THE HOLLYWOOD DREAM."

He sounded confused, his words halting.

I walked over to Sandy. "He's drunk," I said.

She rolled her eyes. "Oh, Lord. I hope there aren't any cops around." By this point we were surrounded by them, Vic pulling them in by pairs to tell them about the crashes and the young stars cut down in their prime. Others slowly walked around the cars, leaning in the broken window of Jayne Mansfield's car, giving a tiny round of applause when Sandy finished her song. Roman paced around us, his words distorted through the bullhorn.

"COME ON UP, BOYS. TAKE A CLOSER LOOK." I half expected him to say, "I dare you." He kept looking at me. I leaned against the fender of the Porsche, tugged up the collar of my leather jacket. Two of the off-duty cops stood near me, pointing to the crumpled hood of the car, talking about the speed of impact. One of them bent down to peer under the car, then motioned for his partner to join him. I watched them, holding my breath. Sandy stood by the Jayne Mansfield car, her arms around two men, all of them smiling as Vic snapped a Polaroid. Roman motioned me over.

"You gotta *talk* to them, son. You're standing there looking like you're guilty of every unsolved crime on the books."

I nodded. "You're pretty drunk," I said.

He smiled. "Hey, I do some of my best work drunk." I thought of the last time he'd been drunk in dealing with the police, in the driveway of Dr. Ballister's house when he tried to bribe Officer Mitchell and ended up spending the night in jail.

"Did you tell Vic?" I asked.

"I thought *you* told Vic."

"No, I mean tell him that you're on to this whole thing."

Roman nodded. "I told him. He thought I was going to beat the shit out of him. I said I was keeping my options open. He offered to buy me out."

"Buy you out?" I watched the two cops open the door of the Porsche.

"For what I put in."

"Let me guess, you said no."

Roman frowned. "Of course I said no. Break even, when I'm up forty thousand already? Not too smart, Gabe."

I nodded. "I guess not."

"Listen, son, you have to distract these guys. Show them every last inch of the car, but keep your mouth moving. Divide their attention, so they don't think about anything for too long." He rubbed his stomach. "Dammit, I need some buttermilk. Go talk to them, Gabe."

As I walked toward them, one of the cops, a big football-player type with slicked-back gray hair, waved and smiled at me. "Here's the man right here, with hardly a scratch on him." His partner waved and moved off toward Sandy and the Jayne Mansfield car.

I laughed, my brain searching for something to say. "Did you know," I asked, "that James Dean was traveling in excess of a hundred and thirty miles per hour when he crashed?"

He smiled again. "You ought not drive so fast, son. See, if I had pulled you for a ticket, you'd have cursed me, but I might have saved your life." He laughed out loud at our little game of pretend.

"You might have. In fact, he, I mean I, was pulled over for a speeding ticket, right outside Bakersfield. And there were two survivors of the crash." I rambled on, realizing I was merely repeating things I had heard from Vic over the last couple of months.

He interrupted me. "What year is this Porsche?"

"One of the survivors was a college student by the name of Donald Turnipseed. He was the driver of the Ford Tudor that James Dean . . . that I crashed into."

"Interesting," he said. He opened the door and sat in the driver's seat, wiggled the gearshift. "What year did you say?"

"It's a '54 Spyder," I said quickly. "Mr. Turnipseed walked away from the accident, as did Rolf Weuthrerich, who was—"

"A '54, you said?"

"That's right." I felt my ears warming. Behind us, I heard Roman talking through the bullhorn, no longer shouting, but merely talking, as if no one were listening. I heard him say, ". . . everything good hurries toward its end. . . . It's true ladies, gents. You can be a movie star, some high-priced celebrity, and it all gets wiped out in an eyeblink. . . ." He was slurring his words. Vic was snapping Polaroids, the camera flashing every few seconds. Sandy leaned back across the hood of the Buick Electra, posing for a photo.

The gray-haired cop put his hands on the wheel, looking out

over the crumpled hood. "This doesn't much look like a '54. I think you have some of your facts mixed up, son."

I laughed, too loudly and insistently, as I had heard Roman do all those years he'd stood on countless doorsteps, trying not to let the door slam. "I think I know what car I died in," I said. I laughed again and gave him a friendly slap on the shoulder. He didn't look at me.

"I think you ought to, but this isn't what you say." He climbed from the driver's seat and stood looking down at me. "Do you have the title for this car?"

"I think you just might be right," I said. "I was killed in a '57, not a '54. Sometimes these little details are hard to keep straight." *You have to sell this*, I told myself. *You know how to do this.* "You've been dead twenty years, you get a little confused."

He smiled, no humor in his face. "I never said it was a '57 either."

Just then Roman circled past and saw what was happening. He clicked off the bullhorn and stepped over toward us. I could smell the alcohol on him.

"Roman Strickland," he said, and shook hands.

"Sergeant Meschery."

I reminded myself, as I had so often, that Roman could sell anything.

"Enjoying the show, officer?" Roman said.

"Well, let's say I'm learning a lot. I was just asking your partner here if he could show me the title to this car. We had a little disagreement about what year it was made."

Roman looked at me a moment, his face white. "The title?" He shook his head. "It's not like we plan to register these and go racing around the streets. We don't have titles. Hell, we don't even have engines in the damn things." He pulled out a cigarette and lit it up. The cop watched him for a minute.

"You aren't allowed to smoke except in designated areas."

"That's fine by me." He stamped his foot on the floor. "I hereby designate this a smoking goddamn area." He laughed out loud, thinking that his jokes were breaking the tension.

Sergeant Meschery took the cigarette from Roman's lips and handed it back to him. "Put it out."

"I thought we were getting a busload of *off*-duty cops." Roman dropped the cigarette and stepped on it. What happened to them? Stuck in traffic?"

At this, finally, Sergeant Meschery did genuinely smile. He looked us over a few moments longer. "I'm keeping you from your show, boys," he said.

"Flat rate, so don't worry too much," Roman said.

"Meaning what?" He picked up Roman's cigarette butt and tossed it in a trash barrel.

"He means we're prepaid for the show, so there's no reason to work too hard," I said.

"You make out pretty well with this?" he said.

"Oh hell yes," Roman said. "Sometimes three thousand a night, few times a week." *Don't push, don't push*, I thought.

Sergeant Meschery raised his eyebrows. "Impressive."

"Let me tell you, Sarge," Roman said. "We make out like bandits."

"Dad, I think it's time we got back to it," I said.

"That's for sure a lot of money," Sergeant Meschery said. "If you don't mind, I'd like to swing around later today and check this out a little more. Maybe look over whatever papers you do have on the cars."

Roman cut his eyes at me. "Be happy to show you the ropes. Maybe around six or so?"

"Last day of the show," the sergeant said. "Doors close at four today."

Roman tapped the side of his head with his knuckles. "That's absolutely right. Completely slipped my mind." He was weaving a little as he stood there.

"I'll be back in a bit," Sergeant Meschery said. We watched him walk away, his leather shoulder holster bumping against him.

"We're fucked," I said.

Roman took off his hat to run his hand through his hair. "Almost, yeah. But he isn't coming back for a while, so we have some time to think of something."

"What do we have time to think of?"

He smiled. "You're asking the big questions, son." Behind us, Sandy started up singing again, slinking around in her silver dress.

"What if we just left? Right now."

He shook his head. "If we duck out, they'll be on the wire to every podunk police department up and down the coast."

"What, then?"

"We'll ask her." He nodded toward Sandy. "She's always the one with the good ideas."

I watched her smile and blush as the little group around her clapped. I turned back to Roman. "No," I said.

He squinted at me. "What do you mean, no?"

"I mean I have not asked you for one thing this entire trip, maybe my entire life—"

"You asked for money at the little golf course."

"I mean something that costs you, Roman. Not money. And right now I'm asking you not to tell Sandy. Don't ask her, don't let her know."

"You didn't tell her?"

"No, and I'm not going to. And neither are you."

Roman replaced his hat on his head, took a deep breath, and let it loose. He looked at me. "Okay, son. If you say."

Two hours later we were watching every golf shirt and shoulder holster to see if they might be attached to Sergeant Meschery. All afternoon I had watched Roman pull the tiny airline bottles from the deep pockets of his trench coat, one after another, like a magician producing scarves. He kept talking through the bullhorn, rambling on drunkenly, and twice Sandy asked me if I ought to take him back to the motel and bathe him in hot coffee. Vic largely avoided us. I think he thought himself an honorable, forthright man in his own cheating, lying way, and was mortified that we knew he had taken us. Or been taken; I couldn't decide which.

I looked up, and there they were. Sergeant Meschery with two of his friends in tow, the three of them circling the Buick, bending under it, leaning over the windshield and writing down the vehicle number. Roman had circled around behind the Bonnie and Clyde car, and I motioned to him, pointed to the three cops conducting their investigation into our new life. He looked at me, the bullhorn held away from his mouth as if it were waiting for words he did not have. He rubbed his mouth, fumbled in his coat for a cigarette. His hands shook as he lit it, then popped the bullhorn, the smoke swirling out around his hoarse, amplified voice.

"What would you do?" he said, not shouting, just speaking. "Stop and think about it as you look at the ripped metal of these cars, as you finger the jagged glass, touch the bloodstains on the upholstery, and ask yourself what you would do in those final half seconds when you see it coming. When you round that curve and know it's too fast or cross that center line and watch the headlights coming up at you, and in that second you know. What would you do, ladies and gentlemen?"

He stopped long enough to take a drag from his cigarette. By now people were pausing to listen to him.

"How about it, Sergeant Meschery? What would you guess was James Dean's last thought? Vic? Gabe? Sandy? Anybody? The last second, you see it coming, it's the end and you damn well know it, what do you think about? Do you have time to wonder about your life? Wonder if you fucked it up? Maybe you see it all and you think what you could have done different? Are you with me, anybody?"

Sandy looked at me, confused. Vic stood between the cars, watching and listening. Roman looked at us as if searching for the next thing he could say.

"Mr. Strickland, we'd like to talk to you a minute or two, if you could shut that down a minute," Sergeant Meschery said. "We have a couple questions." I moved to help some elderly woman up out of the driver's seat of the Porsche. I heard Roman speak again through the bullhorn.

"We have one response. Sergeant Meschery would spend his last moments looking for answers. We aren't too far apart in this, sergeant."

The crowd of onlookers started to move on. A moment had passed, and somehow in that space of time he had become only a drunken man with a bullhorn, rambling and slurring.

"Mr. Strickland," Sergeant Meschery said.

"Let me make clear one point, the difference between us, sergeant. I would . . ."

Roman turned his head to the side, his face twisted in a hard grimace. "Dammit," he said. He gripped his stomach, as he had so often when he needed another carton of buttermilk. I took a step toward him. Something was wrong.

"Let's end this nonsense now, Mr. Strickland," Sergeant Meschery said.

"Shit." Roman lowered the bullhorn and sat on the fender of the Electra, his hands moving from his stomach up toward his chest, fingers tangled in the belt of his trench coat. I tried to get my mind around what was happening, wondering how this was meant to get us past Sergeant Meschery.

Roman looked at me, wincing. "Gabe—" He slid down and sat on the concrete floor, his legs splayed out before him, his face red and shiny with sweat.

Sergeant Meschery started toward him. "We might be looking at a heart attack," he said to the other cops. He grabbed my arm. "Find a blanket and ask your friend to call an ambulance."

Sandy kicked the high-heel shoes off her feet and ran for the phone booth at the concession stand. I moved halfway toward Roman as the officers helped him lie back on the floor, pillowing his head with his brown fedora. All around me swirled the noises of piped-in music and PA announcements. Over and over I said Gladys's name under my breath as I grabbed one of the blue tarps and ran with it toward Roman. I sat down next to him as Sergeant Meschery spread the plastic over his chest. The tiny airline bottles had rolled over by the feet of the people who stood around us. Roman's keys and lighter spilled on the floor beside him.

"Ambulance will be here shortly, son," Sergeant Meschery said.

Thin trails of sweat covered Roman's face. The blue tarp crinkled and puckered as his chest moved beneath it with his quick, shallow breaths.

"If it's bad, call Gladys," he said to me, his voice thin, watery.

"I will," I said. I took his hand, holding it through the tarp, feeling the hard angles of his wedding ring and wristwatch. "You're going to be okay," I said.

He cut his eyes up at me. His voice was barely audible as he spoke, his fingers slowly gripping mine. "Yeah," he said, the word falling somewhere between vow and question.

Chapter 13

Vic, Sandy, and I sat in the orange-carpeted waiting area, the evidence of renovation all around us: ceilings draped with plastic, wires and cables hanging down, scaffolding crowding the corridors. We sat in silence, still in our costumes, Vic with his eyes locked on the TV screen, watching *The Midnight Special*. Finally, Sandy spoke.

"You'd think they'd finish the place before they start inviting patients." She looked at me, her knot of hair unraveling. "I'm sorry, I shouldn't joke. I joke when I get nervous."

"It's okay," I said. She smiled at me, touched my hand.

Vic looked up from his reverie. "The difficulty is in finding the right words at a time like this. Rod McKuen said, 'Who kills a man kills a bit of himself.'"

"Which bit?" Sandy asked.

"He's not *dead*, Vic. Nobody killed him."

"I fear I might have, young man," he said. "God help me if I have."

"They're just running him through some tests. That's what they told me," I said.

"They always say that," Sandy said. "It's one of those things doctors learn to say at doctor school. They spend a lot of time practicing saying, 'We're running some tests,' or 'It's too early to tell.' Oh, and also, 'The next twenty-four hours are crucial.' I almost forgot that one."

Vic drank from a paper cup of coffee. "We should have word by now. Perhaps we should inquire again at the nurses' station."

"You asked them three times already, Vic," I said. "I asked twice."

Sandy rubbed her hands together. "I'm losing. I only asked once."

"It's too early to tell," I said.

"You should be a doctor, Gabe," Sandy told me. "You say that so professionally."

By the time we'd arrived at the emergency room, Roman had been talking, giving me instructions, worrying about his lost hat. He kept telling me that I should check on the cars, that I should call Gladys and let her know. The last part I had done, pouring all my change into the slot and spinning the dial for Dutchland as I had so many times in the last two months. Gladys began crying almost immediately, saying over and over that she knew this would happen, she knew it, as if my call had been something she'd waited for a long time. By now it was nearly midnight, and I imagined Gladys and Dutch making their way to the airport, flying over lighted cities in the dark, her fingers nervously twisting strands of her hair. She didn't know when they would be there, she said, but they would be there. As soon as they could. As she hung up, she told me she loved me and that she still loved Roman, even though I could hear Dutch right there in the room with her, asking questions.

Finally, a Dr. Fernald walked out to see us, his paper booties rustling across the floor. He wore thick, square-framed glasses. "Are you Mr. Strickland's father?" he asked Vic.

"His business partner."

"And you?" He looked at me.

"I'm his son."

"I'm the daughter," Sandy said. I looked at her but said nothing.

"Here's where we are. He's stable in ICU, we're running fluids, he is talking and watching TV. We've run an electrocardiogram and a routine chest X-ray, and so far so good."

"So far so good what?" I said.

"No blockage that we can see thus far. No arterial damage has revealed itself. We have more tests to run. An angiogram seems in order. In any heart patient, the subsequent twenty-four hours are crucial, of course, as we try to devise a strategy."

"Can we see him?"

"He's resting, and his roommate is just getting settled in. Maybe we should wait till morning." He shook my hand and abruptly left.

"Hey, he's good," Sandy said. "He got in the test thingy and the twenty-four-hour thingy in one breath." She rubbed my shoulder. "He's going to be okay, sounds like, sweetie."

"They have more tests," I said.

"I know, but he'll be fine. Wait and see."

We sat down again in the waiting area. On the TV, Wolfman Jack gave us the history of Sly and the Family Stone, then a commercial came on for the Pocket Fisherman. I looked out the narrow window, cars slipping by on the wet pavement, a pawnshop sign flickering, a man pushing an empty wheelchair under the lights in the parking lot.

I glanced at Sandy. Her silver dress looked wrinkled, wilted. "You're the daughter?"

She smiled. "That's right, little brother. They only let family in to see him. I want to see him." I nodded. We watched Sly and the Family Stone singing "Everyday People" while Wolfman Jack stood offstage dancing and making his eyes bug out. Vic ignored the TV and took out his itinerary book, going through the back pages where he kept his accounting of all the money we'd taken in and spent.

"Let's find the cafeteria," Sandy said. She pointed toward the TV. "He's scaring me."

"Who?" I said. "Wolfman Jack or Vic?"

Vic looked up. "You two go on. I have a little figuring to do here."

"Come on, Gabe," Sandy said. "We'll let Scrooge McDuck count his pennies."

We walked through the halls filled with gurneys, clusters of IV stands, sawhorses surrounded by power tools. Sandy picked up a circular saw and asked me if I needed my appendix out. She was trying hard to distract me. We rode the elevator down to the first floor, where the cafeteria was closed, its entrance blocked by a steel chain. Instead we found a tiny room with soda and snack machines, and we sat together in old high-back wooden wheelchairs, drinking Pepsi and eating Ding Dongs. I kept rolling my chair a few inches back and forth.

"I don't know what's going to happen," I said.

"You are going to wait to hear that Roman is fine, then in a week or two we'll get moving again, start the show back up," she said. "Jayne Mansfield and James Dean will keep inspiring lust in the hearts of men and women everywhere."

I shook my head. "The show is over, Sandy."

"Oh, come on, Gabe. Stop sounding so apocalyptic. I told you, everything will be fine."

I let my chair bang into the snack machine, then watched the food inside shake. A pack of peanuts dropped down the chute.

"I mean it. The show is over. We're done."

She put her hand on the arm of my chair to stop the rolling. "Mind telling me why?"

I hesitated. "Roman needs time to recuperate," I said.

"That's bullshit," she said. I looked at her, the tangle of hair around her face. I was surprised to see her blinking back tears. "I don't need to be protected, Gabe. I'm all grown up. Why don't you tell me what's going on really?"

I shook my head. "You don't need to be protected, but maybe I need to protect you anyway." She started to speak. "Why don't you just let me?" I said. She was quiet, watching me, her eyes shining.

"Just like that," she said.

I snapped my fingers. "Just like that, yeah."

She shook her head, wiped her eyes with her knuckle. "It's always about what's over. I mean, that could be the title of life. We could call it *Just Like That*. The whole thing."

I nodded. "After today, that's what I worry about Roman. That he'll be gone someday, just like that."

She rubbed my arm. "He'll be okay, Gabe. I swear he will."

I retrieved the peanuts from behind the plastic door of the vending machine and handed them to her. "Don't say I never gave you anything," I said.

She laughed. "You gave me a lot, more than you know. It's nice having somebody you can't mess up with. Maybe I'm assuming a lot."

"You're not," I said. "It's true, you can't."

"But that might not always be true, though," she said. "Things change. I don't have to tell you that."

I thought about this. "What if we just decided, right now, that it wouldn't change? That no matter what else changes anywhere else, there will be this little island where you can't ever mess up with me."

She looked at me. "God, that would be . . . just, so perfect."

"Okay, then. You got it."

"Really?"

"Yeah, really. But vice versa too, that's part of the deal."

She leaned across and kissed me softly on the lips, then held me for a moment.

"Where are you going to go?" I said.

"Well, I was thinking of racing you down the hall in this thing." She rolled forward in her wheelchair.

"I don't mean that. I mean, what are you going to *do*? Later."

She shrugged. "Visit Roman? Flirt with doctors?"

"Sandy."

"Now, Gabe, what did we learn about golf?"

I squinted up toward the ceiling. "Keep your eye on the ball."

She frowned. "Wrong."

"Both eyes?"

"Strike two." She spun around so her chair banged into mine.

"Remind me," I said, only because I wanted to hear her explain herself again.

"Here and now. That's all that matters, all that's worth worrying about. Breakfast to dinner. Self-validating acts. Is it starting to come back to you now?"

"Slowly."

She opened the peanuts and dumped some in her mouth, then poured some into my palm.

"This has been a great now, a thrilling now. One of the best I ever had," she said, chewing. "But that's the problem with now, it keeps insisting that it wants to be then."

"A promotion," I said. "Moving up the ladder."

She shrugged, brushed hair from her face. "Demotion in my view. When nows become thens, I'm through with them, and then I go looking for another. Haven't failed to find one yet."

"So Skip is the next one?"

She smirked. "Maybe for a bit. He doesn't have much permanent now potential, though."

"Well, here's my idea. Hang around a couple of years, then you and me will get married. I can always be now."

"If you have your father's genes, I don't doubt it. Roman . . ."

She shook her head. "By force of will, he keeps everything now, doesn't he?"

I laughed. "No matter how gone it is. It's selling that made him that way. Always the next moment."

"A bunch of nows standing in line, right?"

I smiled. "Does this mean we're engaged?"

She laughed, reached and stroked my face. "Aw, sweetie. We'd get divorced someday, you'd become a then, and I'd have to watch you pout for the next thirty years. That little island you just made for me would sink right into the ocean."

I shook my head, unlocked the brake on my chair. "I'm already Gladys's then. I don't think I could take being yours too."

"More likely I'll be *yours* in a few years. But you aren't Gladys's, and I think you know that. And you won't ever be mine either. I promise."

"Are we still going to race? I should get back upstairs."

"We'll race if you're not scared." I smiled at her, let my chair bump hers. "Here, hold this," she said. "I'm still hungry, and I want to go ahead and buy my victory Ding Dongs ahead of time."

She set her tattered **MISS NO   ROLI**   7 bag in my lap, dug her coin purse out, and fished around for quarters. I watched her wheel herself to the machine and drop the money in, the little coils in the machine pushing her junk food over the edge.

"Talk about your thens," I said.

"What?" She opened the package, took a bite of her Ding Dong.

"This." I held up the tattered bag, the red embroidery threads hanging down in thin curls. Sandy looked at me as if I'd slapped her, a lump of food bulging her cheek.

"I mean, look at this thing, Sandy. You don't need this."

She did look at it, as though for the first time in a long while. She ran her fingers over the front of the bag, where her old title had been stitched, the letters now mostly gone, the memory of them outlined in tiny needle holes. Her face flushed red and her throat moved as she swallowed her mouthful.

"Now you've gone and hit on the problem of thens," she said. "Pretty soon they're just yellow photos on some scratchy slide projector screen somewhere. No one much cares but you."

"And you still care," I said, not as a question.

"It was the one time it felt like everything lined up the way it was supposed to. That one time when things worked out just the way I'd imagined. So, yeah, I do care. Not that I should."

I looked at her and saw she was crying, as I sat there still awkwardly holding the bag in the air between us.

"Life isn't built around things working out, Gabe," she said.

"I know."

"I'm not sure you do, but I want you to keep it in mind. You're going to need to."

I nodded. "Okay."

She took the bag from me, tipped it over, and dumped its contents into her lap. Wallet, keys, lipstick, comb, movie stubs, coupons, compact, wadded Kleenex, all piled around the unfinished Ding Dong. She handed the bag back to me.

"Pitch it," she said.

"Really?"

"After all *that*? Hell yes, really. Toss the damn thing."

I threw the **MISS NO   ROLI   7** bag toward the wall, where it slid down into the plastic bag that lined the trash can, the rope handles hanging out over the edge.

"Nice shot," she said. "Now hold this stuff." She dumped the contents of her lap into my hands.

"What do you want me to do—"

"On your mark, get set, go," she said, then turned and wheeled out of the snack room and down the hall, her arm muscles making tiny jumps as she worked the gray wheels. I pitched her stuff into an empty chair and followed, my own rubber wheels squeaking and sliding. I caught up within ten feet of her, just in time to see her approaching the corner toward the hallway, where she slowed and glanced back at me. All these years later, it is this image I have kept of Sandy, looking back over her shoulder, her mouth open in a wide smile, wisps of her hair lifting with the breeze she made, the long folds of her silver dress shushing along the tile floor. She waved goodbye, then braked enough to steer around the corner, her wheelchair leaning a little. I braked with my hands to a stop, and sat watching the blank air where she had just been, watched the image of her leaving flood into my brain. I sat there, letting it, until I heard her call my name to ask if I had gone and died on her, why it was taking me forever to catch up.

Early the next morning, Dutch and Gladys arrived, waking Sandy and me from our fitful sleep in the orange waiting-room furniture. We all exchanged hugs, and as soon as I touched her, Gladys started crying, as though I'd hit some hidden switch. Though she still looked tanned and fit from her swimming, her eyes were dark, rimmed with a night's worry. Dutch stood looking grim and embarrassed, watching a game show on the TV, where a woman joyfully tried to guess the price of a pineapple. Sandy left, offering to get all of us coffee from downstairs.

"What have they told you, Gabe?" Gladys said. "When can we see him?"

"I don't know, to both. They said they are running tests, that they haven't found what they're looking for."

"Well, are they looking for something good or something bad?"

"I don't know."

She bit her lower lip. "I hate doctors. So elitist. They withhold their information like it's divine revelation."

"Don't start that, Gladys," Dutch said. "You know it won't help any."

"What else?" she said to me.

I shrugged. "He is resting comfortably."

"That's a first," she said. This annoyed me, suddenly, as if in the last few months she'd given up the right to make jokes about Roman. She bit her nail.

Just then a nurse walked up to us, looking us over. Her hair swung in a long, dark ponytail against her green scrubs. She stood there until we stopped talking.

"Are you James Dean?" she said.

"Well, yeah," I said. "I used to be."

"Mr. Strickland said to get James Dean in there to see him. At least we know he's not hallucinating." She smiled and asked me to follow her. Dutch and Gladys followed behind.

"I'm really sorry," she said to them. "Only one at a time in CICU."

I walked with her down the long, pale halls, her ponytail keeping time with our steps. We kept edging around patients in wrinkled bathrobes, slowly pushing their IV stands.

"How's he doing?" I said to her.

"Every time I say something about CICU, he pretends he's holding binoculars and says, 'See, I see you too.' He's pretty funny."

I smiled. "But how *is* he?"

"Dr. Fernald is there to talk to you. Ask him." She pointed me into Roman's room. "You were really good in *Giant*," she said, then patted my shoulder and left.

The first thing I saw in Roman's pale green room was a security guard with a shotgun in his lap, who sat watching Merv Griffin on the wall-mounted TV. Dr. Fernald was nowhere around.

"Hey son," I heard Roman say. He leaned forward to peek around the striped curtain that separated the two beds. "Did you meet my roomie?"

I noticed then, under a rumpled pile of blankets and sheets, a wiry, wrinkled, gray-haired man, his ankles shackled to the steel bedframe. He waved to me, his eyes yellowed and rheumy. The chains clanked as he shifted in his bed.

"That's Warren," Roman said. "He came here for a vacation."

"Fuck you," Warren said, his voice deep and watery. The guard laughed at something on TV. Warren grinned, his teeth small and yellowed.

"Dad, are you okay? They won't tell us anything." Roman was sitting up in bed, tubes in his arm and nose, a monitor sounding out its green blip with steady beeps. His hair was messed up, and he'd thrown his suit jacket around his shoulders, to cover the hospital gown.

Roman gestured toward Warren, the thin IV tube following his arm. "Can you believe this guy, Gabe? In prison fifteen years already, never picked up a nickname. I mean, you think everybody in prison has a nickname, right?"

Warren was nodding his head and laughing, pleased with all the attention. "He's crazy, your old man," he said.

"Think about it: *Warren*," Roman said. "What kind of name is that for a career criminal? Bet his middle name is Egbert or something. No wonder they put him away."

By now Warren was laughing and wheezing, wiping his eyes.

"Dammit, Roman—just tell me about your heart."

He waved me away, frowned. "I'm fine."

"What do you mean, you're fine?" I said.

He pointed at the foot of the bed. "Read the chart. An 'esophageal spasm' or some such thing. Turns out that frazzled nerves don't mix well with eleven shots of bourbon. It's not even my heart. They're keeping me for observation, a couple more tests just to clear the decks, then I'm out of here."

I looked at him. "You were faking, weren't you?"

"God, no, Gabe. It felt real. It scared me bad. I swear, I thought my train was here." He rubbed his mouth, looked at me, then smiled. "Got us out of a jam, though, didn't I?"

"Yeah, now all you have to do is plan on a heart attack as part of every show."

"The show, the show." He patted his mouth, thinking. "I'll tell you what, Gabe, I was thinking that maybe the show is over for now." He held my gaze a moment, then looked away. "What do you think?"

"That's what I told Sandy already. Except the 'for now' part."

"What did you give her for a reason?"

I thought about this. "Why don't you tell me why."

He shook his head. "I have no doubt we could keep pulling in money, keep selling it. No doubt whatsoever. But . . ." He took a breath, let it out. "I don't think I'd ever love it again, Gabe. It feels, I don't know, *broken* somehow. The cars . . . the whole thing seems messed up now."

I nodded. "I know what you mean."

"I remember feeling bad that you were there and had to see it, Gabe," he said in a low voice. "See me cheat was bad enough, then see me *die*? And worse that Gladys wasn't there, because I knew she would eat herself up with guilt if I did die."

"She's here now."

His head jerked up. "Gladys? *Now?*"

"I called her. Like you said, Dad, I thought you were dying."

He nodded. "That makes two of us."

"I am dying," Warren said.

"Pipe down, Egbert," Roman said, and Warren laughed his wheezy laugh again, his chains clanking.

"So, damn. She's here. How does she seem?"

"Upset. Dutch is trying to comfort her, but it's not working much."

He nodded, watching out the window, the dirt baseball field

across the street where a man was walking three dogs, their leash-
es tangling.

"Did your mother talk to the doctor yet?" Roman said.

"Nobody talked to the doctor yet, much. I think he only has a
part-time job here, maybe for the summer or something."

"Wouldn't matter much, she doesn't trust them anyhow."

"I used to think that was because they have money. Now I'm not
sure why."

He nodded, half listening. "We gotta do this thing right, Gabe,"
he said.

"Do what right?" I said. Warren kept ringing for the nurse,
saying he wanted a chocolate milkshake. The guard watched *As
the World Turns* and polished his shotgun barrel with a paper napkin.

Roman motioned me over by his bed, and I stood up close,
looking down at him. "I'm going to need your help, Gabe," he said.
I waited for him to go on, reminded of all those nights in the basement when I spotted weights for him, or earlier, when he brought
me along on door-to-door calls as a sales tool (especially on rainy
days), or during any of a thousand afternoons on the road, when I
drove for him and acted as some small-scale version of a drinking
buddy, and it was always this, always this needing of help, until I
thought right then, standing beside his bed, that someday Roman
would just wear me out, exhaust me out of ever again wanting to
give him help. There was, I knew even then, no end of need, his or
anyone's; it seemed the engine that drove the world, various needs
firing like rocket boosters, pushing us from one place toward
another we would soon take leave of.

"What kind of help?" I said.

"How upset was your mother?"

"Very."

He studied my face. "Scale of one to ten?"

"I don't know, Roman. She looked like she's been crying all night."

"I can't believe she wants him back," Warren said in his ruined voice.

"Never learns, that one," the guard said. He clicked the safety of his gun on and off, absently. I wondered for a moment exactly how much Roman had told them about Gladys and all that had happened to us, until I realized they were talking about the woman on the TV screen, who was at the moment standing around in a red bathrobe, drinking brandy from a snifter. The two men seemed transfixed by her and her history of troubles.

"Okay, listen up, Gabe," Roman said. "Your mother is out of the loop here, and we can use that. You go along with whatever I say, back me up, and we'll be fine."

"What do you mean? What are you talking about?"

He looked at me, quickly looked away. "From here on out, son, I'm damaged goods. I need her to help me recover. My heart is fragile, a second heart attack could come at any minute. And my God, how in the world will I take care of you?"

"Second? You never had a first. You said so yourself."

"Try to keep up with me, son. Your mother doesn't *know* that. She knows whatever we tell her. And what we tell her is that she has to come back and take care of me. She brings me back to health, takes a year, say. By that time, we're back to where we started. Dutch is out of the picture."

I shook my head. "You can't be serious."

"Hell yes, I'm serious. You tell me why it won't work. All I need is one chance, Gabe. I know what went wrong now, I do. One more chance, and this is it."

"She'll talk to the doctor. He'll tell her it's nothing."

"Probably. And who will she believe, him or us? All we have to do is make it look like we're hiding something."

"You will be hiding something."

"I mean hiding the truth."

"That's what I mean too," I said.

"Well, see, we agree."

I looked up at the TV in time to see the woman in the robe smash her brandy snifter against the wall. I knew how she felt. Warren and the guard cheered for her.

"You can't do this, Roman."

"Like hell."

"Okay, you can, but you shouldn't."

He took a drink from the cup of water on his nightstand. "That's your reason? I shouldn't?"

"What did you just fucking tell me about the cars, Roman? You told me you had never once in your life cheated, that you were sorry I had to see it happen. So now you're going to cheat again. Over this, over *her*."

He was quiet a few moments. "When you were a little kid, I used to read to you, you remember that?"

I nodded. "You used to read *The Art of Winning*."

"No, before that, when you could barely talk. We read nursery rhymes, all these little cute animal books. Your favorite was that story about stone soup. You remember that one?"

"No. And what does this have to do—"

"Just listen a minute. In the story this guy comes into this town where everybody is starving but won't give up the one carrot or potato they're hoarding away. So this guy says he's going to make stone soup, puts a rock in this big pot, then says it's perfect, all he needs is one carrot. Somebody comes up with the carrot, then it's perfect, he tells them, except it needs one stalk of celery."

"So everybody ends up chipping in their food."

"Exactly, and they all eat this big pot of stew and nobody starves."

"Well, thanks, Roman. I liked that a lot better than *The Art of Winning*. I should tell Skip. If it involved body parts instead of vegetables, it could be his next movie."

"See, son, the stone was a lie, but it was a necessary lie. Just to get things moving. Okay? So that's what this is. I use this lie to get Gladys back in the house, and then everything will be okay. I know what I did wrong now."

"Yeah? What did you do wrong?"

He shrugged. "Most everything, except love her. God knows I love her, Gabe. Just never the right way."

I sat at the foot of his bed. "You can pull this off, and she may never know it. But you'll know it, Roman. It'll be like the cars. You will always know you cheated. I'm going to know. And somewhere inside her, Gladys is going to know it too."

"You want to talk about knowing, I know her, Gabe. I know how—"

"Maybe you *don't* know her. Maybe that's your whole problem. Like you assume she's miserable with Dutch. You ever think she might be happy?"

He shook his head, looking out at the empty baseball diamond. "Gabe, just tell me right now if you are in on this thing or not. Tell me if you are bailing out on me after we've gotten this far."

"Like you said, once you cheat, the whole thing is broken. The cars are broken, Dad. If we do this, everything we ever had in that house will be broken."

"Tell me. Right now."

I looked at him, thinking how old he looked in the bed, his hair messed up instead of slicked back, dark circles under his eyes. Part of me wanted to put him back into his shiny suit and his Tiger Rose hair tonic and his striped suspenders and his fedoras and all his old life and swagger, even if we had to cheat Gladys and ourselves to do it. Without those things, I wondered, what was left?

"It's not only cheating, you're cheating the best part of her. The part that still loves you."

"I can make her happy, Gabe."

"She is happy."

He shook his head. "Last time I'm going to ask, son. So I'll know if you're with me when this whole thing plays out."

I took a deep breath. On the other side of the curtain, Warren and the guard were discussing prison food versus hospital food. I could hear the soft clank of Warren's chains beneath his blanket, the low hum of an air conditioner.

"I tell you what," I said. "I'm going to let it be just like all those porches we used to stand on in the rain. I'm going to watch you, Roman, and listen, and I'll go along. I will. You decide. If you need me to nod my head, that's what I'll do. I'll let you make me a cheater too."

He was quiet a moment, his nose whistling across the oxygen tube. He nudged me with his foot. "It's going to be fine," he said.

"I better go find her," I said. I couldn't look at him.

"Okay. You don't have to say anything, Gabe. Just get her in here. But give me a while, so I can think this through, okay?"

I nodded, got up from the bed. On the way out I waved to the guard, who was thumbing through a copy of *Field & Stream* during the commercials. Warren was dozing in his bed, his mouth open.

"What is he in for?" I asked.

The guard looked up. "Armed robbery, habitual criminal."

"No, I mean in *here* for."

"Congestive heart failure. Heart's too big and he's drowning in his own fluids." He held his hands out to show me how large Warren's heart had grown. He nodded toward Roman. "What's wrong with him?"

"Nothing," I said.

"Nothing?"

"Not that he can see."

As I walked out, I heard Roman shout, "I heard that," his words muffled as the heavy door closed behind me.

I found Gladys, Dutch, and Sandy in the orange waiting area. Vic, they said, had been gone all morning. I told them that Roman seemed okay for the moment, that he was going to clean up a bit, then he wanted to see Gladys.

She nodded. For a moment I nearly admired the beauty of this setup, that as long as he was sick, he got to call all the shots, with nobody questioning anything. Sandy and Gladys decided to pass the time by finding some breakfast in the cafeteria. I started to follow, but Dutch held me back, saying he wanted to talk to me. We watched Sandy and Gladys move off down the hall, talking together in the quiet, secret way of women.

"Your dad is a fighter," Dutch said. "He's going to pull through." It was hard not to laugh, knowing as I did that Roman had pulled through about twenty minutes after he sat on the floor of the exhibition hall. Dutch kept plying me with feel-happy lines that sounded as if they'd been pulled from the late-night movies where he advertised his cars.

"I'd like us to offer up a prayer for Roman," he said.

I shrugged. "Be my guest. But don't do it on my account."

"He is my brother, Gabe."

"Pray away," I said.

"Well, not here. There must be a chapel somewhere in this hospital."

After asking at the nurses' station we rode the elevator down to the first floor, where the Henry H. Axelrod Memorial Chapel was located, its stained-glass doors decorated with various nondenominational images—garlands of flowers, rays of sunlight. Only it was closed, part of the renovations. The front doors were tied shut with a length of rope, the opening draped with plastic. A hand-lettered sign directed us around the corner, where, temporarily, the chapel had been relocated to a back corner of the gift shop. We moved past shelves of Holly Hobby statues, display packs of bubble gum and 3 Musketeers bars, get-well cards, bottles of aspirin, rolls of film, and coffee mugs with the hospital name printed on them. In the back corner were four folding chairs and another hand-lettered sign designating that corner the temporary Henry H. Axelrod Memorial Chapel. I wondered if Henry H. Axelrod would have been bothered to learn that his namesake was really only the *idea* of a chapel, instead of a particular place, and could be attached to any empty corner they happened to find. Two votive candles burned on a small table, and mounted to the wall were a crucifix and a Star of David, near the sign which said that checks should be made out to Hospital Gift Shop. We sat in the folding chairs. I picked up a plastic toy helicopter and made the propeller spin around.

"Not exactly a holy place," Dutch whispered.

"I guess if you sell crappy little toys it is," I said. Just then an elderly woman with blond hair stepped out from a door marked STOREROOM. She wore a green smock and was carrying a pricing gun.

"Do you boys need help with anything?"

"No, thank you," Dutch said.

"When do you pass the collection plate?" I said. Dutch shushed me and frowned.

"I don't think this is the time for jokes, Gabe," he said. I apologized, having forgotten that I was the only one who knew that there was not a damn thing wrong with Roman beyond his general approach to his life and to the people who, somehow, loved him. Dutch closed his eyes and laced his fingers and knitted his brow tightly, making a good and earnest show of offering up prayers for the brother whose wife he was sleeping with. Right then, I felt angry at everyone, for what we had done to all of us, and at myself too, for my own part in it all. As a family, we seemed to have an amazing capacity for screwing everything up. I watched Dutch finish his prayer, then I reached and opened a bag of M&M's. The lady looked at me and smiled, and I handed her a quarter.

"I'm sure Roman will bounce right back, Gabe," Dutch said.

"I'm sure he will too," I said.

"That's the spirit," he said, and I offered him some M&M's, which he took, cupping them in his hand.

"As to other matters . . . your mother and I have made wedding plans, and I would like to make sure you will be there."

"I don't think this is the time for wedding plans," I said.

He nodded. "You're right, but there won't be another chance when we are all together, and time is short."

I nodded. "So what are the plans?"

"Well, first off, your mother wants you to give her away. It's an important gesture to her, Gabe, and of course her father . . . well, they haven't spoken for years. You know that."

"Yeah, but don't you think, since we're talking gestures and giving her away, that maybe Roman should be the one? Seems like a better fit."

Dutch's face flushed deep red.

"Or maybe," I said, "you could substitute for the giving-away part of the ceremony, and have a *taking* away. Right in the middle of the church aisle, you two could wrestle, like you did on the beach. That would be perfect."

"I didn't take her away, Gabe."

Inside I knew this was true, but what do you do when you have a whole big bag of blame saved up, and nowhere to put it? I sighed.

"That's it? She wants me to give her to you?"

He took a breath. "The hard part is, she would like Roman to be there too. By then the divorce will have been finalized, and she

wants to put much of this behind us. She wants the wedding to be
. . . how did she put it?"

"A time of healing?" I said. It was a phrase I'd heard many times
over the years.

"Something along those lines. But we need you to get him to go.
I don't think it's going to work coming from me or Gladys."

"I think you're right," I said. The woman in the smock worked
beside us, straightening a shelf of decorative thimbles.

"After that, since your mother has never really traveled, I plan
to take her to Rio de Janeiro for our honeymoon."

"Then you are off into your new lives," I said.

"That's our hope, Gabe."

I nodded. The whole plan seemed so easy. A fifteen-minute ceremony, see some old friends, then hop a plane into a whole new
version of yourself. A do-over, just like God and Noah's ark, Roman
and me left behind, treading water. The other plan was easy too:
stand at Roman's bedside, nod when he looked at me, trick Gladys
back into her old life. And all her old misery? Roman swore not,
but starting off with a lie did not reassure me much.

"So," I said. "Where is the commercial tie-in?"

"What do you mean, Gabe?"

"You know, the 'Off to Rio' sale or something. You could dress
up like Ricky Ricardo, and make a few bucks off the whole thing."

I think I expected to piss him off by saying this, but instead he
started laughing, trying to quiet himself since we were in this
makeshift church.

"Actually, Gabe, that's not half bad. I like that."

I laughed with him. "Maybe even Carmen Miranda instead of
Ricky Ricardo," I said.

He thought about it. "The Off to Rio sale . . ."

"The savings are hot," I said, and we laughed again, and again I
had one of those twinges of liking him and of knowing that Gladys

could find a way to be happy with him. Or that, at least, minus all the distraction of the last twenty years, she could find her own happiness.

"Well," Dutch said. "The wedding. You'll come, Gabe? Try to bring Roman?"

I thought of Roman up in his bed, probably rehearsing his chest pains, silently trying out the words he would say to her, polishing his lie, Gladys waiting to see him.

"Let me think about it. I'll get back to you."

"That seems fair enough. But soon, okay?"

"Okay."

Upstairs, Gladys told me that she had not yet been in to see Roman, that she wanted to wait until she knew it was okay. Already, she was worried by what she imagined to be his fragile condition.

"Well, come on," I said. "It's okay right now." I wanted to get this over with.

She hesitated. "They said only one allowed in."

"Yeah, but I think I need to be there."

We walked down the long, white hall, around the gurneys and cans of paint. Gladys wrapped her arms around herself, her face drawn with fatigue. I put my arm around her, struck by how small she was, how thin. I wondered how I had missed that for so many years.

When she saw the guard and the gun, Gladys jumped a little. The guard smiled and waved at me, tipped his hat to Gladys. Roman had arranged himself so that he was all slunk down in his bed, arms limp at his sides, the IV making its slow drip. She saw him and put her hand to her mouth, whispered "Oh my God" to herself. She moved to his bedside and hugged him, then kissed him at his hairline.

"Did you meet my roomie?" he said, his voice a thin whisper. He once told me that every sales call was a gig, an acting job. "That's Warren and his baby-sitter. Boys . . ." He paused to take a deep, labored breath. "This is my wife, Gladys."

She turned and half-smiled, said hello, and I could see her holding the word "ex" in her mouth, not letting it loose.

"Roman, Dr. Fernald said there is no evidence of a blockage so far, that they are going to run one more routine test."

He nodded. I sat down in the bedside chair, a front-row seat. Gladys sat on the edge of the bed. "That's good," Roman said. "He didn't tell you anything else?"

"No. I mean, what else is there?"

Roman cut his eyes at me, making sure she saw it. "Nothing important."

"What then? Roman, are you not telling me something?" She took up his hand in hers.

"No, I'm sure everything is fine, right Gabe?" He looked at me, his eyes flat, dull. As cued, I nodded my head.

"Roman," she said, "you're hiding something from me. I know you." I wondered if she did, in the least.

"Gladys, I wouldn't hide anything. Like I said, it's nothing to worry over."

She shook her head, crying a little. "You're protecting me from something, Roman. Just tell me what it is."

I watched him, the small hesitations he allowed himself, the tiny, faked winces. So far, it was a great pitch.

"Tell her everything is okay, Gabe."

I looked at him, saw in his eyes how near he was to closing. "Actually, they did a little surgery," I said.

"What?" Gladys said.

"Son, what are you talking about?" Roman cut his eyes at me. I was breaking the bubble.

"They planted a few new ideas in his head," I said to them. "For example, they put in the idea that if you cheat, you ruin things. And the surgery worked too. He was telling me that very thing not half an hour ago, weren't you, Roman?"

Gladys started crying, her eyes moving back and forth between us. "I don't understand. What is this about?"

"Gabe . . ." Roman said.

"Wait, here's another new idea. He loved you more than anything else, Gladys. But it came out wrong. See, he knows that now, thanks to modern medicine."

"Gabe, I want you to make sense, just tell me," Gladys said, her face confused. Their hands were still loosely joined.

"But you're exactly right, Gladys, we are hiding something."

She put her hand to her mouth. "Oh, God."

"Tell her, Roman."

He looked down at Gladys's hand in his, as if it were some mysterious thing he'd found while walking along. He turned his gaze to me, and looked at me for a long space of time, the tiny green blip on his heart monitor beeping steadily. He watched me as if it had been years since he'd seen me and he was having trouble placing me. Behind us, the metallic clank rose from Warren's bed, and the guard lightly dozed in his chair, chin on his chest. Roman lifted her hand, looked at it, then placed it back in the palm of her other hand.

"I'm fine, Gladys," he said.

"Roman, I know you are not fine, so just——"

He held up his hand, pushed himself up in the bed. "Really, honey, I'm okay. It's just this esophageal thing. Not my heart. My heart . . . it's fine."

"Roman . . ."

"I mean it, Gladys. I'll be out of here this afternoon." He looked at me. "Though some of my activities may be restricted, that's what the doctor said."

"Really?" Her hands shook. "Are you telling me the truth?"

"Never been more honest in my life, Gladys. I really am okay."

She closed her eyes and let loose a shaking sigh. "I'm so relieved," she said.

"So am I," I said.

She hugged me, then Roman, holding him tightly and awkwardly, leaning down. I stood watching the slow movement of the fluid that pushed through the tube in his raised arm, imagining that the liquid was something running out of him instead of into him, the worst of his need drained away. Gladys wiped her eyes, gathered her purse.

"When you get out, I want us to talk about some things," she said to him. He nodded, unable to look at her.

"Talk soon, Gabe, okay?"

"Okay," I said. "And Gladys?"

"Yes, honey?"

"Tell Dutch I said yes."

By late afternoon Roman was out of bed and dressed, making arrangements for signing out. He sent me to check on the cars, though I didn't know exactly what I was supposed to check. Roman didn't either, but told me I would figure it out, he had faith in me. I later found out that while I was on my way in the Chevy, driving toward the exhibition hall, Vic had returned and paid Roman's hospital bill in cash, from out of our gray box of profits, and had given the rest to Roman, bundled up in a grocery sack. He kept only the gray box itself and the first dollar we had made, which I had put aside back in Valdosta and kept sealed in a plastic sandwich bag after Vic insisted that all of us sign it. He apologized over and over to Roman, torn by his guilt over Roman's attack and over his cheating of us, the fakery he had sold us on. Roman did not set him straight on the nature of his attack, as he'd done with Gladys, and I didn't mind. There was nothing Vic loved more than a meaningful gesture; Rod McKuen would have wanted it that way.

The sky edged toward dark, the sunlight a dim, slanting orange as I drove the Chevy slowly around the exhibition hall, the empty lot strewn with paper cups and trampled programs. The big rolling steel doors were closed over all the entrances, the mercury-vapor lamps beginning a faint pink glow. I found the cars around the back, beside one of the big doors, wedged up next to the wall beside a green dumpster, the Lincoln parked nearby. I got out and walked around them, kicked the dented quarter panels a few times and heard the shush of rust flakes dropping to the pavement. I opened the door of the Spyder and sat in the driver's seat and held on to the steering wheel, closing my eyes for a second as a warm breeze washed across me. My hand moved to the gearshift, and I ran through the pattern, upshifting as though I were flying into the final straightaway before Dead Man's Curve. Then it seemed silly; this car had likely never seen Dead Man's Curve, and any fame it would ever have we had given it during two quick months of money and hope. I opened my eyes and noticed something stuck beneath the twisted windshield wiper, reached around to grab it. It was Sergeant Meschery's business card, his name printed beside the *To Serve and Protect* logo. "See you next time," he'd written across the top. I read it over, lifted my hand, and gave the card to the breeze, then unscrewed the wooden gearshift knob and stuck it away inside the pocket of my leather jacket. I got out and moved around the rest of the cars, touching them, letting their ruined paint color my fingertips.

I had there with me both the Lincoln and the Chevy, with no way to drive both back. I figured I could wait for Roman, or bring Sandy back out here with me, but there would always be this problem, our old car and our new. I let out the brake on the Chevy, put it in neutral, and with my foot out the door rolled it over beside the

Death Cars until it lightly bumped Jayne Mansfield's Electra. Inside the glove compartment were Roman's old Crown Royal bag, his empty packs of Pall Malls, old road maps. I took out the title and signed it, then left it on the driver's seat with the keys, giving to whoever might want it this other old heap with its tens of thousands of miles of neighborhoods and rain and sales samples and the memory of a teenage boy trailing his father, tracking the next sale. Inside the Lincoln, I noticed that someone had swiped the tiny TV. Already the paint had chipped away from the dent in the shining hood, and a thin layer of rust had formed around its edges. But it started right up, ran smooth. With Pogo on the dash, watching me, I slipped into drive and pulled away.

Chapter 14

The wedding took place on Thanksgiving weekend, during a cold and snowy blast that slid across the mountains, across the Little Chapel in the Woods where the ceremony was held. The chapel had been built in the thirties by a group of WPA railroad men who wanted a place to worship, then added onto over the years until its own name seemed a lie, which the current owners had tried to compensate for by putting the now-mistaken adjective in quotation marks: the "Little" Chapel in the Woods. I imagined that if the woods were torn down and replaced by subdivisions, they would have to call it the "Little" Chapel in the "Woods." It was Dutch's kind of place, and he had filled it with long strands of purple garlands, a carpet of yellow rose petals leading down the center aisle. Since they had no flower girl, the petals had to be predropped, and by the time of the ceremony early that afternoon, they had browned and curled at the edges, looking as if the aisle was littered with potato chips.

By midmorning, I stood in the parking lot, watching for arriving guests, hearing the distant rumbles of salt trucks and plows along the narrow roads. The sun finally slipped from behind the clouds and the air stilled, my breath blowing out in white streams. Most of the guests had stayed away because of the weather. Dutch

had arranged to have him and Gladys arrive in a horse-drawn car-
riage, but they had scrapped these plans because of the weather,
and I knew Gladys was grateful that day for icy roads. Dutch's
salesmen sat together near the back, pouting over having so few
takers for their business cards. Several of Gladys's artsy friends
arrived together, and they told me that for wedding presents they
had given Dutch and Gladys a tree and a boulder for the front lawn
of Dutchland. I said that those must have been tough to gift wrap.

While I was watching the roads, Roman was inside the chapel,
leaning against the back wall. All day and during the ride up that
morning he'd had little to say, though he'd had nothing to drink and
had even gotten his hair cut for the occasion, all razor-trimmed and
slicked back with hair tonic. After that day in the hospital, I'd had
little trouble talking him into showing up. Once he had let go of his
plans for selling her on their reconciliation, it was only one more
step, a deep breath or two, for him to let go of her. As he'd said at
Vic's party, a door in your face means no. Only this time he'd closed
that door himself, given up on making that deal. If Gladys wanted
her sense of closure, her time of healing . . . well, all free gifts—jar
lid grippers, refrigerator magnets, gestures of kindness—were
write-offs anyway. It cost him nothing he hadn't already lost, I figured, and he'd spent on this day only a small defiance by way of his
insistence that all he would do was show up.

But he had plans, as he'd shown me during the drive up. He'd
driven us through a section of Winston-Salem, near an elementary
school, on a street lined with porch-swing houses and tiny grocery
stores. He steered the Lincoln slowly down the street, then swung
into a concrete parking lot, the surface stained with faded oil spills.
He broke off the fire of his cigarette and put the unfinished half
back in the pack. This was his way of cutting down, as Dr. Fernald
had advised him. He had slowed down drinking too, and had lost
some weight, his old suits a little baggy around the shoulders.

"What are you doing?" I said. "We're already late. I have to give her away, remember?"

"Give her away . . ." He started to say something, then stopped himself. He pointed toward the back of the lot. "What do you think," he said.

"About what?"

"About this place." I looked around. This place, it turned out, was an old Shell filling station, with two glass-topped gas pumps, regular and high-test, looming tall and rusty, and an old oil pit filled in with weedy dirt. The station itself was made of poured concrete, shaped to look like a giant scallop shell.

"Back in the forties, all of them were made like this. You know, Shell and shell, an advertising gimmick. This is the last one in the country. It's on the National Register of Historic Places."

He popped the door of the Lincoln and stepped out, and I followed him. We peered in through the dusty window of the door cut in the middle of the shell, the inside cramped by a small desk, a chair with a broken seat, a metal rack meant to hold motor oil or snack foods. On the desk was the ghost tracing of an old cash register outlined in heavy dust.

"Pretty cool place," I said. "Why are you showing it to me?"

"Because I bought it. With Vic's money, our money, most of what was left." I knew that he had given five thousand to Sandy, and I silently calculated how much he had spent on this place.

"Mind telling me why?" I said.

He shrugged, his face still pressed to the dusty glass. "I was thinking that maybe it's time I got off the road, Gabe. Just for a few years. I'm not old yet, but I guess that's coming, isn't it? And this hospital thing. I don't know . . ."

"So this is your place to land."

"Something like that," he said. "There isn't another filling station for eleven blocks. Plus the elementary school just up the road, all

those moms picking up their kids every day, you know, let the customers come to me for a while. I think it can pull in a good income.
Nothing spectacular, but steady."

"A steady income," I said, as if repeating it phonetically. Finally,
he had hit on what Gladys always wanted: a little bit of sure money
to bolster her love. Only Roman, as ever—as with his forays into
muscle-building and tie-dyed clothes—was a little too late. I imagined Gladys at that moment, standing before a mirror, nervously
pinning the flowers in her hair, her strong, brown arms lifted, the
ice burns long since gone from around her eyes.

"Not right off, of course," Roman said. "And God knows we
have some fixing up to do around here. But we handled the beach
house, right?"

"We?"

"Well, if you want to. I was thinking we might go in this together." He rattled the knob on the door. "I pick up the keys next week,
after the papers are signed."

I nodded. "You know, I'm doing pretty well now that I'm showing up for school all the time. Turns out that's about all they really
expect anyway."

"You're a smart one, Gabe. Never any doubt about that."

"Gladys wants me to apply to some colleges for after next year.
She thinks I can get in."

He kicked at the concrete around the base of the shell. "I'm sure
you could get in. I mean, what else could they want?"

"So," I said. I wrote my initials in the dust.

"So, what do *you* want to do?"

I looked at his wavy, dusty reflection in the glass. "I don't know."
I shook my head and shrugged. It hit me then that no one had asked
me what I wanted since I was seven years old and got to decide if
we ate dinner at Tastee-Freez or the K&W Cafeteria. Most of what
I thought I wanted lately had been connected to them, Roman and

Gladys, only now there was no more them. All tangible evidence of this thing I called my past was now only memory, my future some cloudy assemblage of half-plans handed to me for reasons that had only a little bit to do with me. I suppose I could have then treated myself like a Death Car, invented for myself some celebrated and tragic past, a story to haul out and sell myself on. But real loss seemed enough, quiet and inevitable as it was, and with the past dismantled there was little else for me to do but turn around and move toward some future. I couldn't see what, but movement was movement, I figured. I shook my head again. "I'm just not sure."

He looked at me and nodded, tried the door once more. He wrote his own initials above mine, then beneath both wrote OWNERS.

"Come on," he said. "We've got a wedding to get through."

Sandy showed up in the same tiny red dress she'd worn the night of the beach party, with Skip following close behind her, nodding his head at most everything she said. The two of them were living at the beach house, using her share of the money to finish fixing it up so they could rent it out. Roman had told them they could keep half the rent if they looked after the place and kept the ocean from swallowing the whole thing. In the meantime, she told me she had gotten a job pouring beers and shots at the VFW post, and made, she said, several pounds of tips every night. With the rest of the money she was producing *Goon with theWind* for Skip, which would end up playing at a string of drive-in movies across the Southeast before finding its way into rotation for years on local late-night TV. Sometimes I will see it on some three-a.m. cable channel, and there is Sandy for her five minutes of screen time, forever twenty-three years old, playing one of the newspaper reporters who keep hounding the local sheriff. She told me once she felt like some North Carolina version of Dorian Gray, with commercials.

We stood around at the front of the chapel, waiting for things to begin, Sandy and Skip in the front row and Roman in the back, sitting with his arms crossed on a pew by himself, like some tourist who had wandered in to watch out of curiosity. I wore my Roman Junior suit with the fox-hunter tie, Dutch the same white suit he wore for his commercials and billboards, his Ford and American flag pins neatly aligned on his lapel.

"Nervous?" I asked.

"We should have rehearsed," Dutch said. "I don't like doing things off the cuff." He took a big breath and let it go. I wanted to tell him that if you gave off the cuff a fair chance, pretty soon you could fall in love with it.

"You'll be fine," I said.

"What about you?"

"I'll be fine too."

"How is Roman with all of this? Your mother is very worried about him."

"Well, he's here. I wouldn't push for much more than that."

"Listen, Gabe, I told my advertising boys about your Off to Rio idea, and they liked it. They wish they'd thought of it. I think if they'd had enough advance they might have gone with it."

"Next time you get married, I'll think of something weeks ahead of time," I said.

"Oh, I don't believe there will be a next time." He looked momentarily confused. "In any case, my guy at the ad firm wants to talk to you about an entry-level position, starting in the summer, then carrying over indefinitely, maybe involving some help with tuition. Not a lot of money, of course, but you could learn the ropes, get your foot in the door." He smiled, brushed a speck from my lapel.

I nodded, watching the piano player settle into her spot and begin to turn the pages of her songbook. I thought about trying to explain to Roman that I was going off to help Dutch put together his TV ads, but for little money. It would be like that night in the

Lincoln, when we sat together laughing in the motel parking lot, inventing the worst jobs we could imagine. I turned so that Dutch would not see me smiling.

"Sounds good, Dutch, really it does. But I already have a job lined up next summer."

"Well, then, that's that, I suppose. Doing what, may I ask?"

"Pumping gas." I didn't know if this was true yet, but I liked the sound of it anyway. Part of finding out what my years ahead would be, I figured, was carving away what they would not be.

"*Pumping gas?* Gabe——" He said this loudly enough that everyone craned their necks to look at us. Dutch shook his head and started to say more, but then the music started up and Gladys began her slow walk down the carpeted aisle, where I met her halfway and offered her my arm. She seemed so happy and pretty, ignoring the potato-chip rose petals at her feet, ignoring for that day and those to follow what she would know in three years' time: that if Roman's wild, blind stabs at love did not work, if what she called crazy love could not be sustained, then neither for her could Dutch's version of it: practical, ordered, systematic. Maybe a guitar could be played the way an engine is repaired, but a woman could not be loved that way. It would not be until her third marriage that she discovered what she couldn't find in all her mediocre poetry: the way in which love could find form, could mean, and could keep at its center something at once hidden and known, the constant, steady hum of longing and surrender.

The reception took place in the adjoining banquet room, with a couple of tables filled with food and a friend of Gladys's playing the hammered dulcimer. Sandy walked over to me, complaining that it was really, really hard to dance to the hammered dulcimer, saying that we needed Vic there with his record collection. She kept slapping Skip's hand every time he reached for his notebook. Finally he gave up and stood by the champagne fountain, drinking.

"It was a nice ceremony," Sandy said. "Lots better than mine."

"How so?"

She rolled her eyes. "Oh, the Miss North Carolina thing. Had to keep the marriage quiet or they'd have booted me. Planning the whole thing was like one of those movies where the troops are trying to break out of some POW camp."

I laughed, and Sandy took my arm. "You okay with all of this?"

"I feel happy for Gladys, bad for Roman. I'm trying to balance myself somewhere in between."

She thought about this. "What are you going to do? What do you *want* to do now?"

"You know, it's really weird," I said. "I don't get asked that for ten years straight, then now I get it twice in the same day."

"That is weird."

I shrugged. "Well, the question was never really askable before, I guess. And anyway, according to you, I'm only supposed to worry about making it to dinnertime."

"For yourself, yes. The rest of us get to worry our heads off over you."

"Well, don't. Actually, I'm kinda looking forward to worrying about me for a while. I'm easy."

She laughed, nudged me. "That's what I hear. Listen, Gabe, if you ever have some scheme for making big money—" she squeezed my arm—"try real hard to talk me out of it." She hugged me, rubbed my back, began to move off toward Skip.

"Fine," I said. "After I'm a veteran of some foreign war, I'm going to move to Carolina Beach and spend my days in your bar, giving you bad tips and trying to pinch your butt."

She waved to me. "Promises, promises."

Roman kept his own promise to himself and me not to drink, and made a good show of his own happiness, smiling at Gladys, talking shop with Dutch's salesmen, even shaking Dutch's hand. He kept frozen in place the same face he'd worn on a thousand porches, and I was the only one that day, I think, to notice the tiny winces he allowed himself, like those that followed the slamming of a door.

After half an hour of this, he made his way over to me.

"They're going to end this soon, and then we will all line up to say goodbye."

"Off to Rio," I said.

He nodded. "I don't think I can be here for that part. Hugging, kissing—" He took a cigar from his coat pocket and occupied himself with unwrapping it. All during the reception, Dutch had been running around handing out cigars, as if he and Gladys had just had a baby.

"Listen," I said, "why don't we get out of here."

He put the cigar in his mouth. "Just leave?"

"Yeah, exactly. Let's just leave."

"I don't know about that, son. Think we should?"

"I think we should. Sure."

"Okay." He nodded. "Let's go ride."

The Lincoln seemed not to like the cold weather and was hard starting, misfiring as we turned out onto the road. We drove the twisting roads as we always had, looking out the windows, carried along by a slow patience. Roman reached across me, opened the glove box, and pulled out a bottle of Crown Royal, still inside its purple bag.

"I thought you were cutting back," I said.

"Cutting back, yes. Not cutting off." He uncapped the bottle and took just one short swallow, then handed it to me. I took my own taste, then put it back in the glove box.

"You think your mother is going to be all right with this?" he said.

"I don't know if she's going to be, but she is right now."

"Right now."

"Yeah, today she's happy, at least until dinner."

He looked at me. "That's reassuring."

I shrugged. "Sorry. That's the best I can do."

He thought about this for a while. "So, where are we headed, anyway?"

"'Away' is all I think you really had in mind."

"Yeah, but we have to go *somewhere,* don't we?" he said.

"Too bad the Land of Oz bit the dust, I think we're near it."

"Hard to believe somebody could not make a go of that place. I mean, it had everything, location, zero overhead." He frowned as the Lincoln misfired, hesitated.

"What about that other place you told me about?" I said. "Mystery Hill?"

He shook his head, took the cigar from his pocket, and put it in his mouth without lighting it. "It's around here too, but it must be, damn, close to twenty years since I went there. Don't know that I could find it."

Roman steered the car through small towns, down unmarked roads, squinting at the highway markers we passed. Every time the Lincoln misfired, he slapped his hand on the dash, shaking Pogo. "Damn, this looks familiar," he said, though I imagined that all the roads looked familiar to him. Finally we came to an overlook, the black ribbon of road curling before us in small hills and dips. He pulled off the road, let the engine idle.

"This is almost it, I swear. It was a road just like this, and I remember Mystery Hill started right where a big white barn stood beside the road."

"Maybe it's on ahead. Maybe the barn isn't there anymore."

"Could be, Gabe. We might sure enough be close."

We drove on slowly, the speedometer barely registering, Roman scanning the landscape for familiar signs and shaking his head. By now we had the heater on full blast, the air in the car dense and hot, the engine struggling up the hills. Finally, at the bottom of a steep incline, the Lincoln missed twice and died. Roman cranked the engine over and over, thin blue smoke billowing out behind us.

"Shit," Roman said. Across the road was a tiny gray clapboard building with signs advertising bait and beer. Roman motioned at it.

"Guess I should call for a tow truck," he said.

"Okay."

He headed across the road, the icy slap of air filling the space of his open door. I got out and opened the hood of the Lincoln, staring at the oily parts as if I could make some sense of them. I gave up, then sat on the trunk and waited. Roman walked back toward me, the collar of his suitcoat turned up against the wind. He shook his head.

"The store doesn't open till one," he said. "We're gonna be stuck for a while."

He retrieved the bottle of Crown Royal and we shared a drink, sitting together on the frozen trunk lid. Roman fired up two of Dutch's cigars and passed one to me. We sat there, frozen and puffing.

"We should be able to fix this," I said. "You always say we're the idea men, right?"

"That's true, we should be able to." He shrugged. "We don't have any tools, though."

"We'd have to know this stuff if we were in the business. We'd need tools, too."

He turned to look at me. "I think your mother might be right about the college thing, son. She was always smarter than me about what's best for you."

I nodded. "It could turn out I'm smarter about that than both of you. Now is probably a good time to find out. And besides, I need a summer job, so I might as well work for you. The hours are bad, but at least the pay is lousy." This was one of his own old jokes.

He laughed. "All right, then, Mr. Smart Guy, what do you think is wrong with this car? Think of it this way: there is an answer. The only thing between us and it is figuring it out."

I took a drink, feeling its warmth spread through me. I passed him the bottle. "Well, just think for a minute then. I know a car needs fire, needs fuel, needs air. That's basic stuff."

Roman took a drag from his cigar, a long drink from the bottle, then a deep, slow breath. "Well, I don't know about the car," he said, "but we have everything we need." I laughed.

"Too bad about Mystery Hill, though," he said. "I really wanted to show you that. It is something to see."

"Hey," I said. "Maybe *this* is it, right here. This hill."

He looked back over his shoulder. "Don't think so."

"Maybe you just don't recognize it anymore."

He thought about this, nodded slowly. "It has been twenty years. Could be, I guess."

We looked at each other a moment, then sat back in the warmth of the car, in the pale clouds our cigars made. Roman shifted the car into neutral, let out the parking brake, slowly lifted his foot from the brake pedal. The car inched backward, down the small incline, then stopped.

"Nope," he said.

"I guess not," I answered. We smoked our cigars in silence, let the ashes grow. The pale sun eased across the tops of the pine trees surrounding us, its thin yellow light the color of the chill that surrounded us. I looked ahead, up the black, curving incline of the road before us. There was, I knew, no mystery in this hill, or in the one behind it or the one behind that, other than what mystery is in every anticipated and unseen thing, the mystery of moving forward, leaving empty road behind you, of betting against hope for some next perfect moment.